Don't be afraid, said the Voice. *I am your friend.*

Oh, what'll I do, thought Pidge fearfully.

Am I hurting you? the Voice asked with infinite gentleness.

"No."

Believe in my friendship.

"But I'm afraid."

Listen! said the Voice.

Music flooded down the chimney as if it were water surging over the edge of a fall. It hushed—and there was a downpouring of perfumed light, in accord with the clear and perfect notes of a solitary flute, in which the light rejoiced and danced.

It all faded and whispered away.

Look up!

Pidge looked up and saw the night-time. It was filled with glittering stars.

I write my name, said the Voice.

Out of the multitude, the biggest and the brightest of the stars formed the word: DAGDA.

PAT O'SHEA, who grew up in Galway, Ireland, now makes her home in Manchester, England. This is her first novel.

the hounds
of the
MORRIGAN

PAT O'SHEA

LAUREL-LEAF BOOKS bring together under a single imprint outstanding works of fiction and nonfiction particularly suitable for young adult readers, both in and out of the classroom. Charles F. Reasoner, Professor Emeritus of Children's Literature and Reading, New York University, is consultant to this series.

Published by
Dell Publishing
a division of
The Bantam Doubleday Dell Publishing Group, Inc.
1 Dag Hammarskjold Plaza
New York, New York 10017

Laurel-Leaf Library ® TM 766734, Dell Publishing

ISBN: 0-440-20001-6

RL: 6.9

Reprinted by arrangement with Holiday House, Inc.

Printed in the United States of America

June 1988

10 9 8 7 6 5 4 3 2 1

KRI

To
Jimmy and Sheena
and Geoff.

THE
HOUNDS
OF THE
MÓRRÍGAN

Prologue

RISING up into the air, they took to the sky and flew. From west and beyond west, into the wind and through it, they came past countless moons and suns. One laughed and briefly wore a scarf of raindrops in her hair, and then with wicked feet she kicked a cloud and caused rain to swamp a boat.

At times, they dived into the track of the moon in the dark sea-water and opened their mouths to swallow the silver. At times, they plunged into the path of the sun in the green-blue ocean and opened their mouths and drank the gold.

All the time invisible; except once, when they swooped down on a basking shark and frightened it silly by making faces at it. Then they showed it their *real* faces and it dived down, down, to the bottom of its world and stayed quivering for hours.

All the time silent; except when they tapped their teeth with their finger-nails and sent lightning; or when they laughed with elation and caused thunder.

They had been silent for so long.

Silent, while man followed man as tiny blushes of life.

They laughed when they flew in over Connemara, where the wild, greedy Atlantic takes long, blue bites out of the green land, and that laugh alone destroyed a field of yellowing oats, turning it ash-grey.

They reached Galway city and for fun sculpted three supersonic bangs out of thin air, so that all the people ran into the streets and looked up to see a plane that wasn't there. Then they turned left, spinning and rolling up the east side of Lough Corrib *until they reached a certain signpost, ordinary and artless, which they blew on and set spinning like themselves*, before a final dive to earth behind a small hill. There they paused and took

7

form, and rapidly emerged into view, *two strange women riding a powerful motor-bike*.

All the time, their hounds followed them.

When they conversed, they called each other Macha and Bodbh, and they were in advance of and watched for the coming of the third one—The Mórrígan—who is the Great Queen. They made for a place called Kyledove, changing their names and their characters as they went . . . .

All this, because a boy was about to try to buy a book in the second-hand bookshop, in the small grey city of Galway.

Part One

Chapter 1

AFTER making sure that the shopping for Auntie Bina and his folded jacket were safely stowed in the saddle-bag, Pidge wheeled his bike through the crowded streets. The day was unpleasantly hot. People were moving slowly, as though drained of energy, and even the young Garda on point-duty looked half-asleep. He was swaying on his feet, beckoning the cars forward with only small movements of his wrist; and when at last he raised an arm in the air to stop the traffic, and turned to allow the waiting people to cross the road, Pidge saw a large damp patch of sweat on his shirt. It looked like the map of Australia.

The clock in the steeple of St. Nicholas' Church struck the half-hour.

Only half-past two, Pidge said to himself. I don't have to start for home for a good while yet.

He walked on, pausing once to stare after two nuns who walked through the lightly-dressed crowds.

How hot they must feel in their heavy clothes, he thought. And they have to wear stockings as well. It can't be much fun.

He turned into a side-street and saw, with pleasure, the newly opened second-hand bookshop. The window was pasted with red stickers announcing the event; and books of all sorts were displayed to their best advantage. Three brass balls still hung above the doorway.

That place has been boarded up for years and years—for as long as I can remember, anyway. It used to be a pawnshop long ago, he reflected. I'm really glad it's a second-hand bookshop now.

The outside of the shop hadn't been touched; the signboard under the brass balls was still impossible to read, just the same old flaked blue paint that had once said a name.

11

He wheeled his bike to the window and looked through the glass.

Inside all was bright and cheerful with fluorescent lighting; the shelving that was already well-stocked with books was of new wood, and from the parts of the floor that were visible, he could see that a new dark-brown carpet had been laid. The counter was just inside the window and the bookseller sat behind it. He was arguing with someone over the phone.

A small sign on white card at the front of the window offered to buy books, but stipulated that they must be in a good, clean condition. As Pidge examined the contents of the window, the bookseller covered the mouthpiece of the telephone with his hand and shouted:

'Don't lean that bike against the glass!'

Pidge was taken aback. He felt like answering:

'I wasn't going to!' But he was far too polite and instead, he wheeled his bike a little further on and propped it against the shop wall, thinking: They're all the same, these shopkeepers. I wouldn't mind but I've never actually seen anyone break a window with a bike.

The picture that this conjured up made him smile. He was still smiling as he went into the shop through the opened door. The bookseller scowled.

The shop was filled with books. The shelves were all tightly packed; and boxes and piles of books were stacked in low walls almost everywhere, allowing only a bare passage by the shelves and down the middle. Pidge moved along, picking out a book to dip into from time to time.

At length he was right at the back of the shop. Here a door stood open, leading into a small back room. Intrigued, Pidge went inside.

It was dark in the little room. The one source of light was a small lancet window set very high up; and with the light having been so bright in the new shop, it took time for his eyes to adjust.

It was full of junk, all sorts of junk; there were boxes and bags of it. Some of the things had once been elegant, made of silks and satins and bedecked with sequins, but all was tarnished and spoiled now by time and dust. There were tea-chests full of mouldy shoes and boots. On top of one of these there was a concertina with a rip in it, and on another there was a collection of old fans, some with feathers that had moulted ages ago, leaving only the once-white ribs with a few tattered wisps of their former glory. There were tennis racquets that looked wavy and were without strings, a mirror that was dim with grime and a pair of rusted ice-skates.

'This must be all that's left of the old pawnshop,' he said quietly, feeling saddened.

At this point there were three loud bangs in the sky.

In the shop the bookseller leaped to his feet, and when Pidge craned his head to look, he saw him rush into the street. Just as he was about to follow after the bookseller to find out what was happening, a thin finger of sunlight beamed in from the little window above.

It was incredibly bright and it shone on a small package on the ground. Pidge picked up the package and found that it was simply some pages from an old book, tied in a bundle with string. The covers were missing but there was still a title-page. He examined it to see what the book had been about, to find out if it was worth reading. Even though the print used had an unfamiliar, squashed look about it, he saw that it said 'A Book Of Patrick's Writing'. All of the pages were dog-eared and had chewed edges; the top and bottom pages were rather grey.

It might be very boring, he thought.

While he was looking at the title, the finger of sunlight moved and lit up the pages in his hands. Pidge thought nothing of this, knowing that light moves all through the day, even though this seemed a bit fast; but suddenly he felt that he must have them! He must have these pages!

Not even caring now about the cross bookseller, or the sudden bangs in the sky, he marched back into the brightness of the shop.

The bookseller had not yet come back, but someone else was behind the counter, a thinnish old man with a great white moustache. He was deeply engrossed in the study of a paper with strange foreign writing on it.

He's a scholar, thought Pidge.

He stood for some moments waiting to be noticed. Just as he was about to speak, the man looked at him.

'Are you serving now?' Pidge asked.

13

The man nodded and smiled.

'I've always served,' he said.

Before Pidge could say anything else, the man added:

'You want to get rid of that in your hand? It's condition is bad—any price would be too high.'

'Oh no, you misunderstand,' Pidge hastened to say. 'I found this package in the back room. How much do you want for it, please?'

'Ah,' the man said softly. 'An old pledge from far-off days. Are you sure you want it?'

'If it doesn't cost too much,' said Pidge.

'Cost—ah, cost,' said the man thoughtfully. 'The price could be great, as I've said before. But money isn't the thing, is it?'

'No,' Pidge answered, not quite understanding his meaning.

'All that will burn in that back room is for burning, but we don't want that burned, do we? You would save it from the fire?'

'Yes, I would,' Pidge said.

He looked at the package. I don't know why I want it so much, but I do, he thought.

'Is there anything I could say that would stop you wanting this?' asked the man.

'No,' Pidge said, wondering at this peculiar question. 'I feel it's important to me.'

'Take it then and good luck to you,' the man said.

'No money?' Pidge asked.

'No money.'

At the front of the counter there was a small pile of cards, saying:

The New Second-Hand Bookshop Tel: 7979

I'll take one of those just to show that I mean to be a proper customer in the future, he thought; and he slipped one into his trouser pocket.

'Thank you very much,' he said as he left the shop.

'Thank *you*,' the man replied, rather fervently, Pidge felt.

There was no room in the saddle-bag so Pidge stuffed the pages inside his shirt, flat against his chest. The bookseller

14

passed him by without noticing him, and he was muttering 'Supersonic Jets or similar rubbish!', in an angry way as he went back into his shop.

I'm glad that *he* didn't serve me, Pidge smiled to himself, while he carefully buttoned his shirt.

The clock in the steeple struck four.

'Good heavens!' he said. 'How time has flown—and if anything, the day has grown hotter!'

As soon as he began to ride his bike through the town, he at once saw that a change of some kind had taken place. There was an unusual atmosphere and the crowds in the streets were wildly excited, as if it were Race Week again, or some sort of Festival time. People were rushing everywhere and the young Garda on point duty was as frisky as a racehorse. He was leaping about with flailing arms as if he were trying to herd quick-silver. One or two people stood looking and pointing at the sky, gabbling, but not listening to each other. Pidge looked up but there was nothing to see.

As he made a right turn after he had passed the Franciscan church, he glanced back and saw the two nuns again, and he had the illusion that one nun was turning a cartwheel and another was trying to stand on her head.

He pulled up, got off his bike and really looked back. Disappointingly, all was normal.

'I could have sworn I saw it,' he said. 'It must have been my imagination unless they were men dressed up. Mummers or such.'

He cycled on. Very soon he turned up the rough track to The Dyke by the side of Lough Corrib, making his way to Terryland and then on to Shancreg where he lived.

Now he was alone, with only the mild wind from the lake and the scratching, rattling sound it made in the dry rushes that grew so thickly by the water's edge.

For no reason at all, he shivered.

He had left The Dyke and was well into the country when he realized that darkness seemed to be creeping in very early in the evening for August.

He looked west towards the lake which was now at some

15

distance, and saw that the sky beyond the Connemara mountains was dark blue with darker streaks of purple, and the waters of the lake were coloured violet and mulberry, and the mountains themselves were a blurred mistiness of astonishing darkness. These near mountains were the familiar Maamturks. Beyond them stood the Twelve Pins, a region of mountains which Pidge had visited more than once on days out.

His mind drifted from one thing to another, the strangeness in the city already half forgotten. His father would be coming back from Dublin to-morrow. He had been at the Horse Show all the past week.

He was going to buy a magnificent mare who would be the mother of wonderful young horses. She would be the best mare in the whole country and her foals would be the wonder of the world.

Pidge hoped that she would be the colour of milky coffee with a long, blonde tail and mane. He knew that she would have a beautiful head and that her muzzle would be a soft warm velvet. He could hardly bear to wait until he looked into her gentle and intelligent eyes for the very first time. Then there would be the lovely gradual friendship, growing stronger day by day.

'Could I have a few syllybyls with you, young sir?'

Pidge looked round him.

Sitting on the wall in amongst the bushes, so that he was almost hidden from view, was a very ancient looking man wearing the appearance of an angler. His face was as wrinkled as dried apple skin; his tweed hat was stippled with artificial flies and there was a basket and rod standing up against the wall beside him. His eyes were a bright blue colour and they twinkled as dew drops lit by the sun.

Pidge got off his bike and walked over to him.

'Are you the young sir who's just been buying in Galway?'

'Well, I'm one of them, there must be dozens of others,' Pidge answered politely.

'That's a fair oul' catch you've got under your jumper,' the angler said, in an admiring way.

'That's not a catch at all,' Pidge smiled, thinking that fishermen all have one-track minds.

'Isn't it?' the old angler said with some doubt.

'No. Just some books.'

The man looked satisfied for some reason.

'I'm to tell you to watch out,' he said, 'there's danger at the crossroads.'

'At the crossroads up ahead? What kind of danger?'

'Too soon to say—but danger there is.'

Pidge could think of only one possible danger.

'You can't mean traffic, it's so quiet round here?'

'I can't mean traffic, young human sir—but you are to use the eye of clarity when you get to that spot. There's deluderings at the crossroads, such as would confound Geography and Cartography; such as would make Pandora's Box into a tuppeny lucky bag,' the old angler said earnestly, and added: 'Bad work and not many knowing it; quiet as water under the ground. You be careful, young mortal sir, as there's more than one kind of angling and you could be sniggled in a flash! There's lures and lures. That's my message!'

What a lot of strange things he said and I don't understand the half of it, Pidge thought. Aloud he said:

'Who told you to tell me? Was it the Gardai?'

'Couldn't say it was. But that's the chatter that's filling the place and I was to put you wise.' The old angler looked with dreadful earnestness straight into Pidge's eyes as if trying to impress the importance of his words on Pidge's brain. His concern was clearly very great.

'Well, thank you very much,' Pidge said.

'All the small wild things know it,' the old angler said. 'It's them that chatters.'

'They usually do,' Pidge replied, thinking of forest fires and how animals are said to scent danger from a silent wisp of smoke.

Not knowing what Pidge was thinking, the old angler looked surprised at Pidge's apparent knowledge.

'You know more than the Minister of Education,' he said and he swung his legs in behind the wall with great agility. He began to walk off.

'Don't forget your rod and basket,' Pidge called after him and put them over the wall.

'What rod and basket?'

He turned and came back. He smiled just a bit ruefully,

17

Pidge thought, when he saw that he had forgotten what should have been his most treasured possessions.

'Time has made a Nutmeg of me Brainbox, I fear,' he said and picked them up. 'My thanks to you and a safe journey.'

'My thanks to you and goodbye now,' Pidge said.

The old angler vanished from sight in the bushes. Probably on his way to the lake, Pidge decided.

He got back on his bike and rode on, his head turned towards the lake to try for a glimpse of the old man. He stood up on the pedals and looked at the expanse of fields and bushes. There was no sign of him anywhere and the only person visible was a distant youth with flowing fair hair, dressed in something white that looked like a tunic, who was running at an exuberant and impossible speed, just for the joy of it.

It must be the distance deceiving me, he thought. He's probably wearing some sort of sports kit and is running fast all right but not impossibly so. But I wonder where the old man has gone? He was nice. I liked him and he was so odd and interesting.

Before he could puzzle further about the old man, he was surprised by a large, freshly painted signboard stuck in by the side of the road. It said:

> THIS IS A VERY SAFE ROAD
> A BOY CAN CYCLE ON IT WITH HIS EYES SHUT.

And then there was another almost immediately after, saying:

> THIS ROAD HAS BEEN AWARDED THE
> VERY SAFE ROAD PRIZE
> IN
> THE ALL-IRELAND COMPETITION
> FOR VERY SAFE ROADS.
> ANY BOY CAN CYCLE ON IT WITH HIS EYES SHUT
> TRY IT TODAY

Pidge burst out laughing.

'It's just like a students' trick, although it isn't Rag week and they are all supposed to be gone home for their holidays. Maybe some of them are back early and they've got some kind of game going on for Charity. I wish I knew more about it and where the real fun is.'

He reached the summit of a small hill, stopped and got off his bike. The road rolled down ahead of him, and there below him and not too far away, was the crossroads.

And it was just the crossroads.

There was nothing there.

All was just as usual: the signpost, the stone walls and the few trees, growing slender and young in the corner of one of the four fields bordering the road. They were too few to be a good hiding-place for a would-be trickster.

A sense of disappointment was beginning in Pidge until he realized that he was standing in the middle of a dead silence.

There was no lowing of cattle in distant fields; no barking of dogs from farms even further distant; no soughing of the wind in the solid old trees growing right beside him on the hilltop; no birdsong or chatter; no clicking of grasshoppers in long grasses. No thing made any sound at all and there was only a stretching and continuing silence; stretching all round him and continuing far away.

Everything seemed to be holding its being in check, waiting for something to happen.

'My imagination again,' Pidge reflected. 'I wonder how many dead silences I've been in before and just not noticed because my head was busy with my own thoughts? Anyway, there's my road home—and home I must go.'

The silence persisted as he freewheeled down the hill.

It magnified the sounds of the bicycle; the squeaks that needed oiling; the whirr of the wheels and the click-clicking of the chain as he rested his feet on the pedals. Small stones rattled sharply against the inside of the mudguards as they jumped out from beneath the pressure of the wheels.

Each one sounded like a sharp handclap.

The bike sounds like a real old rattle trap; I'm sure it can be heard for miles, he thought.

A moment later he was there—at the crossroads at last and

about to cycle on when he happened to glance at the sign-post.

It was all turned round the wrong way.

All the four fingers were pointing in wrong directions.

'So that's it!' he exclaimed. 'Those rascals of students are trying to send people astray! What a funny idea and won't Auntie Bina have a good laugh when I tell her!'

He got off his bike again and inspected the signpost.

The finger that said 'Shancreg' was pointing in the direction of Kyledove.

Shancreg was the place where he lived and Kyledove was a great, tangled wood, dark and wild and frightening even in the bright middle of a summer's day. In its heart and centre there was an ancient, moss-covered ruin that had slipped and crumbled over long ages of time until its stones had the texture of old, damp biscuits.

Kyledove means Black Wood and that was because it never saw sunlight.

Just to think of it gave Pidge a cold feeling because of its darkness, its whippy thorny traps and its great age, stretching far, far back in local tradition.

I hate to spoil the students' joke, he thought, but I'd better change that back in case any stranger would get lost.

He hesitated for a while, looking round to see if he could see someone to explain how he felt about strangers getting lost, in case such a thing had not occurred to the jokers; but there wasn't a soul to be seen.

Still the silence was unfailing.

It began to annoy Pidge a little bit. He tried to break it and attract someone's attention by shouting out as powerfully as he could 'Hallooooooo!'—but there was no resonance so it was like shouting into cotton-wool.

The sky changed to a strange green colour. There was a curious mesmerizing atmosphere as the green light filled the pools of the brown bog away at a little distance to his right. Something nudged at the borders of his mind and for a little while, he was puzzled. Then he realized that his surroundings held a definite element of menace.

'It's not the students,' he said suddenly and loudly. 'It's magic.'

Just then, the pages seemed to move of their own accord, inside his shirt.

The skin tightened on his head from shock and freezing goosepimples stood out all over his body.

'I *must* change it back!'

He threw his bike down and ran to the signpost. He gripped it and the sky began to spin; and Pidge *knew* that if he didn't put it right, the country would somehow obey the signpost and twist round and that, even though he was headed directly for Shancreg and home, he would end up in Kyledove. Pidge knew this with his whole body though he didn't understand it with his mind.

As he gathered his strength together and prepared for a hard struggle, the sky went even faster and the clouds raced round and around above his head. There was a low zooming sound like the whirring of a toy paper whizzer.

He gave the signpost a good, hard twist.

To his amazement, it spun round quite easily, as if turning on oiled wheels. Pidge set it in the right position and the sky became blue and tranquil and the countryside all round him woke up. There was no more soft silence.

In the near-distance, he could hear the sound of a motor-bike. It seemed to be going cross-country from Kyledove to join with the road up ahead of him.

'The old angler was right,' Pidge said quietly to himself, there *was* danger at the crossroads and I was all but sniggled, whatever that is. But for him, I wouldn't have given a single thought to the crossroads and I would have just cycled on and ended up at Kyledove. And whoever painted those daft notices was just trying to snare me and undo the good the old angler had done. Goodness knows why. But, as to the pages—I must have jogged them somehow and imagined they moved, because there was a funny feeling about, with the sky so strange and everything; I'd have jumped at my own shadow, just then. I won't stop now because I don't want to hang about in case the sky means there's to be a storm—but I'll have a good look at them when I get home.'

Cycling on home, he searched in his mind for a reasonable explanation. He was begining to think that he had made much out of little and that, really, there was nothing sinister about the signpost or the excitable people in Galway, or the sky or anything, and that he was only having a wonderful day full of interest, when he arrived at the roadworks.

There were two big signs standing smack in front of him on the road. One said:

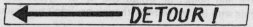

HALT! ROADWORKS AHEAD

The other one had a big, yellow arrow on it and the word:

← ——————— **DETOUR!**

The arrow pointed to a gap tumbled carelessly in the roadside wall.

There was a simple barricade cutting off the road. It looked as if it had been thrown together in a hurry; only some barrels placed at the sides of the road with planks laid across them. Nothing else. No materials or tools of any kind. Not even a shovel to work with.

'I'm not going to be put about anymore,' Pidge said firmly and he was off the bike in a flash. He pushed the planks off the barrels and cleared a way through for himself. While he was doing this, he heard the motor-bike again in the distance. It seemed to be going further on, past his own house, which was now not *too* far away.

Only five minutes or so, thought Pidge, and I'm home—if I put my head down and go fast. The same thing that wanted me to go to Kyledove tried to stop me just now and get me off the road and into the fields. Maybe then, I would have been wrapped in a sudden mist rolling down on top of me from nowhere and I would have been lost in a whiteness that could be worse than any darkness. But the trick with the signpost hadn't worked, thanks to the old angler. And there hasn't been enough time for *it* or *them* (he gave a small shiver because he didn't know which and both ideas were frightening) to do the job properly and make that road-block look convincing enough to fool a hen. Or maybe I'm being plain daft?

Determined to look neither to the left or to the right, he rode on.

'I'll soon be home now and a good job too,' he said loudly.

Chapter 2

*T*HEY *had blown on the signpost and set it spinning so that when it stopped it pointed in wrong directions. They had sent their servants to trick him into a false sense of safety. The trick had failed.*

'*Imbeciles! Couldn't you have thought of something better than painted signs?*' *was the question they asked.*

'*In the time given, we wrought at our best,*' *the reply came in servile, cringing tones.*

'*A boy can cycle on it with his eyes shut!*' *they mimicked in derision.*

The servants hung their heads and with their tails drooping in abasement, they made little whines that asked forgiveness.

'*And roadworks, you dumb-bells! Such roadworks! Why, it wouldn't have fooled a hen!*'

The servants lay humble on the ground and covered their eyes with their paws.

Now, the two strange women on the powerful motor-bike, and followed by their servant hounds, pulled up at the little house where Old Mossie Flynn lived.

In the space of three minutes they told him a string of lies as long as the Shannon river and bedazzled him with smiles of great brilliance and jokes of great wit, while they muffled his good sense by plastering him with outrageous flattery until he was like raw dough in the hands of a master baker.

They persuaded him to rent them his glasshouse.

The befuddled Mossie thought this very comical and said that they and their beautiful hounds would be an addition to the locality.

'We will be,' they said. They smiled at each other; Mossie's glasshouse stood only three small fields away from the house where Pidge lived.

The stupefied Mossie then offered to give them all his furniture.

They thought his concern was truly amusing. Don't worry about furniture, they said in their funny voices as they clouted each other on the backs with merriment.

It's ordered.

It's coming.

It's on its way.

They thanked him and gave him a week's rent and had impelled him outside the glasshouse door before he had even realized that he was on his way out.

He stood staring at the glasshouse in fascination. The two women encouraged him to leave by waving 'bye 'bye at him while their smiles grew harder and harder. At last Mossie went back inside his cottage and sat by the fire chuckling as he lit his pipe.

Inside the glasshouse the two women looked at each other, sending a message of deep meaning from brain to brain with one glance. Then they clutched each other and fell about laughing for ten whole minutes before they set to work to furnish their glasshouse home.

A little while later, a young Swedish rock-climber, who had been misdirected in Galway by a stranger who didn't know his right hand from his left, found himself far from the mountainy district of Connemara where he *wished* to be and on the east side of the county close to Mossie's little farm. To his mystification, he saw a wardrobe make a perfect landing on the area in front of a glasshouse. Its landing was assisted by a couple of strange women with the aid of two table-tennis bats. The women appeared to be treating the whole thing as an extravagant joke.

He looked upwards and saw a succession of domestic objects appear in the sky above the glasshouse, where they circled and waited their turn to land.

In a big departmental store in Galway, there was turmoil. People were astounded as objects became flying objects and took off out of various windows. There was boundless panic as floor managers tried to grasp the fleeing items and customers hid under the counters or tried to climb into boxes.

Two people fainted and were brought round with brandy.

Then they were recognized as two people who *always* fainted when there was a chance of being brought round with brandy and to their disgust they were told to pay up.

A fearless country-woman was having a fight with a pair of sheets that she was trying to buy, as they struggled to escape from her and become aerial. The sheets broke loose and joined all the other articles to vanish from sight in the sky.

Everybody saw them go; only the Swedish rock-climber saw where they landed and who became their new owners.

Which is it? he wondered to himself, crime or magic? And what should I do? He decided that all he could do at that moment was walk on, and that's what he did.

By this time the distracted Manager of the store had sent for the Gardai, who threw a living cordon round the block, while a sceptical Sergeant made notes in his notebook.

They all waited for something else to fly away.

The two women laughed now that the supernatural shop-lifting was over. They put out a sign saying 'Beware Of The Frog' and closed the door.

Mossie came out and sneaked a look across at the glass-house. Except for some (stolen) venetian blinds covering all the glass, everything looked the same. He wrongly supposed that they had had the blinds in their saddle-bags all the time.

Then he saw the sign.

He nipped over to read it.

'They've done another funny thing,' he said happily and went back indoors.

The Sergeant and his Gardai waited patiently until closing-time. Looking at him very suspiciously, the Sergeant asked the Manager if he had drink taken? The Manager nearly exploded with rage. The Sergeant said, well, maybe it was all a mirage? The Manager pointed out that there were witnesses to the day's events, up in the hospital suffering from shock.

'Mass hypnosis,' said the Sergeant.

'Where's all me stock gone so?' asked the Manager.

'Where indeed!' said the Sergeant drily, 'I'm keeping my eye on you from now on!'

The Sergeant went off for his evening strut.

25

The Manager wished that his trousers would fall down.

'Granted!' said one of the women in Shancreg.

The Sergeant's trousers fell down in folds round his ankles. He pulled them up angrily and went home to write a letter to The Irish Times about how the climate had rotted his braces.

Whenever the Sergeant and the Manager met after that day, hostility lay like a force-field between them. This was very sad as they both loved growing roses more than anything else in the whole world and they could have been friends for many long and happy years.

The two women were gleefully conscious of all this, even though they were miles and miles away in Shancreg.

The end of a perfect day, they said to each other and shrieked with laughter until the tears came hot and glittery to their merciless eyes.

Auntie Bina was watching for him and waved when she saw Pidge turn in at the boreen from the main road.

'Isn't it strangely dark!' she cried out to him in her high, careful voice, 'I'm thinking there might be a storm tonight!'

Pidge knew instantly that she had been worrying about him; there was something extra about the tone of her voice that told him so. He felt a sudden rush of love for her and, then and there, he resolved not to tell her everything about the journey home—just the bit about the roadworks, because nothing extraordinary had really happened then.

Now that he was safe, he wanted to reach out and grasp hold of everything that was familiar and trusted. Instead, he quietly began to take Auntie Bina's shopping out of the saddle-bag.

'Where's Brigit?' he asked.

'Is it me you're asking?' said Auntie Bina. 'You know Brigit; she could be anywhere.'

'Maybe we should call her in? In case it storms?'

He tried to make his voice sound casual and ordinary. It bothered him to think that Brigit was happily wandering around on her own. She was so daring and innocent. She could easily get sniggled, being only five years old and five years daft.

'Brigit!' he shouted loudly.

'What?' she said, climbing out of an old unused water-butt, using blocks of wood for steps. 'What are you shouting for?'

'I thought you were lost,' Pidge said foolishly.

'*Me* lost? I never get lost. I've just this minute been down to the inside of the world and I met a mad earwig and we went to a Battle and then I came back and I never got lost, not even for a second.'

'Did you bring anything back from your journey?' Auntie Bina asked.

'Only the mad earwig. I brought him up to give him some cough mixture to make him better, but you can have him if you want him.'

Auntie Bina thought it over.

'I don't think I need one,' she said. 'Better leave him free.'

Later, when they were finishing tea, Pidge told them about the roadworks.

'Wasn't there even a rheumatic drill?' Brigit wanted to know. She took a great bite of bread and butter and scraped the last of her egg from inside the shell.

'Maybe it's The Martians,' Auntie Bina said, because she was very interested in Outer Space and was always reading books about it. Sometimes she would stand on the small hill at the back of the house, with a seaman's telescope held up to one eye as she looked for Flying Saucers. Pidge laughed at the idea of the Martians doing roadworks for the County Council and then he was conscious of the lovely lightness of feeling that filled his whole body after laughter.

'It wasn't The Martians,' he said and he was really sure of that.

But, he thought, *somebody* must have done it, after all. Apart from the old angler—who else was on the road at the time? He had a vague feeling of missing out something important. Then suddenly he asked:

'Did you see anyone pass by on a motor-bike?'

'No,' Auntie Bina said.

'*I* did,' Brigit said matter of factly. 'Two queer ones with loads of dogs. One of them had two miles of red hair floating out behind her like a cloak and the other one had sort of blue hair twisted round her head like ropes. The blue one was smoking a cigar. The dogs were skinny and they ran like water. They waved at me but I pretended I didn't see them, 'cos I didn't like the look of them.'

'Ah, they must be tourists,' Auntie Bina said, laughing at Brigit.

'Brigit! We have enough with mad earwigs,' Pidge exclaimed sharply, because he wanted to really know and not just be amused by one of Brigit's stories.

'It's true,' she said calmly. 'They went to Mossie Flynn's.'

Strange tourists, thought Pidge.

Brigit began to yawn and immediately said that she wasn't a bit tired. The more that she declared that she wasn't tired, the bigger the yawns.

'Honest!' she lied, 'the rest of me isn't a bit tired, only my mouth.' Her eyelids started to close.

'No nonsense now, Brigit. You couldn't keep your eyelids open if you pinned them up with clothes-pegs,' Auntie Bina said.

'Could we try?' She chanced.

'Bed for you. Come on now.'

Reluctantly Brigit submitted to being washed, said good-night to Pidge and went ahead of Auntie Bina up the ladder-stair, that led to the two small bedrooms in the loft.

Pidge left his place at the table and went to the old-fashioned hearth.

There were two little stone seats built into the hearth, one on either side of the fire. You could sit in there and see right up the chimney to where a patch of the sky showed at the top. He hunched up his knees to make a bony lectern on which to rest his pages of Patrick's writings. He settled himself to examine them in comfort.

They were old but Pidge couldn't guess how old. There was a musty smell from them with some other fragrance mingling in; something like camphor mixed with old rose petals. The pages were stiff and held together by worn leather thongs.

'I know what they are!' he cried joyfully. 'They are part of an old Celtic manuscript, written and painted long ago by a monk sitting all alone in his little beehive cell in one of the monasteries. Well, isn't that a piece of luck! I can just imagine him—making his own colours because he couldn't very well buy them when there weren't any shops, and probably his fingers nearly dropping off with cold in the winter—his nose too, I wouldn't be surprised!'

He turned the title page and saw that the next page was decorated with many colours, now faded.

At first glance, he had the impression of an elaborate pattern rolling smoothly in loops and spirals all over the page, but worked at with careful control. Then he saw that the pattern had some animals inside it; impossible animals, created not by nature but out of the dreams of man.

Oh, he wondered, am I really touching paper that was made and used by one of those far away monks? Did he have to do a lot of this work by rushlight in the evenings or in the dark days of winter? Whatever would he think of electricity or printing machines or photography or anything you could buy in Woolworths? But how can I be? All the old manuscripts have long since been gathered into museums and universities and are looked on as great treasures. This one must be some sort of fake.

He was turning to the next page when a loose bit fell out. He managed to grab it before it fell into the fire; and it was then that he heard the voice in the chimney.

Imprison it in iron, it whispered.

Pidge froze into a statue of himself. He didn't dare move. He sat with his eyes staring straight ahead, not seeing anything, but *feeling* with the back of his neck. After a long, long moment of this, he tried to make his head vanish inside his body like a tortoise pulling into his shell.

It was as though he were getting ready to receive a blow on the head.

Don't be afraid, said the Voice. *I am your friend.*

Oh, what'll I do, thought Pidge fearfully.

Am I hurting you? the Voice asked with infinite gentleness.

'No.'

Believe in my friendship.

'But, I'm afraid.'

Listen! said the Voice.

Music flooded down the chimney as if it were water surging over the edge of a fall. It hushed—and there was a downpouring of perfumed light, in accord with the clear and perfect notes of a solitary flute, in which the light rejoiced and danced.

29

It all faded and whispered away.

Look up!

Pidge looked up and saw the night-time. It was filled with glittering stars.

I write my name, said the Voice.

Out of the multitude, the biggest and the brightest of the stars formed the word:

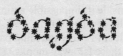

Pidge felt his whole body shaking violently. Slowly he realized that it was Auntie Bina and she was saying:

'Wake up! Are you mad? You could fall into the fire, sitting there asleep.'

So it was a dream; a marvellous dream and so real.

He stared up the chimney.

It was as always; vast and wide and sooty—nothing wonderful there. The sky had clouded over. Not one single star shone through the heavy blanket of darkness.

Auntie Bina was in a typically talkative mood. She flung herself into a humorous retelling of the principal events of her day. Mostly it concerned her daily battle of wits with a very cunning little hen. For over a week now, she had been laying her eggs in a secret place. Auntie Bina had been tracking her. Even so the little hen was still winning. She wouldn't leave the farmyard if anyone were looking, but pretended to search for delicacies on the ground, while she watched with her bright eyes all the time. But as soon as the yard was deserted—she was off. She was clever enough to keep in cover as well and kept to the hedges and walls, and she wouldn't dream of walking down the middle of a field, in case she'd be seen.

Pidge couldn't listen at first while he still marvelled at his wonderful dream—but, gradually, his mind was opened to her voice. Every word she said took him a little step away from the marvel, yet it seemed to him that he would never entirely lose it. It made him happy to think that he owned it forever and that, whenever he wanted to, he could recall it in his mind.

At length, it was time for bed.

He raised the latch on his bedroom door and stepped inside the little room's tight snugness. He closed the door gently, so as not to disturb Brigit, whose breathing he could hear through the partition. He sat on his bed and carefully opened the tattered book. As he did so, the loose page fluttered out again, almost as though it were trying to get away from him. Pidge snatched it up before it touched the floor and leaned forward to get the best of the light.

Now that he could see it properly, he discovered that it wasn't one page at all but two stuck together. At least, they had been stuck together once, but they were now splitting apart.

The top page was undecorated except for a large drawing of a cross. Beneath the cross there was some faint writing in big letters. The writing was in latin.

He could read it but he could only understand one or two of the words. He read:

O Serpens Vilissimus
Et Hic Signo Et His Verbis
Te Sic Securo In Saecula Saeculorum
Amen
Patricus

Well, *In Saecula Saeculorum Amen*—meant forever and ever, so be it. That was simple. He had heard it said in prayers. And *Patricus* must be latin for Patrick. There was something about *Sic* in it. Did it mean someone was sick? And *Verbis*—did it mean that someone was sick of his verbs? *His Verbis?* Or was it an ancient cure for someone who was ill?

What a pity I'm only ten and haven't started to learn latin yet or I could easily solve this puzzle, he told himself. I'll find out what it means, if I can. A scholar would know. I wonder if the underneath page will be more interesting?

It was funny but he couldn't really see what it was all about. As soon as he looked at any part of it, the bits that he wasn't looking at began to shift and change on the page. He could *nearly* see it happening out of the corner of his eye. He made his eyes search every inch of it as fast as he could but he was never quick enough to see anything happen. Each time, as soon as his gaze moved on from one piece of it, that piece began to move. No matter how quickly he returned his attention to it, he couldn't catch it in time. That bit would then be still—while the bit beside it would tempt him to look *there* by seeming to glide or dance or just tremble.

He shut his eyes tight and squeezed his lids together with all the strength he could manage. When his eyes were as tight as tight could be, he opened them as suddenly as could ever be possible and looked commandingly at the page.

He saw it then.

It was a snake.

Serpens! he thought. That's what the writing is about.

It was odd in that it didn't look painted on the page at all. It looked carved somehow—carved out of green glass. It was extraordinary as well, that one moment he could see nothing, the next moment, there was this vivid, brilliant thing; as if curtains had been pulled aside by an invisible hand.

As if the snake had wished itself to be seen.

It was long and thin and twisted into the most intricate of looping patterns. Its head looked as though it might be alive but was pretending not to be. The split tongue seemed to flicker, and did its eyes just slide a fraction of an inch?

A pinpoint of light appeared in its eyes and flared into a blue spark. Pidge stared, as it grew bigger.

The light appeared to have the power to hold him and draw him into a perilous other world; it was so compelling. To his horror, he found that he was unable to resist. The eyes vanished and he was being pulled into a dark forest where the trees were evilly alive and pale wicked flowers waited to catch hold of him. It was a hideous world and its grasses were reaching out to whip round his ankles and imprison him forever.

Then Auntie Bina finished her prayers and got into her bed and made the springs creak. This ordinary thing broke the dream in pieces and Pidge woke up to find that the page had gone!

It had been in his hand and it had vanished!

The first feeling that rushed into him, filling him from top to toe with the most exalted relief, was pure delight that the ugly thing had gone. Instantly came the memory of the Voice in the chimney-dream which had said, or *commanded*, that he imprison it in iron and he knew that he must find it whatever happened. He dropped to his knees to look under the bed.

There it was, half-way through a crack in the floorboards; could it have been trying to escape?

Pidge reached in under the bed and caught it. He took Patrick's page with the latin writing and in it he wrapped the snake page. He roughly folded them in half and then in quarters and held them tightly in his fist. He waited for Auntie Bina to fall asleep. He listened for her first snore.

When it came, it sounded beautiful and musical and human. I'd never have believed I'd think that, Pidge remarked to himself.

He left his room and crept down into the dark kitchen. There was no light at all from the fire. Auntie Bina had banked up the burning turf with soft white ashes to keep the fire living all night. Some houses had fires that hadn't gone out for two hundred years or more.

Kneeling down, he blew some of the ashes away and coaxed the turf to provide a little light.

By the side of the hearth, Auntie Bina kept her bastable oven; a strong, iron pot oven with a flat lid and a lug at each side to hook onto the crook that hung down the chimney. It had three little legs so that, if you liked, you could cook with it on the hearth by lighting a small, separate fire under it and laying the red sods of glowing turf on the lid. It could stew, bake or roast food.

Pidge glanced at it and realized at once that it was exactly the prison he needed. He lifted the heavy iron lid and laid the folded pages on the oven's floor. They fluttered, seemingly in protest. He stood up and reached from the mantle-piece an old flat-iron and he laid it on the pages as an iron obstruction, before putting on the lid. To be really safe, he inserted the tongs through the half-oval handle on top of the lid and left them resting their iron weight as a further hindrance.

He carefully scooped up a few small shovel-fulls of ashes and re-banked the fire.

Then he went cheerfully to bed.

The night had turned wet and it was so pleasant to lie in bed listening to the rain picking at the windows.

He was snug and felt safe and warm. The spectacular sky must have only meant rain, after all. He turned over and snuggled further down, keeping an ear outside the covers to listen to the rain.

At that moment, a very powerful motor-bike roared into life just below his window. It revved a couple of times and then it was off. By the sound it made, he judged that it was leaping over a wall and then the noise began to diminish, as the bike went further away.

Pidge jumped out of bed and ran to look out. But he was too late.

Whoever it was had now gone and he could see almost nothing anyway, through the glaze of the rain.

He got back into bed.

It wasn't very nice to think that whoever it was *might* have been watching him through the window while he was in the kitchen.

The iron prison must have done the trick, he thought.

He was just beginning to wonder why Auntie Bina or Brigit hadn't been disturbed by the noise, when he fell asleep.

Chapter 3

PIDGE woke suddenly, his heart banging a little bit, but it was only the morning light on his face that disturbed him. He lay still as a stone for a while, thinking over the strange events of yesterday. The long, calm hours of sleep between evening and morning had taken away the realness of it all and diminished it of its life, so that now it was no more than something experienced in a passive way, like a film. But the gap of night did not blot out a small core of knowledge that remained inside his head, stripped of drama and standing true; yesterday, and all it had held, had happened all right.

He slipped out of bed and began to dress. He had better retrieve the page before Auntie Bina decided to bake bread.

It must be very early, he thought. I'm the first one up. No sound from the kitchen and quietness everywhere.

In the stillness, the latch on his bedroom door squeaked loudly enough to awaken even Brigit. He waited a second before going down to the kitchen but nobody stirred.

The fire looked lifeless and grey in the sunlight and the tongs still rested on the lid of the oven. In two seconds, he had the dreadful page in his hand. He unfolded it and looked at it, half expecting the snake to leap out of the page and strike its fangs into his hand.

But the snake dutifully decorated the page, and what struck him now was its beauty. There was no trace of the wicked white flowers, or the trees with evil life, or the ensnaring grass. He must have completely imagined them.

Still, there was something about the snake that was more than just painting. He re-folded the page, stuffed it inside his shirt and went back up to his bedroom.

'Hallo,' said Brigit's voice as he closed the door behind him. 'Where were you?'

He looked up. Brigit's hands gripped the top of the partition but the rest of her was lost from view. She was striving to look over at him and was pulling herself up with her toes dug into the wooden wall. Her head appeared briefly and then she slid back down. Having disappeared for a few seconds, she struggled back up again.

'Well?'

She vanished once more.

He waited until her head was there again.

'I was just downstairs.'

Brigit accepted this answer without question; she was often just somewhere herself.

'Did you hear the rustlers in the night?' she asked, hooking herself over the edge of the partition with her elbows.

'What rustlers?' he asked, startled.

'Didn't you hear them? They made their getaway on a motor-bike.'

So Brigit had heard it too.

'Maybe you were dreaming,' he offered hopefully.

'No, I wasn't. It was too plain. Dreams are fuzzy and they've got chocolate and sweets in them. And icing sugar and bikes. I'll bet you anything, they've rustled the pig.'

'Ah, who would want to rustle a pig!'

'Pig-rustlers! Gangsters on motor-bikes; "Steal a pig one minute and off to a Dinner Dance the next," is what they say. They don't care a straw for anyone.'

'I don't know where you get your notions, Brigit.'

'I get them from nowhere. They just come—and why are you up so early?'

'I thought I'd go and look for mushrooms,' he said. He felt guilty about telling her a lie, but for the moment he didn't know what else to do.

'Good!' she declared. 'I won't be long getting dressed. Wait a few minutes, will you?'

Right away, they found mushrooms enough for breakfast in the top half of Grangefield; and feeling very hungry now, they were just deciding to turn for home, when they saw Old Mossie Flynn huffing and puffing as he climbed the stone wall into the field.

'Grand day!' he cried out when he came close enough to salute them.

'We've been up hours and hours,' Brigit said proudly.

'Have you? Aren't you the great girl.'

'Yes. Chasing pig-rustlers and God knows what!'

'Did you catch any of them?'

'Not yet but I will later. I have to get some handcuffs first.'

'Where will you get them?'

'Oh, somewhere,' she answered vaguely.

'Did you get many little musheroons, this morning?' Mossie asked.

'We got fourteen hundred or so,' she told him.

Mossie was laughing. Everybody knew about Brigit and her stories.

'Well, I hope you left a few for me,' he said cheerfully.

'We didn't go near the bottom half at all; there should be plenty down there,' said Pidge. 'We only got about a capful.'

'Good. Now, wait'll ye hear my news!' Mossie said with great satisfaction. 'I've two right queer ones below on my place!'

'How do you mean?' Pidge asked.

'Two ladies, they are. You'll never believe it but one of them dyes her hair blue. She has golden wheels in her ears and I declare to God, she smokes cigars! She says her name is Melodie Moonlight, if my hearing is not gone astray entirely. Melodie Moonlight,' he repeated wonderingly. 'Did you ever hear the beat of it for a name?'

'What's the other one called?' asked Pidge.

'As good as the first or nearly. She says her name is Breda Fairfoul! And if the first one smokes cigars—well then, the second one is not far after her, for she chews tobacco. The likes of it I never saw in a woman! Anyway, to go on! The first one has blue hair—like a sort of bluestone spray for potato blight, and begod, the second one has orange hair hanging in flames down her back like a horse's tail.'

'Oh, them two!' Brigit said scornfully. 'I saw them yesterday. They have dogs and an oul' motor-bike!'

'What are they doing on your place?' said Pidge.

'Renting my old glasshouse! They are paying me good money to live in it. What do you think of that now, hah? It isn't everyone has the like of them to stay is it?'

'Living in your glasshouse? They must be daft,' Brigit said because she was feeling a bit jealous.

37

'Why are they?' Pidge wanted to know.

'Because they're artists and a bit touched,' Mossie said with pride. 'They told me they do it out of bits of old bikes and tractors and the like. They said it delights them to make Works Of Art out of old rubbish. They are very funny as well. Such jokes they have between themselves, always roaring laughing at something, they are.'

'Do they do any painting?' Pidge thought he must ask.

'Painting?'

'Signboards, for instance?'

'They didn't say so. I don't think they do.'

'Oh,' Pidge said.

'Well, I'll be getting on,' Mossie said.

'Mind they don't make a Work Of Art out of you, Mossie,' Brigit said, half as a joke and half in resentment that Mossie liked them so much.

As they walked towards the gate, she kept looking back and waving.

'I don't like them two at Mossie's,' she said.

'Not them two, those two,' Pidge said.

'Why not them two?' she demanded.

'I don't remember but it's those two, anyway.'

'Well, I don't like those two and if you meet them, sure you won't like them either, sure you won't Pidge?' she asked him.

'Not if you don't,' Pidge promised.

'I suppose Mossie likes them 'cos they'll give him a spin on that oul' motor-bike. I wish I had one myself.'

They walked along in the sunshine. By the time they had reached the bend in the road, Brigit was saying that she wouldn't have a motor bike if they went down on their bended knees and begged her to have one. She'd far rather have a foal or a 'hellercoptor'.

There was a phone-box tucked in by the wall at the turning. It gave Pidge an idea.

'Wait here a minute, Brigit. I just want to phone someone,' he said.

He went inside, took the small card from his trouser pocket and dialled the number of the second hand bookshop.

After a few seconds, the bookseller's gruff voice came down the line.

'Hallo!' He sounded as cross as ever. Pidge's heart sank.

'Hallo. 'Is that the bookseller?' he asked politely.

'It is!'

'Could I speak to the assistant?'

'What assistant?'

'The old one with the white moustache'

'What? What nonsense is this?'

'Could I please speak to the old man with the white moustache—the scholar?'

'What scholar? What are you talking about?'

'He was there yesterday. I saw him.'

'No one works for me as an assistant.'

'But he was there yesterday.'

'Must have been a customer. A scholar you say?'

'Yes.'

'What kind of scholar?'

Pidge thought for a moment.

'A latin scholar,' he said, crossing his fingers.

'I'm a scholar of latin myself.'

'Oh?' said Pidge. 'Could you translate something?'

'I could!'

'Well, will you?'

'You're a boy, aren't you?'

'Yes.'

'Don't they teach you latin at school?'

'Not yet. I'm not old enough.'

'Are you trying to fool me into doing your homework for you?'

'Honestly! It's the summer holidays. I haven't got any homework and I don't learn latin. Honestly!' Pidge said earnestly.

'All right so. Fire away!'

'Right. Here it comes,' said Pidge. ' "O Serpens Vilissimus! Et hic signo et his verbis Te sic securo, in Saecula Saeculorum, Amen. Patricus." '

'That's simple!' the bookseller said loftily. 'It means: "O most vile serpent! By this sign and these words, thus I secure thee, forever and ever, Amen, Patrick" Or words to that effect. Ask me another one. Go on! I'm in the mood now.'

'I haven't got any more to ask,' said Pidge politely. 'Thank you very much for your help.'

'Your latin pronunciation is atrocious—don't know what the world's coming to.' said the bookseller.

'Is it?'

'Are you sure there isn't any more for me to do while I'm in the mood?'

'No.'

'That's it then!'

'There *was* an old man serving in your shop. You didn't see him because you ran outside to look at "supersonic jets or similar rubbish" '

'Don't be so cheeky!' the bookseller said and he hung up.

Brigit was sitting on a wall.

'Who did you phone?'

'I can't say just yet,' Pidge answered, feeling mean.

'Is it a secret?'

'Yes.'

'Tell me.'

'I will later. Let's get home. I'm starving.'

'So am I. I could eat an elephant.'

Pidge laughed and gave her a little friendly push.

'No you couldn't. It'd never fit inside you.'

Brigit imagined what shape she would be with an elephant inside her. It made her forget to ask any more questions about the phone call.

Pidge caught her by the hand and they ran together towards the boreen and home. All of the way, he wondered about the old man in the bookshop.

To Brigit's deep disgust, the pig hadn't been rustled after all. He was in a field close by the house, grunting and rooting in his normal happy way.

'Bet you they tried but he was too clever for them,' she said.

Breakfast was delicious; thick rashers of home-cured bacon, fresh field mushrooms, and wholemeal bread with yellow home-made butter. Auntie Bina had cooked it for them before going out to shadow the little hen.

While they were eating, there was a hesitant, sly sort of knock on the front door; a sort of searching whisper of a tapping rather than a bang-bang-I'm-here knock. A knock to find out if anyone was in.

Pidge opened the door.

A strange man smiled into the kitchen. He was extremely tall and thin—stretched out like elastic and on his back rested a large, brown bag that bulged in places.

'Good morning to you, young sir,' he said and showed his teeth again in a smile. Pidge hated his smile because his teeth looked so sharp and needle-like. For the sake of politeness however, he gave him a good morning in reply.

'Is the lady of the house in?' asked the man.

Pidge had the impression that the man was well aware that they were alone in the house without the protection of an adult.

'*I'm* the lady of the house,' Brigit said rudely. 'What do you want?'

The man smiled again and pretended to believe her.

'Oh?' he said. 'So young for such work! I wonder now, ma'am, if you have anything you'd like to sell? Any old gold or silver?'

'No,' said Brigit brazen-faced. 'All my old gold and silver is brand-new.'

'What about old pictures? Have you any old pictures— paintings, drawings, gilt frames or anything like that to sell?' and he looked at her so sharply, while the tip end of his tongue flickered over his lips, that Brigit lost a little of her courage.

'No. I'm sorry,' she said.

'No old pictures? No old gold or silver? What about old books?' said the man.

'No,' Brigit said.

'Are you sure?' he asked. 'Are you positive?'

'Of course I'm positive,' she replied. 'I never tell lies!'

Pidge went bright red at this declaration from Brigit. Some people might think she seldom told the truth. At least she's got her courage back, he thought.

'So sorry to give offence,' smiled the stranger, and his pink tongue flickered again. 'I only meant to jog your memory, in case you had something to sell, and it had slipped your mind for the moment.'

'My memory doesn't need jogging,' said Brigit. 'I've got cups and medals for it.'

'What about you, young man,' said the stranger, turning to

41

look at Pidge. 'Any old books to sell today?'

He knows, thought Pidge. He really knows I've got that tattered old book.

'No,' he said.

'Not even one?' said the stranger in false tones of amazement.

'Not even one,' Pidge repeated firmly and turned his head away.

'Hard times for pedlars and dealers,' said the man. 'Still, you've got your health and health is more than wealth, they say!'

This was said with a dark look from soft brown eyes and seemed to Pidge to be a threat. He felt sure that the soft brown eyes were not a real indication of the man's true nature.

He stole another look at the pedlar.

He was reminded of something but he couldn't think what it was. Even though he was unusually tall and thin, the man was beautifully built. There was a litheness about him that suggested strong muscle underneath the clothes. His waist was lean and his face long and narrow. The soft brown eyes held yellow glints. Then Pidge knew of what he was reminded, for the man had the look of a finely bred animal; something like the horses his father bred.

The pedlar stared back at Pidge and then he smiled again.

Pidge saw the pointy teeth so sharp and creamy-coloured and the pink tongue flickering over them. He saw the great strength resting quietly in the fine slim build of the shoulders and he realized as well, that all of the time the stranger had been at the door his nostrils had never stopped working—as though the man were smelling at every single thing that lay inside the house. Smelling and identifying without having to think while he was doing it.

He's like a greyhound, thought Pidge. Not a greyhound but a hound of a more ferocious breed? And maybe he has smelled the book?

'I'll buy your thoughts if you'll sell them?' the pedlar said softly.

He stood for a moment waiting for Pidge to reply and then he went away down the boreen towards the road. He left Pidge feeling very stunned.

'Well,' said Brigit. 'That's the strangest looking creature

I've ever seen. I didn't like him the smallest bit.'

'Neither did I,' said Pidge.

'What a funny thing he said about selling your thoughts, Pidge. I wonder what he meant?'.

Pidge wondered if he should tell her all the things that had happened since his visit to the bookshop the day before.

But, suppose all of the strange things hadn't truly happened? Suppose it was real in the way that say—a painting was real? A painting is canvas, wood, paint and things; but the artist could make a bowl of oranges, or a whole valley somewhere, or a battle, or anything he wanted to, out of his materials and they always looked real, didn't they? It was something in the artist's mind that did it. Maybe, he was doing the same thing in another way? I'll leave it for a while, he decided.

'Your guess is as good as mine,' he replied truthfully.

They washed up the dishes and then the whole day lay stretched before them like a sheet of white paper with nothing written on it. There was the feeling that time was not passing at its correct speed. The day would be long in passing, because today their father was coming back from Dublin with the new mare.

An ordinary day unfolds itself bit by bit and is sometimes full of surprises; a day with an expected high point built into it is hard to bear.

'It's going to be a long day today,' Pidge said. He wiped the last plate.

'Why?'

Brigit was stabbing soap-bubbles with the tip of her finger.

'You know what it's like when you're waiting for something.'

'Yes. It's like being kept in a bag and hung up on a nail.'

Pidge thought he knew what Brigit meant but he wasn't sure.

'How do you mean?' he asked.

'I mean it's like being kept in a bag and hung up on a nail on the back of a door in a shed!' Brigit said with deep significance. 'And you don't *want* to be in the bag and it's too hot inside it and all you can do is bang yourself against the door and you're too soft to make any noise and no one can hear you. Now do you know what I mean?'

'Yes.' he said.

'It's just like trying to break the sky with your fist, isn't it?' she said. She sounded as if she'd tried it many times.

'Yes.'

'I'd get so hot with madness because no one would hear me in the shed. Wouldn't you?'

'I would.'

So that was how Brigit felt when she only seemed impatient or thwarted.

He looked at the kitchen clock. Only a quarter to ten.

'I know.' Brigit offered, 'We could go down to the stony field and pick hazel nuts!'

'They won't be ripe for a long time yet. It's only August, don't forget.'

'We could go to the lake and row out to an island?'

And that was it, of course.

'Good old Brigit!' he said. She grinned proudly.

'We can take bread and hard-boiled eggs and a bottle of milk with us. And you can take a book, Pidge.'

'What'll you take?'

'My knitting.'

Pidge laughed. Brigit was learning to do her first knitting. It was supposed to be a scarf. Brigit herself admitted that it looked sort of bocketty. She didn't mind that Pidge laughed.

By the time they were ready, Auntie Bina was back from her hunt. She was feeling hot and bothered because the little hen had dodged her again. They told her of their plan.

'That's a good idea,' she said. 'It'll be nice and cool near the water. It's so hot today! It's enough to make the tongue of a crow hang out.'

'We'll call in and see Tom Cusack on the way,' said Brigit.

'Do. Your father will be taking the new mare in to him for shoeing in a day or two, I've no doubt.'

Before setting off, Pidge went into the barn and took a few pieces of an old, worn out bridle from the tack box and put them in his shirt pocket. These old rings are made of iron, he said to himself, and it's just as well to be on the safe side.

He checked that the pages were safe inside his shirt against his skin.

Chapter 4

Tom saw them coming into his yard.

'Aha, you two!' he cried. 'I was hoping I'd see you today. I've made something for you, Pidge.'

He showed them a small thing made of iron. It looked like a little flat book.

'What is it?'

'What is it? Well, it's a thing! A kind of case. For handkerchiefs or the like.'

Tom sounded puzzled and he looked at it as if he didn't know what it was or why he had made it.

'You could keep paper money in it when you're rich,' he joked.

'It's very good.'

Pidge held it in his hands. It was quite heavy.

'It opens, doesn't it?' he added. 'I can see where there are little hinges.'

'It opens all right.'

'Where did you get the idea of making it?'

'I don't know. It just came into my head, yesterday. There was a couple of old tinkers playing a banjo and singing just outside the yard at the time, I remember. They kept smiling and nodding and, when I started to make it, they waved at me and went off somewhere. They didn't come and beg at all though. I feel it was to do with them, in some way. I know it sounds cracked.'

No, it doesn't. Not at all, Pidge thought.

Brigit was standing in the sunshine outside the wide door of the forge. She was feeling very left out of things and a bit hurt because Tom hadn't made anything for her. She saw a spider hanging from the door-post on a long, silken thread. She hooked the thread onto her finger and the spider immediately began to climb up the thread to her hand. It was trying to get

45

back to its web and knew that its web was upwards.

When it had almost reached her hand, Brigit gave a little jerk to the thread and the spider dropped down again. At once it began to climb back up.

'What are you doing, Brigit?' asked Tom.

'Playing with a spider,' she said, pretending to be unconcerned.

'Don't hurt it, it's unlucky,' Pidge said quickly. He thought it was no harm to have luck on his side.

'How can I hurt it?' asked Brigit scornfully. 'I'm only playing yo-yos!'

'Come here, Brigit! Come and see what I've got for you,' said Tom.

She dropped the spider who instantly ran into a crack at the foot of the door. She ran inside the forge to Tom. He held out his hand and showed her a piece of metal that looked like dull silver.

'What's that?'

'It's only a piece of metal yet. A small piece of silver.'

'Are you going to make something for me?'

'I am.'

'Now?'

'Yes.'

Brigit's face brightened.

Tom opened a small drawer in a little wooden chest, a bit like the kind of chest that people keep spices in. He took out delicate tools and started to work. He reddened the fire with his bellows and took the small piece of silver in his great hands. He secured it in the grip of his tongs and heated it with great care and attention in the warm heart of the fire. Then he took it out and began to work.

His hands moved so fast the children could hardly see what he was doing. As he shaped the silver, he talked to them about smiths' work. He told them about metals and the great smiths of long ago who did marvellous work in silver and gold and were rated by the people as artists.

Then Tom was finished. He had fashioned for Brigit a tiny silver bow and arrow. There was a minute groove in the bow where the arrow could fit and clip in and the whole of the beautiful little object shone in the light of the fire.

Brigit had never felt so pleased. Pidge was full of admiration.

'Now we will string it,' said Tom, and he got something else from the small chest. It was strong hair from a horse's tail.

And then he finished it; fashioned, burnished and strung, and with a small clip and chain so that Brigit could wear it on her dress as a brooch.

The sight of its perfection seemed to astonish Tom.

'I never knew I had it in me to do that well,' he declared.

'Oh Tom,' whispered Brigit. 'It's beautiful! When I learn how to turn the heel, I will knit you twenty pairs of socks.'

He was delighted with Brigit's response.

'That seems very fair,' he said.

'When did you get the idea for that? Was it while those tinkers were singing and playing the banjo?' Pidge asked.

At this Tom appeared even more puzzled.

'Now that you mention it, it was,' he was looking completely perplexed.

More of it, thought Pidge. Here now, we have people who sing and put ideas into other people's heads.

'Is there anything special about iron?' he asked, only half-wanting to know.

'There's a lot I could tell you about iron. What do you mean in particular?'

'Well,' Pidge hesitated, not wanting to look a fool.

'What?'

'Anything magical? Is there anything about magic?'

'Oh, I think there's a fair bit. It's said for instance that witches can't touch it, though I don't know about that myself.'

Witches! I hadn't thought of witches. I'd been thinking of something, well, *stronger*, Pidge realized. And if it's witches, at least I have iron and it will secure me against them.

Now being prepared for almost anything, Pidge with Brigit said goodbye to Tom and thanked him once more. They set off along the boreen towards the lake.

The island was only a short row from the shore.

Brigit sat in the bow admiring her brooch as she listened to the oars dipping into the water and the drops falling back into the lake. They moved slowly over its surface. It was such a hot day and so still and quiet. They could hear every creak the leathers of the oars made as they rubbed against the rowlocks. They could hear every little squeak from the boards in the bottom of the boat. The boat seemed to have its own language and its own song. As he rowed, Pidge stared dreamily over the side of the boat, watching the swaying of the long weeds in the water and the darting minnows whose shadows followed them over the clearly-lit sandy bed that was the bottom of this shallow part of the lake. Some parts of the lake were said to be bottomless. They were places where the water was always dark green and glassy and impenetrable to vision, even on a bright day such as today, Pidge knew.

When they landed on the island, Pidge felt overwhelmed by the sudden loudness of the insects, as they busied and buzzed amongst the tall, flowering grasses and in the thickets of sloes, wild roses and woodbine. He flopped down in a grassy dip. Brigit said that she was going to pick some wild flowers.

When Pidge was alone, he took out that dreadful page, still wrapped in Patrick's writing, from where he'd hidden it inside his shirt. He opened his little iron case. He was about to fold the pages once more to fit them inside it and secure the manuscript properly in iron.

It jerked out of his hand, slipping out from Patrick's page, and pretended that it was being blown by the wind.

There was no wind.

Not a whisper.

He dived after it. In seconds he had it folded again within the covering page. Then it was inside the iron case and he snapped it shut.

And now I have you! he thought happily. You are really imprisoned in iron!

Brigit came back, her fists full of daisies and the brooch pinned through her hair as an ornament, right on the top of her head.

'It's far too hot,' she complained and she threw herself down beside Pidge. She began to make daisy chains, selecting the ones with the strongest stems. Pidge lay on his back, thinking about witches and trying to remember everything he had ever heard about them. This wasn't easy, for not only had he heard very little on the subject, but he couldn't exactly remember what he had heard. Just broomsticks and black cats, really.

After a time, Brigit held up her daisy chains triumphantly and said:

'Know what these are?'

'What?'

'Handcuffs! In case those pig-rustlers come back and try again.'

She put them on her wrist as bracelets. Already they looked wilted and lifeless.

Two swans sailed into view and steered in towards them. Brigit opened up a paper bag and broke up some bread to throw into the water for the swans to enjoy.

The heat made throwing an effort. The last piece she threw fell far short of the water. One of the swans glided into the shore and waddled onto the land towards the bread.

'Do you think that swan could be a fairy?' she asked.

'I wouldn't be a bit surprised!' Pidge said sitting up; and that was exactly how he really felt.

Brigit threw another piece of bread. She deliberately aimed to bring the swan closer. It stood for a while and looked at her with its black button eyes.

She sang to it:

'Come swan! Come swan! I'll give you bread and butter!' It turned and waddled back to the lake.

'What about a hard-boiled egg?' Brigit shouted. 'Would you come for that?'

The swan settled back on the water like a cat on a cushion. The other swan came to meet it and they sailed in circles close to the shore. All the time they watched the children with their intent black eyes.

It was as if they had been on the island for hours and hours. Again Pidge had the feeling that time was not passing at its correct speed. Brigit was restless, and Pidge felt impatience rise inside him like a large bubble, threatening to burst if he didn't do something soon.

'Why don't we go and explore the island?' Brigit suggested.

'We already know every stick and stone of it.'

'Will we row to a different island?'

'Too hot.'

'I'm fed up sitting here. Do you think Daddy is home yet?'

'No. It's only about twelve o'clock.'

'I'm going into the little wood. There might be something to see in there.'

'What?'

'Oh, an animal or butterfly or fairy—any old thing at all. It's too hot to do anything, we might as well go home.'

Pidge raised his head.

'Listen!' he said.

It was the sound of a banjo.

Two figures appeared, walking towards them from behind a small hill. Two tatterdemalion figures dressed in what looked like the sweepings of a Jumble Sale. They were an old man and an old woman.

'Tom's tinkers,' Brigit murmured.

The old man was wearing the remains of a battered old billy-cock hat and a ragged faded mackintosh; and he had tattered trousers fluttering around his thin ankles. He was wearing a pair of torn tennis shoes and no socks. In his buttonhole, he sported an enormous pink rose and his face was split into a smile of ecstatic happiness.

The old woman was wearing the motley found only on rubbish tips, topped by an outrageous hat which had every flower of the wild pinned all about it; all overpowered by masses of dandelions. It looked like a bowl of flowers on top of her head. She it was who played the banjo.

She had a red concertina tied on a long string and fastened to a big button on her coat and it dangled and swung round her knees in time to the rhythm of her swaggering, dancing walk. She was singing 'The Lark In The Morning' in a voice that sounded far too young for her age. The old man was dancing by now. He held out the hem tips of his mack in a dainty way and did a little spinning turn.

The song finished as they neared the children. The old man clapped his hands, laughed, flung his old billycock up into the air and caught it on the point of his walking-stick as it came back down. He twirled it round a few times and bowed to the children.

From amid the flowers at the crown of the old woman's hat came the pure beauty of a blackbird's song. A butterfly fluttered onto the old man's nose from a dandelion fastened to the hat's brim. The old man at once went cock-eyed as he tried to see it.

'Oh, I wish it would come on me,' said a hopeful Brigit before Pidge could stop her.

'Go on the little girl,' said the old man.

Oh botheration! Pidge thought uneasily. I wish I'd told Brigit all about it. She's gone and made friends with them as if everything were just as usual because she doesn't know any better. It's my own fault—I should have told her!

The butterfly obeyed the old man and presently it was standing on the very tip of Brigit's nose; opening and closing its magnificent wings to show its beauty to the world. She could feel its delicate little legs barely resting on her skin. She held her breath and was as still as she could be. But after a moment, it tickled and she just had to sneeze. The butterfly wafted back to its dandelion.

'Do you know,' said the old woman, 'I could do with a bite to eat. I could do with a pancake or two. Let us sit down a minute, Patsy, while I just have a rootle in me bageen.'

'Do, Boodie, do. A good rootle is what's needed, for a small hunger wakes in me at the thought of hard-boiled eggs.'

'I don't know about hard-boiled eggs!' said Boodie. 'I wonder now, did I put any fairy cakes in?' And she smiled.

'I hope not indeed!' said Patsy. 'After eating Boodie's fairy cakes your stomach would feel like a bag of rocks.' He smiled at the children to show that his remark was addressed to them.

Boodie took a fit of laughter.

'Will ye look at me shoes, Patsy! Curling up at the toes like two little rocking-boats! We're all dressed up and nowhere to go!'

'We look as if we're dressed in potato peelings,' agreed Patsy. 'But, wise eyes will see beyond that and maybe even wish that they had shoes that were comical too.'

'I wish I was the Queen of England, so I do,' said Boodie. 'Sitting down to High Tea in the palace. I'll bet it's so clean in there it'd make you want to spit on the floor.'

Brigit giggled.

She nudged Pidge. He was laughing too.

'I'll bet she's even got someone to blow on her soup! I'll bet she's that rich; not like old Go-The-Roads such as ourselves!' Boodie said, so cheerfully that it was plain she didn't mind at all. It was all said with a twinkle and only for fun.

'Who's rich?' yelled Patsy.

'We are!' Boodie shouted back.

'That's right. I've got my black hazel stick from Lugduff and you have your white hazel stick from Cregbawn; do we want more and we having the wealth of Wicklow?'

'Well, a few pancakes wouldn't be amiss,' Boodie replied, 'but you're right as always, Patsy me ould Champion!'

Patsy took off his hat and stuck it up in the air on the tip of his black hazel stick.

'It's grazing time!' he announced. 'Lunch is about to be served!' He looked across, grinned and winked at them and said:

'Would you like to eat some food with us?'

'Not if you're eating grass,' Brigit said. 'I've never grazed and I don't think I'd like it.'

'See now, Patsy, you have made confusion in the small one's head. Drollery nor waggishness is not what's needed, but lashin's and lavin's of edibilities, I'm thinking,' Boodie said.

'Yes! We have full and plenty for all,' Patsy replied. He held up a spotless white bundle. 'There's a few farls of oaten cake tied up in this handcloth so that they can't escape, a hambone and a pot of jam.'

'A hambone is sweet; but a pot of jam is the supreme comforter!' Boodie declared.

'*We* have hard-boiled eggs,' said Brigit, and she walked forward at once. Pidge held back. Suppose *they* were not what they seemed? Suppose they were the ones doing all the strange things?

Patsy appeared to be marvellously pleased about the hard-boiled eggs.

'Now we have everything!' he cried.

'Yes, and twice-offered too,' Boodie said with a secret smile at him.

Whatever does *that* mean? wondered Pidge.

Boodie took Brigit by the hand.

'And what's your name?' she asked.

'Brigit.'

'The lovely name. Patsy, this child has the lovely name of Brigit.'

Patsy scattered his rose petals.

'Ah, the lovely young Goddess—here's to her honour. Did you know that there was the Goddess Brigit here in Ireland in the old days, young sir?' he asked Pidge.

'I've heard of *Saint* Brigit.'

'Ah, I'm persuaded 'tis likely the Goddess was before your time,' said Patsy sadly.

'Don't be downhearted, Patsy. See what flowers the child wears on her wrists?'

'Daisies!' Patsy exclaimed, and his eyes seemed to light up. 'Do you like daisies?' he asked Brigit.

'I do. I love them.'

'That's the word right enough!' Patsy said, adding, 'It's a potent word and a mighty flower for all its littleness.' He patted Brigit on the head as if he were her grandfather.

Pidge came over to stand beside him. He touched Patsy's sleeve.

'My name is Pidge—short for P.J. It's quicker than saying P.J., you see.'

'And what's P.J. short for?' asked Boodie.

'Patrick Joseph,' said Pidge.

'One of the new-fangled ones—but, good enough!' Boodie observed. She was taking things from inside the bag and setting them beside her on the grass. 'Look here! We have yellow meal bread!' she continued.

'That's the ticket!' Patsy said, rubbing his hands together and cheering up. 'The yellow meal bread washed down with a good mugful of buttermilk.'

'No buttermilk,' Boodie said.

'Well then, we'll have spring-water.'

'No spring-water. The can is empty.'

'No spring-water?' He sounded quite horrified.

'Rest aisy,' Boodie said. 'There's some on the island.'

'There isn't!' Brigit said smartly. 'We know every inch of this place and we never saw a spring, did we, Pidge?'

'Not on this island anyway.'

'Back a piece the way we came, I saw a waterspout sticking out over the path and it gushing out glittering water that fell to the ground like a shower of diamonds. Would you carry some here in this little milk can—to please Patsy?'

'It's me legs or I'd go meself,' Patsy said. 'The screws do be

53

terrible by times. I'd *like* the adventure of going for water but for that. For you'd never know who you might meet or what mysteries would overtake a person going solitary for water. Such a gift it is—the whole world might die for lack of it, as I've said all through the years.'

'I'll get it, gladly,' Pidge said.

He took the milk can and set off. As he turned in towards the centre of the island, he looked to see if the swans were still swimming in circles close to the far shore.

There was no sign of them anywhere.

Chapter 5

H E ran and half-trotted along the path of short-grown grass. All of his boredom and sense of time dragging had vanished. Now he was curious to see the sudden waterspout, which he had never seen in the past although he had been coming to the lake islands for as long as he had memory.

The soft turf was springing under his feet in response to his weight and again he had that feeling of deep happiness that he had experienced after the voice in the chimney dream. In a while he heard the sound of falling water, and going faster he followed the path skirting a corner made by trees and bushes; and there it was!

He stood amazed.

There was a towering moss-grown rock that he had definitely never seen before and the water spouted down from it, gushing from a dark hole not very high up. From the darkness there, it streamed in a bright shining flood to the ground. Pidge was astonished and he stared at the water, watching its force. He saw how the sunlight made streaks of radiance on parts of its surface and that the more transparent places of falling clear water, seemed full of colour—soft browns and greens. Staring at all of this, he wondered if he had somehow made a mistake and rowed to an island that he had never previously visited; but he knew well enough that he hadn't, and that this new rock, that looked so old with its moss, and this surprising waterfall, were only more of the things that he didn't understand.

He held out the milk can and listened to the sounds the water made as it rushed in to fill it.

When the can was almost brimful, he dropped it in alarm and it clattered on the clean washed stones on the ground. He made three or four hasty backward jumps and he stared at the falling water with fright.

55

Through the movements of the falling waters, there was another, a different movement; and a head was suddenly there, the head of an Eel.

It was enormous!

Fear gripped Pidge. Unable to move, he stared into the water with horror. The whole of his body was trembling while a small part of his mind hoped desperately that the water had somehow exaggerated the head's size; but when it swayed and moved out of the flow to look down at him, he saw it quite clearly. It was huge, bigger than the head of a calf, and the terrified Pidge knew that no freshwater eel should be so big. He couldn't help but stare at the mouth, seeing the way that the bottom jaw came out under the top jaw to curve upwards at the front, and he saw the bone formation that went all around the edge and looked like hard lips. As if in a dream, he noticed that the skin under the jaw was yellowish white with olive tinges and that the skin on the face had a sheen to it that was bright. The face looked very old and the eye that he could see, was silver with dark flecks. The eye moved in its socket as the Eel looked down at the boy.

As soon as the eye moved, Pidge was ready to run; but when the Eel spoke, Pidge struggled with his terror and stood, trembling.

'Do not be afraid,' it said. 'The Dagda is my father.'

At the first sight of the head, Pidge's heart had given a ferocious twist inside his chest and now it was knocking around inside him so that he could hardly breathe.

'Fill your vessel with water, and leave with me that which is a burden to you, that I may bind him in my own strong coils; even though I may not hold him for very long,' the Eel said. The voice was slow and deep. It seemed to have a quality of gentleness. But still Pidge stood woodenly for he was incapable of movement now. He knew that the Eel was talking about the page from the book and he fought to get his breath.

The Eel spoke again.

'I see that you are fearful and in dread at my size and to hear me speak. Do not spend yourself on trifles such as these, for many amazements may confront you, and your store of bravery will wear away uselessly on matters of no consequence. Where is your burden? Come closer!'

But Pidge didn't move.

A long sigh like the wind in the reeds escaped from the Eel.

'Take your courage from The Dagda and come near to me. Be not afraid, I shall not harm you.'

A timid bravery came into Pidge and he took a step forward.

'Where is your burden?' the Eel asked again.

Pidge's mouth felt as dry as dust.

'I have it locked in iron,' he whispered, his voice collapsing. The words all came out as if broken in bits because now his heart seemed to be jumping in his throat.

His hand shook as he held out the little case that Tom had made for him.

'That is well,' the Eel said.

Pidge forced himself to speak again.

'Why is it well? What is this all about?' he asked, his question ending on a sort of squeak.

'The one you first released and then imprisoned is Olc-Glas, a thing of poison and terror. Those who desire him and seek for him, pretend at present to be less than they are—to deceive you and others. Because of this deceit they cannot touch iron, for all that they have evil power. As for an explanation? You are needed. Be content with that for now. A time will come when more will be told.'

Suddenly Pidge wanted to ask many more questions but the Eel's authority was so striking that he thought he had better not.

'Beware of the One who is Three, She who is also They— for she will be angry that she comes too late. Tell her nothing,' the Eel said sternly.

'Tell who nothing?' Pidge had to ask in spite of all.

'I do not know how she will name herself, or how she will come, or what form she will take; but she is The Mórrígan and her second and third parts are Macha and Bodbh. She is The Battle Goddess. She is Scald Crow. She is Queen of Phantoms. She feeds on the miseries of humankind.'

Pidge waited until it became plain that the Great Eel wasn't going to say anything more. All at once, he was calm; he knew that he was in the presence of a friend.

'Who are you, please?' he asked.

'I am the Lord Of The Waters,' said the Great Eel, and

reaching his head forward, he took the iron case between his jaws. He pulled backwards and upwards into the dark place from where the water surged and in a moment, he vanished from sight.

'Wait!' Pidge cried. 'Who is the Dagda?' But he was too late. There was no answer.

He stared for a few moments longer at the dark place, his mind filled with the image of the Great Eel and the brief sighting he had had of the body that swelled amazingly from just behind the head, when the Eel had reached forward to take the iron case.

Knowing now that the Voice in the chimney had been real, he filled the milk can and turned to go back to the others.

He was only mildly surprised to find that Brigit was sitting by herself, when he returned.

'They're gone,' she said. 'They told me to tell you they were sorry but they had to go.'

'Why? What happened?'

'I don't know, unless they were frightened by the dogs.'

'Dogs? What dogs?'

'They were barking over there,' she pointed to the mainland, 'and they really sounded terrible; barking and snapping and growling. It'd give you a pain just to hear them. Boodie and Patsy just stopped what they were doing and they said to tell you they were sorry but they had to go. Boodie got our picnic ready, look! They said to eat it and leave the things in the bag and put it near the waterspout. Was there a waterspout, Pidge?'

'Yes.'

'Where?'

'Not far away. What happened then?'

'They went away. They were gone in a flash. You'd think they were on wheels.'

'What else?'

'A big pack of dogs tried to get into the water to swim over here. And do you know, Pidge? You'll never guess! The two swans came again and they were fighting the dogs. And then, all of a sudden, another swan came and he was really fierce.'

'A third swan?' Pidge interrupted with a quickened interest.

'Yes. He rushed at the dogs and beat them back to land, all

58

by himself, really. He was standing on the water and beating his wings so fast and hard that at times you'd think there were two hundred swans out there. Look! The swans are still there but the fight is over now.'

Three swans were gliding backwards and forwards, watching a strip of the opposite shore.

'It's a pity you missed it,' Brigit concluded, 'it was the best fight I ever saw!'

Then she beamed with pleasure and said:

'Look what we've got! Presents from Boodie and Patsy and it's not even Birthdays or Christmas and we already had presents from Tom Cusack, as well! What do you think of that? Isn't it just great? And we thought it would be so slow and empty today! This is for you.'

She handed him a packet.

He opened it and inside he found an ordinary glass snowball ornament; the kind one shakes to make snow fall on a miniature alpine scene. In finest copperplate handwriting, on the label attached to it, was written:

Scrying Glass
To see where you cannot go

There was something else as well as the snowball. A leather pouch. Embroidered on it in silver thread was:

Wonderful Wonders & Co.Ltd.
Satisfaction Guaranteed

He looked inside and discovered clusters of ripe hazel-nuts.

It's only nuts, he thought. We can get those ourselves when they're ripe.

Then it flashed through his mind that they were freshly ripened and not from last year's saving; they were pale and they still had crimson markings. Older nuts were brown all over and he wondered where these had come from? Maybe from another land where they ripened earlier, he decided.

'What did they give you?' he asked.

'Patsy's own penny whistle,' she said proudly, 'and a box of sweets. But I can't open it. It's stuck.'

Pidge tried the lid. It was stuck fast. He turned the box over and saw a manufacturer's imprint:

The Old firm
Secret Sweets
Not to be opened until Swapping Day

Brigit was thrilled.

'Oh, I love secret sweets,' she said.

'How do you know? You've never had any before.'

'Well, I've got some now and now I know. I wonder when Swapping Day is?'

'I'm sure we'll find out later,' Pidge answered abstractedly.

He was thinking about the dogs now and wondering why they had tried so hard to get to the island. It must be that page again. It couldn't be anything else. Although it was now out of his hands and in the care of the Lord Of The Waters, he felt uneasy. What if they thought he still had it? Suppose they came back? What would he do if a whole pack of dogs attacked them? They might be torn in bits before the dogs found out that the page was gone.

'We must go home now,' he said decisively.

'We're not going now, are we, when we are having such a fine old time? I can't believe my ears!' Brigit said in surprise.

'It's not all nice, is it? What about those dogs?'

'So what about them?'

'I think something very serious is happening and they might be part of it.'

'What? Tell me.'

'I don't know if I should.'

'Oh! I suppose I'm too much of a baby to know about anything serious?'

'It's not that, Brigit. I don't know if you're meant to know, that's all.' He looked unhappy.

'Aw Pidge, cheer up! Tell me and you won't have to worry by yourself. Who cares if I'm meant to know or not? There isn't a law against me knowing, is there?'

Pidge glanced round him. The island didn't seem to be the familiar safe place it always was before. There were too many places where an enemy could hide.

'We must be safe and not overlooked. We ought to be somewhere secret.'

'Where?'

'I don't know.'

They thought about it for a while, Pidge's mind still half-engaged in thinking about the dogs. Then Brigit's mind went straight to the answer.

'I know!' she cried brightly. 'Out on the lake! If we were out on the lake no one could hide near us; no one could hear what we say!'

'You're right! That's it! We'll put the stuff back in Boodie's bag and leave it near the waterspout; and then we'll row out a bit and you can hear everything. I'll be glad to get it off my chest.'

Brigit was thrilled and excited by the waterspout. She wanted to stay and dabble with it for a while but Pidge said that they should hurry and get out on the lake as soon as possible. He looked up at the dark place but there was no sign of the Great Eel.

'Isn't it the loveliest waterfall you ever saw?' Brigit said. 'You could wash your hair under it.'

'Yes, you could.'

'Isn't it funny how it just suddenly appeared? It wasn't here ever before, was it?'

'No. Come on! I'm sure there's going to be a storm.'

'All right—just let me have one more minute with my hands under this lovely waterfall—'

'Brigit! Stop it and come on!' Pidge interrupted her as forcefully as he could. 'Do you want to hear about this serious thing or don't you?'

'Oh, all right, but it's a pity to leave it though, isn't it?'

She followed him back along the track turning to look over her shoulder at the waterfall with every second step she took.

Halfway between the island and the mainland, Pidge stopped rowing. He told her the whole story, right from the very beginning in the bookshop in Galway. She listened, her face alive with interest and fascination, and it changed from mood to mood as Pidge talked. It was just like the sky on an unsettled day.

'I think it's wonderful,' she said when he had finished. 'I hope and pray that some more things happen and I'm in it with you.'

'But it could be dangerous,' he said seriously.

Brigit shrugged her shoulders.

'What do I care,' she said. 'I'm not afraid of danger.'

'Well, you would be if you had any sense.'

'Ho! Would I, indeed!' she said and she grinned.

And Pidge was very glad that he had told her, for the sharing had lifted some of the weight off his mind. It made him feel better just to look at her cheeky grin. It's her nature to be light-hearted and doesn't it come in useful at times, he thought.

The heat of the day bore down heavily on them. It seemed to be getting even hotter. To the west of them, the lake was a vast expanse of shimmering bronze. If he gazed at it for too long, the effect would be entrancing, hypnotic.

The swans were gone, he noticed.

He dipped his oars and began to row to the mainland.

They had dragged in the boat and were walking back along the boreen, feet trailing in the dust. Trickles of sweat were running down Pidge's back like rain on a window-pane. Brigit's forehead glistened and her hair was curling in little damp ringlets at her temples. She was looking down at her feet; looking at the way the dust was gradually covering her sandals as though sprinkled with talcum powder. She saw a fat worm on the ground, whiplashing in silent pain.

'Oh! Look at this poor worm, Pidge!' she cried.

'A bird must have dropped it,' he said. 'It's dying from the heat.'

'We must save its life!' Brigit said dramatically.

'We'll find somewhere damp.'

Pidge bent down and picked up the worm.

'It's all covered in dust, poor thing,' Brigit said.

Pidge looked round for a damp place to put the worm. The grass verges were dry and parched and useless. Lying against a small stone was a solitary white wing feather, speckled with droplets of blood now dried brown.

'One of the swans got hurt in the fight,' he said.

'Oh no!' Brigit cried, full of concern.

'It's all right, Brigit,' Pidge said. 'Look, only a few little drops of blood. It wasn't hurt badly.'

'All the same,' Brigit said, her face instantly pugnacious, 'I don't want them to be hurt at all. I'd like to get my hands on the bully-dog that done it.'

'*Did* it,' Pidge replied automatically.

He thought of a small coppice a little way further on, where there was a tiny stream running like a ribbon of music. The stream came out under the boundary wall of the little wood and ran alongside the road in the ditch. The earth would be soft and moist and the worm could easily burrow in and be safe.

'We'll put it by the stream,' he said.

They had just finished covering the worm with damp grass and moss, when they heard the murmur of low voices coming from inside the coppice. Brigit's eyes widened and she opened her mouth to say something but Pidge stopped her by putting his finger to his lips and shaking his head in warning. He motioned that they must get in closer. They crept in close to the wall.

One voice was talking:

'And so, it was defeat. A third one fought. The victory was with the Daughter and Sons of the Twelve Moons.'

'This time, Findepath!'

'And which of us is brave enough or foolish enough to take the news to Macha and Bodbh? Great indeed will be their anger! What will our punishment be, when we report that we were too late?'

'Not too late, Findepath.'

'How so, Lithelegs?'

'Is it not well-known that the Lord Of The Waters must rise to the temptation of the Brandling Breac?'

'Lithelegs speaks truly,' said a third voice. 'But the Breac must be offered in the shifting-time; when morning changes to the second quarter of the day or when night changes to the fourth of the fours.'

'Greymuzzle! You are truly well-taught in Mouth Knowledge!' said the first voice, (must be Findepath, thought Pidge) 'Speak further!'

'The day is theirs but the night is ours. So, it must be at middle-night when we are at our fullest strength and The Dagda's people are low.'

Then other voices spoke:

'Wolfson speaks! It is true that we are not at our best in the light hours. Greymuzzle is wise!'

'Fowler speaks! Because of this alone did the White Walkers, who are the Sons and the Daughter of the Twelve Moons, defeat us!'

'But who is to do the telling of this defeat to The Queens? It is Silkenskin who asks.'

'What were the words spoken to us? "Have a care and keep a good watch!" It was thus did Scald Crow speak!' said yet another voice.

'Well does Rushbrook remember! I, Swift, remember also The Mórrígan's final words: *Do not fail on your peril! Let not Olc-Glas by you—or it will be the worse for you!*" And even now, Olc-Glas is in the jaws of the Lord Of The Waters, imprisoned in iron!'

('They're talking about that green snake on that page I told you about,' Pidge whispered.

'Who are they?' asked Brigit.

'I don't know,' whispered Pidge again.

'They have funny names, and do you hear the daft way they talk?' Brigit said and she began to giggle.

'Sssshhhh!' said Pidge.)

'A question, Findepath!'

'I hear you, Fierce.'

'Would it not be pleasing to The Mórrígan, Scald Crow and The Queen of Phantoms for us to kill the two-legged cubs, who are like gnats in one's eye or two specks of sand between one's teeth, and meet again in the ending of this day and seek then the Lord Of The Waters?'

Other voices approved:

'It would please The Mórrígan indeed!'

'There is but one middle-night to each day and think how she would delight in not waiting one more day.'

'NO!' said Findepath forcefully.

'Why so?' asked Fierce.

'The striplings are under the protection of The Dagda, The Lord of Great Knowledge. There are bonds on us not to kill them except in the hunt.'

('Findepath is the boss!' murmured Brigit. 'Sssshhhh!' Pidge said again.)

'We must find a way of making them run. I, Gnawbone, undertake this.'

'Not yet. It is not time. Now that there is a beginning, there is an imperative on us to follow the course. It must be so. We must play our correct part,' Greymuzzle declared.

'Our chance will come,' said the voice of the one named Fierce.

A small breath of wind touched Pidge on the back of the neck.

'Be still!' commanded Findepath. 'I have a scent. We are not in close concealment here and the two-legged cubs are close-by. It is time to disperse. Let us melt away like snow-flakes!'

Then there was silence, broken suddenly by some magpies chattering in their castanet-like way. They sounded louder than was normal, as though they had held their noise for so long that it was unbearable.

Pidge peeped over the wall.

The coppice was empty. The tall bracken was moving and swaying as if battling against a gale and yet there was the merest breeze blowing. He saw the hind-quarters of a hound disappearing through a white cloud of marguerites before it vanished from sight completely, in the cover of the thickly-growing bracken.

'Did you see them, Pidge?' Brigit asked breathlessly.

'I saw the back-end of a hound, that's all.'

'I don't like them. They talked in a funny way and I had the feeling that they were talking about us some of the time,' Brigit said.

'So did I!'

'Did you really see a hound?'

'Yes.'

'And no people? Who was talking?'

'To judge by the names they called each other—a whole pack of hounds!'

'Dogs! I don't want any old dogs thinking they can kill me!'

'They said they couldn't because of bonds or something.'

'Unless they can make us run. Wasn't that it? Well, I'll tell you one thing, Pidge. They'll never make *me* run. And I hope they all get worms!'

'And the mange,' Pidge said fervently.

'Do you really think that hounds were talking?' Brigit asked.

'I don't know. It seems too strange. Maybe there were people there and we just didn't see them.'

It really does seem too strange a thing to be true, he thought. But then, well, there were the peculiar names.

'I only saw the back-end of one hound you know,' he said aloud.

'I wonder who daft old Mórrígan is? And Scald Crow. And the other one they talked of, Queen of something.'

'Well, we know already that they are one and the same person. The Great Eel said so. She's The Battle Goddess or something.'

'Who does she think she is, coming here to Shancreg and messing about with us? Herself and her oul' Battles. Whoever she is, she'll find out a thing or two from us.'

'I think she must be very powerful,' Pidge said.

'Powerful, me eye!' Brigit said gruffly and they set off again on their journey home.

Chapter 6

SUDDENLY, there was the roar of an engine and a motor-bike came behind them as if from nowhere—as if it had been skulking behind a hedge waiting for them to pass and then leaped out and chased after them.

Pidge jumped on to the grassy verge just in time.

The motor-bike almost grazed his right side, travelled on a few yards and then pulled up. The children saw that it was being ridden by the two ladies who had rented Mossie's glass-house. Pidge thought he heard the one with the blue hair say:

'Oh drat it! We missed him!'

'Sssshhhh! They'll hear you,' the one with the red hair replied, and then she sniggered. She looked back over her shoulder and shouted:

'I say! Are you all right?'

She dismounted from the pillion and walked back.

'Frightfully sorry, old bean. Let me help you up.'

'It's all right. I can manage,' said Pidge.

'He's able to stand by himself,' Brigit said firmly.

'Nonsense!' said the woman. 'I must assist you. After all, what are fiends for? I *beg* your pardon! What I meant was—what are *friends* for. Dear, dear, I really must learn to listen to what I say.'

She leaned forward and grasped Pidge by the arm and jerked him to his feet. She closed her eyes and held him for a moment like one in a trance.

Before letting him go, she gave him a nasty, nippy little pinch. She smiled at him and then she aimed and spat a tobacco spit over the roadside wall.

'My name is Breda Fairfoul,' she said chattily. 'This is my friend, Melodie Moonlight.'

Melodie turned the bike round and purred back to where they stood.

'Why do you chew tobacco?' asked Brigit.

'Like to bite something that bites back. Puts me in a hot mood,' she said. She smiled again.

Melodie Moonlight looked penetratingly at her.

'Well?' she said.

'Too late,' said Breda Fairfoul. 'Another moment in time, peradventure.'

'Foiled, then,' commented Melodie Moonlight. 'The question is—by whom?' She turned to the children.

'Do come home with us and have some tea,' she said silkily.

Pidge thought that her voice sounded like a cat singing the death song of a mouse.

'No thanks,' he said.

'Try and persuade him, my little duck,' said Breda Fairfoul turning to Brigit.

'Yes do, my fubsy one,' said Melodie Moonlight, 'and you shall have Red Cap Pasty, Peggy's Leg, Kiss Pie and Walking Stick, Hafner's Sausages and Soup Of The Day.'

'No,' said Brigit. 'I've took against you.'

'You've took against us? But why?' Breda Fairfoul cried theatrically.

'Cos you're a pair of road hogs. You might have killed Pidge just then.'

'Yes—we might have, mightn't we,' said Melodie Moonlight, rather regretfully, Pidge thought. He wasn't quite sure what she was regretting; nearly killing him or just missing him.

'Oh dear!' said Melodie artificially while she lit a cigar, 'now I'm feeling in a fuss. Forward Fairfoul! We must regroup.'

As she got back on the motor-bike, Pidge noticed that she carried a dagger in her garter.

'Don't boggle at me, it's rude!' she snapped.

'Bogglers get fits of the braxy if they're not *very* careful,' Breda added. 'Especially when they boggle into things that don't concern them—don't they, Melodie?'

'Not half,' said Melodie and she kick-started the bike. Breda remounted the pillion and with a roar of the engine, they shot away ahead of the children, shrieking with loud laughter.

Before they were lost to sight over a small hill, Breda made her hair stand up and wave goodbye.

'Aren't they queer,' said Brigit. 'They gave me the running willies up and down my backbone. What's this they dropped?'

She bent down and picked up a small white card from the road. Pidge read it aloud:

M. Moonlight and B. Fairfoul

Licensed to deal in Runes, Spirits & Tarot
Bogglers Braxied Hedges Trimmed
Sunny Spells Cast

'What does that mean?' asked Brigit.

'It means that they're witches, I think.'

'But they told Mossie Flynn that they were artists!'

'I know,' said Pidge. 'That must be to throw people off the scent in case they did anything peculiar.'

'Brazen Liars!' said Brigit.

They walked on in the heat.

As soon as they were back inside the glasshouse, Melodie Moonlight filled a crystal dish with water. She set it carefully down on the floor and then she sat on a little stool beside it.

Breda Fairfoul sat ready with her harp.

The surface of the water became a picture; a moving picture like a film. It showed Brigit and Pidge as they trailed along the boreen.

Melodie Moonlight laughed.

'Begin the Calling Music,' she said.

Breda ran her tapering fingers over the harpstrings.

A faint, delicate music whispered into the air. It was lighter than a summer breeze, it was more quiet than dust-motes in a ray of sunlight, yet its strength was greater than iron chains.

Pidge and Brigit stopped walking. The music touched them and caught hold of them and yet they heard nothing. It began to pull gently. It was inaudible and very powerful, in the same way that electricity is invisible but full of force.

'Don't you suddenly feel that it would be very nice to take the footpath across the fields for the rest of the way?' Pidge said.

'I feel that nothing in the whole world could be nicer,' said Brigit.

They climbed over the wall into the field.

As they walked along the little footpath, a wonderful feeling reached the soles of their feet from the earth, so that every step gave a marvellous tingle of pleasure. It came right through the soles of their sandals. The awful heat of the day seemed to lift and the air felt gentle on their faces. It was all part of the way the harp music called them. They began to hop, skip and jump along the path.

Ahead of them, the track split in two directions. One way, turning right, led to home; and the other way, turning left, went to Old Mossie Flynn's. As they approached this division, Brigit shouted exuberantly:

'Why don't we go to the glasshouse and peep in at the witches?'

'Why not!' Pidge shouted back, and that was strange from someone as cautious as Pidge. Neither of them gave the matter another thought but skipped along the left-hand way in obedience to the music.

As they neared the glasshouse, they went on tip-toes, making it a game of spying. When they got closer they noticed the closed venetian blinds,

'They've got some of those slatted blinds, but there might be a place to peep in,' Brigit said.

Then they noticed the sign saying:

: BEWARE OF THE FROG :

and they burst into delighted laughter.

'What you laffin' at?' said the frog as he sprang into view from behind an old up-turned bucket. Then he remembered that he was on guard and said:

'Halt! Who goes dere? Friend or Foe?'

Pidge and Brigit were astounded and delighted and they stared at the frog in happy disbelief.

'You can't talk,' Brigit ventured after a while, her eyes wide

70

and her voice full of doubt and hope at the same time.

'You hear me awright,' the frog said accusingly.

'A frog just spoke to us, Pidge,' Brigit whispered and she looked at him with a broad smile.

'It's wonderful! I don't really believe it,' Pidge answered with laughter breaking into his speech.

'You did, didn't you?' Brigit asked, gazing down at the frog a little doubtfully.

'I did, didden I? I'm doin' it again,' the frog asserted as though answering a slur.

'How can you do it?' Brigit asked in a conspiratorial way. She knelt on the ground beside him.

'Same as you!'

'But it isn't possible,' said Pidge, kneeling down as well for a closer look.

'Doan tell me it izzen possible when da times are so queer,' the frog replied tartly.

Then Pidge asked:

'What is it? Is it magic?'

The frog looked wildly at the glasshouse before whispering:

'It's da queer ones, doan ask me any more.'

'What do you mean?' Brigit whispered back.

But the frog pretended not to hear. The children were waiting for an answer to Brigit's question, and were perplexed when, instead, the frog said:

'Well?' loudly, and then nothing else.

'Well what?' Brigit demanded after a time.

'Who goes dere? Friend or Foe?'

'Neither,' said Pidge and he laughed.

'Doan know what to do about a Neither,' said the frog looking baffled. Then he remembered that he was supposed to say something more.

'Tress . . . um, tress . . . ah! . . passers! Tresspassers will be . . . will be . . . ' He forgot the rest.

'What?' asked Brigit.

'Tresspassers will be kilt stone dead!' the frog said brightly.

'Oh really?' said Brigit.

'Yis!' said the frog. 'Thim's fonda kids, mingled wit' herbs in a big black pot wit' onyins bilin' in it. Thim's not fonda frogs, thanksfully.'

'Who do you mean?' whispered Pidge.

'Thim two in dere.'

'Don't you like them?' asked Brigit.

'Hate um. Dey is pisen—pure pisen. Hate um wit' da whole strength of me back legs, so I do.'

'Why do you work for them so?' asked Pidge.

'Cos of da mallet,' said the frog. 'Dey got it inside da door an' "One False Move From You" dey said, an' I get a crack on me pate.'

'Well, if they're like that, why are you working for them?' asked Brigit.

'Cos I diden know. I haden any idea. Oh, dey shambizzle me nicely,' was the glum reply.

'How?' asked Brigit.

'Lass night in da gloamen, I wuz hoppen along as is me wont, when what did I see but dis big blue van. Its back doors wuz wide open and dere wuz happy, careless music comen out of it, an' it made me feel all rollicksome an' skipperish. An dere wuz a big sign on a Neasel. I hop over to da sign. It said: "Gala Night Tonight. Frogs Free 'Till Ten O'Clock." I never even stop to dither. Oh, what a froggy fool I wuz!'

At this point, the frog's eyes glistened and he looked as sad as a soggy bun.

'What happened?' whispered Pidge.

The frog sniffled for a moment or two and then he carried on with his story.

'All lighthearted, I hop inside. I taught I'd be dancin' a fundango and de pokey-hokey, an' atin' thim Roshyian fish eggs—Havacare, dey's called or sumthin like that—thim that comes from far away over the Ballthrick Sea—an' drinkin' cordials an' everythin' until the cows come home. I taught wrong, diden I?'

'Then what happened?' asked Brigit.

'Dey got me inside an' clang da doors. Den, off on a joy-ride, so I taught, until dey ended up here at dis glass-house. I knew sumthin wuz wrong, when dey made da van vanish.'

'The van vanish?' Brigit repeated in a puzzled voice.

'Dey made it disappear an' dere I wuz standen on dis very spot. "Are you up to da mark?" dey said. "What mark?" I ask

72

nawnchalonkly. "No lip from *you*," dey said. I taught to meself, "Dis creshin is da better part of valour," so I kep' quiet. "You're mean an' ugly an' you got big eyeballs," dey said, "You'll do fine." I said nuffin. Den, dey learned me all about "HALT" an' "TRESSASSERS" an' den dey showed me da mallet. "See dis?" dey said. I seen it awright. "One false move from you an' you get a crack on yer pate. An' after you've been batted on da crust," dey said, "we'll give ya to thim Frenchie Ones an' dey'll ate da leggies off ya. Or failen dat," dey said, "We'll putcha down a swally-hole an' you'll get swoggled." Oh, dey gev me da wobblies when dey said dat about me legs. Still, dat's life—as da Philloppytors say.'

The frog made an obvious attempt at perking himself up by means of Philosophy. He managed to look more cheerful.

'Is that all?' asked Pidge softly.

'Dat's all, an' if you ask me, it's moren enuff,' said the frog.

'What's your name? Have you got one?' Brigit asked.

'Course I got one! What do you think I am, a nonny mush? I doan go round all nonny mush like a bit of pondweed,' the frog said scornfully.

'What is it?'

'I never tell. Wild Frenchie Cooks cudden drag it outa me.'

'Then you're only an oul' nonny mush, after all,' said Brigit.

'No I'm not,' the frog said. 'But, "Dis creshin is da better part of valour," is what I say; an' I wudden like dem two in dere to find out me name, in case dey got more power over me. Oh! I could end up turned into a prince in a sailor-suit, or sumsuch calamity, if I diden watch out. Oh!' And he went quite glassy-eyed with horror.

'I'd look cute in a sailor-suit,' he continued after a moment, 'an' I'd never see Miss Fancy Finnerty, me own true love again.'

'Who's she?' asked Brigit.

'What? Never heard of Miss Fancy Finnerty? Her what I'll never see agen?'

'Of course you'll see her again,' Pidge said gently.

'No I won't,' said the frog. 'I gotta stay here.'

'Why don't you just hop off?' asked Brigit.

The frog gave her a stupid look full of pity.

'Cos dat'd be one false move, wudden it?' he said, in a tone that implied that Brigit was a fool who couldn't see the obvious.

'But, if you hopped off when they weren't here, or when they weren't looking, they couldn't do anything to you, could they? You're a bit stupid, aren't you?'

'I got me quirks,' muttered the frog.

'How much is two and two?' Brigit asked briskly.

'A lot!'

'That's not the answer.'

'A few?'

'No.'

'Not a lot an' not a few—dat's what two an' two is,' said the frog.

'You're hopeless,' said Brigit.

'What are they doing in there now?' Pidge asked softly.

'Doan know. Torchurin' sumthin wit' dat mallet, I serpose. Or knocken back da crab's blood cocktail, or da orange juice wit' sumthin in it to give it a kick.'

'I'm going to try to get a look inside,' said Brigit, getting to her feet.

'Brigit! Don't!' said Pidge, scrambling after her.

'What harm is it?' she said, and she pressed her nose to the glass where there was a gap between the blinds and the glasshouse frame.

'Whose little nib is that, pressed against our window?' called a mocking voice from within.

Pidge froze for a second, then he grabbed Brigit's hand and prepared to run. To his horror, he found that they couldn't move. And then, the two women were standing in the door-way.

'If it isn't Bo-Peep!' said Melodie Moonlight. 'How nice!'

'It's the little bogglers!' said Breda Fairfoul. '*Delighted* that you could come to tea after all. Do step inside.'

Pidge, still holding Brigit's hand, stood firmly where he was. They're not getting us inside that glasshouse no matter what happens, he decided in his mind.

The friendly expression on Breda's face vanished and was replaced by a strange knowing sort of look that seemed to say 'We'll see about that!' She smiled sweetly and threateningly and turned to the frog.

'Well, frog?' she said.

'I halted um an' I whogoesthere'd um an' I trespassed um, so I did,' the frog said smartly.

'Clodpate,' murmured Melodie Moonlight.

'Scallywag!' said Breda Fairfoul. 'Keeping our guests in idle chatter.'

'Can't tell the difference between a friend and a foe,' Melodie said severely.

'Wouldn't recognize quality if it jumped up and bit him on the nose,' said Breda, shaking her head in disapproval.

Pidge felt that he should say something.

'It's not his fault. I'm sorry we looked in at you, we didn't mean any harm,' he offered politely.

For the moment, the women chose to ignore him and continued to admonish the frog.

'Setting himself up as a Freethinker with powers of decision over who comes and goes,' said Melodie Moonlight.

'Oh, I wudden do dat!' the frog declared fervently and his eyes seemed to bulge even further than before.

'I'm afraid, frog,' said Breda Fairfoul regretfully, 'there'll be no Cup for Good Conduct for *you*. Coming here, pretending to be a First Class Watchfrog, indeed! I've heard that types like you have been frizzled for less than that.'

'Oh, I diden! I never did!' cried the frog in a shocked way.

'Testimonials from the Tower of London! Said you had watchfrogged the Crown Jewels. Forged, were they?' asked Melodie.

The frog didn't answer. He appeared to be dumbstruck.

'Described himself as six ounces of sheer muscle and sinew, he did. Alleged that he had been a considerable All-in Wrestler working under the name of "The Throttler!" And we now know for a fact that he had a fight with a Daddylonglegs once and *he* lost,' Breda jeered in a low way.

Two big, fat tears welled up in the frog's eyes.

'He is nothing less than a blot on his family's escutcheon,' Breda continued. she turned to Pidge.

'Did you know that two or three of his ancestors were munched in *one* sandwich by Louis fourteenth, a fair toff in his day?'

'Leave him alone,' Pidge said.

'You're a big brazen bully,' Brigit said with spirit. She was fingering her daisy chains distractedly.

'I'm not a blod,' snuffled the frog, as the tears ran down his face. 'I'm not a blod on me famblies scutchun, cos it hadden got one.'

'Still, in spite of everything, we've got a soft spot for that frog, haven't we, Breda?' said Melodie.

'Oh yes,' Breda said. 'And when he's dead, we're going to have him stuffed.'

'And that might be sooner than he thinks!' Melodie said sharply.

'That's enough!' Pidge said courageously, for he had never spoken in this way to an older person before. 'If you don't leave him alone, I'll report you to the Society for the Prevention of Cruelty to Animals.'

'And I'll report you to the Minister for Angryculture and Fishes,' Brigit said cockily. 'He's a great friend of my father's.'

'Any more lip from you, madam—and that frog is a dead duck!' Breda said to Brigit.

The frog howled.

Breda smiled and winked broadly to show that she was joking.

'I don't think you're very funny,' Pidge said, feeling even braver because nothing had happened to him when he had dared to check Melodie, a moment before.

'You've made him cry; you're about as funny as a gumboil,' Brigit declared.

'Ask um about dat mallet,' mumbled the frog.

'What mallet?' Breda said innocently.

'You know well what mallet,' Brigit said.

'Do you mean *this* mallet? Melodie asked sweetly and she produced a large, wooden mallet from behind her back. She reached forward and snatched up the frog who immediately squealed in despair.

'Dear, dear! We shall have to put it out of its misery,' she said. 'Don't know whether to pop it like a blister, or squash it with the mallet.'

'You couldn't do a thing like that,' Pidge said. 'It's a disgusting thing to do!'

Melodie smiled at him amiably.

76

'Such a thoughtful little object,' she said. 'But you mustn't worry about me dear; I shan't mind doing it one little bit. I was bred for it, you know, and Nanny helped, of course.'

'We don't care about you. Pidge is thinking of the frog,' Brigit said.

'Thinking of the frog—oh, is he?' crooned Melodie and with that, she and Breda, with the poor frog as a prisoner, were back inside the glasshouse with the door closed behind them, before the children could properly realize what had happened.

After a few moments of bewilderment Pidge said:

'We can't just walk away and go home and just leave him with them.'

Without saying anything, Brigit walked over and very deliberately, kicked the door as hard as ever she could, though the softness of her sandals wasted some of her boldness. She wished she were wearing football boots to let them *really* know what she thought of them.

'Open up in the Name of The Law!' she shouted.

Immediately, the door opened and she was snatched inside and the door shut with a bang.

Pidge ran and began to hammer on the door with his fists. Two hands reached out and he was twitched inside and confronting the two strange women.

In a jolting split second, the amazed Pidge noticed the furniture, the dish of water on the floor and the harp standing by the table. On the table itself, the frog was cowering on a plate under a meat-cover of metal gauze, which stood horrifyingly close to a dish of stuffed olives, buttered bread and an arrangement of condiments and pickles, as if he were part of a meal. Melodie Moonlight was holding Brigit by the arm. All this he observed in a twinkling without once taking his eyes off Breda Fairfoul, who held him captive in a pincer-grip from which there could be no escape.

In coaxing, gentle, but perplexingly quick words, they commenced to ask questions—so fluid, so vague, so indefinite and blurred that they might be questions formed in a marsh instead of a brain. And each one hard on the heels of the one before, baffling, seeming to be about the horrible page and who had it, and over and over they asked—Was There Anything Said?

They went on and on, with voices that were somewhere between a twitter and warble, as they delicately sought answers without really asking questions—in case a question would contain too much and suggest an answer, and so give to the children information they hadn't already got.

Pidge thought it was like being pecked to death by doves.

Throughout all this, he stood blank-faced and bewildered and Brigit wore a grimly stubborn expression on her face that would have put the wind up a Gorgon.

At length there was a lull in the quizzing.

Melodie Moonlight and Breda Fairfoul, without consulting each other, decided to try another tack.

'We are not trusted,' they remarked miserably to each other, and Melodie Moonlight began to cry. Tears like golf-balls dropped from her eyes, going splat as they landed on the floor. Brigit half-expected them to bounce.

'There, there, Melodie my pet,' Breda droned soothingly.

Melodie's eyes took on the appearance of large wet oysters and her nose turned into a shapeless, overblown scarlet poppy, whose copious drips she mopped charmingly with a small table-cloth.

'All we wanneb wab to be frens wib you—swab bleasantries and' be balsy-walsy—gossib, an' exchange our harmbless segrets,' she sniffled dismally as the golf-balls thundered down her cheeks as would crystal globes on a ski slope.

She looked like someone who had been crying bitterly for at least a week.

'We *had* hoped to break bread and get a Social Circle going where we could practise our After-Dinner Speaking, with a few Soirées and Musical Evenings et cetera. A few tunes on the Harp, we thought,' Breda said, and her voice expressed a great sense of loss.

'Pretty pieces well within the scope of the Tonic Solfa; something catchy like The Howls Of Hoffman or The Turning Of The Screw; and now—hopes dashed!' added Melodie and she sobbed pitifully.

Pidge wondered what he should do as Miss Moonlight looked so anguished, though her nose now seemed to be unblocked. Brigit had no doubts at all.

'Aw shut up, you big cry baby,' she said scornfully. 'Stop pretending!'

Again there was an instant change in the women's behaviour and, releasing the children, Melodie whisked the meat-cover off the frog while Breda grabbed the mallet in both hands.

'Softness got us nowhere,' Breda said with quiet menace.

Melodie seized the frog and held him cupped in her hands, all marks of her tragic weeping now casually and unaccountably missing from her face.

'It's up to you, dear children. You've got a choice. Do you talk, or does the frog get the coup de grâce? Look at him; and look at this mallet; and give him the thumbs down if that's your whim. Do you *want* him guttled and guzzled or not?'

She thrust the prisoner forward to within inches of their faces.

Breda did likewise with the mallet.

Pidge and Brigit looked with dismay at the helpless frog who was by now in a trance of horror. And Pidge was on the verge of gabbling out every single thing that had happened to him, when Breda mistakenly added a few more deciding words.

'Speak or he joins his forefathers!' she commanded.

Something was released in Brigit at this. She took her gaze off the wilted frog in amazement and glared up at Breda Fairfoul.

'That's stupid!' she declared. 'He hasn't got four fathers, no one has!' And for some strange reason and without even thinking, she threw her wilted daisy chains over the women's wrists.

'Handcuffs,' she said.

At once, the daisy chains snapped tight shut. Melodie Moonlight dropped the frog who lay on the floor, inert as an empty paper bag.

'Nóiníní!' screamed Breda Fairfoul.

'Angus Óg's flowers!' screamed Melodie Moonlight.

The daisy chains had turned to steel shackles of remarkable beauty; the yellow hearts and white petals being of a radiant enamel; the pollen was a dusting of glittering gold.

Pidge dashed forward and scooped up the frog, knocking over the crystal dish filled with water and breaking it in his haste.

'Quick Brigit! Run!' he cried.

Holding the frog carefully, he grabbed her hand and, in a kingfisher flash of speed, they were gone.

Chapter 7

THEY ran very hard.

Pidge, who was holding the frog in one hand and gripping Brigit's hand tightly with the other, ran faster than he had ever done in his whole life before. Brigit, pulled along by Pidge's speed, was skimming over the ground as would a low, purposeful wind. After a while, they realized that they were not being followed and they flopped down to rest in the lee of a stone wall.

'Oh!' said the frog, who was by now greatly recovered, 'Dat's better! Dey gev me da Quakers when dey said dat about Lousy da fourteenth of France. It made my blood run cold, if I had any warm to begin with. I wuz like a . . . . like a icicle!'

They sat still for a few moments to recover their breathing.

'My heart is still galloping. Doesn't it know that I've sat down now and it can go slow?' Brigit gasped.

'Hearts is like dat—dey got dere quirks,' the frog said knowingly. 'Mine wuz goin' like knackers when I wuz trapped on dat great plate.'

Pidge, breathing a little better, said:

'What did they really mean to do, I wonder?'

'I wudden like to speckerlate, but I serpose it wuz to be a leg each wit' torchure sauce,' replied the frog, who was not at all breathless because of being a passenger during the mad, punishing dash.

'Seems ta me,' he went on, 'I nearly got swoggled, an' not by no swally-hole neither, cos dey said to me lassnight: "Lissen Gormless! Just you remember dat fried frog's legs are by no mean to be despised an' you'll be welcummed in wit' open jaws!" Seems ta me, dey nearly done mathematics on me, an' made a short division sum of me: One into Two an' None Over. Dey said I would be quite wholesome, trussed an' stewed; not only a nibble but a novelty too, dey said. To think I nearly ended up in fractions! Oh dear, oh dear, I feel quite sweltered just to think of it,' he finished a little shakily as some of his horror returned.

'Let them try a trick like that and we'll soon see who gets swoggled,' muttered Brigit with a terrible scowl.

'Don't worry about it anymore, you're safe now,' Pidge said reassuringly. He didn't truly believe that they were entirely out of danger but he hoped to make the frog feel better.

'Tanks to you two, I am. I doan know what I would hev done but for you. I'd follow you to da ends of da earth for it, so I would,' the frog said, emotionally.

'Really? All the way to the ends of the earth?' Brigit wanted to know.

'But no furder. I'd follow you to da ends of da earth but no furder,' he answered earnestly. He honestly tried to make himself plain and wanted them to understand that the ends of the earth seemed far enough, to him.

At this, they both laughed.

'You're laffin' agin,' he said.

'We can't help it,' Pidge replied.

'Muss be a disease.'

He looked at them anxiously.

'You should take a bottle for it or hev your chests rubbed wit' emanations.'

They laughed even more and he looked very puzzled.

'You're laffin'—an dose two could be the other side of dis wall,' he said, and instantly looked as if he'd frightened himself to near-death.

Brigit stood up and looked over the wall.

'Nobody there,' she said, and sat down again. 'You know, you never told us your name?'

'It's Puddeneen Whelan,' the frog said, with pride. 'I cudden tell you before 'cos of dem. Dey should hev dere heads banged togedder, tête-à-tête as da Frenchies say. Pickin' on da likes of me an' making me feel like a cabbitch—born to be biled.'

'Fried, more like,' Brigit said.

Sitting and laughing had done much to restore ease of breathing to Brigit and Pidge, but Pidge's mind had not stopped running on the behaviour of the women in the glass-house.

'I've been thinking about that,' he said slowly. 'I'm sure now that they wouldn't have hurt you, anyway. I think you were only like bait to trap us—so that they could ask all those questions. I don't think they would have harmed you really and I don't think they would have harmed us either. They only wanted to find things out because they are after something, so you see you were only like bait after all.'

'Only bait? ME? What a cheek! Squorms is bait—frogs isn't.'

'Squorms?' said Brigit.

'Thim little pink wispies that squorms an squiggles in da ground. Dey's only got faint, skinny figures wit' no mighty back leggies; in fack—dey got no leggies at all. Frogs is different. If I'm nuthin' else, I'm a Nathlete. Any swimmin you ever want done—I'll do it.'

They were just about to thank him for his kind offer, when another frog sprang into view and landed on a stone beside them. He looked very surprised and said:

'Where you bin, Puddeneen? Miss Fancy Finnerty hev bin fit to pop.'

'Hev she?'

'She hev bin poppin' mad at you. Bin doing her gypsy dance an' bashin' her tangerine, wit' a bitta watercress clenched in her mouth. You know how she gets when she's poppin'?'

'I hev bin at death's door. Dat's where I bin,' said Puddeneen.

'How'd you get dere?'

Puddeneen told his story again, just as he had told Pidge and Brigit, but this time with all the things that had happened afterwards, added on. The other frog listened with astounded attention. Puddeneen dwelled at great length on the threat of the mallet and finished by saying:

'Dey took all da GO outa me an' it's only tanks to dese two, dat my brain is still in puffect workin' order an' I still got me legs.'

'I kin harbly believe it,' said the second frog.

'I kin harbly believe it myself but the trufe is bitter when it's told.'

'I muss go an heva gawp at dem. I love gawpin' at anything

like dat, so I'll go now an' hev a good gawp.'

'You better not. Dey set a booby trap to ketch boobies; dey cot me an' dey might ketch you.'

'It appeals to me sportin' instinck; an' ye know me, Puddeneen —if it appeals to me sportin' instinck—I'm sunk!'

'Oh Bagsie,' pleaded Puddeneen, 'doan go. Dey'll ate ye if ye do. Lissen to your elders an' betters Bagsie, an' be led by da wise.'

'Dat'll be da day!' Bagsie said cheerfully, and he sprang away.

'Come back, Bagsie Curley! Come back or I'll tell yer Grannie!' shouted Puddeneen but there was no reply and Bagsie had gone from sight.

'Where do squorms—meaning worms—come from, I wonder?' Brigit asked.

Pidge thought about it for a while.

'I don't really know,' he said.

'I do,' said Puddeneen. 'Dey come out of holes. Well, I'll be off now. See you again sumtime, I hopes.'

He sprang.

He had meant to go forward magnificently, but his legs were still weak from shock so he went sideways instead and fell over.

'Oh, oh! I'm jumpin' crooked! I'll never make it to da lake. Me nerbes are all shattered an' me legs is outa tune,' he wailed.

'I'll carry you,' Brigit said kindly and she picked him up.

She stroked the top of his head gently with her fingertips as they walked along towards an inlet of water that led back to the lake. He kept blinking his golden-ringed eyes but said nothing for a while. Presently he said:

'Dis hev bin a lesson to me an' from dis on I'll be more clever. But you two hev bin friends in need an' in deed, an' if you ever want any doings done—or if I can ever do anything dat would help you—I woan let you down, an' dat's my sollum word.'

'You're very good, Puddeneen,' Brigit said. She kissed the top of his head.

'I know I am. Doan do dat—you'll get warts.'

'Yes, you are good,' Pidge said. 'That's a very brave offer.'

'Is it?' Puddeneen asked and looked instantly worried.

83

Brigit set him down carefully at the edge of the little inlet where the water was slapping lazily into white lace.

'Dis is da ends of da earth,' he declared, 'here begins da water.'

'What do you mean this is the ends of the earth! Is that as far as you'd follow us? I don't think much of that,' accused Brigit.

Puddeneen looked down and turned his head from side to side.

'Dere's no more—look. Dis is da furdlingest place in Ireland izzen it? See for yourself—no more ground cos dis is da brim of it, and da water starts here,' he answered with honest surprise at her response.

'You're daft,' she said.

'Doan matter what you think of me,' he said generously, 'I'll never think less of you.'

He looked at the water nervously.

'What's wrong?' Pidge asked.

'I just hope I heven't got a puncture after all I bin through, dat's all. I could get swamped an' go down like a ton of bricks.'

'We wouldn't let that happen.'

'Well—here goes den!'

He jumped in.

Finding that he floated, he spread out his back legs and said grandly:

'See me leggies? Puffect, izzen dey?'

And he swam off doing the breaststroke and singing:

'One Alone . . . To Be My Own . . . .'

They watched until they could see him no more.

'He's gone,' said Brigit sadly.

'Yes. I hope we see him again.'

'I suppose we won't; the lake's too big and wide. He's gone off now to see Miss Fancy Finnerty and we'll probably never lay eyes on him again. He's the most stupid thing I ever saw. But I wish he'd stayed here near us, so that we could see him and play with him sometimes.'

'Maybe we will,' Pidge said.

They made for home.

As they walked across the field, Brigit said:

'We never got our Hafner's Sausages, nor the Kiss Pie and Walking Stick—whatever they are. Wait 'till Auntie Bina

84

hears about those two witches; she'll be fit to be tied.'

'Don't say anything about them or what's happened, Brigit.'

'Why?'

'She might get worried or frightened.'

'Auntie Bina? What could frighten *her*? She'd face a mad bull with only a feather in her hand.'

'If she went over there to them to tell them off, they might turn her into something.'

'What?'

'Anything. A chicken or an . . . eggcup or anything.'

'Oh!'

'And she mightn't let us out, if she knew. She might keep us in or just near the house.'

'Oh! What about Daddy when he comes back?'

'Don't tell him either. They'd have no peace; they'd just be anxious all the time. And somehow we're part of what's going on and how could we do anything, if we weren't let out?'

'What might we have to do?'

'I don't know . . . yet.'

'If I just told about Puddeneen, or about my handcuffs?' Brigit said wistfully.

'Better not.'

As they climbed up the last wall that was nearest to their house, they saw a Garda sergeant riding by on his bike. He was going in the direction of Mossie Flynn's.

'I hope he arrests those two for something and they get six months each in the jug,' said Brigit.

'So do I.'

'They didn't follow us, did they? That's cos they're afraid I'll do more magic on them. Remember the way I made them scream?'

'Oh, they're not afraid of you and me; don't think it, Brigit. Something else must have stopped them or they'd have caught us easily—if they wanted to.'

'I wonder if Auntie Bina would like me to saw her in half? I bet I could if I had a box. And a saw.'

'Brigit!'

'All right. I won't say anything. I wouldn't really like to have an eggcup or a chicken for an Aunt.'

They sat on top of the wall for some moments. Their own

house was just across the road. They saw the horsebox standing empty in the farmyard and knew that their father had come back from Dublin with the new mare.

She had come at last.

It's queer how I had forgotten all about this with the adventures of the day, Pidge thought; and I had longed for it for such ages too.

They jumped down and ran to see what she looked like.

Michael, their father, stood alone in the yard, holding the bridle in one hand and stroking the long slope of the mare's face with the other.

She was as creamy and silky and beautiful as Pidge had hoped her to be.

He tried to notice everything about her at one sweeping glance: the marvellous head and the whole shape of her; the way her flanks shimmered and the strands of gold that appeared in her thick mane, in the light of the afternoon sun. He saw the strength in her body and the quiver of her shapely muscles; the beauty of her fine head and the elegance of her slender legs. He marvelled that such legs could support that strong body and wondered why it didn't look very wrong and daft, instead of just right.

Pidge looked with a broad smile at his father; but Michael was so wrapped up in his ownership of such a beautiful animal that he didn't even notice.

Brigit was asking to be lifted up which was the normal thing whenever their father came back from anywhere, if it was only from working in the fields; but he couldn't seem to hear her.

'Where's Sally?' Pidge asked.

Sally was their good, loving, faithful, humorous and playful sheepdog and she always went where Michael went. People called her Michael's Shadow.

His father didn't seem to hear his question so he asked it again.

'Sally? Oh, she ran away or got lost when I was buying the mare,' his father answered carelessly and continued to stroke the long and lovely face.

'What?' said Brigit. 'Is Sally gone?'

'It would seem so.'

Pidge couldn't believe his ears. Sally lost or run away and his father caring nothing about it? But he loves that dog, he said to himself, he must have searched everywhere for her, broken-hearted; and he's not saying much so that we won't be upset.

'Couldn't you find her anywhere?' Pidge suggested.

'Why would I bother to look for her?' Michael answered, without once taking his eyes from the mare to look at them or really notice them, and his words sounding queer and hard-hearted, somehow.

He's like one in a trance, Pidge thought; and the mare turned and looked at him.

He was shocked to see something like flames flickering wildly inside the eyes, that blazed for an instant only and then dwindled to something that might be two red stones or two small fires, deep within the pupils. They looked so strange and frightening that Pidge shuddered and stepped back.

Two swallows came looping through the air and came to rest on the roof of the barn where generations of them had made their nests under the eaves. They were happy and began to sing.

The mare held Pidge's eyes for some seconds in a very deliberate way and then she looked upwards and stopped the swallows' throaty song with one glance. The little birds huddled and went very small. And then the mare returned her stare to Pidge's startled face.

A picture came into his mind; flocks of superbly coloured butterflies, some with wings of an amazing size—all dropping to the ground dying, and turning to dirty ashes; trees of great magnificence whose leaves fell in great flurries until the branches were stark; and then smoking branches and trunks splitting open and falling all twisted and in pain, and becoming ashes like the butterflies and then lying as pools of horrid, dark, treacly water; and people in fields becoming queer, warped, creeping things, full of tears.

Amazed Pidge looked at his father in horror.

'Her eyes are funny,' he said, slightly stammering, 'they're all red inside.'

Michael laughed loudly, with a strange, hard edge to his

voice, and he looked at Pidge with a piercing cold stare, as though he didn't know him and cared as little for him as he cared for Sally.

Pidge felt a kind of pain inside his chest and was full of misery. He tried to smile at his father, but it was too difficult; there was such a lump in his throat and the tears prickling behind his eyes.

The mare drew his gaze once more. There was a hint of pleasure or satisfaction in her eyes, if such a thing could be possible. He just caught a glimpse of it before it was replaced by a look of the most ferocious intelligence, that made Pidge wonder if he were seeing aright.

Auntie Bina called out that dinner, or supper, or whatever they liked to call it at this hour of the day, was ready; and would they come in at once, please.

Pidge stood and stared as his father a moment longer and then turned to go inside.

And he was downcast and unhappy as never before, and wished for night-time and the end of the strangest day that he had ever lived. He felt worn out. His legs were solid and lifeless and he could hardly drag one after the other.

Brigit, however, was entirely herself, as if she had noticed nothing odd about the mare or Michael; though she did say, perhaps by accident:

'Oh good! I could eat a horse!'

Chapter 8

INSIDE the glasshouse, the women looked at the daisy chains and laughed derisively.

'Such fun,' Melodie murmured. 'We haven't had such fun for ages!'

'This won't take long,' Breda said.

They held their wrists up close to their mouths and began to lick the metal. Their tongues became as rasps directly and the glasshouse was filled with the noise of scratchy filing—exactly the sound that cinders munched by horses would make.

After a while they grew angry as the metal held and would not give way.

'That pest Angus Óg, himself and his daisies! I might have known,' Breda fumed.

'Tears are required, I think,' said Melodie.

They held the bracelets where their tears might fall on the metal and began to cry. Drops of acid fell from their eyes, but still the metal remained callous and would not soften.

They fell into a fury of anger and danced round and round the glasshouse in a frenzy of licking and crying, until after a long time, the beautiful little bracelets fell to the floor.

They were on the point of leaving to see if they could catch up with the children and the frog, when there was a knock on the glasshouse door.

'Who's this?' Breda asked in surprise.

'Hush, listen!' Melodie whispered.

Outside, a voice was saying:

'There's a glasshouse all right—in the position stated—that much tallies anyway.'

'Open the door,' Melodie murmured.

The Garda Sergeant stood at the opened door of the glasshouse.

'It's a Noble Savage,' said Breda, turning back from the door to look at Melodie.

The Sergeant glanced behind him, to see who it was that she meant. As there was no one standing behind, he realized that she was talking about himself.

'I'm not a Noble Savage, madam,' he declared.

'It's an Ignoble Savage,' Breda informed Melodie.

'I'm not a savage at all, my good woman. I'm a Garda Sergeant!' she was told very firmly.

'It's a Police Sergeant,' Breda told Melodie.

'Anyone can make a mistake,' the Sergeant said gallantly.

Melodie looked at him through a pair of binoculars.

'I might have guessed!' she cried. 'Look at the fine pair of shoulders he has to support his neck and noddle, and the thigh muscles breaking the seams of his trousers. He really is a picture!'

'Now that you mention it,' said Breda as she squinted at him through a magnifying glass, 'I can't help observing what a wonderful physical specimen he is, indeed. The manly jaw! The eyes of steel! The magnificent brow! The strength of his nose stuck on to his face like a figurehead! A housetrained thoroughbred! Le dernier cri!'

'Anything else?' asked Melodie

'That's all,' Breda said.

Melodie glittered a smile at the Sergeant.

'Were you fed on minced kelp as a child? What is the secret of your superb personal body?' she asked, simpering.

'It was the buttermilk that done the job,' the Sergeant confided, shyly pleased. The ladies' open admiration had disarmed him completely.

'You don't say,' Melodie said with interest. 'Well, well, well!'

'Say "cheese" before you go, if you please. I always like to snap any celebrity, exhibit, curio or bric-à-brac that crosses my path,' said Breda as she unstrapped a camera and pointed it at him.

The Sergeant smiled foolishly. He could feel himself doing it but he didn't know how to stop.

'There's a terrible draught, Breda,' Melodie chirruped from within. 'Won't you shut the door?'

'You see how it is, Dear Sergeant,' Breda said apologetically.

'Yes indeed,' the Sergeant replied, without knowing what it was exactly that he was supposed to see.

'So, pip-pip and farewell,' said Breda and she quickly shut the door.

The Sergeant stood for a moment in bewilderment. He felt that something had gone wrong somewhere. Something had been left out! Ah yes. *He himself* had been left out when he had really expected to be invited in, before the closing of the door. That must be it, all right. It had been done so quickly—he had been surprised; but so politely that it must have been a mistake on the part of these charming and sensible ladies.

Thinking about this, he began to walk slowly away, rubbing the side of his nose with his thumb because he was perplexed.

When he had walked a few yards, he stopped. Goodness! he said to himself. I was bedazzled entirely and forgot me duty. It's me *duty* that got left out!

He went back to the glasshouse and again knocked at the door.

This time Melodie opened it. The Sergeant waited, confident of a warm, even gushing welcome.

'Who's there?' Breda called from inside.

'It's that fool with the face like a bashed crab,' said Melodie.

'What?' said the Sergeant, not at all sure if he had heard aright.

'Policemen get faces like that when they drink illicit liquor after confiscating it from hard-working poteen-makers. That's what happens when they drink illegal booze!' Breda said.

'Shouldn't drink the evidence,' Melodie said severely; and she wagged her finger in his face.

The Sergeant went red from shame and anger. How do they know that? he thought. Is it true about me face? It was all right this morning when I was looking in the mirror. They're just guessing. He squared up to them.

'That'll be enough of that,' he said, 'or you'll be scrubbing floors in a House of Correction!' He got out his official notebook and pencil.

'Information has been laid against you,' he intoned pompously, 'by a passing Swedish rock-climber—'

'A rock-climber? Round here? East of the Corrib? Nothing to climb round here,' Melodie interrupted him.

'He was on his way to a rock!' the Sergeant said masterfully. 'Anybody could guess *that*! And it was then that he saw a certain occurrence.'

'What certain occurrence?' asked Breda sweetly.

'He alleges that items of furniture descended from the sky in the near vicinity of this glasshouse. The description of the furniture matches exactly some furniture that was taken from a store in Galway, and it is believed that you are in possession of these objects. He states that he saw you assisting it to land. What do you say about that?'

'How was it stolen in the first place?' Melodie asked, as if daring him.

The Sergeant blushed before replying sturdily:

'The suspicion is that it was conjured in some way, for it certainly flew out of the windows in a manner not at all natural! Shoplifting in a new way no doubt; but there's a law against it!'

'You're a buffoon, sir!' said Breda.

'And I under the impression that he was a scholar and a gentleman!' Melodie said shaking her head sadly.

'I never heard such misguided twaddle,' said Breda.

'Swedish hallucinations are no concern of ours,' said Melodie.

'Had *he* been at the alcohol too?'

'Did you get him to blow up one of those balloons of yours to measure the amount he had drunk?'

'Don't tell us that he was as sober as a Judge—held up by string, most of them!'

'The accusation is outrageous!' said Melodie.

'Monstrous!' agreed Breda. 'If we shoplifted—where's the evidence?'

She stepped outside into the sunshine.

'Inside that glasshouse,' said the Sergeant.

Melodie emerged and stood beside Breda. She carefully closed the door of the glasshouse after her.

'Oh really?' she said.

'We are very lambs of innocence,' said Breda. 'You have only to look at our faces to see that we are without a speck of guile.'

'Speckless,' murmured Melodie.

Together, they presented two guileless faces to the Sergeant's view.

Bashed crabs, he thought vengefully. 'I've got a search warrant,' he smiled.

'Unspeakable Sergeant!' cried Melodie. 'Does that mean you are going to have a look inside?'

'That is my intention, madam,' the Sergeant replied stiffly.

'Without evidence it becomes mere hearsay by a common informer, doesn't it, Breda?' said Melodie and she turned a very significant look in her friend's direction.

'Swedish people are not common!' the Sergeant said severely.

Breda winked at Melodie. Then in perfect time, they snapped their fingers extremely secretly and slyly so that the Sergeant didn't notice or even hear.

'Go in and case the joint, don't let us stop you,' said Breda.

'You are using the criminal idiom, madam; and with great fluency, I notice,' said the Sergeant and he opened the glasshouse door and stepped inside. He paused to make a note in his notebook about Breda's fluency in the criminal idiom and then he looked round the glasshouse.

It was bare.

Empty as a balloon.

Not one stolen object to be seen.

The Sergeant looked utterly crestfallen. When he came out, he was silent.

'Well?' sneered Melodie.

'I'm keeping my eye on you two from now on,' the Sergeant said darkly.

Unexpectedly, her whole manner changed. She became cold and terribly threatening.

'If you are not very careful, Sergeant, my dear,' she said and her words came like splinters of ice, 'you could very easily find yourself Up The Amazon On A Rubber Duck. Be warned.'

The two women went inside the glasshoues and shut the door. He could hear them inside, sniggering.

As he walked away, he could hear that one of them was playing a tango on a tuba. He was too dispirited to even wonder where it had come from.

'You'd want to keep your eye on those two,' said a passing frog.

That's it, he thought. I'll never again touch another drop. I swear it. By the shiny buttons of my stainless predecessors, I swear it. Frogs talking to me. What next?'

The Sergeant went round the corner and had a good cry.

Chapter 9

PRESENTLY, the Sergeant wiped his eyes. He undid the buttons of his tunic and reaching inside, he produced a small, interesting bottle filled with poteen, which he had personally confiscated only the day before.

'This'll put fizz in me,' he said.

He unscrewed the top while scanning quickly in all directions to be sure that he was unobserved and then he had two or three stiff belts.

'A belt of this is better than five pounds spent at the doctor's,' he said.

Feeling much better, he remounted his bike and pedalled along towards Galway. He hadn't gone very far when he saw a great number of hounds approaching. They padded quickly past him and he dismounted to watch where they were going. To his delight, they went to the glasshouse, where they were admitted at once.

'I have them now, the rogues,' he said.

He cycled back to where he'd had his good cry, parked his bike and then he went and knocked at the glasshouse door. This time, he gave his very official knock.

Melodie Moonlight opened the door.

'I see you are fond of dogs,' the Sergeant said with a smiling innuendo.

'Blow your nose!' snapped Melodie Moonlight authoritatively.

For the tiniest moment, a small reflex jumped in the Sergeant's right hand, fleetingly eager to obey her command, but he controlled it without any difficulty.

'Who's there this time?' Breda called out.

'It's that nosey Sergeant again, trying to work his way indoors for a cup of tea,' Melodie responded.

'That pest? He's becoming as well-known as a begging donkey!'

These two could cause a row in ten convents, the Sergeant remarked to himself, but they won't get me going *this* time. Aloud, he said:

'Have you got licences for those dogs, Madam?'

'Don't brandish your nose belligerently at me like that!' said Melodie in a ratty tone.

Breda came to the door. She scrutinized the Sergeant carefully and then turned to her friend.

'Don't you think he has a nose like a duck, Melodie dear?' she suggested gently.

'Plug up your gob or I'll blister you!' quacked the Sergeant threateningly.

He stopped, thought for a moment, and then allowed his eyes to slide together so that he might take a peep at his nose.

He hadn't got one.

In its place was a duck's bill.

It wavered for a few seconds and then it was gone and his own comfortable old nose had returned.

I'm seeing things, he thought.

'My,' said Melodie admiringly. 'Aren't we pale blue today!'

'And those ribbons in your hair—aren't they madly wicked? How very pagan of you,' said Breda and she smiled a secret smile.

The Sergeant drew his truncheon and took a step forward to assert his authority. As his foot moved, a flash of white caught his eye.

He looked down.

With horror he saw that his legs, his own beefy, well-muscled, hairy legs, were wearing dainty white ankle-socks and his feet were in buckled hornpipe shoes. As his gaze travelled upwards, he found that he was dressed as a little girl in a pale-blue frock with puffed sleeves and a tie belt, and instead of his truncheon, there was a skipping-rope with wooden handles and tinkle-bells, in his great, big fist.

Resting on his broad chest were the ends of two fat, flaxen plaits, tied with lavender ribbons. He touched one of the plaits, found that it was real and felt all the way up to his head, where he discovered that his Garda headgear had somehow changed into a cotton sun-bonnet.

Worst of all, one of the legs of his pretty pink knickers was hanging down below his knee, exposing all his frills to the world, because the elastic had given way.

'The leg of your drawers is hanging down, Sergeant,' Breda said vulgarly.

Oh mother! I'm bunched altogether now, he thought sadly. Thanks be to Providence, the lads can't see me like this. The young Gardai would be sniggering at me, and then they'd be whistling after me and after that, they'd be laughing and mocking and pointing openly, until I'd be driven daft.

Angrily he went to throw away the silly skipping-rope. To his confusion, it was a truncheon again and he was very properly dressed in his uniform. He touched the peak of his cap for reassurance.

It's that blasted poteen! It's giving me visions, he decided, and felt a little comforted, his flummoxed brain not allowing him to realize that the women were playing a part in his discomfort and were even remarking in words, the changes that were taking place. He thought it was all happening inside his own head.

He struggled to carry on doing his duty.

'Now you two! What about those dogs? Are they licensed or not?' he asked crossly.

'You won't be told, will you?' Melodie said with an impatient wave of her hand.

The Sergeant found himself Up The Amazon On A Rubber Duck.

He paddled madly with his hands towards the distant bank of the river before the piranha fish found out that he was there.

Chapter 10

'WELL, here I am Up The Amazon On A Rubber Duck and the light bad. I haven't felt this weird since I won a medal at a Feis,' he said.

He reached the river bank.

Ireland seemed so far away; the vegetation round him was exotic and composed of secrets.

'All I can do now is follow my nose and see where it takes me,' he said and glanced round nervously.

Some seconds later, his nose was back in the Garda Barracks in Eglinton Street, Galway, with the Sergeant at his usual close distance behind it. He was sitting by the fire in the duty room. Hastily, he inspected his appearance to see if he was himself again. Finding that he was and that his trouser-legs were dry, he let out a sigh of relief.

A young Garda entered, holding a mug of tea.

'Gimme that,' the Sergeant said.

Startled, the young Garda handed him the tea.

'Didn't you go yet, Sergeant?' he asked. 'I thought you were off out in the country somewhere, doing your duty?'

The Sergeant swallowed the tea in almighty gulps.

'Where'd you get that idea?'

'I thought that a young Swedish rock-climber phoned in from Annaghdown to report something about flying furniture?'

'Flying furniture? Don't make me laugh! Do I look the kind of eejit to be taken in by a half-baked hoax like that? Thought made a fool of you, my lad, didn't it? Nip outside now and see if me bike's all right and don't be talking out of turn.'

The young Garda turned to go—poking out his tongue when he thought he was out of the Sergeant's view.

'Keep that tongue where it belongs!' roared the Sergeant.

'Sorry, Sergeant.'

'If it ventures out again—I'll tie it in a knot round your nose.'

'Yes, sir.'

The young Garda went outside thinking: He'd run his mother in and out of a hole after a fox, that fella. He has no mercy.

Alone, the Sergeant sat cogitating and feeling cowardly.

'After all,' he said finally, they hadn't got any furniture in that glasshouse and as for dog licences—a minor offence. We mustn't lose our sense of proportion here. And nothing on earth would get me near that glasshouse again; facing two such sarcastic little judies for the sake of furniture stolen from that gobdaw of a Manager. There's always some poor woman with drink taken— I'll go after them, instead.'

Immediately he was struck by the unworthiness of this thought and he cast it out of his heart.

For the present, however, he sat and brooded, while the cowardice in him struggled with the anger in him, but the thought that simmered most deeply in him was, sadly: Wait 'till I get my hands on that damnable poteen-maker, I'll see that he gets a long stretch!

'The bike's all right,' the young Garda said, re-entering.

'Get on with your work!' the Sergeant said fiercely.

Chapter 11

IT had been such a long, tiring day.

Pidge was glad to sink into the feather mattress, feeling his limbs as heavy as stone in the soft bed. A strong drowsiness came on him and his eyelids closed and opened and closed again, very slowly, as he drifted into a beautiful daze of sleep. He thought it the most wonderful feeling in the whole world.

After a little while he felt his mind spinning off into a dream. There was a slow whirling of his being, as if he were inside a silent and gentle tornado that was taking him off on a journey of delight. It lifted him up to a great height and he was swimming like a dolphin in the sky and then it laid him back on the cushion of his bed, like a snowflake landing on water.

In his dream he heard a sound.

It was a cold, hissing, tinkling sound and it came from the landing outside his bedroom door. He sat up, eyes wide open.

There was something coming in under the door: a thin, snaky tendril of fog. It crept into his room, keeping low on the floor. It began touching things and creeping into things. It whispered to itself as it crept towards his chest of drawers and then it insinuated itself through all the cracks, until it had been in and out of every drawer. It withdrew then, and paused as though to think before turning towards his wardrobe, as if it had an intelligence and could make decisions for itself.

Pidge felt his skin prickle. He was almost breathless with shock.

He hoped that he was still dreaming because one always wakes up from a dream. More than anything, he wanted to wake up.

'If I wake up now, it will be gone. I must wake up! I hate this dream, if it is a dream. It's horrible!'

Someone touched him and in his mind he had the notion that a small voice was saying: *Pidge!*

There was no one else in the room, just a little golden moth resting on his wrist where he had felt the touch. In his mind the voice went on:

Don't be afraid.

'I can't help it,' whispered Pidge, 'I hate it.'

When it leaves—follow it.

'What? No! I can't.'

Follow it through the scrying-glass. You'll be quite safe.

The moth fluttered across to the window where a second moth waited for it.

Two of them, thought Pidge. Like there were two swans at first.

The fog finished searching the wardrobe and it began to swirl round the floor seeking under the floor boards. In seconds it was satisfied that nothing lay hidden there; it approached the bed and began sensing the covers. Pidge shut his eyes tight.

After some time he opened one eye to see if the fog had come any nearer to him and he found that it was just withdrawing back to the landing, whisking away under the door.

He reached under the pillow where he had, for safety, put the presents left for him by Boodie and Patsy; and he scrabbled about until his hand closed on the scrying-glass. It still seemed a very ordinary thing. After giving it a quick shake, he watched the artificial snow inside it as it swirled and rolled. In a moment, the little snowstorm had vanished, and he could now see a picture of the landing in the small glass globe. The fog was moving there and it was going in under the door of Brigit's room. He followed its movements in the glass. He saw the inside of the room and there was Brigit fast asleep and well snuggled under the bedclothes. He was almost certain that she wasn't in any danger; the fog had shown that it was only searching when it had left him unharmed. Brigit was so deeply asleep, she would never know that it had been there.

Inside the scrying-glass, the scene changed. It showed him the stable and there, standing in the bright light that came from the moon, was the new mare.

The fog was coming from her mouth.

I might have known it would be something to do with that one, he thought grimly.

He could see that the fog was made up of particles or atoms or something and they were all flowing out of her mouth in a thin, cold stream; a narrow white river filled with a kind of life and all of it moving in one direction, away from her. He found himself looking into her eyes and he pulled back from the scrying-glass in case those eyes would see him. They were cold and dark, the colour of wet granite; as cold and dark and grey as the winter sea. There were no pupils in those strange eyes and as he watched, they began to gleam; two ovals of hard shiny metal, where there should have been only softness and the gentle colour of brown.

As the eyes began to gleam, the fog changed direction and began to flow back inside the mare. Pidge watched spellbound and suddenly totally unafraid.

Soon it vanished completely and not even one wisp remained to show that it had ever been there at all. The mare came back to life and shook herself. The eyes were now brown but still with those red glints of tiny fires.

She walked to the stable door and stepped out into the night. She lifted her beautiful head and smelled the night air. She turned, searching out a direction, and started to gallop off across the fields towards old Mossie Flynn's place and the glasshouse.

In spite of everything, it was thrilling to watch the magnificent way that she moved. It all seemed to be in slow motion and her mane and her tail streamed out and undulated behind her as if made of the lightest silk. It was a picture of beauty and movement. If only she hadn't this strangeness about her, how I would have loved her, thought Pidge.

As she neared the glasshouse she slowed down and stopped.

She stood utterly still.

Something appeared to be coming out of her again and before Pidge could see properly what had exactly happened, a woman stood beside the mare.

She was tall and blonde and very beautiful.

She wore a long, filmy dress that floated around her like shadows on grass. In her hand she held a small, glittering object. She tossed it into the mare and the mare trembled slightly. Pidge suddenly knew that the little shining thing was part of the mare; it was what made her a living being. He also knew that the mare had been used by the woman like clothing and nothing had been the mare's fault.

Poor animal, thought Pidge, as the mare began to walk back across the fields. She was obviously worn out. Her lovely head drooped and she hardly had the strength to move her legs.

The door of the glasshouse opened and Melodie Moonlight and Breda Fairfoul rushed out. They seized hold of the fair woman with eager hands and cried:

'Come! Come! Let us see you!'

The three looked at each other.

'How beautiful you look,' said Breda Fairfoul.

'Exquisite,' murmured Melodie Moonlight.

Something seemed to tremble in the air between them.

Laughter!

They giggled and laughed and shuddered, as if they would shake to pieces.

'Beautiful!' gasped Breda Fairfoul at last.

'Oh, peachy!' whooped Melodie Moonlight.

And then Pidge knew that they were laughing at the *idea* of beauty as the height of nonsense.

The fair woman suddenly stopped laughing. Her outline went fuzzy and shapeless and then she appeared as a skinny, grizzled old hag, whose face looked as if it was carved out of yellow soap. Her nose was like a walnut with long and strong black hairs that closely resembled prawn whiskers sticking out of her nostrils. Her moustache was a fringe of wiry white, stuck out in a nimbus round her mouth, like a chimney-sweep's brush. She had at least five hundred warts, some—one on top of another, four or five times over. Her ears spiralled out of her head, looking like two pink, fleshy corkscrews and each lobe was as big as a duck egg. The eyebrows were two tufts of coarse red hair. Her eyes were purple and her eyelids hairless. Her teeth hung down over her chin; they were so long that they grew in tangles and they were as grey as Dead Men's Fingers. Her hands were as big as dinner-plates, blackish-green with grey scales and her feet were twice as big as meat-platters, fat and glistening white with wrinkled edges. Her toes moved about in a hesitant way like blind worms, seeking.

103

'Now you are more like yourself,' said Breda Fairfoul.

'But not entirely yourself,' said Melodie Moonlight. 'We have not the satisfaction of seeing your fullness of ugliness, which is known to deprive men of two thirds of their strength.'

'Only on special occasions,' croaked the hag and she became the beautiful fair woman again.

'What colour is your eye make-up?' asked Breda Fairfoul.

'Deadly Nightshade.'

'And what is that fabulous perfume?'

'Flowers of Brimstone.'

'Oh, you're a fizzer and no mistake!' said Breda Fairfoul, and they all broke out laughing again like mad hyenas.

They clasped hands and formed a circle. Moving slowly at first, they began a round dance. They gathered speed and went faster. Soon, they were spinning at a scorching speed, all the time shrieking with mad laughter; making a circle of flashing colour and light.

Then the outline of the circle blurred and trembled. The three women rushed to its centre and crashed into each other. Incredibly, they became One—and spun round and round so fast that all Pidge could see was a sort of smear of colour. After a while, a slowing down came, and he could glimpse the flash of a face. The face held aspects of all three women but it was one face. As he watched, it began to dissolve from being just one entity and, where there had been one pair of eyes, there were now three. Three noses and mouths appeared, and all the extra features then slid off to the sides and there were three heads, instead of one.

Gradually, the women broke away from each other and stood separately, still screaming with laughter.

He was beginning to think that they would spend the whole night in fits of merriment, when the fair woman abruptly stopped the fun.

'What of Olc-Glas?' she hissed. 'He has not come though I whispered.'

'Ill news. Our web has been broken.'

'Explain!'

'Meddling by The Dagda. Even now, Olc-Glas is in the keeping of the Great Eel.'

'Good! There will be sport.'

'You are not angry?'

'No. It will be like following the stag or a board game; fidchell, the Royal Game. The Dagda reached the boy first?'

'He was warned even before the first snare.'

'There will be pleasure in considering our moves.'

She smiled, a dazzling smile; and Pidge almost forgot how she had looked as a hag.

'And you, with your blue and orange hair—how is it with you?'

'Our pretence is, that we are merely witches from the country to the east of us. Thus we are frightening which is amusing; but not too frightening for the sake of wisdom,' said Melodie Moonlight.

'We have a most wonderful chariot that moves without horses and it is called A Harley Davidson,' said Breda Fair-foul.

'Let me see it,' the fair woman said with a slight smile.

Melodie straddled the bike and kicked it to life.

Breda leaped and sat behind her. The fair woman's leap was like a salmon's; she wriggled through the air and then she was sitting behind Breda.

Pidge watched as they raced off at a fearful speed, screeching with wild laughter and a crazy kind of delight. He watched until the scrying-glass, clouded over and he could see no more. The scrying-glass as he held it in his hand, seemed very small, the pictures that he had seen within it, no bigger than photographs. Wishing to see more, he gave it another shake but although the snow fell as before, no further picture appeared.

He put it back under his pillow.

She was no oil-painting, he thought, and he lay back and closed his eyes in sleep.

They raced on, stopping only once at seeing a solitary cottage. Leaving the motor-bike under a tree, they approached the house on foot. Inside, two old people sat on either side of the fire and talked drowsily together. They were the best of old friends and they spoke of their long lives lived in the little house; and of the children they had once had, that were now grown up and getting old themselves. Their talk was calm and

105

there were many pauses where the little silences carried on their conversation for them.

As the three women approached the house, their footfalls made no sound. At the keyhole, they listened to the drowsy, affectionate words. Disgust filled them and they sent a spiteful wish into the house. In a moment, the drowsy words were changed and grew rapid, savage and bitter. The two old people said terrible things to each other and threw wrongs in each other's faces. And the three women listened with pleasure.

In the end, even the silence was tainted; and the old woman sat with tears pouring down her cheeks and the old man sat staring desolately into the fire.

Then the three women flew to the motor-bike and raced away again, saying to each other:

'A little evil, a very little evil!'

And they didn't stop laughing even when they were back inside Mossie Flynn's glasshouse.

Chapter 12

LATER there was a dream.

'It is middle-night and The Dagda's people are low,' a voice said.

Pidge saw the coppice lit by a full moon, mysterious and strange in the bright darkness; so bright for night time and so cold-looking.

As he watched, shapes prowled here and there in the under-growth. There were shadows everywhere.

He knew that Brigit stood beside him. It was odd that without seeing her, he *knew* that she was there.

The shapes melted in and out of cover and at last came clearly into the moonlight, to stand before an old oak tree that grew deep within the coppice among all the new trees.

He saw then that they were the hounds.

They sat in a half ring round the tree and they said:

'Come forth, Brandling Breac.'

A testy voice from inside the tree asked:

'Who calls me?'

'Mórrígan,' a hound answered.

An object emerged from the tree.

It appeared to be wonderfully lit up from inside itself and it shone brilliantly. It was striped red and blue and to Pidge it looked like a barber's pole. Then he saw that it had spots as well. They were many, many coloured and as the stripes revolved, the spots began to pulsate.

The hounds dipped their heads once and sat regarding what Pidge thought of as The Pole. The hounds' manner was deeply respectful.

'Why?' said the voice, sounding even more crusty, and Pidge felt an intense curiosity to see what the owner of the voice would look like, when he finally would appear.

'She desires your bright beauty.'

The Pole quivered and a strong tremble ran the whole of its length. The stripes went faster and the spots glowed and pulsed even more brightly. For some moments there was a silence, while The Pole suffered its emotions. It bent from the middle and twitched and seemed to be in pain. In a short while, it straightened itself with a deep sigh.

The moon sailed on across the sky and the shadows moved to obey a natural law. Shadows were now gathering more deeply and darkly beside the oak tree.

Then Pidge fancied that he could see the semblance of a head at the end of The Pole that was furthest from the trunk of the tree; and he realized that The Pole was not a pole but a marvellous sort of worm.

It swayed.

It whispered.

'Must I?' it said and the whole of the dream was filled with sadness.

The hounds waited.

'For what purpose this time must I obey?'

'To bring her Olc-Glas who is her heart's desire. He has been given into the care of The Lord Of The Waters by two mortal pups, under guidance from The Dagda.'

'No,' said the marvellous worm, who was the Brandling Breac.

At this, the hounds appeared puzzled beyond belief.

'What means this?' they asked each other. 'We have obeyed in all things; he may not refuse.'

'It means that the bond on me has been crossed out by a debt on me. I will not go against the two young mortals. I am beholden to them.'

'What is this debt?'

'The sun was fierce today and one of my tribe was weak and exposed. His small body twisted in pain as he struggled in vain against scorching. The two you speak of saw and understood. They placed him in safety and I may pay what I owe. I am not in revolt in this.'

'This is true,' the hounds agreed among themselves.

The Brandling Breac went smaller and smaller until he was as little as an ordinary earthworm and then he suddenly dimmed and went back inside the tree.

The dream changed.

The hounds were approaching the glasshouse where the three women stood in awful vividness. So clearly did Pidge see, that he remarked to himself the hounds' eyes; soft, shiny butterscotch brown eyes, full of fear.

'Oh, Great Queen,' they said, 'forgive us, we have failed.'

Although three women spoke, there was only one voice reaching Pidge's mind.

'What message?'

'The bond on him is broken.'

'Impossible!'

'The human pups were kind to one of his people who was distressed.'

'Interfering brats!'

The beautiful fair woman who was The Mórrígan herself, felt a slight anger and her eyebrows worked rapidly like two small electric eels on her forehead. She muttered a mild triple curse which she sent in three directions, not aimed at anyone in particular; but causing three unhappy things to fall on three innocent people in different parts of the land.

'Go and tell that worm,' she said, 'that if he doesn't do as I say, I've only to flex my big toe and all of his people will die. When they die, the earth will go sour, the grass will not grow and everything that lives will sicken and die. Better still, I'll come myself and bring such trouble with me for him if he persists in this conceit, that he'll wish he had never seen the light of day.'

Once more Pidge saw the coppice, with the Brandling Breac and The Mórrígan staring at each other. The Brandling Breac was as large and as bright as he had been before and he was saying:

'If you kill everything, where then will you get your sport? And, forgive me for reminding one as great as you, it is not within your power in these times. Your old strength belongs to other days long past.'

The Mórrígan made a sign and out of the dense shadows which had now thickened on one side of the tree, a single shadow leaped and snatched the Brandling Breac and then everything was swallowed into a deep blue-green darkness that devoured the whole picture from Pidge's sight.

In moments, the Brandling Breac, full-sized and in all his brightness, was there again; hanging in deep water, still in the grip of the shadow. He was being offered as bait to the Great Eel.

The Eel lay at the bottom of the lake, moving only with the weed.

His eyes were shut tight, and his whole being was one passionate wish not to look at what was being dangled up above his head. Every ounce of will and wish was focused on this one thing.

'Alas,' said the Brandling Breac. 'I know you are there, Great Eel; and I know that you try not to see me.'

The Eel's mind was a tight knot of will-power.

'You may give way in the end and look.'

'I know it,' the Great Eel said.

'This is not in the terms of the bond. I am here against my will.'

'I know that too, but hunger is despot here.'

Hundreds of little faces, trout, chub, bream, moor-hen, wild duck, and a vast multitude of insect faces, appeared and lurked in shadows to watch the terrible drama. A strong feeling of sadness was everywhere and sympathy was fused with horror.

The Great Eel trembled and his head moved a fraction of almost nothing upwards, causing a shock of greater horror to ripple through the watching faces. They all joined their unified will with the Eel's will, and his head was steady again and his eyes were firmly shut.

Pidge saw water-boatmen rowing like maniacs all over the lake. Three of them found Puddeneen Whelan who was lying on a lily-pad. The water-boatmen twittered excitedly as they told him what was happening. Puddeneen looked terrified.

Again Pidge saw the Brandling Breac dangling in the dark water and the Great Eel struggling to keep his eyes closed.

Then BLINK; the eyes finally opened and they were full of hunger.

The Great Eel looked upwards.

A murmur arose from the onlookers and a whisper:

'The Lord Of The Waters is about to be ensnared.'

The Eel's body began to drift and he moved upwards towards the Brandling Breac.

All of a sudden, the whole thing was interrupted by what seemed to be dozens of frogs who leaped between the Brandling Breac and the Great Eel and began to perform the most spectacular and amazing underwater ballet imaginable. The Eel recoiled and lay on the bed of the lake again. At once the Brandling Breac went very small and the horrible tension was completely broken and the terrifying hunger was gone from the eyes of the Great Eel. The multitude of watchers laughed and created a great wave of happiness and Puddeneen in a magnificent leap upwards clasped the Brandling Breac and, holding him tightly and safely, he swam away.

In an eye's twinkling, the Brandling Breac was safely beached on a broad lily-pad and was being given artificial respiration by a team of frogs who queued to take turns: a healing-fish came to apply medicinal-slime for his wounds and when these things were done, a frog recognized by Pidge as Bagsie Curley, did up the Brandling Breac in a splint and a bandage.

Last of all, a sign was hung up on a bending reed which said:

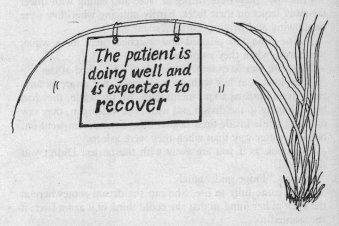

The patient is doing well and is expected to recover

This pleased all the waiting well-wishers and it especially pleased Pidge because near the end, the Brandling Breac had looked so horribly pale and languid.

111

Chapter 13

THEY both slept late the next morning. Auntie Bina had to call them several times.

In the end, she shouted that she would come and pull them out of bed by the heels, if they didn't hurry up and come to their breakfast, because she had to begin the churning and they were delaying her.

In the summer, Auntie Bina churned the gathered cream twice a week and she liked everything to be out of the way, before she began.

'If you're not down in two minutes I'll give your breakfast to the hens,' she threatened from the foot of the ladder-stairs; and they reluctantly dragged themselves away from sleep and out of bed.

Presently, they were sitting at table and eating with queer far-away looks on their faces, hardly noticing what they were swallowing and Brigit peculiarly silent.

Auntie Bina was puzzled and watched them for a while, wondering when they would notice her.

'Why are you so quiet this morning?' she asked at last.

They looked at her with great surprise, not aware of anything at all unusual about themselves. All the while, they had been clinging to the dream and with eyes wide open, they saw nothing; while inside their heads, bits of the dream went on, but in a softer way than when they were asleep.

'You look as if you are away with the fairies! Didn't you sleep well?'

'Oh yes,' Pidge said vaguely.

Brigit came fully to life. She put the dream somewhere at the back of her mind so that she could think of it again later, if she wanted to.

'Like a snuggard,' she said, thinking it sounded right.

'You're sitting there—with the eyes falling out of your heads for want of sleep, and showing about as much life as two dead

112

bees; you look as if you didn't get a wink.'

Pidge, too, let go of the dream for the present.

'I slept very well Auntie Bina,' he assured her.

'And I slept like a baby. It's just that I had a funny dream and I was thinking about it,' Brigit said.

Pidge looked at her with curiosity and said nothing.

Auntie Bina laughed at Brigit and, missing the important part about the dream, said:

'I'm glad to hear you slept like a baby, Brigit. The sooner you finish eating and get out in the fresh air, the better. And if you haven't sparked up by dinner-time, we'll have to see about a remedy.'

'Malt?' Brigit asked.

'Senna,' Auntie Bina said brightly.

'Yerk!' said Brigit pulling a horrible face. 'It's a poor look-out if you get senna for only not saying anything.'

They finished eating and went across the yard to the stable to have another look at the new mare.

Michael was up in the hay-loft over the stable, forking down hay to her manger—and there she was, calmly standing and champing as normally as could be.

When they came in, she turned and regarded them and her looks were gentle and her eyes were innocent. She just looked like a nice-tempered animal.

They fussed and patted her, and she was pleased and nuzzled them and made friendly sounds of horse-gossip as they got to know each other.

Michael came down.

Pidge looked at him anxiously, in dread that he would be as strange as he was the night before.

'Oh,' said Michael. 'Here you are, at last! She's lovely, isn't she?'

He spoke with pride; but now he was entirely like himself, with nothing left of the distant and cold stranger he had seemed the night before.

He doesn't even remember yesterday, Pidge thought, and he was very happy about that, but he wondered in his mind about Sally and what had happened to her.

'She is,' he replied.

'Good enough for a King,' Brigit said.

113

'If only Sally were here; I'd be the happiest man in the county. It couldn't be known, how much I miss her. What came on her at all—to run away like that, I'll never know,' Michael said softly.

'Maybe she'll find her way back?' Pidge suggested.

'You often hear about things like that,' Brigit said. 'They're always doing it—going off somewhere just to show they can find their way back. I've heard about it, often.'

'We couldn't reply on *that*—we might never see her again,' Pidge said.

'I'm going to phone all the newspapers in Dublin to advertise her loss and offer a reward for her safe return,' Michael said.

'Oh good,' Pidge smiled.

'I'm keeping the mare in here for today, so that she gets used to things. She can have the place to herself. You two could take a walk down as far as Fouracre and Thornfield and see if the others are all right. I'll go and phone the papers; I'll feel a lot better when that's done.'

All the other mares and young horses were out to pasture on the summer grass.

'I should have gone down myself last night to look at them, after the heat yesterday. I can't think why I forgot,' Michael continued, looking very uncertain as he tried to remember the evening before, exactly.

It was obvious that he couldn't remember how he had been, at all.

Everything was wonderfully right.

Pidge knew that, throughout the day, interested neighbours would be calling in to see the mare and to nod their heads wisely and knowingly as they admired her many fine qualities, and, in the ordinary way, he would be sorry to miss any of this clever talk. Now, however, he was glad of the chance to get off somewhere with Brigit, to be by themselves so that he could find out about her dream, at last.

They had left the farmyard through the way between the cow-house and the turf-shed, when Pidge suddenly remembered something.

'Have you got your brooch?' he asked.

Brigit opened her cardigan; the brooch was pinned on her dress.

'Where are your other things?'

'Under my bed; hidden,' she said.

'Wait here a minute; I won't be long,' he told her, and ran back to the house.

The kitchen was empty and the churn was scalded and standing ready to be filled. He could hear Auntie Bina in the dairy, humming to herself as she skimmed the cream from the big, wide-necked crocks of milk. So that was all right; he wouldn't have to answer any awkward questions.

He hurried up the stairs to his room and got his scrying-glass and the bag of nuts and put them into his pockets. He went into Brigit's room and put her Swapping Sweets and her penny whistle inside her school satchel and fastened up the buckle. And then he came back downstairs, glad to find the kitchen still empty, and went out into the farmyard again.

The mare was in her loose-box, gazing out over the half-door at a small part of her new world; so, his father must have already gone to the phone-box to ring the papers. That meant that there was no one to ask: "What have you got there?" or: "Where did you get those things?" and he didn't have the difficult problem of trying to explain without really explaining, and that was an ease to his mind. Later, perhaps, he could tell everything; but not yet.

He caught up with Brigit.

'I went back for these,' he said, showing her.

'Why?'

'It might be as well to have them handy. They were given to us for a reason, even though we don't know why, yet. I want to know about that dream you had, Brigit.'

'It was the most real dream I've ever dreamed. Now I don't think dreams are fuzzy anymore; only that I wake up too fast and all the lovely colours and things go away, because my eyes are too wide open and the eyes inside my head don't get a chance to see anymore.'

They walked along and Brigit told her dream.

Pidge listened, impulsively butting in from time to time, as detail matched detail and Brigit told him his own dream. So she really had stood beside him and they had indeed shared it all.

115

He explained this to Brigit, who wasn't in the least surprised, and he told her about the scrying-glass and the mare and the fair woman.

'Why didn't you wake me up and let me look too?'

'There just wasn't time; it all happened too fast and I would have missed some of it.'

'Couldn't you have missed a bit for my sake?'

'If I had, I couldn't be telling you all about it now. Neither one of us would have known the whole thing. This way, we both know.'

'That's true; I suppose,' she said a little begrudgingly. 'I wish I'd seen the ugly one though.'

'You're lucky you didn't!'

'The nerve of her, getting inside our mare like that! Tell me it all again!'

Again Pidge told her all that he had seen in the little glass ball.

'How do you mean they crashed into each other when they were dancing? I don't know what you mean?'

'They sort of became one person for a while and then they broke away in three again.'

She asked many more questions and had heard it all twice over in pieces, by the time they reached Fouracre and Thornfield.

Fouracre was first.

They went in, shutting the gate after them, and walked among the horses. Everything seemed to be fine; the horses were all busily tearing at the grass, moving at a steady pace from one cropping-spot to another.

They went through the wide gap that led into Thornfield and found all as it should be. There was a large three-sided shelter there, where the animals could take refuge from the flies or the heat, or when it was unpleasantly windy or wet. From the amount of droppings there, it was plain that the horses had spent a good deal of time inside, during the heat of the previous day. Between them, Pidge and Brigit cleared it all away to the heap, using shovels and a barrow, that were kept beside the shelter for that purpose.

When it was all tidy, they left Thornfield by the gate in the farthest wall, which bordered the little boreen. A thorntree

116

grew there and the field was named after it. As they passed by the tree, Brigit plucked a few leaves and put them in the pocket of her dress.

They walked along the little road, turning for home.

'I gotta message for you from P. Whelan, Esquare,' said a familiar voice and to their great delight, there was Bagsie Curley, sitting on a flat stone.

'Oh! It's Bagsie Curley!' Brigit cried.

'That's me. Yes, Bagsie Curley,' said Bagsie.

'Where's Puddeneen?' Pidge asked him.

'He is Lordin' it on a desirable lily-pad, in a detached, perminint puddle; and I gotta message for you from him.'

'What's the message?' Brigit asked eagerly.

'Dis is it: "Tell dem," he said, "I hev done da doings an' dat it's a wonder me hair heven't gone snow-white from shock, after all I bin through—if I had any".'

'Why didn't he come himself?' asked Pidge.

'Miss Fancy Finnerty is kickin' up a racket an' woan let him out today, dat's why. She is watchin' an' clockin' over him like an old hen. She sez he's gotta stop where he is, cos of all da shocks he got, lass night an' yesterday. Now, I gotta tell you what happen lass night.'

'We know; we saw it all,' Pidge said.

'In a dream,' Brigit added.

'You mustave ett cheese,' Bagsie said knowingly.

'Is Puddeneen all right?' Brigit wondered. She looked concerned.

'Accordin' to *her*, he's prostherated an' flattened an' not worth washin' dis mornin'. "Tell dem," she sez, "dat he's not worth a rat's ransome; dat he hev about as much pep as a washleather, an' he look like a wackwork. He's a wrung-out frog," she sez, "an' dere's no more pitiful sight on dis earth, den a frog wit' no puff left in him. An' I wudden be serprised," she sez, "if he doan come down wit' da hoopy-cough or queasles, cos of all he bin through. He look like an old prune from Outer Magnolia," she sez, and he can't go out today.'

'She sounds very bossy,' Brigit observed.

'Oh, she's a Perfect Polygon,' Bagsie answered, 'da kind we ought to take our hats off to—if we had any. She's spittin' wit' temper; she's like a wasp!'

'Is Puddeneen really sick? I hope he's all right; he was so brave last night. He's not really sick, is he?' Pidge asked hopefully.

'His Grannie, Big Julia—nearly threw him out wit' da tea-leaves dis mornin' he wuz dat dessicrated. Dey are spoonin' him now wit' herbaceous tea, but he keeps askin' for grapes.'

'I don't want Puddeneen to be sick like that,' Brigit said.

'Oh, he's not really suffrin', you know. He's just got brain-fag an' is a bit underblown. He's goin ta get a big plate of muffled betaytas an' onyins an' gravy in a little while, to plump him up. An' after dat, dey're given him a mugga brawth wit' barley an' thin, buttered toast. An' after dat, he's gettin' a big dish of strobberies an' cream wit' nuts an' chocklit an' minced chickweek. An' after dat; he'll just rest for a while an' read da Connacht Tribune; atin' a bitta tuffy an' a Chester cake or two; until he rises up again wit' his figure back nicely. Miss Fancy Finnerty wuz all for takin' a short-cut wit' a bicycle-pump, but Big Julia wudden hear of it and said da old-fashioned remedy wuz da best, an' she don't want no new-fangled Nightingales round da sick bed of no Whelans. Dere'll be trouble dere yet, mark my words,' he finished significantly.

'She could have burst him with a pump,' Brigit said indignantly.

'Tell him that we hope he gets better soon and thank him for all he did. I don't know what would have happened if he hadn't got that ballet going,' Pidge said.

'Doan worry; he'll be awright. It's a day's work gettin' him up in da mornin' his grannie always sez; so he's only too pleased dat he kin lie dere all day, stuffin' himself,' Bagsie said, sounding envious and looking hungrier with every word. 'I fancy a mouthful or two, meself; I'll be going now.'

One spring and he was gone.

They watched to see if he would re-appear in jumps, and they saw him bob up and down from moment to moment, going really fast. They saw him hop up a wall by doing it in stages, from perch to perch where the stones stuck out, and then he jumped over and was out of sight.

They turned away and walked slowly on.

'I love Puddeneen, he's my favourite; and I love Bagsie, too,' Brigit said.

'So do I. I think Puddeneen was really great last night and truly brave.'

'Pidge,' Brigit said, dragging her feet.

'What?' he stopped and looked at her.

'I wish we didn't have to go home yet. I'd like to stay around and about to see if any more things will happen. I don't want it just to finish.'

'Neither do I,' Pidge said, understanding perfectly. 'It's good fun, really. And a wonderful adventure.'

'I was hoping you'd say that,' said a friendly voice to the left of them, and they stopped at once and looked to see who it was.

119

Chapter 14

'COULD I have a few more vocables with you, young sir?' It was the old angler and, as before, he was sitting in among some bushes by the roadside.

Pidge felt a wave of pleasure at seeing him again. Brigit looked at him with great interest.

'Are you the old fella who warned Pidge about the cross-roads?'

'Brigit!' Pidge said sharply. He hoped that the old angler would realize that she wasn't really being rude and ignorant.

'That's me!' the old angler chuckled. 'The Old Fella! As old as the bush behind the house; as old as the far-away bygones; an eld and a hearty friend to many old bones, once audacious,' and he laughed a wheezing laugh like a ruptured bagpipe.

'Older than mardykes, highways, byways and broadways; older than ring-a-ring-a-rosie; older than boats and even older than that brazint serpint, if all is known.'

'I thought so,' Brigit said, looking at him intently. 'Your face is as wrinkled as a curly cabbage; it's got lines on it like a chicken's leg.'

'Brigit!'

'What?'

Pidge's face was going red with embarrassment, but the old angler didn't seem to mind.

'Never mind that the truth is not good manners; it seldom was,' he said. His old face smiled and was more wrinkled than ever, but somehow the wrinkles looked delicate and perfect, and reminded Pidge of poppy petals, newly opened and all creased and papery. 'Especially in babies,' he finished and winked at Pidge.

Luckily Brigit didn't catch all of his meaning but she knew that he was excusing her.

'See?' she said.

'You didn't get sniggled like an eel, then?' the old angler said to Pidge.

'No. Thanks to you, I didn't.'

'You came this far without damage, anyway.'

'Yes.'

'If a good-willing party was to say—can you go further?'

'How do you mean?' whispered Pidge, beginning to wish now that he hadn't said it was all a wonderful adventure.

'What is the pretty name of this place?'

'Shancreg. It means Old Rock.'

'Yes, Shancreg,' Brigit said, not to be left out.

'Ah,' the old angler murmured, 'it's a nice name.'

Something in the way he said this made Pidge feel that the old angler had known well that the district was called Shancreg, and that there was an old, old rock standing in the middle of one of the fields, with other old stones tumbled down around it, like fallen trees. Once, they had all stood upright in a pattern, with one or two arranged as capstones, so the old people said; once, they had a purpose and a meaning, way back in ancient times; but the knowledge of these things was now lost.

'If you go further, young mortal sir—Shancreg is your path.'

Pidge was sure that the old angler had only asked about the name, to be able to give him this information. This must mean that the whole thing had been bound in some way to the district in which he lived, right from the very beginning.

'Will you tell us some more, please?' he asked.

'It might be beyond your liking. It might raise your hair and quiver you and even cause you to refuse the venture, though it has been in your hands now since the beginning.'

'The beginning was in the bookshop?'

'Two long fingers have been moving you, but you spied that soon enough.'

'Yes. Was one of them someone called—The Dagda?'

'To be sure.'

'Who is The Dagda?'

'The Dagda is the Good God. He is God of the earth and the life in it; he arranges the run of the seasons. He is the Lord of Great Knowledge.'

'And the other one—was The Mórrígan?'

'Oh her!' Brigit said with a fine show of scorn. 'Cabbages to her!'

'Do not be cabbaging nor slighting such as would make Nero look like a bit of fried bread. She has set her evil heart—which is so small it would flap about inside a midge's skin—on gaining Olc-Glas; but such a thing would be ruin and destruction and full of sorrow.'

'Who exactly *is* she?'

'She is the Goddess of Death and Destruction.'

'What?' said Pidge. He thrilled with horror and fright and remembered the ugly fires in the mare's eyes. He caught hold of Brigit's hand and wanted to simply walk away and go home.

The old angler looked at him searchingly and said:

'If she adds the vile poison that belongs to Olc-Glas to the evil that still sleeps within herself, all creation will suffer for it.'

Pidge made no answer. He just stood and wondered what on earth he could do to get out of all this. It's too much for one boy and one little girl, he thought.

'The Dagda is your strong friend in this,' the old angler said softly.

Pidge hardly noticed.

'I freed Olc-Glas when I peeled away St Patrick's words,' he said miserably.

'He must have been an elegant, powerful Druid, that Patrick,' the old angler said admiringly.

Brigit was shocked.

'He was a Saint, not a Druid; I thought everyone knew that! I can't imagine how *you* didn't know it,' she said.

'Ah well! Sometimes we miss the latest news. I'm a bit behind the times and I never did go to school,' the old angler smiled.

'Why don't we just destroy Olc-Glas?' Pidge asked.

'It's your task, if you'll do it.'

'Couldn't we just tear the paper up or burn it?'

'That would only release him.'

'Is that why he couldn't be burned with the rest of the rubbish from the old pawnshop?'

'Yes.'

'How could we do it?'

'With The Mórrígan's own foul blood.'

'What!' Pidge cried again, appalled at the dangers and horrors that this suggested.

'One drop.'

'But we'd never get it. She'd kill us first.'

'Kill us?' Brigit said. She looked around wide-eyed at the idea of anyone even thinking such a thing. Everything the old angler was saying was miles above her head; all that she really understood was that there was some sort of game going on. 'I don't think that's a very nice thing to say,' she said, 'it hurts my feelings.'

'Could it be,' the old angler asked wistfully, 'that you have ever heard the name of Cúchulain?'

'Of course. He was the Great Hero who lived long ago in olden times, who was the most skillful warrior ever known,' Pidge replied.

Delight spread across the old angler's face: 'The prophecy was true,' he whispered to himself. 'On the day he first took arms, it was said that his life would be short but his name would be greater than any other in Ireland.'

'I've often heard stories of him and there are some in my schoolbooks as well.'

'Cúchulain spilled three drops of The Mórrígan's blood. To find even one drop would be enough,' the old angler said quietly.

'Was she around in those ancient times?' Pidge asked.

'Indeed she was,' the old angler replied emphatically. 'Three times she went against Cúchulain during the battles of The Cattle Raid Of Cooley and three times he gave her a sharp answer. It was while he was standing in the waters of a ford fighting his enemies that she came the first time as an eel. She wound herself three times round his feet to trip him and hinder him in his striving, but he struck back at her and crushed her ribs against a green stone in the waters, and a drop of her blood turned them dark crimson. That was the first drop. Next she came as a grey she-wolf and attacked him again. He fought back using his slingshot, and his swift pebble wounded her in the eye. The third time she came as a red heifer without horns, with a herd of cattle following her, and they stirred up the waters of the ford so that Cúchulain lost sight of it and couldn't tell deep from shallow or where he would be safe, so he flung a second stone from his sling and broke her legs. The first blood-drop was lost, but the two pebbles of her wounding are stained with her blood and lie somewhere in this land. If one could be found! If only one could be found,' the old angler finished, even more wistfully than before.

'Is it a sort of quest?'

'Yes.'

Pidge had once read a story to Brigit about a quest. She looked stern.

'I'm not slaying no dragons or anything like that,' she declared.

'Any,' Pidge said. 'I'm not slaying *any* dragons.'

'Neither am I!' she nodded solemnly.

'There never was dragons to be slayed in this,' the old angler said, smiling at Brigit, 'unless all things graceless are dragons. It's more seeking than slaying.'

'It sounds too terrifying,' Pidge said. It's no good pretending it doesn't, he told himself.

'The Dagda and all his people will serve you well in this.'

Suddenly a great power came into Pidge. This time, he really took in the fact that the Dagda was his friend. He remembered the music and the way that the stars had moved. What on earth have I been afraid of? he asked himself. With Dagda as my friend, what on earth have I been afraid of?

The old angler watched the changing expressions that showed Pidge's thoughts and then he spoke again:

'Don't look for it—find it. Don't search for it—come to it. This is the best and the oldest way, for maps can be read by many eyes and maps can't show the crooked path of sensing. She will send her hounds after you, but they will be obliged to send eyes and ears in many directions before they find the path you follow; there are no patterns that declare an unknown path. All who are true creatures will help where they can. As to the hounds, when they hunt—do not run. No harm will come from running unless you run *from them*. If they are not in view when you turn your head, you can run as you will.

124

Nor the grass won't grow under your feet until you return. If it is your will?'

'I don't understand everything, but I'll go,' Pidge said fearlessly.

'Me too,' Brigit said, not understanding much at all. 'Because she's awful. She'll make a name for herself one of these days, the way she goes on.'

Pidge laughed because Brigit didn't realize that the Mórrígan had made her name thousands of years before.

A look of relief and joy lit up the old angler's face and he clapped his hands for happiness. Then they saw that he had a bandage on his left hand.

'What happened to your hand?' Brigit asked at once.

'Something bit me for a joke,' he said.

Pidge recalled the day before on the island and Boodie and Patsy and the three swans that fought with the dogs. He saw again in his mind's eye, the sad feather with the dried blood spoiling it. Before he could ask about any of this, however, a voice from behind them said quietly:

'I am very well—how are you?'

Chapter 15

THE voice was so gentle and musical that the children, when they turned round, expected to see a very lovely woman standing behind them. Instead, they saw the heavy head with the mild, patient face—an ass. Her eyes were lustrous and calm; her face asked to be stroked, it looked so smooth and warm. Brigit threw her arms round her neck and cuddled her.

'You're beautiful,' she said.

'Go along with you!' the ass said shyly, but she was pleased. 'If you're ready, we will go now.'

'Oh yes,' Brigit said. 'We'll go now.'

She gave the ass a kiss.

'I am Serena Begley and I am your diviner,' the ass said.

'Great at dowsing is Serena, better than Old Moore,' the old angler said. 'She'll find the path you need to take you rightly through the Old Rocks. It's a secret line under the ground, invisible but to those with a very great gift. For the second sight and the mysticals, there's no one like Serena.'

'Could anyone find the secret line under the ground?' Pidge asked.

'No, by that and by this!' the old angler replied. 'They couldn't even smell it and it would take a fair, long time to discover it by accident. It runs like fire under the ground, the way lightning runs in the sky. Serena will find it.'

'If you would like to climb up?' Serena suggested.

Pidge gave Brigit a leg up and then got on behind her.

'Are you sure it's all right?' he asked.

'Right as turnips,' Serena answered reassuringly.

'Apples!' the old angler said. 'Here is one each, if you like them.'

He handed them an apple each.

'What about one for Serena?' Brigit asked.

'I'd rather have a carrot or a handful of barley. I cut my eye-teeth on apples, in my time. But we must be going, it's time we got the feel of the road.'

She started to move off.

'What springs to mind now is safe journey to you,' the old angler called to them and before anyone could even say "Thank you", he went in over the wall and was lost to view. Pidge watched for him for a while and soon he saw him running.

He nudged Brigit and as they watched, he grew more and more like a wild, young man instead of one that was old.

'He's a good runner for an old fella, isn't he, Pidge?' Brigit said.

'I wonder if it's really him?' Pidge replied.

Serena walked unhurriedly along the road. There was nothing to show whether or not she had found the secret path. Pidge wished now that he had asked the old angler a good many more questions while he had the chance. He was sure that there were a lot of things he still did not know. I don't even know the right questions to ask, he thought, but even wrong questions might have led to right answers, some-how.

Serena turned in from the road and went through a small gap into a field.

Suddenly, her ears sprang upright and then splayed out rigidly on either side of her head. She stopped walking for a second, drew in a deep breath, closed her eyes and concentrated hard. The result was almost instant and, very carefully, she took a neat-footed step forward. Her ears began to move. She took another step and her ears began a graceful sweep, circling and closing towards each other, like a crab's front claws. One step more—and the ears whipped across each other and stayed still but for the slightest tremble, showing some kind of strange force at work.

'That's it,' she said. 'We've got it.'

Walking along at a brisk pace now, she followed the invis-ible line. From time to time, her ears would start to splay outwards again; but she would simply take a step this way or that and the ears would twist across each other and, once more, show the way.

'Those are great ears you have, Serena,' Brigit said. 'I wish I had ears like those.'

'Eat your apples now,' Serena said, 'we're nearly at the field where the Old Rocks stand.'

'Oh, it's so exciting!' said Brigit with great delight, and she took a great bite out of her apple.

Pidge quickly bit into his apple. It tasted of—apple; with an apple's sweetness. Goodness, he thought, I'd half-expected it to taste of something else; I'm expecting miracles all the time now. He took another bite and happened to glance thought-lessly up at the sky. There was a plane, high up there, leaving a vapour-trail behind it like the track of a sort of skysnail. And that's just ordinary too, he thought, nothing magical about that except that it's a marvellously clever thing. Not all miracles are magic.

'Quite right,' said Serena.

'You knew what I was thinking?'

'It's these ears of mine; I can't help it.'

'Oh!'

'What were you thinking of, Pidge?' Brigit asked, and Pidge told her.

'I wish I knew what everyone was thinking,' she said. 'I'd set myself up as the best spy in the world. I bet I'd be rich in no time and I'd know everyone's secrets and what Auntie Bina was getting me for Christmas and everything.'

'But you'd never have any surprises, then,' Pidge said.

'Who cares about surprises?'

'You do.'

'Well, I wouldn't if I knew what everyone was thinking. I'd give up surprises for that.'

But Pidge was thinking of Auntie Bina and Michael. Oh dear, he thought, they don't know where we are, or what we have got into; and I don't know how long we'll be or if we'll ever see them again.

'Believe me, the grass won't grow under your feet until you return,' Serena said to reassure him, just as the old angler had said it earlier. Pidge felt comforted and was just about to ask her to explain it better, when they went through another gap and into the field where the Old Rocks stood.

With horror, he saw that there were people there already,

ahead of them; tall, thin people gathered in small groups. They looked like part of a procession that had lost its way.

'Who are they?' Brigit asked.

Pidge had known the first second he saw them.

'They are the hounds,' he said and he couldn't help but shudder.

Chapter 16

THE tall, thin people stood about in little groups, talking in low tones and nodding as if they were having interesting conversations, but really they were just pretending not to notice Serena and the children.

'They hope to follow us through the stone way, by picking a path in my footprints; but they'll find that more than difficult, I can tell you,' Serena said quietly.

'Plishpeens!' Brigit said rudely at the top of her voice.

Pidge thought it would be the easiest thing in the whole world for dogs to find any path they wanted, because of their talented noses.

'Are you sure, Serena?' he asked doubtfully.

Serena's ears parted company and went sideways again, causing all the heads in the field to turn at once and watch her. So much for the way they pretended not to be interested, Pidge thought. Serena didn't answer his question until she had found the path again, after her ears had waggled a little bit and then jumped forward, before jerking together again in front of her face.

'I'm sure,' she said. 'Remember, this track cannot be smelled out like a perfumed truffle or a rotten bone. Keep your head cool and all will be well.'

The tall thin people had stopped pretending and were openly watching, with eager eyes, every step taken by Serena. The long, pink tongues flickered over the creamy teeth.

'Look at them licking their lips, the whelps!' Brigit said. It felt really strange and bold to say such a thing about them, when they looked just like people—grown-up people, at that.

By now they were at the Old Rocks.

Someone had been working hard. All the tumbled stones had been raised, making a wide circle, and there was a capstone bridging over the two most massive rocks. Pidge and

Brigit were astonished by all this and the odd sort of difference it made to the nature of the field.

Serena stopped walking.

The dog-people had been creeping closer and closer as Serena had followed her path and now they stood in a half ring, watching intently to see where she would put her feet.

Pidge took a last bite out of his apple and reached inside his pocket for a hankie to wipe his mouth. His fingers touched something small and round and hard, and he found that he was fingering one of the hazel-nuts. It must have fallen out of the bag. He took it out and looked at it as it lay on his palm. A fine hair-line crack appeared in the shell and the nut lay open in two halves.

'One of my hazel-nuts has broken open,' he said to Brigit. 'Let me see.'

Serena stood and waited, her ears vibrating now with the strength of the signal from under the ground.

There wasn't a kernel inside the nut, just the soft white stuff that was like cotton wool but silkier, the stuff that's always there before the nut grows from the tiny, pearly seed.

Just an unripe nut; a dud, he thought.

As quickly as the crack had appeared, three minute dots showed in the whiteness. And as they watched, the little specks grew bigger. They took on colour; two green and one pink. They grew faster and, in mere seconds, an outline could be distinguished and to their great delight, they saw the pretty face of a white cat; no bigger than a quarter of Brigit's small fingernail.

Pidge had to drop his half-eaten apple quickly to cup his hands, so that he could hold her, as she grew faster than thought. And there she was, calmly washing her face and sitting on his hands. She was lovely.

She looked at Pidge with her green silver-foil eyes and rubbed her pink nose with her delicate paw. She looked at Brigit and purred.

Flicking her tail, she studied the half-circle of dog-people with her flaring, wide, unconcerned stare. She slowly turned her head from side to side as if assessing them, while her tail flicked, flicked, as she dismissed them as creatures of no worth, in her clear, uninvolved mind.

The dog-people watched her as if mesmerized.

Small, involuntary movements betrayed their desire to be at her and tearing; a tremor from one, a fidget from a second, a tiny spasm and a step forward from a third. One of them made a low, fretful, complaining sound.

With a scream that was exquisitely cattish, she suddenly leaped from Pidge's hands high into the air above the heads of the dog-people, flew right over them and landed well behind them, muscles already bunched and back legs in place for a swift springing start. She landed lightly on the ground and was off in a glorious white flash of pure speed, leaving the tall thin people stupidly baffled for some seconds, until one of them made a noise like baying and they were off, giving chase, muscles just as efficient and brains now concentrated only on the enticing chance of catching her.

This was the moment Serena chose to step under the capstone portal and through the stones by the secret path.

The children saw briefly that the tall thin ones would never catch that particular cat; and once again, there was the music Pidge had heard from the chimney; hours of complicated beauty experienced by them in almost no time; and then everything round them dissolved rapidly and they were wrapped in a thick, white mist, dense as fleece, but insubstantial as drifting cloud.

It swirled and spiralled and eddied all round them, and muffled the whole earth.

Part Two

Chapter 1

I T was a strange world.

Serena's steps might have been the breathing of butter-flies; completely silent. So they moved in mystery, and but for the motion of Serena's body under them, they could have believed themselves to be floating far above the solid earth.

It was not at all clammy, this curious enfolding of mist; and it didn't cling to them or bead their hair. Breathing was easy and Brigit liked the way the mist rolled away in little puffs from her face as she breathed out.

They moved on.

'Look,' said Brigit, her voice all but smothered, 'over there.'

There was a candle burning brightly through the mist. Yellow, orange, blue and white like opal, flared and danced in waves over a tall, white wand. The tip of the coloured flame was pointed and it swayed and bent, sending shudders down to the dark, curling wick. The body of the candle seemed to be only a thickening of the mist.

Serena walked past the candle flame and it fluttered for an instant longer and died.

Ten paces further on a second candle appeared just like the first one, and it too failed and vanished as they passed by.

They looked so beautiful and so eerie in the thick whiteness, with nothing else at all to be seen.

Another one appeared; they passed it by; and then another and another and to Pidge it was plain that the candles were there to guide them only; but not to guide anyone following after.

This lovely thing went on for a long, long time and when at last Serena came to a standstill, she said:

'You see how the candles keep appearing? I can leave you now.'

'Oh, must you?' Pidge cried.

'I wish you wouldn't. I like being in this funny, misty stuff and the candles are lovely, but I want you to stay with us, Serena,' Brigit said most coaxingly.

'Please stay with us. All the way; wherever we're going,' Pidge urged her.

'No. I must go back and lay some false trails to confuse the hunters when they find their way through.'

Pidge felt shocked. From what the old angler had said, he had known that this was possible; but in his heart he had hoped that only Serena could do it.

'Do you think they will?' he asked hopefully.

'It might be a day's work, or two days' work, or only an hour's work, but they'll stumble their way through in the end. But don't fear too much. You'll be as safe as a bird in a thornbush, so long as you don't run from them. You can run like ten mad hares if you like, so long as they are not in view. Only, if you see them behind you, do not run for any reason whatsoever. Promise me that.'

They promised.

'Don't worry. I wouldn't run if they paid me,' Brigit added cockily.

'Hunting is one thing; catching is another thing entirely. You have a long way to go and you have started gently. Don't think it is easy not to run. You are only thinking it's easy because you have never been hunted by a beast of prey.'

'Beast of prey?' Pidge echoed with a shiver. 'Are we prey?'

'Not unless you run. *Only* if you run. You will be followed but not hunted, do you understand? *You may run but never within sight of the hounds*. All right?'

'Yes.'

'I must tell you now that there is still time to change your minds and ask if you are still willing to go on this journey of wonder and fear?'

Pidge felt that Serena couldn't lie to them and must be telling the truth about their not being hunted. He thought over what she had said and made up his mind not to run on any account while the hounds were in view.

'I have to be willing; it's my fault about Olc-Glas being free,' he said.

135

'We are willing but we have no experience,' Brigit said.

It was very odd to get down from Serena and find the ground, without being able to see.

'Safe journey. Goodbye,' whispered Serena and she was gone; lost in the mist, silent as a flower.

'You can hold my hand, Pidge, so that you won't get lost.'

'You always make me smile,' he said, and he clasped her hand tightly.

'Do I? Why?'

'You just do.'

They started walking.

It needed courage just to walk for fear of unseen things like holes or bogs or even cliffs. After a few steps, however, it began to feel quite natural and, anyway, Serena would not have led them into such a danger.

'Pidge, are we going the right way?'

'I can't tell yet. If there's a candle soon, it's the right way.'

Well, he said to himself, the die is cast and no mistake. We're on our own now. Whoever would have thought that Shancreg could have been the setting for all these supernatural events. In my heart, I'm glad that I'm mixed in with it. Not everyone gets this kind of chance.

They walked along gently, like thieves.

Brigit asked:

'Are we still in Ireland, Pidge?' And Pidge wondered before replying:

'I think we are; we must be I think,' because he really didn't know.

A candle blossomed ahead of them through the white mist.

'There's one! We're on the right track,' Brigit said.

She tried to hurry towards it, her hand squirming in Pidge's, as she attempted to be free to rush ahead.

'Don't let go of my hand, Brigit. Be patient for a second.'

Presently they were standing and staring at the candle-flame. It flared and danced, grew long, rippled and bowed and lit up the ivory-white wax drippings, and these were frosted by drops of moisture. A little anchored flame, with glowing blue frills at its edges, quivered with life and tried all ways to pull free from the wick that was its mainstay.

Of course, Pidge thought, if it did manage to pull free, all the life would instantly die.

'It's as if the mist is the sea and the candles are lighthouses showing us the way,' he remarked to Brigit.

'I'd like to stay here and watch it forever,' she said. 'I like candles much better than electrixity. It's all right though, I know we can't, just like that waterspout.'

They walked on.

The candle flame shuddered, went to almost nothing, and vanished.

'I'm just so surprised that they burn in this mist,' Pidge said.

'I'm not. It's only magic. There's a lot of it about at present, just like the old days.'

'There's always a lot of magic, but our way of seeing is very small and we mostly just call it Nature. Why, we are not at all surprised that we can pick an apple in the autumn that was a pink flower in the spring. That's natural magic and we don't really notice it.'

'Yes, and what about butter?' Brigit said.

'Butter?'

'Yes. It's hard and it comes out of something soft. It's yellow and it comes out of something white. Just by battering the cream with the dasher. It comes in little, weeny graineens and when you rock the churn, it turns into lumps. That's magic.'

'There used to be spells and charms about making butter in the old days, and even up to when Auntie Bina was a child.'

'That just proves it,' Brigit said smugly. 'I knew I was right.'

They continued walking and passed many more candles, without stopping to admire each one, though they would have liked to. All the time their steps were as soft as the wingbeats of a wren.

Pidge kept on chatting and holding Brigit's interest with anything that came into his head that would make magic sound natural. It was a way of not thinking too much about the dangers that might face them and a way of reassuring, not just Brigit, but himself as well.

For he had decided quietly to flow, as a leaf on a river, without fear. But, through all his resolution, the beauty of the

137

mist and the candles and the chatter, he was listening intently for any sounds behind them, that might say that they had indeed been followed through the stones.

It was with a start, then, that he heard a voice up ahead of them, calling through the mist:

'All ha'pennies and pennies, this way, please!'

Chapter 2

THE mist began to thin and, as it thinned, the children heard the sounds of many people bustling about and they were in the midst of footsteps, conversation and laughter, the rattle and squeak of wheels and the clucking of hens.

The mist parted like a curtain before their faces and then vanished completely.

To Pidge's very great astonishment, he found that they were standing on the platform of the railway station in Galway, surrounded by people, baskets, parcels and luggage, crates of chickens, sacks of potatoes and meal, and some very busy porters wheeling trucks piled high with trunks and umbrellas and bags of every description.

Pidge was utterly unprepared for this. I expected lots of things but I didn't expect this. I expected at least half a dozen magical things; but not this, he thought.

Brigit, who had been expecting nothing at all, was excited and happy. She had only been inside the station once before in her whole life.

We were definitely going in the wrong direction for this and we haven't gone half far enough to be in Galway City, Pidge said to himself; it's certainly a surprise.

'How did we get here, Pidge?'

'I don't know,' he said.

A diesel train was coming in from Dublin. People waited and chatted as they stood to welcome their visitors. Some were gathering their things together, to be ready to get on the train for the return trip.

'All ha'pennies and pennies, this way, please!' shouted a man with a megaphone, who was sitting on the ground a few yards from the exit. He had only one leg. It was stretched out in front of him on the ground.

'Pity the man who has only half his share of underpinnings,' he said.

He caught Pidge looking at him and winked. He beckoned discreetly.

'That man over there is calling us with his finger,' said Brigit.

They went across to him.

Pidge wasn't really sure if the man meant to call them or some other one in the crowd. As they drew nearer, Pidge hesitated.

'Come closer,' the man said.

'Yes?' Pidge said, feeling in his pocket for some ha'pennies and pennies.

'Thank you, young sir!' the man said loudly as Pidge dropped the money into an upturned cap, which lay on the ground with a few coins already lying in it, just by the man's one leg.

'I see you took the job then?' he whispered.

'Yes,' Brigit whispered back.

'That's good.'

He looked about him carefully before speaking again and then said:

'Find the man with the spray of oak leaves on his coat and follow him no matter where he goes.'

'All right,' Brigit whispered back.

Pidge felt an absolute trust in this man.

'How did we get here?' he whispered.

'No time for ins and outs, hows or whats,' the man whispered back, 'but follow my advice.'

'All right. We will. Thank you,' Pidge whispered.

'Thank you very much,' Brigit whispered dramatically.

'Not at all,' the man said. 'And should you happen to have thorn leaves in your pocket, keep them there.'

'I will.'

The man put the megaphone to his lips again and shouted out his command about pennies and ha'pennies.

Pidge took this to mean that the man had no more to say to them. He turned away and looked round to see if he could spy the man with the oak sprigs.

The station seemed less bright—why, it was almost dusk in

140

some corners. He had to look really hard to see some things, especially things that stood in against the wall. As he peered into the gloom, an object caught his attention.

'Look, Brigit, at that old chocolate machine.'

'Where?'

'Just there.'

They ran over to it. They were very excited as it looked so queer and old. The slot for money was very big, but Pidge put some of his money in anyway and pulled a lever. Out came a bar of chocolate. It seemed much bigger and thicker than any he could buy in the shops.

'You open it, Brigit, while I keep a watch for that man. We could easily miss him in this crowd and with the light going, you know.'

He looked round.

'That's odd,' he said.

'What?'

A steam engine stood breathing out clouds of steam by the platform.

'That train. I thought it was a diesel coming in, but it was a steam engine after all.'

The engine whooshed out a massive jet of steam from a valve at the side. The noise it made overpowered every other sound. Brigit stuck the chocolate bar in her other pocket and clapped her hands over her ears.

'It's marvellous!' she shouted. 'Like an ORMOUS giant. I'd like to drive that. I really would.'

Pidge didn't hear her. He kept looking everywhere for the man they were supposed to follow.

I didn't know they still had steam engines let alone used them, he thought, as he searched here and there with his eyes; and the chocolate machine was a nice surprise too.

He noticed that the paint had been changed on the wood-work round and about the place. And the doors and windows of the Ladies' Waiting Room, Parcels' Office, Station Master's Office and General Waiting Room were changed too. Well! Even the people dressed differently, he thought. They must be a different lot and the other lot went off somewhere, perhaps on the diesel—while we were talking to the man with the megaphone? And even *he's* gone, and that was quick and clever of him; a man with only half his share of under-pinnings, like that. And the porters and the man who takes the tickets, they look different, too. They've all got different uniforms on and waistcoats with watch-chains draped across them and they've got moustaches. And they look so kind and friendly, and very proud in some way. Because they're working with that big, massive steam engine, maybe? And those large advertisements nailed high up on the walls: "Fry's Chocolate" and "Guinness Is Good For You" and "Ah, Bisto" and "Clarke's Perfect Plug"—all solid and shiny. It looks like enamelled tin and I'm sure positive, they weren't there before.

And while he was thinking and marvelling at all this, the steam still rushed out, making a great cloud on the platform, and as he glanced once again at the engine to admire it, a newcomer appeared from the steam; a tall man, dressed in dark clothes and wearing a shapeless soft hat well pulled down, so that his whole face was not visible. All that Pidge could glimpse was a brief showing of a cheekbone, the flash of an eye and a quick showing of the tip of a strong nose. The springs of oak leaves were pinned to his lapel.

Brigit, who hadn't taken her eyes off the steam engine from first sighting it, said:

'There's that man.' And as the steam jet was now going quiet, Pidge heard what she said.

The man walked to the ticket barrier and they followed him. They were both wondering how they would get on when the ticket-collector asked for their tickets. The man simply walked through the barrier without the ticket-collector even noticing him.

'Come on,' Brigit said while pulling Pidge after her, 'I think it's free today.'

They were through and out into the town without an official word being said.

As they left the station behind, Brigit gabbled on about the steam engine and how much she liked it.

The man crossed over the turning into Forster Street and walked up a slight incline.

On the left was Eyre Square.

Pidge kept his eyes steadfastly on the dark figure up ahead.

'They've put railings all round the Square,' Brigit remarked.

142

'Have they?'

Pidge took a quick look and saw a low, granite wall as a boundary and tall iron-wrought railings surmounting it.

'They weren't here the other day; they must have worked very fast,' he said.

Trees as well—just inside the railings, a row of trees grew. Some children had made swings on the trees with ropes.

'What will we do if he goes in for a pint?' Brigit asked.

'Follow him in and buy some orange crush.'

'*I'll* have a glass of champagne,' Brigit said grandly. 'And a packet of biscuits.'

'Trust you,' Pidge said smiling.

When he reached the great open space in front of the Square, the man looked carefully in every direction before crossing to the left and walking past the two massive cannon, that stood huge and threatening and pointing (rather insolently, Pidge thought) across the space at the Bank of Ireland.

They followed after him past the Browne Doorway and the statue of Pádraig O'Conaire, sitting inside Eyre Square itself. The statue looked newer somehow but, oddly, the new railings didn't look at all new, despite a fresh coat of green paint. It was possible to see that parts of the iron were corroded and pitted. They looked old-fashioned and very elegant. Brigit spied a drinking fountain built into the wall by the Browne Doorway. It was a sort of stone bowl and there was a heavy copper cup on a chain.

She wanted to stop and try it but Pidge said no.

The man carried on into Williamsgate Street.

Pidge looked back and thought for a moment that the Square, and all the objects that were part of it, had disappeared and that there was just a space filled with people dressed in rough clothes, having a fair day or a market, but that didn't last long. In seconds, he found that he was looking back through a massive gate in a great stone wall with a tower, and all the people had moved off somewhere or other. He knew he would have seen them through the open gate if they had still been there.

The man turned round the corner at Dillon's Jewellers and carried on through the town. They hurried to keep him in sight.

Pidge now noticed that among the ordinary people in the street, there were some who seemed the poorest he had ever seen, with eyes that were like dark rags in pale, gaunt faces. Others among the crowd wore unusual dress and some gentlemen, looking very proud, were riding on fine horses.

They went on, past the Four Corners and still on past the Cathedral of Saint Nicholas of Myra. In the crush of people they lost sight of the man with the oak leaves and so didn't know which way to go—on towards O'Brien's Bridge, or left into High Street.

Making a quick decision, Pidge grabbed Brigit and ran full tilt down High Street; looking both ways at the Cross Street intersection and on, down to the quays.

Here the streets opened out and there was more space and fewer people. Across where the Claddagh should have been, there were dozens of thatched white houses built higgledy-piggledy all over the place. Sometimes this is Galway and sometimes it isn't, Pidge thought. And then he had a sudden insight. Times! I think we are seeing different *times*; it's always Galway, but not always the Galway of today.

They went back up and turned left at Cross Street and then left again and on to O'Brien's Bridge in a few minutes.

The river below the bridge rushed in mad white froth towards the sea and it seemed to be at a higher level than even in the rainiest weather. People moved over the bridge and to Pidge it seemed that they too were like a river moving endlessly forward, all the time. So many people and all so different. Who built this bridge anyway and who was O'Brien? It's a funny thing that I don't know really, he thought. And all these people! How often I've walked over and thought—this is Galway; this is my town— just like anyone would. And all these hundreds and thousands of people from the past; they thought this very same thing, I shouldn't wonder. And what about the ones who are to come? I can't imagine them walking here and not knowing about all of us. This town has belonged to so many.

He studied the faces passing him by; all different, all human. And he suddenly realized, all beautiful in a special human way.

But where is the man? Have we somehow passed him?

He looked back to see, and there was no spire on the Church of St Nicholas. And then he heard from a distance what sounded like the dull thud of cannon and he saw puffs of smoke. But oddly, the spire had gone before the cannon-fire, as though one thing had nothing to do with the other.

Suddenly, there was riot and confusion and the sound of trumpets, and again the sound of cannon and the air thick with the stench of gunpowder. He could hear the long low whistling sound of cannon-balls rending the sky and landing with that awful 'crump' sound that said death and destruction and fire and pain. The city was under siege.

The moment was brief and soon over and they saw the man standing at the other end of the bridge, which was now unaccountably made of wood instead of granite. The man was turning right, into Nun's Island.

They hastened after him.

Everything was ordinary again and through one window, they saw a man sitting reading a newspaper in the front parlour.

Most of the houses had lights on early because there was an early dusk that was brooding, and the sun turned to a vivid red disk in a sky that was purple and awesome.

Leaving the houses behind, they followed the man past tall mills and mysterious yards behind high wooden gates.

On the left, there was a high stone wall built in a broad sweep. It should have been the new Cathedral of Our Lady and Saint Nicholas, but Pidge knew that it was the old jail which had stood on that piece of ground before being knocked down to make way for the Cathedral.

The man turned right on to the Salmon Weir Bridge. Brigit ran and peered through the balustrades and Pidge ran after her and looked too. Down below, the fat beautiful salmon lay packed as tightly as sardines; rising in layers on top of one another and all facing upstream, waiting to jump the weir and get up to the lake.

Pidge urged Brigit to hurry and they carried on over the bridge and saw the man, who had waited for them, at the back of the old Courthouse. He turned to the left and went down the Waterside.

Once more Pidge looked back, not expecting to see very far

because of all the tall buildings in the way. But the buildings had vanished and in the distance was a walled city with fourteen towers. He couldn't understand how he could know at a glance that there were fourteen, but he did. As he looked, the city seemed to shiver and go like a dream, and all the buildings were back in their usual places.

Reaching a short wooden jetty, the dark man stopped and waited for them to catch up. He motioned them towards a small boat with sails. Holding hands, the children climbed on board.

After untying the mooring rope, the man too climbed aboard. He stood tall and proud in the stern and pointed to seats in the bow, and the children immediately scrambled forward and sat down. Then the man simply pointed with great authority towards the lake and the boat began to move of its own accord. The canvas filled out and the boat sped forward, up the river towards the lake.

The sky was dark now and full of menace. Lightning like whips of fire appeared in the sky, lashing and cracking and belting the clouds which scattered like sheep from dogs. Then it hit the earth on either side of the river with savage, venomous spits.

The sails cracked loudly as the wind caught at them and the boat moved at an unbelievable speed. Still the man pointed and the boat moved forward tight on its course, as if the boat and the wind were linked in obedience to the man's wishes.

They were passing the Dyke already. To think I only cycled up there the day before yesterday, without any idea in the world of what was to happen, Pidge said to himself, marvelling. He was holding Brigit tightly. He thought that she must be too terrified to talk.

The lightning stopped and a terrible blackness came, through which they could see nothing at all. Brigit clutched at him and he held her as hard as he could, to comfort her. Rain poured down and drenched the sails.

'Darkness and Light are old companions, two sides of one thing. They are part of the great natural balance. One wouldn't even have a name if the other didn't exist. Do not fear Darkness,' the man said very plainly and matter-of-factly. The tone he used made it clear that he thought little or nothing of this strange, impenetrable blackness.

But it persisted for some time and was dense and horrid and very hard to bear. It was eerie being out in a small boat and not knowing where they were going. If only it were possible to see *something*, even the surface of the water!

The lightning began again and, against all reason, it seemed preferable because it took away the sense of being smothered and enclosed. They were now approachng the Friar's Cut—a narrow channel cut through to the lake as a quicker way than following the river.

This means we've passed Menlo Castle already, Pidge knew.

They were within yards of the Cut, when lightning struck like a snake, at the banks on either side and at once, two walls of flame roared on both sides of the channel. Pidge dragged Brigit down onto the floor of the boat and shielded her with his body.

The dark man continued to point and the little boat obeyed and sailed through the walls of flame. After what seemed to be ages and ages, the boat emerged with sails not only dried, but scorched; and they now sailed out on to the lake.

The lightning kept on beating at the sky and the earth, and in its light the children saw that the tall, dark man had a face that looked noble and handsome, and that he was dressed in flowing robes and had long hair under a strange head-dress. In his hand he held a staff of oak with some leaves still growing on it and mistletoe twined all around it and, beneath his belt, there was a golden sickle.

'Why! You're a Druid!' cried Pidge.

147

Chapter 3

THE wind snatched the words from his mouth and took them away ahead of them to the side of a quiet river in County Mayo, where an angler, who had a poor opinion of himself in everything, stood hopefully.

'Why! You're a Druid,' the wind said into his ear and at that second he hooked the biggest salmon ever, onto his line.

'Why! I am! I am! I *must* be!' he cried, and took a different view of himself from then onward. And was the better for it.

The tall, dark man in the boat heard the words quicker than the wind taking them away.

'I am Cathbad,' he said and Pidge now knew for sure. He had read of Cathbad, the wisest of the Druids.

The bottom of the little boat scraped on shingle and Cathbad, by a sign with his hand, showed them that this was where they should land.

They climbed out and on to the dry earth, both of them amazed that everything, including themselves, was not wet through after such rain and wondering where exactly they had landed.

They were now on the west side of Lough Corrib, but it was so big a lake and with so much shore-line, they could be anywhere.

There was heavy cloud and the sky was still dark with unspent storm. Rain was still falling in the distance and as he looked about, he fancied he saw the shapes of mountains to the right of him through the haze. If that's north, they should be the Maamturks and we've come ashore below them. If I can see other mountains in the west, they'll be the Twelve Pins, he surmised.

He tried to pierce the rainhaze by focusing his eyes in a narrow stare. If he could just see the shapes of the Twelve Pins on the skyline he was sure that he would recognize them and get a bearing. But it was no use.

He turned to ask Cathbad but the Druid had gone, and all that was to be seen was the speck of white of the sail, where his boat was a dot far away on the expanse of the water. It was small enough to be only a seabird.

'What do we do now?' he said.

There was another flash of lightning.

'There's no hounds; run for shelter,' Brigit said and they ran.

As they ran, the blackness came down again like a thick quilt of sorrow and the thunder exploded across the sky and sounded as if it were overthrowing temples and ethics and crashing them down like sixpenny plates. Lightning darted and streaked in long, crooked daggers of white fire; a knife-throwing act of some mad and wicked God.

That's what it is, Pidge was thinking. So it's magic and there's no realness in it and if it hits us—it would probably be no more dangerous than a blow from a bubble.

But, just in case, he still ran with Brigit.

The blackness was even more solid and they had to rely on the light from the flashes to see ahead and know where to run when the light had gone. They saw before them the low wall of a field and ran to climb over. Just as they reached the wall, the blackness came down again and they could barely make out the stones, but their hands were on them, so feeling their way, they climbed in.

And then, the singing began.

The thunder stopped and they were in the field and running.

The singing was the singing of men; a choir of men's voices; and they sang a song of bravery and courage and it was very powerful.

The very last flashes of lightning came and they spat at the walls of the field.

There was no sign of the singers: all that could be seen was that the field was a bit uneven and bumpy, and that there was a natural shelter of trees grown tall, with their high branches arching and meshing together like a blueprint for a Cathedral roof, dense enough to obscure the sky.

Knowing full well that to be under trees in a storm is to be utterly mad and foolish, still Pidge ran with Brigit for the sake of feeling covered and protected; and, for all that he thought it

149

was magic and not true lightning, he was afraid.

Thankfully they crawled into an opening like a little nest in the undergrowth and sat down on the sweet, dry earth.

'I wonder where we are?' Pidge ventured.

'In the Field Of The Seven and safe from danger;' said a voice.

'That's good news,' said Brigit.

Is it though? Pidge wondered silently.

There was a long pause and a small slit of light appeared in the sky; and in a little while it widened and brightness spread and streamed; the darkness moved away and small, brave birds reclaimed their own place, singing.

And then the voices began to speak, as though making conversation:

'There is nothing like having a head,' said one; 'it is a bag full of treasure.'

'A head is like the earth,' said another; 'the more you put in—the more you get out.'

'Every head is a secret,' said a third; 'and everyone wants to know a secret.'

'Every head has a sweetness curling up inside it somewhere,' said a fourth; 'and who is there who wouldn't like to taste it?'

'Every head has a cunning hiding in its little caves,' said a fifth; 'and who would not like to find it?'

'A head holds its mysteries like a periwinkle,' said a sixth; 'but you can't get them out with a pin.'

'Every head is the head of an artist,' said the seventh and last voice; 'because it can see and hold beauty if it's only once in its life.'

Pidge and Brigit had listened to this with amazed interest. Brigit was especially fascinated.

'I didn't know all that about heads,' she said. 'I thought it was just the way we got finished off at the top, the way we get finished off at the bottom with feet. Heads are really interesting.'

The voices spoke again and recited a list:

'The harp came out of the human head.'

'The pointed tip of a casting-spear and the sharpness of the sword-blade with three edges, came out of the human head.'

'The proper teaching of wolfhounds and young warriors, came out of the human head.'

'The elegance of coloured dress, the use of threads and the twisting of ornaments in gold and silver, came out of the human head.'

'The making, remembering and chanting of songs and genealogies and the words for each little thing, came out of the human head.'

'The love of the dawn and the sunset, came out of the human head.'

'The art of roasting meat and the knowledge of good herbs, came out of the human head.'

Brigit was dying to have her say and, when she was sure that everyone who was going to speak had spoken—she announced proudly:

'The steam-engine came out of the human head! Rock cakes came out of the human head and so did sausages and bicycles.'

She stood up and walked out of the sheltering trees and looked around to see if she could see the speakers. Quickly Pidge followed her, to try to protect her if there was any danger.

They looked everywhere.

It was quite a bumpy field, all right.

Small bumps.

Seven of them in a straight line.

'Knives and forks came out of the human head,' she said encouragingly, 'and so did toothbrushes and hellercopters and chocolate biscuits.'

'How sweetly she talks,' one voice remarked in a sweet sound of its own.

'Where are you?' Pidge asked with some caution.

'Here,' said another voice.

'Aw come on, do,' said Brigit in her most coaxing way, 'let us see you—don't be shy.'

And the reply came:

'Tell us your names and where you go, to know if you are the right ones.'

'I'm Pidge and this is my sister Brigit, and we go on a journey for The Dagda,' Pidge said shyly; it felt odd to say grand things about The Dagda and themselves.

'Ah! These are the ones!' the voice told the others.

'Good,' Brigit said briskly. 'Now, come out 'till we see you.'

'First you must consult your sighting-glass and see how your enemies fare.'

Pidge felt very embarrassed that he hadn't thought of this himself, though really there hadn't been time. How stupid of me not to realize that I could do this whenever I wanted to, he said to himself.

He got out the little glass ball and gave it a shake. Brigit was excited and jumped up and down in eagerness. This time, when the snowflakes had cleared, they saw the great stones at Shancreg and the hounds still running this way and that, as they searched for a way in. They were no longer disguised as people. Pidge felt the most enormous sense of relief surging through him, even though he was by now unafraid. It was good to know that they were well ahead. In a few seconds, the alpine scene was back as before.

'It's all right,' he said happily.

'And now, Brigit must play her pipe for us,' one of the voices instructed.

'Is it me?' Brigit said, with the beginning of a horrible smirk on her face.

'You, indeed.'

'I haven't got a pipe,' she said, her face falling.

'Yes you have,' Pidge said, opening the schoolbag and taking out the penny whistle. He handed it to her.

'I've never learned to play it but I'll give you a blast, anyway,' she said confidently.

She put the whistle to her lips and covered the holes as well as she could with her small fingers. She drew in a breath and blew.

A little tune that nobody ever heard before came out of the whistle; a tune that was a musical crinkle, there were so many notes in it.

And then something happened to the seven bumps on the ground and in their places were seven heads; men, all young, all with long hair and bright eyes, and each one wore a necklet of twisted gold, a little dulled.

Brigit dropped down to her knees and said:

'Hello!'

152

Pidge knelt down too and asked:

'Who are you?'

'I am Maine Mingor, the Gently Dutiful,' said the first one.

'And I am Maine Morgor, the Very Dutiful,' said the second.

'I am Maine Andoe, The Quick.'

'I am Maine Mo-Epert, The Talker.'

'I am Maine Mathremail, like my mother.'

'I am Maine Athremail, like my father.'

'And I am Maine Milscothach, the Honey-Worded,' said the last.

'And we are the Seven Sons of Maeve and Ailill,' concluded the one named The Talker.

'Oh! I've heard of Queen Maeve!' Pidge said with delight.

'So have I!' Brigit said quickly.

'She was our fierce, wild, courageous, boastful, proud, laughing, loving mother, and we loved her and she loved us.'

'Sometimes, she was a bit mad,' said Maine Athremail—reminding them.

'I won't deny it,' said Maine Mathremail, 'but she smelled lovely.'

Brigit was looking at them critically.

'You've all got dirty faces and your hair is all in tangles,' she said.

All the faces looked at each other and smiled.

'She sounds just like our Mammy, the Queen. Many a time she hammered us when we were small for the same fault, and said not to be walking around as if we were minding pigs and disgracing her; but to try and look like the sons of a Queen, or she'd skin us,' said Maine Mingor, the Gently Dutiful.

'And other times, she said that we were her own lovely boys and she loved us for personal reasons, so she did,' said Maine Milscothach, the Honey-Worded, and his voice was indeed as sweet as honey.

'Would you like me to wash you and comb your hair?' Brigit asked.

'That would be the right thing to do, plain enough,' said Maine Andoe, The Quick.

'Where's the nearest water?' she asked.

'Not the lake,' Pidge butted in quickly. 'Not as far as the lake.'

'Over in that corner, to the right of you, there is a spring; we hear its soft chanting night and day.'

Brigit went over and wet her hankie; Pidge searched his pockets for a comb.

'Now,' Brigit said, kneeling by Maine Mingor, 'hold up!'

Maine Mingor held his head up, delightedly.

'Shut your eyes!'

'Just like our Mammy when we were no higher than a heifer's knee and plump as bolsters,' he said, and turned and beamed at his brothers, who all beamed back at him as they remembered Queen Maeve, fondly.

'Keep still!' Brigit commanded, turning his face back square in front of her and rubbing vigorously.

'Not *too* hard,' Maine Mingor said.

'Don't be a baby!' she replied sternly, and all the other Maines whooped with joy.

'Shut your eyes.'

Maine Mingor was gently dutiful, as he closed his eyes obediently.

'This bit is a bit hard—it won't come off,' she said and spat on her finger and rubbed harder.

'How often our Mammy spat on her finger in just that manner and struggled in the same way with a defiant bit of dirt!' said Maine Morgor, the Very Dutiful, his voice gentle and the look on his face, very loving.

'There now—you'll pass. I'll comb your hair.'

Pidge had the comb ready.

'No! No! Let your brother do the combing and you do the washing. And you must say everything to us that you said to Maine Mingor—to be fair,' Maine Mo-Epert, The Talker said.

'And you must spit on the finger for us and everything,' said Maine Milscothach, the Honey-Worded, 'and not leave anything out at all.'

So, Brigit moved on and Pidge combed Maine Mingor's hair, being very careful not to drag the tangles. Some of the hair came out, trapped in the teeth of the comb.

'Don't throw any of the hair away; you'd never know the

154

hour when it might come in useful. I say this thing most seriously for there is marvellous power in our hair,' Maine Mingor said gravely.

And soon they were all washed and combed and handsome, and Brigit gave all the gold necklets a bit of a shine, and told them that she had once got one in a Lucky Bag; quite sure that hers was gold too. They smiled and wished they could see a marvel called a Lucky Bag. Pidge carefully gathered all the hair in a soft, glinting ball. He rolled it small between his palms and put it inside the leather bag with the other things.

'Now,' said Mo-Epert, The Talker, 'there is one other thing you must do. In each of our mouths there is a little seed. We will bring them out so that you may gather them off our lips. Keep these with great care, as well.'

And then there was a wheat seed waiting to be taken from each of the Maines.

'It is time for you to ask us a question,' said Mo-Epert.

Pidge thought hard. There were too many questions. After a time he said:

'I'll just ask—do you know which way we should go?'

'The feathered flight is your direction,' Mo-Epert answered, as if this were the question he had expected.

'Which way is that?'

'You will soon see. Wait a little longer.'

Brigit had a happy thought.

'Can you come out of there? Would you like us to dig up the rest of you?' she offered brightly.

The Maines all exchanged glances with each other.

'The rest of us is somewhere else; our heads alone remain here,' said Maine Milscothach very kindly and gently.

'What do you mean?' Pidge asked, appalled.

The Maines all looked at each other again.

'Don't be alarmed by this,' said Milscothach soothingly, 'It was a holy thing to do; other warriors took our heads in Battle.'

'Our heads were highly prized and so were carried off when all was over,' said Mo-Epert. 'We, ourselves, took many heads in our time; to gain all the valours and virtues and quicknesses that were in them.'

'I myself,' said Maine Mathremail, like his mother, 'always

gave great amusement to any head I took and never left one of them out of my decisions; but asked its advice. I always told them every bit of the latest news and recited stories for them, every night.'

'Did they ever tell you stories?' asked Brigit. She was so much at ease with the Maines that she didn't feel any surprise at what they said. She didn't realize that people had been killed.

'Oh yes, very good stories too, they were indeed,' said Maine Mathremail.

'Were you headhunters?' Pidge stumbled over the idea and the word.

'I understand the word but the meaning is foul. No. After the Battle, we took the heads. It would be a shameful ending to leave them for the crows to pick out their eyes and their brains; an infamous, blasphemous last thing, for Warriors who had fought so bravely; bad payment for courage,' Maine Mathremail answered with a soft smile.

'We know this is hard for you to understand, for what is believed in one man's time, is despised in another man's day. To be sure, there will even be revulsion in some future years at things you hardly notice, that are happening in what is known to you as the present. It's nothing new,' Maine Mathremail said kindly.

Pidge thought about this and knew that it was true.

'I begin to know what you mean,' he said and all the Maines were satisfied.

'That is good enough,' said Maine Mo-Epert.

In a moment, there was the creaking of wings in the sky and everyone looked up at a string of wild geese flying in a broad V in from the lake and across the sky above them.

'There goes your direction,' said Maine Athremail sadly. 'You will leave us now.'

Pidge watched the geese to see their direction and get it firmly in his mind.

'I'm sorry to leave you,' he said.

'So am I. I'm very sorry,' Brigit said and went to each one in turn and kissed him goodbye.

'Just like the Queen, our Mammy,' said Maine Andoe, The Quick, and the tears ran down his face.

All the Maines cried silently.

Brigit did her best to wipe their tears but her hankie was still damp.

'Oh, poor boys,' said Pidge, and he took Brigit by the hand and hurried away from Maeve's sons, before he cried too. It didn't seem wrong to talk like this to young men who were a good deal older than himself; they seemed so lonesome, somehow.

He wished that Maeve were there to cheer them up, even if it was by giving them a hammering, they seemed to miss it so much.

But he would much rather that she could tell them stories and be nice to them.

Chapter 4

O N the same morning that Pidge and Brigit had met the Old Angler and Serena the ass, the Sergeant woke up much earlier on, with a groan. He lay on his side for a good while, trying hard to put off turning over onto his back.

He knew that if he changed his position, his eye would light on the text that hung on the wall opposite the foot of the bed. The text had been given to him by his Horrible Auntie Hanorah, in honour of the day that he got promoted to Sergeant. It was there every morning, staring him callously in the face.

After some minutes he began to get pins and needles.

With another groan, he turned over and his gaze was drawn against his will to the text.

It was done in poker-work. It said:

DUTY IS BEAUTY.

Every morning, the Sergeant answered it:

'It's not. A rose is.'

This morning, however, he just said:

'Why?'

Before his startled eyes, the text—giving out a hissing and crackling sound—changed. It now said:

BECAUSE I SAID SO.

'What?' said the Sergeant, sitting up in bed: 'Am I seeing things, again?'

The text crackled even more loudly and emitted sparks. It changed again and said:

GET UP OUT OF THAT YOU DOZY

158

LUMP AND GET OFF TO YOUR WORK.

'That poteen!' exclaimed the Sergeant. 'I always heard that the effects stayed in your system for days; but it never happened to me before!'

While he stared with his eyes popping, the text continued in a series of messages:

GET UP!
WASH AND SHAVE YOURSELF.
GET DRESSED.
EAT YOUR BREAKFAST AND
GET OFF TO YOUR WORK AT ONCE.

'I wish the effects had been nicer,' the Sergeant said glumly.

I WON'T TELL YOU AGAIN.

'All right, all right! Stop nagging!' the Sergeant answered crossly.

WHAT'S DELAYING YOU?

'All right, I said!' shouted the Sergeant and he got out of bed.

He started to obey all the orders.

WASH BEHIND YOUR EARS.

'Can't you see I am washing behind my ears?' he roared.

AND WHAT ABOUT YOUR PRAYERS?

'I'm sorry: I nearly forgot. God help me,' said the Sergeant and that was the best prayer he said—he was so distracted by all the strange things that kept happening to him.

Later, he strode into the Garda Barracks.

'Good morning, Sergeant. Isn't it a lovely morning?' said

the young Garda with a bright smile.

'Oil me bike!' the Sergeant responded abruptly.

After all, he said to himself, what's the use of being Sergeant if you can't get your bike oiled?

But he was sorry in his heart for being nasty. It's not the young fella's fault when all's said and done, he told himself severely. It's Horrible Auntie Hanorah's fault—a woman constructed on a frame of sharp bones, with a thin nose that could slice cheese, a tongue like a leather strap, and a heart that wore corsets of steel or was coated in concrete, at least.

When the young Garda came in to mutter that the bike was oiled and what else would the Sergeant like him to do, the Sergeant smiled a warm, expansive smile.

'Don't you be minding me, now. I'm not too well at present, you know. Here's a couple of quid—take your young lady to the hop tonight,' he said generously.

The young Garda blushed.

'I haven't got a young lady, Sergeant,' he said.

'WELL GO OUT AND GET ONE,' the Sergeant roared in an immediate temper, feeling thwarted in every possible way.

He sat by the fire, brooding and drinking cocoa.

Chapter 5

WHEN one of the hounds went to the glasshouse with the news that Pidge and Brigit had gone through the path under the stones, Breda Fairfoul, wearing a fashionable apron and a chef's hat, was frying up a panful of Stinking Parasols, Death Caps and Destroying Angels for a late breakfast. Melodie Moonlight was brushing her hair with a hedgehog who was pretending to be in a coma; and the Great Queen was playing with a chessboard on which all the pieces were alive. She made her moves with the help of a sharp pin, using it to coax the figures to bustle from one square to another. She was smiling.

'O Great Queen,' said the hound speaking with a whistle, as though he had a bird trapped behind his teeth, 'they were helped through.'

There was a squeak from the chessboard as she stabbed at something, with her pin.

'Have you found the track?'

'Not yet. It is elusive.'

The hound bowed and began to slide out the door with little backward steps, trying very hard to be insignificant. He held his tail in tight and moved slowly on the ground. He had almost reached the outside, when the Great Queen said with a mild, benign air and a terrifying gentleness:

'Eating on duty, my pet? Come here.'

The hound came back, his jaw dropped open and a thrush flew out. The door shut itself.

'O Mórrígan, be not angry,' the hound pleaded. 'I make no boast of skill. It flew so low it all but flew into my mouth of its own accord. Out of the sky, it came and seemed like a gift from yourself, Great Queen,' he finished desperately.

'Did it?'

'Did it?' echoed Melodie Moonlight.

161

'Did it?' said Breda as she deftly flambéd the mess in the pan.

The hound cringed and stayed silent.

'What will I do with you?' asked The Mórrígan thoughtfully.

'Turn him into a sausage while I've got the pan on,' said Breda Fairfoul.

'Dogskin slippers might be romantic,' Melodie Moonlight sighed sweetly.

The Mórrígan looked at the thrush where it had struggled to a perch near the roof of the glasshouse. It looked bedraggled and extremely flustered. She had a thought of her own.

'Change,' she said.

And now, the thrush became the hound. And the hound, who was the one called Fowler, turned into the thrush.

They had become each other.

In the instant that the change had happened, the real thrush had jumped down because it had lost its perch with its form and would have fallen. It was now snatching and snapping at the terrified Fowler who flew in a demented panic all round the glasshouse.

'How funny,' said Melodie Moonlight.

'Very merry,' said Breda.

But the fair woman, who was The Mórrígan, soon tired of it and allowed each of the creatures to turn back into being itself.

Fowler looked humbled and wilted beyond description. The thrush looked slightly drunk and a little bit cocky. It found an open pane and flew away, dizzily. It hadn't a true idea of how lucky it really was.

'Eating on duty is forbidden, Fowler,' The Mórrígan said.

He was far too shaken to reply.

The Mórrígan threw her chessboard and its men aside. As the pieces fell, they lost the artificial life that she had put into them for fun; and were made of insensible wood.

'Findepath must sharpen his nose. I am not pleased with his lack of craft. Do you understand?'

'Yes, Great Queen,' Fowler whispered faintly.

'You have leave to go.'

'Thank you for my life, Great Queen,' he whispered almost

162

inaudibly; like the true subject of any tyrant, showing gratitude for being allowed to keep what was his own.

'A modest gift,' was the reply, in a tone that clearly said his life was not worth thinking about. The glasshouse door opened.

Fowler left the glasshouse as quickly as he could, grateful to be alive and with his legs still shaky from terror. But a small seed of anger spasmed inside him and bold thoughts came into his head.

'I don't think I care much for Domestic Science,' Breda remarked and she threw the disgusting and poisonous mess out.

Melodie put the hedgehog down on the floor and plaited up her hair in a high crown on top of her head.

'Let us begin,' The Mórrígan said, and picking up a cat, she dusted a great big table that now appeared in the middle of the glasshouse.

'You have made the inside of this place bigger than the outside and broken some Laws of Physics,' Melodie observed admiringly.

'You have your charm bracelet?' Breda enquired.

The Mórrígan showed a wrist, where a charm bracelet, hung down with all kinds of gold replicas of things, dangled heavily.

The table-top shimmered and now it was a very small version of the landscape where Pidge and Brigit walked. It was possible to see them—two tiny, live figures travelling along.

The Mórrígan detached an object from her bracelet and placed it on the landscape at some distance ahead of the children.

Then the three women sat round the table and waited. They had long, pointed sticks which they held ready.

In time, another little live figure appeared on the scene but as yet, only just on the edge. He was only just discernible before he was enveloped in mist, but they knew who he was.

'Findepath is through!' they all shouted triumphantly.

Other little figures appeared on the edge. The women prodded them with their pointed wands.

The hedgehog, lying on the floor in a ball, waited until they were deeply engrossed in what they were doing, before he

163

quietly uncurled himself and crept soundlessly out of the door that was slightly ajar, from when Fowler had left in his highly disturbed state.

The hedgehog shuffled along outside and wouldn't have looked back if he'd been offered his weight in slugs.

'It was only a funny dream,' he told himself firmly and kept his nose to the ground.

Chapter 6

THE outsides of the walls of The Field Of The Seven Maines were blackened and scorched from the lashes the lightning had given, and when Pidge saw this, he blamed himself for being foolish and thinking it couldn't hurt them; but he was glad and very relieved indeed that they had been lucky.

Leaving the field behind, they went on the diagonal the geese had flown and every so often, Pidge gave the glass ball a shake and saw that the hounds were still not able to find their way through.

Pleased by this, they walked on, and sometimes they found little sheep paths and sometimes they did not; and sometimes they climbed over walls and other times they crossed ditches and went through gaps and round bushes of thorn and hazel and such things.

All this time Brigit watched the ground, looking from side to side, mostly; but now and again, she stopped and looked at the ground behind her, as if he might have missed something.

'What are you doing?'

'I'm looking for that bloody pebble,' she said with a glint in her eye.

'Brigit, you're not supposed to use language like that.'

'Like what? You know he said it had that one's blood on it?'

'You're just being smart. You just wanted the chance to say it.'

She didn't say anything but made her face look very innocent and affronted.

'Anyway,' Pidge continued, 'we're not *supposed* to look for it; we're just supposed to find it.'

'How are we to do that?'

'How do I know? We'll just have to see what happens.'

'Would you like a bit of chocolate?' she asked and took it from her pocket.

'Oh good. I'd forgotten about that.'

'I hadn't. I wish I could have given a bit to the Maines. I *was* going to at first; but I didn't, 'cos—you know.'

'What?' he asked.

'There was nowhere for them to eat it to. They could bite it and taste it and chew it, all right; but there was nowhere to swallow it to. Isn't it an awful pity about them, Pidge?'

She broke the bar of chocolate in halves and gave Pidge his share.

'Yes, it is. Sometimes you're very kind, Brigit.'

'I know,' she said.

They ate their chocolate as they went.

Sometimes they walked on soft grass and sometimes they walked through coarse sedge and other times they tripped over stones and snags; but they were not at all tired. Brigit didn't like the times they tripped over stones and other inscrutable nuisances and said so. Pidge didn't like them either but he didn't say anything. Mostly, they talked of the Seven Maines and Queen Maeve, and Brigit kept wondering things like: what kind of a Crown did she have, and did she have silver dresses and diamond shoes, and what kind of things would they have for their breakfasts, in the olden days.

Then a moment came when Pidge looked again in the scrying-glass and had to realize that the hounds had found the way through the stones; for he saw that the place was deserted but for the last hound of all, going through purposefully; and he saw its tail disappear in the mist.

'If they come near *me*,' said Brigit, 'they'll get a swipe on the gob and I mean it.' Her eyebrows went together and her bottom lip stuck out as she practised how she would look, if they caught up.

But Pidge wasn't really listening.

They had been warned it would happen and he knew that he should have expected it; but it seemed too soon. He had hoped for a better start.

At first he could barely believe it and stood in a bit of a daze, not thinking at all, while he stared into the glass ball with eyes that saw nothing.

And when he did believe it, he accepted that it really was so; and with Brigit keeping up with him easily, he strode resolutely on.

'They still have to get our scent and even find the right spot where we got off the boat. They'll have to run over every inch until they find it.'

'There's enough of them, the whelps!' Brigit said, glaring.

Presently, they came to a small hill and they got a view of the mountains in the west at last; but there was a deep, screening haze like many thicknesses of gauze and only the tips were bare. They were the Twelve Pins, all right; that much, at least, was plain.

But there was a difference in the way they looked: they broke the skyline in an unfamiliar way, so that Pidge couldn't know, even roughly, where they now were from the point in his mind, that said home.

He was beginning to be a bit uncertain of the direction the geese had taken and began to doubt his path. Was he going a bit too much to the left or the right? He couldn't be sure, anymore.

In a short time, it was twilight. It would be dark soon.

They needed a place to sleep for the night. Just somewhere dry and sheltered, for fear of wind or rain, would do: it needn't be a house.

He was half-tempted to keep walking to put an even greater distance between themselves and the hounds, but he well knew that if they walked across country that was strange to them, without light to see where they were going, they really could fall into a bog-hole and get drenched, or tumble over an edge or sprain an ankle; and they would certainly go even further off course than during the day.

He kept an eye out for a likely place. A cart-house would be great, he thought.

The day was almost entirely gone when they found themselves close to a pine forest.

They looked behind and saw no movement of any kind in the broad sweep of land they had crossed. Even in the gloom they would have seen movement, if any of the hounds had actually been following them, Pidge was sure. Hoping he was right in thinking this, he held Brigit's hand and they ran the last bit.

There is nothing in the world as enticing as a wood of any kind, because of its mysteries. They went inside to see what it was like. Pidge was pleased to find that it was dry underfoot and that the air trapped inside by the roof of branches was warmer than when they were outside. It felt cosy and safe.

When it was dark, they had made a snug for themselves and lay down on the thick flooring of dry pine-needles.

The resinous scent was wonderful.

When it was pitch-dark, they fell asleep.

In the morning when they woke up early, so early that it was the day's beginning, they found that they had slept very close to a part of the forest that was cleared of trees, where a small spring came out of the ground and threw itself in a modest waterfall over a few small boulders.

The sky was streaked with long, ruby gashes frilled with apricot clouds and they felt breathless at the sight of it, for there was not only colour but amazing light, so that the whole, mad, beautiful concourse, with the sun glinting behind it, could truly be the doorstep of Paradise.

For a long time they stood—heads tilted—and filled their eyes.

By and by, they went to the spring and drank; and Brigit whispered that she wished this little spring were in the Field Of The Seven Maines, so that they could look at it every day, it was so pretty.

The water tasted perfect.

It was a morning of wonderful stillness and the wood was a beautiful place to be; not the smallest movement of wind to make the trees rustle and sigh. And then the birds burst into the fullest flood of song, almost as if they had waited a little longer than usual to see the dawn themselves and were triumphant that it was so splendid and they were justified.

The boy and the girl touched the trees and smelled them: they saw the bright green of the ferns and the darker green of the pines, with smokey blue shadows all about the trunks of those further away, ready to faint away altogether if anyone came too close. They tasted the air with as much pleasure as when they had tasted the water, and they listened to the sound of the birds.

The forest satisfied everything, and most of all—the sense of mystery.

They walked through it in what Pidge hoped was the right direction, enjoying the birdsong until the very last note was sung. As they walked, they were visited by every wild thing, curious to see the creatures that walked on two legs through their world.

All of the birds flew down to low branches and observed them with their heads cocked sideways, for all the world as if they each had only one good eye to see out of—some old people, and a lot of pirates, seem to do this too. Squirrels scampered all around them, pausing at times to look, pleating the skin round their nostrils as they sniffed and tried to know them by scent. Rabbits sat in groups and did the same thing with greater bravura, as though it was their special skill. Other small animals watched keeping well-hidden, peering from behind boulders or clumps of bracken or fallen dead wood in a shy kind of prying, just as though they were people who were nosey but respectable; but they were only nervous, and far too natural to be respectable.

In the blue shadows, there was the outline of a small herd of deer which kept in a close bunch around a stag—all heads up and alert and his crowned with his proud antlers.

If they made a noise at all, the animals were careful to break the silence gently as if in church, and the dawn chorus of the birds had been a glorification; to be properly followed by a time of quiet, as the day was still so young. Later they would chatter and argue and sing again, when the sun was big enough to give permission.

Pidge and Brigit were totally wrapped up in this quietness: the whole world existed in what they were seeing with their wide-open eyes.

It was shocking then, when they heard from deeper in the wood, the sound of an axe going hard against a tree, as a woodcutter went to work:

BOK! BOK! BOK!

All the small creatures took offence at this brutal sound and, leaving the children, they made for their homes and safety.

And the chopping went on without mercy.

Chapter 7

IT is easy to travel through a pine wood because the undergrowth is always sparse. Apart from the fallen dead wood which may be climbed over or walked round, there is little else that might be called an obstacle. True, there are always the occasional patches of fern and bramble, but these are never dense and are not the stubborn barriers that they can be, in an old wood of mixed trees that is mostly untrodden. Some people prefer one kind of wood to the other; some people are fond of both kinds.

It didn't take long for Pidge and Brigit to come in sight of the woodcutter. When they were near enough, they called out to him; but he, muffled in a heavy overcoat and big, shapeless hat, did not reply. He saw them, Pidge was sure. One hasty look and he turned his back on them very quickly, but not so quickly that Pidge couldn't see quite clearly, that the man did not want to speak. Brigit noticed it too.

'Sir? Why are you chopping that tree?' she shouted, and he paused for just a second before swinging at the trunk again.

He was a hunched kind of a man and there was a curious awkwardness in the way he handled the hatchet.

'I'll bet you he's a rustler; one of the kind who steals trees,' Brigit whispered. 'He didn't want to talk to us did he?'

'Come on, we'd best not bother him,' Pidge said.

Even though he was clumsy in his movements, the woodcutter kept up a good rhythm. Brigit looked back at him at intervals as she trailed after Pidge, holding on to the hem of his jacket for guidance.

'He's no good with that hatchet,' she said derisively, when she knew they were out of earshot.

'It might be that heavy coat hampering him,' Pidge suggested.

'What does he want a coat like that for? It's not cold.'

'Some people feel the cold more than other people; something to do with thin blood, I've heard.'

'Thin blood? What's that! I've never heard of anything so daft. Is there fat blood, too? Have you ever heard of anyone with fat blood?'

'No.'

'That just proves it! If there's supposed to be thin blood— there should be fat blood or it's just silly. Anyway, he's a cranky oul' devil, whatever way his blood is.'

They discovered now that they were at the far boundary of the forest, roughly opposite to where they had come into it the night before. The trees ended at a wall that was partly tumbled and scattered and there was a road running by it, alongside. Across the road, the countryside was hidden by a heavy-grown hedge of fuschia and bramble and other bushes, rising very high.

They went over the scattered stones and out onto the road.

It was hard to leave the forest—they might never, ever, see it again—and it was a perfect place to spend time.

The more Pidge racked his brains, the less sure he was of the way. Again he was puzzled as to whether they should go right or left. Should they not bother with the road at all, but try to get through the hedge and over the fields?

'Where do we go now, Pidge?'

'I can't seem to remember.'

'Don't you know the way?'

'No. I did last night but now I'm not sure.'

'Why don't we go this way,' she suggested, pointing to the right. 'We could try it for a little while, anyway.'

'We might as well. If we get to a place that isn't so boxed in, perhaps I'll get a better idea of where to go.'

And I really hope so, he thought to himself gravely; for what will happen if we don't know which way to try for, and just go any way, hoping it's right? We could just drift around aimlessly and be of no use.

They had gone no more than ten paces and Brigit was just going to mention something about breakfast although she really wasn't hungry, when the sound from the forest stopped and for a little while, there was silence.

Then, from inside the wood, a hound bayed: a long, lingering, unearthly cry.

171

And they knew that the woodcutter was no woodcutter and his hunched back was only a disguise for his height; and the thick old coat was only to hide his thinness and the old hat was for hiding his face.

They stopped dead in their tracks and looked at each other, Pidge overcome by dismay.

'That sounds very bad,' he managed to say after a moment.

A thrill of horror rushed through him and he stood, daunted, not knowing what to do. Brigit watched his face and waited until he would think of something.

He stood, tense with shock and the awful knowledge that one of the hounds had traced them already and was now calling to the others.

A little wind came and smacked him gently in the face, and his hand went into his pocket and reached into the leather bag. His fingers grasped a nut—obeying something other than his mind.

He held it out and they watched it split open.

Something that was coiled up inside it, spiralled out and flew up into the sky, and Pidge was holding a string that was taut and strong, while up above, there flew a kite.

It was the most glorious kite that they had ever seen, with an old ship painted on it and long ribbons of violet satin billowing out from it; and on one of the ribbons were glittering silver words, that said:

THIS WAY PLEASE

The ribbons were long and thick and shiny and they couldn't help but stand and admire, in spite of the certainty that danger was close.

The string in Pidge's hand gave a small tug and lifted him about three inches off the ground.

'It's very strong: grab on to it!' he shouted at Brigit, as he began to get an idea of what was happening, and they each

172

held onto the string with both hands gripping.

As soon as they had a firm hold, the kite began to move across the sky and they were carried along with it.

At first they were only inches above the ground, skimming along above the road's surface. but in a moment, the kite lifted them higher and they were above and over the fuschia hedge. They sailed across the fields, low enough to notice the splashy patterns of yellow lichens on grey walls, the velvet mosses on rocks and the veinings in stones.

The kite lifted them up into the sky where some of the clouds lay thick as spilled cream and others danced along in gauzy wisps.

It was wonderful.

The air was so gentle; and below them was an incomprehensible distance of patchwork fields, spreading in generous colours as a quilting on the earth.

From behind, they heard again the awful cry, and Pidge wondered if the hound could spy on them and work out where they were being taken; just as he himself had been able to get a bearing from the geese flying the day before.

But the earth wore the sunshine like a dress, and a little burst of small birds came quickly from a treetop and flew beside them with curiosity, it seemed. He forgot about the hound when all this was so much fun.

The string wasn't hard on their hands at all; it felt like soft cotton wool.

Lightly they went, like thistledown in the slight breeze, rising higher and higher. A field of rippling wheat went as small as a postage stamp. Pidge turned his head to look back and saw, with surprise, that the forest was not very big, quite a small plantation really, and only about half as big again as the wheatfield below. Still, it had *felt* like a forest while they were inside it. I suppose, he told himself, because even in a gigantic forest, you can only be in a little bit of it at a time, so it doesn't matter if it's big or small.

A small animal was running at his fastest speed along the ground at some distance behind and a long way below them. For a few seconds, Pidge watched it wonderingly, before he realized that it was the hound, trying desperately to keep up with them.

173

He knows that the others can easily follow his scent, he thought.

At that, the little birds left them and flew away into the distance, looking at first like a spray of moving freckles on the sky; and then they were dots as small as grains of pepper spilled on a cloth and at last, they disappeared altogether.

Then came white birds in their thousands, as thick as snowflakes in a blizzard, and Pidge only just had time to notice the hound coming to a standstill, almost skidding in surprise, before they were entirely surrounded by clouds and clouds of birds that flew steadily along beside them. There was an infinity of wings beating and numberless little heads with bright eyes and yellow and orange and black bills. In among the mass, some swans flew, pure white; and it seemed to the children that one pair was linked with chains of silver, before they were swallowed from sight in the masses of beating wings. Look any way they pleased, and try as hard as they could, they saw nothing but white birds flying as thickly below and above as they were on either side. Now and again, there was a glimpse of the swans wearing their chains.

Once, a single feather floated down, dislodged from one of the beating wings up above, and Pidge watched it, knowing that if feathers landed on the ground, the hounds could follow them like a marked trail. It was too far away for him to reach. But even as he worried about it, a bird captured it with its bill and held it fast, and then looked at Pidge with a bright eye, as much as to say: 'You needn't worry; we've thought of that.'

Looking around, he saw that other feathers were lost from time to time and that each one was caught and held. At times, a small gap would appear in the living white floor that was a good bit below them, as a bird dived for, and caught, a stray feather from the bottom layer of birds.

This will put a halt to their gallop, Pidge thought, and giggles bubbled up from somewhere deep inside him and he laughed aloud with great merriment.

Brigit was laughing too.

They both felt intensely happy.

Chapter 8

A TIME came when there was a diminishing of the flocks and flocks of birds that flew with Pidge and Brigit, and when they could see speckles of blue sky through the dense mass of whiteness, they realized that the birds had been quietly going apart from them for some time. The bits of sky gradually went from speckles to scraps and from scraps to patches, until in the end, only a few dozen birds were left and it was possible to see the gorgeous kite again and the earth below.

The swans had gone.

The birds who stayed longest were the ones who had flown closest to them all of the way. Now they cocked their heads and swooped and rose and did tricks of flying such as looping-the-loop and triple-somersaulting and formation-spiralling, before they came in close and dipped, as they said goodbye.

Soon there was only a single bird left in all the sky and they watched it going far away, and at last, it went gliding through a valley and looked like a piece of white paper borne by the wind. And then it was gone, like all the others.

They were near mountainy country now.

Far away to the left, the mountains were high and close together and all of their valleys were narrow and deep, Pidge could guess. On the right, the country was still quite mountainous but in a far broader sweep of land, so that each mountain stood alone like a hermit or a strong chieftain in his own domain.

The kite took them smoothly for a little while more and then came down slowly, slowly—until they could reach the ground with their feet. The pull of the string lessened and they didn't have to run to keep hold of it.

They had come to earth where there were many sheep tracks, and old, bleached rabbit droppings; where the land was poor with sparse grass and lines of granite showing through, like the earth's ribs. The sun was hot. There was a shelf of stone like a low bench nice and handy, so they sat down.

Dreamily they relived in their minds the way they had just travelled and how it had felt to be surrounded by the thunder of whispering wings. Languidly, Pidge still held on to the kite string.

It was strange to be back on the ground and their legs felt wobbly and weak, in exactly the same way that they would be from sitting in the trap after the long journey home from a trip to Galway on market day. The ground always feels wrong after such a journey, because of legs that are benumbed.

So they sat, half-liking the odd sensations and thinking about the birds; and Pidge feeling very safe because he was so sure that The Mórrígan wouldn't have the least idea of where they had got to and the hounds wouldn't have the smallest notion of where to look.

And the kite billowed quietly up above and its ribbons streamed out from it, held by the breath of a breeze.

Well, said Pidge in his mind, this has certainly been splendid and easy up till now. The lightning and hearing the hound cry out were the worst bits and we have been very greatly helped. If it all goes like this, it's going to be easier than I first thought. And I could just sit here all day and think of The Maines and the birds and the little wood, and be really happy and satisfied, somehow. And even the worst bits weren't *too* bad when I think it over: it was mostly the way I was taken by surprise that made me a bit nervous.

He thought about 'a bit nervous' and decided he meant 'fearful'.

Brigit was thinking her own thoughts about the birds. Presently she said:

'I've made up my mind; I know what I'm going to be when I grow up.'

'What?'

'A flyer. It's so lovely up there. I'm going to be a kind of bird myself.'

'It won't ever be as good, you know.'

'I know all right. But it would be near to it.'

'You could be a glider—that would be almost as good, I suppose,' Pidge said after considering.

The kite suddenly tugged out of his hand and drifted away.

'Oh!' he said, taken by surprise.

They both leaped and tried to jump high enough to reach the tail-end of the string; but it was already impossible.

'Come back, Kite!' Brigit cried.

But it went away.

Up and up and up it went and then it was lost altogether, in fleecy clouds.

'It's gone; well, that's that,' Brigit said cheerfully enough, but Pidge had only to look at her face to know how she was really feeling. She looked as if she was holding it together by the power of her will, or stubbornness as older people call it sometimes; and he knew that it would take very little to make her cry.

'That's all right, Brigit. When we get home, I'll make one just like it. I can find out how to do it from a book. It shouldn't be too hard.'

'It was ours! It was in that nut and you owned it, didn't you?'

I don't want her to cry, he thought. If she starts crying she might start saying that she wants to go home and I wouldn't know what to do. What's the best thing to say? If I'm too kind, she'll just bawl.

'It wasn't ours; the journey was ours. Just think, Brigit, we are the only two in the whole world who had that journey! And you are the only one in the whole world who played the whistle for The Maines. Isn't that so?'

'Yes,' she muttered, mollified.

'And on my word, I really will make one for you when we get back.'

'When will that be?'

Oh, here it comes, he thought.

'After our quest is over. I imagine we're going to have a lot more adventures.'

'Good,' she said, without sounding aggrieved.

Pidge was very relieved.

'We should be making a move now,' he said. 'Though I don't know which way we should go.'

177

Trusting to luck, they followed one of the sheep tracks.

'And will it have a ship painted on it and ribbons and everything?' she asked as they walked along.

'Yes. Of course.'

'And will it be mine?'

'Yes.'

'Well Pidge, when I know how, I'll knit you . . . *two* pairs of socks.'

'Only two pairs? You promised Tom Cusack twenty pairs for your brooch,' he answered, laughing.

She heaved a deep sigh.

'Oh dear, don't remind me. It's going to take the rest of my life.'

The sheep track led them to better ground and later to a wider track, where marks from cartwheels had printed two shallow scars. Patches of bilberries grew wherever it was rocky and blackberry bushes were everywhere. They picked a handful from time to time and ate the shiny, ripe berries.

'Brigit,' said Pidge, 'do you feel very hungry?'

'No. I like eating these, though.'

'We haven't had anything to eat since that last bit of chocolate, have we?'

'No. Why?'

'We should be starving and we're not. I wonder what time it is? We don't know if it's breakfast or dinner-time. Our stomachs usually tell us the time.'

'What?' Brigit yelled and got such a fit of laughing that she had to sit down for some minutes.

'I never heard of such a thing,' she snorted, when she got her breath back. 'My stomach telling me the time; it's a wonder I don't have to wind it up at night.'

Pidge was glad that she was laughing and had forgotten her disappointment about the kite.

'I mean—first you're hungry and then you eat, and for a while you feel full up; and then, after a time, you don't feel *that* full up; and then a bit later you know you could eat a bit of bread and butter; and later still, you begin to get hungry. And then, not long after that, you're really hungry again. And it all sort of chops the day up into lumps.'

But Brigit still thought it very funny and kept saying: 'What time is it by your stomach?' to beetles and butterflies and every kind of live thing that they met for a long time afterwards.

Occasionally Pidge would stop and look all round to detect any movement that might be a following hound; not because he really expected to see one but because he thought he should. He was pleased to find each time that they were alone but for the insects and a couple of crazy hares sparring with each other, a long way away—too far to be worth watching. Larks sang high above them; everything was as it should be. The cart-track took them through heather and clumps of harebells, with a blackthorn growing here and there; and it wasn't very long before the growth around them was richer, as the land was better.

While he was deciding that the leaping boxing hares were too far away to repay time spent watching them, Brigit gave an unexpected whoop of delight and shouted:

'Look Pidge!'

He saw that a little distance from them, there grew a pear tree. It was thick with ripe pears and the branches drooped low with their weight. They ran to it, with Pidge marvelling that everything should be so ripe this early in the year; and thinking that maybe this particular place got a lot of sunshine, or was some way protected from frost in the spring, so that everything got off to a good start.

Even though they were not really hungry, he reached and plucked as many as he could hold. Finding anything like a fruit tree—even a crab-apple—always seems marvellous; a free gift. Many a time, they had eaten crab-apples just because they had been lucky enough to find them and not for any other reason at all.

But pears! Ripe pears!

They sat under the tree and Pidge selected a pear and started to wipe it carefully on his sleeve. It looked mouth-watering and would tempt even a person who was as full as a sausage, or make a composed monk break a vow, laughing. It was a luscious, inviting yellow with lovely brown marks and pin head dots on its skin. The smell made them long to bite into it.

He was in the act of passing it to Brigit, when he froze.

She was urging him to hurry and not be too fussy, when he went like a statue.

179

Something was wrong; he knew it before he recognised it.

All about them, the insects made a soft racket as they went from flower to berry and back again, as if spending their lives in furious indecision; but beneath the tree there was nothing at all to be heard. Not one insect was there paying a visit; not even one wasp. Not a leaf of the tree stirred. The tree was the centre of a strange silence and Pidge suddenly knew.

It was that watching silence again, just as it was at the crossroads; but now only beneath the tree.

He sprang to his feet and threw the fruit on the ground.

'Maggots,' he said.

On the grass, the perfect pears dissolved into a sort of grey slush and some white maggots squirmed in the mess. The fruit remaining on the tree shrivelled in an instant and hung in dried-out, twisted tatters and the smell was vile.

They hurried away from the dead, ugly, thing.

'I know who is to blame for that,' he said grimly.

'Who?'

'She—They. The Mórrígan. The Fair Woman, Melodie Moonlight and Breda Fairfoul. She knows where we are but I don't really care; she makes me feel so mad.'

'Dirty tricks to do that with pears,' Brigit replied bitterly. 'I feel like biting a lump out of her leg!'

To think that, in spite of all the birds, she found us, Pidge was thinking angrily, while his eyes grew bright and hot, as tears of pure rage welled and almost spilled over. I imagine it's because the birds were magic and she's good at that herself. It may be that some other thing will work in the end as she can't easily be swizzled at her own game. Now I suppose that the hounds will be nosing after us again quite soon. But even so, we will be helped by The Dagda and if it's not going to be as easy as I thought—well, she's not going to have it all her own way, either.

Not knowing what else to do, he looked back over his shoulder to see if the hounds were there anywhere; and he fancied that he saw a gleam of gold or strong sunlight from the pear tree before it trembled and vanished but he couldn't be sure because of the hot tears blurring in his eyes.

In a moment, the chance that the smarting in his eyes would really turn to a spasm of angry tear-shedding had vanished;

and his eyes were suddenly dry and he felt braver than he had ever felt in his life before.

'Come on, Brigit,' he said forcefully, and they took the chance to run.

Chapter 9

There was a shared snigger from the women sitting at the table in the glasshouse.

An object had just shimmered and fallen over. The Mórrígan reached across and picked it up. There were some mocking sneers about fruit not being the temptation that some people claimed it was.

Smiling placidly, The Mórrígan put the tiny golden tree back on her bracelet. With her wand, she gave the little figure who was Findepath, a poke in the right direction. He howled, calling the part of the pack that was searching nearby.

'Are we cheating?' Melodie Moonlight asked, with a delighted smile. 'I send Fierce.' She prodded a second little figure, who called to his companions in his turn. She made him move in the right direction.

'Greymuzzle for me,' said Breda Fairfoul, and she whacked a third diminutive figure a brisk whack on the head with her pointer and turned him round and round until he too, faced the correct way, although dizzy. He called his team-mates with a feeble cry. The three groups of hounds soon came together and led by Findepath, they ran the way they were bidden.

Melodie Moonlight handed round the cigars. Breda declined and, instead, popped half a plug of tobacco into her mouth and chewed. The Mórrígan accepted one which she examined with great interest. After a few moments of sniffing it and considering it, she opened her mouth and ate it.

'Sweet,' she said appreciatively.

Growing tired of looking at the table landscape, Breda Fairfoul yawned and allowed a small frown to appear on her forehead.

'It becomes tedious between moves,' she remarked and to pass the time, she began to read a book by a great Russian genius whose name was Tolstoy. The name of the book was

'War and Peace.' As she read, she chewed her tobacco quid with relish and spat from time to time.

Melodie Moonlight, too, yawned. She drifted from the table and put a dance record onto the turntable of an old wind-up gramophone. With her shadow as her partner, she danced a number of frenzied brawls, until the shadow was forced to sit down and rest, panting. She allowed it to fan itself with the shadow of a rhubarb leaf, which it picked up off the floor, before challenging it to compete against her at boxing. She kept winning by knock-outs.

Breda closed the book.

'Too much Peace; not enough War,' she complained with a profound, critical air and threw the book out of the glasshouse.

'I believe I might like to invent a new kind of rat,' she added, and dressed in cap and gown and wearing a pair of thick-lensed, horn-rimmed spectacles, she sat at a small laboratory bench, boiling various things in glass round-bottomed flasks; while she studied a Biology textbook and one on Advanced Chemistry, for her B.Sc., because even Gods must work with what already exists in the Universe, especially nowadays.

The Mórrígan herself simply lounged like a fat snake under the sun.

'A little time, a very little time, and they shall hear of me again,' she said, and she watched the table-top from under the lazy, half-closed drapes of her eyelids.

Melodie Moonlight's shadow lay flat on the floor, exhausted.

'Get up and fight, you cur,' Melodie snarled in a sudden temper, 'or you will be sent to the dark side of the Moon.'

And the shadow got up and tried to fight. It crawled and cringed after her and did as she wished, because it knew that the dark side of the Moon would be its death.

A shadow needs light to live.

The hounds were running marvellously. They had covered a great deal of ground when a small herd of deer broke from cover and crossed over the countryside at a point that was not very far ahead of them. The hounds didn't immediately give chase as natural hounds would have done, but they ran on without veering away from the straight path of duty. They had even passed the invisible line on the ground at the place where the deers' spoor must have lain so fresh and enticing.

And then one of the hounds broke away from the pack and went in pursuit of the deer.

This breach in discipline was too much for the others and baying loudly they went after the bold one. They were now running with a terrible purpose after the herd. Soon the leading hound made a sort of leap forward and sank his teeth into the hind quarters of a deer. An indescribable sound came from the doomed animal's throat, and then there was the snarling and the excitement as the victim fell on its side, with its delicate legs moving stiffly in the air. The deer tried to raise its head from the earth but a hound took it by the throat and sank down on it. In the finish the hounds were sprawled all over their kill, dipping their heads to its flesh and nuzzling it. The scene now looked almost affectionate, as the hounds licked at the blood of the deer.

The Mórrígan's fury glittered in her eyes as she regarded the events on the table landscape. With her wand she punished the hounds rapidly and severely and they broke off from their feasting and ran cringingly to take up their duty again. They were desperately eager in their work; all but one.

Fowler complained in a low voice:

'We are treated not as servants but as slaves,' he said bitterly.

'What are you saying?' responded a shocked companion.

'We behave as slaves,' Fowler said.

'Hush!' Greymuzzle warned.

'No,' Fowler insisted. 'I will have my say. Who can blame her if she walks on dirt?'

'Findepath speaks: guard your tongue, brother. The Great Queen will punish any treachery and woe to you, Fowler, if you ever rise against her.'

'What was lost?' Fowler persisted. 'We took a few bare moments of freedom. No loss to The Mórrígan for we still do our duty.'

'Your speech lacks respect,' Greymuzzle said. 'I caution you as Findepath did.'

'You, Fowler, were the first to break away in pursuit of the deer and now we have all been punished,' Fierce said accusingly.

'It is true that I was the first to break away and give chase. But why did you follow? We obey an instinct; was our crime so great? It is equally true that the deer was caught by you, Fierce. My teeth were not the first to bite; I was not first there.'

Fierce shivered and licked away the few red berries of congealing blood that clung to his muzzle.

'Hush!' Greymuzzle said again, this time more strongly.

'Hush! Hush! Hush!' Fowler repeated in bitter mimicry. 'This is the word that puts infants to sleep!'

No more was said.

The hounds ran on and for a while the others ran a little way apart from Fowler, until as time passed—they forgot his queer defiant words.

Chapter 10

At intervals, Pidge stopped and looked back and searched the countryside, his eyes darting here and there; but he saw nothing, except once, a flock of sheep tumbling through a distant gap. He waited to see if they had a man and a dog following after; but they were just running on their own.

He didn't bother looking in the scrying-glass to discover how near the hounds might be; there was no point in doing that. The region they had passed over with the kite had been completely concealed by the birds; so there was no way he could recognize landmarks—a tree, a corner of a field or a ditch—to know if the hounds were far or near. He knew that they must catch up with Brigit and himself eventually. He wasn't even ill at ease, just on his guard.

At length they heard a low whistle coming from a way off and they turned and saw coming after them on the cart-track, two men with an ass.

One man carried a spade over his shoulder and the other one had a scythe. The ass wore panniers.

As the men came nearer it was possible to hear that they were arguing with each other. Their voices carried crisply in the natural stillness of lonely places; loud and sharp against the low sing-song of insects and the random flourishings of birds at melody. One man was old and the younger one was cut from the same pattern as the old one, so Pidge judged them to be father and son.

When they saw that Pidge and Brigit had noticed them, the men waved in greeting and the children waved back. Pidge now became extra watchful, just in case they were something of The Mórrígan's doing and he thought it curious that they didn't stop their squabble now that they might be overhead. Far from it; if anything, the argument livened up and improved for having an audience.

186

The younger man was saying:

'Stop dictatin' to me about the potatoes and onions! And stop layin' down the law about the turnips and cabbages! I'm the one doin' the work and I'm the master of the garden, now. And when we get to the valley of our relations and connections, watch you don't make small of me in front of the other men, with your mean-mouthing!'

'And who are you to talk to me like that? Do you think you are King Of The Aztecs with your prate about gardens and who's master? Master of the garden, who told you that?' the older man responded with spirit.

'Nobody told me. It was time for me and I a man this long time.'

The old man made a great show of being staggered by this.

'Well, hold me up!' he said, and pretended to go weak at the knees.

'See?' said the younger one, taking advantage of this bit of play-acting. 'The legs of you couldn't take the weight of a wren. Isn't it a pity for you that they haven't the same horse-power as your oul' jaw!'

'I'm strong yet—no better! I'm a better man than you, any day of the week!' And with that, the older man took to leaping off the ground in a series of high, quick springs, shouting gleefully:

'Here I am, the real, right, thing! That's me; I'm that man. The real McCoy, in bone, breeding and action! From a long-tailed family that goes back before the flood, and strong enough to gather the world up in my fist and throw it over the sun!'

'Stop tricking around, Da. You're enough to turn an ordinary brain, and you'll unnerve the grass itself below your feet and stunt its growth.'

'Shut up, you bally Normin!'

'I am not a Norman, Da.'

Now that they were close by, Pidge carefully took notice of how they looked.

They were about the same height and their faces too, were alike, except that one was really an old man. Now that he could see him better, he saw that the younger man was not young; maybe about fifty, Pidge guessed. He was wearing a rough jumper of a kind of rust colour and his father wore the same kind of jumper but it was coloured a deep blue. They both wore homespun jackets without sleeves and baggy trousers of the same material. Their faces were tanned as leather from working in the open in all weathers and this made the whites of their eyes seem very white, and the blue, very blue. They were just ordinary country people he decided, looking at their thick-soled boots; a bit like Aran Islanders in dress, that was all. The older man wore a cap.

Brigit stood with her thumb in her mouth, uncertain of them because they were having a row.

'I saw you ahead and whistled so that I wouldn't put a start in you, in a lonely place,' the younger one said.

'Oh, thank you,' Pidge replied.

'Fine day,' said the old one to Brigit. 'How's your health?'

She took her thumb from her mouth and looked at them with a serious expression on her face. She chose one out of the many things that came into her head, all of them untrue:

'I never talk to strangers,' she said.

Pidge had to suppress a smile that stole over his face. He knew well that Brigit delighted in talking to strangers whenever she got the chance. He wondered what the two men would make of this reply and was intrigued to see that they were also trying not to smile. A person would imagine that they knew her as well as I do myself, he thought.

'And what has made you so wise?' the older man asked her, bending down.

'I was born like it,' she answered grandly, losing her new-found wisdom in the same second.

'If *I* had a good, stout-hearted, *wise* companion like you, I'd go round the country on springs,' the old man said and Brigit beamed.

'You're already doing that,' she said impudently. 'I saw you lepping like a hare.'

'And where do you go, this fine day?'

'We're just on a journey,' Pidge said quickly.

'Are you going our way?'

'How do they know that, Da? They don't know which way we're going,' the younger one said.

'Don't be so smart,' said his father.

188

'We follow this cart-track to the road that butts onto it there ahead. We turn left on the road for a good while and after that, we go right through a thick bordering of trees and down into the Hidden Valley,' the younger one explained, adding: 'My name is Finn Spellman and that's my father. Everyone calls him Skin-the-Goat, he's so mean.'

'They do not! They call me Daire for that's my name: Daire Spellman. Don't mind the brat.'

While Brigit was telling them their names in return, Pidge stood doubtful about what to do. While he was considering, there was a cry from up above and he saw just two wild geese flying. They flew straight ahead, turned left for some time and then went right, before dwindling out of sight in the distance. It was the drawing of a map in the sky that matched the directions mentioned by Finn. So that was all right.

'We'll go with you,' he said happily.

'Hup!' said Finn to the ass, who was standing and waiting patiently, and they got going again.

'I was going to say "Hup!" ' complained Daire.

'Why didn't you?'

'Did I get the chance?'

Brigit walked by the ass and looked at her closely. She wasn't Serena but she had a lovely humorous face.

'Woah!' shouted Old Daire. The ass stopped.

'Oh Glory,' moaned Finn, 'what are you stopping the ass for, at all?'

'So that I can start her. Hup!' the old man shouted quickly. The ass started again.

'Don't mind the oul' fella,' said Finn.

'And who are you calling an oul' fella! Are you calling me an oul' fella?'

'You're seventy-seven, Da.'

'And if I am?'

'It's not young.'

'I am in my late middle-age,' Daire said with almighty dignity, 'and don't you forget it, you Sprout, you!'

'He's always like this till he's had his breakfast, and sparring with me keeps him perky,' Finn explained.

'That's true,' Old Daire agreed. The ass stopped dead and brayed, amazed that they had agreed on something. The end

189

of the braying had a kind of gurgling sound.

'Do you know,' said Finn, 'I'd swear that ass laughed.'

'It takes one to know one,' his father responded tartly, and away they went along the cart track towards the road.

'I could ate a holly-hedge and follow it up with a bucketful of nettles, I'm that hungry,' Old Daire declared.

'You've only yourself to blame if you are. Nothing would do you, but to get out and underway to show off to our relations, the Lawless family, and our connections, the Power family, how good you are, that you can get out of bed!'

It was at that moment that a hound wailed from somewhere a long way behind and Pidge stopped to listen; not noticing that the two men, who had also stopped, listened as intently as he did. Brigit halted the ass and stroked its face.

An answering wail came from somewhere even further off, to be followed almost at once by a third cry from a point farther away still.

Pidge felt a hand on his shoulder giving him a reassuring pat and looked up into Old Daire's face and saw a very kind smile. Finn walked to Brigit and placed her on the ass's back, in front of the panniers.

'We'd better walk on,' he said.

No mention was made of the hounds' crying.

In a moment Old Daire had resumed his battle.

'About them potatoes an' onions,' he began.

'Aw Da—stop it.'

'I keep telling you that you put them in upside down!'

By now Pidge and Brigit had realized that the argument was a sort of game being played only for fun. Pidge was glad that the men were with them at this particular time and that they kept talking all the time too. It made the hounds seem less of a threat.

Finn laughed.

'It's true—you put them in upside down!' Old Daire insisted.

'How can I be putting them in upside down—if they grow? They grow well enough, don't they?'

'But half of them come up on the other side of the world! There's a lot of fine, big, strong men in Australia. Why wouldn't there be—when they're 'atin' our spuds an' onions?'

190

They had been walking faster and were now almost at the turning onto the road.

'Will you stop barging out of you? You want a say in everything!' Finn said, and casually looked back over his shoulder. Seeing this, Pidge looked back as well. Not a living thing to be seen.

'Why shouldn't I have a say in everything?'

'You've had your day and this is my day; my turn has come.'

'Well, you've said it now! The last straw to break me back! But I'll put a halt to your gallop. I'll fix you well—I'll get married!'

At this Finn stopped and throwing his head back, he roared with laughter until the tears came running down his face.

'That's what I'll do—I'll bring you a stepmother; as true as there's a nose on my naked face. Now!' Old Daire shouted with passionate jubilation.

Pidge and Brigit joined in the laughter with Finn who wiped his eyes with the back of his hand and exchanged a pleased look with his father and they all walked on.

'And where will you get her?' he asked genially, as they turned left at the road.

'I'll get her all right,' his father answered darkly.

'Faith, I admire your hope!'

'I'll get her,' roared Old Daire, 'if I have to go through the country ringing a handbell.'

Everybody laughed at this, including the ass and Old Daire himself.

'And what kind would you get if you did that?'

'The *worst* kind and isn't that what I'm looking for? I want one that'd raise lumps on you.'

'Be quiet, you old prawn, or I'll pull your nose.'

'Pull away!'

'I will!'

'And why wouldn't you? That's what them oul' Normins always did—went round pulling noses.'

So they went on like this, with sometimes the old man leaping and springing about in pretended temper and Finn answering him back at every stroke. As they went along, Finn glanced in his casual way but more frequently, at the spread of land to their left. Each time Pidge followed his example.

The hounds had not yet come. But he knew that they would and was resigned to it.

Chapter 11

BRIGIT stopped listening to the men and talked to the ass instead. The ass turned her ears back and listened, and Brigit told her a story all about an ass named Serena, while she stroked the rough neck affectionately.

Finn walked at her side, smiling as he heard snatches of Brigit's tale in between answering his father.

Now they had reached the part of the road that was bordered by oak and beech trees, growing in a belt that was about six or eight deep, in to the right of the road. The undergrowth of bracken and bramble had sprung up thickly and reached up to the lowest branches of the trees, so that it could not be known what lay behind it all.

At some mysterious point along this fringing, the men stopped.

Finn went in first, parting the ferns and bushes carefully to let the ass, with Brigit still on her back, come in after him without damaging anything. Old Daire signalled to Pidge to follow them and he came last himself, making sure that everything sprang back into place as they passed through.

On coming out into the open again, Pidge was astonished to see that they were faced with a sheer rising of living rock, that ranged for some distance on either side of where they stood. It looked insurmountable and impenetrable and he could feel his heart sinking; the men had been so quietly sure of where they were going. And now, this unbelievable obstacle!

Calmly, Finn lifted Brigit down onto the ground and he took the panniers off the ass. Daire hooked one of them to the handle of his scythe, replaced the scythe against his shoulder and grinned. Finn did exactly the same thing with the other one, attaching it to his spade.

'Now—suck in your breath and follow me,' he said cheerfully.

He walked in straight at the rock. Pidge followed, with Brigit, the ass and the old man in a line behind him.

Now that he was right up to it, he saw that there was a cleft in its structure; hard to distinguish at first because the main colour of the rock didn't vary. The split wasn't edge-to-edge but overlapped, and the front part was about three feet nearer to them than the section behind. Some bushes and plants had taken root on the rock and reached across the gap and they tangled with each other and helped to hide and match it, like patterned wallpaper.

Pidge followed Finn through the breach. He was obliged to turn left almost immediately, and then right. As he walked along this twisting, narrow and deep passage, he was thinking what a great hiding-place it was and how hard it would be for the hounds to find it. He knew that Brigit was behind him safely; for he could hear her telling the ass not to be afraid.

The passage grew even narrower and he understood why the panniers had to come off; there simply wasn't room to spare. The path now sloped upwards very gradually.

After what seemed a long time, he finally stepped out into the open and the sunshine, to find that Finn was sitting waiting for him. Brigit popped out in a moment with the ass and Old Daire at her heels.

'Here we are,' said Finn, 'the Hidden Valley.'

It was as if they were standing on the rim of an enormous bowl.

They looked down on a broad, shallow valley, bare of trees and scrub, that was a vast mosaic of small stony fields. A road ran down ahead of them, slightly winding. It went all the way to the far end of the valley, where it seemed to come to a finish at the rising wall of rock which formed the opposite end of the bowl where they now stood.

The base of the valley was level. There looked to be miles and miles of it with people all over it working busily, cutting and burning small furze bushes as they cleared the land for cultivation. The distance made each of those who were furthest away seem smaller than a finger-nail. There were a great many fires going and the smoke rose up in straight plumes to the sky as steady as telegraph poles, because there was no wind.

Pidge had never seen such a host of people working together

in one place; so many that they couldn't be counted.

Everything sparkled and was radiant under the sun's blaze. Wherever there was the smallest drop of water even, it shone like a mirror and the bits of quartz in rocks, glittered and flashed. The men wore homespuns and brightly-coloured jumpers, some red as cherries and others peacock-blue, and they were scattered all over the valley in dabs, like spatters of paint. The women's petticoats were of scarlet; the grass was a brilliant green.

As they walked down into the valley, people stopped work and greeted them when they passed by, and some, a long way off, paused to wave.

'There'll be time for you to get a bit of breakfast,' said Finn.

'Good,' said Brigit. 'But no hollyhedges or nettles, for me.'

From end to end, the valley was easily four miles long. The houses of the people were of the traditional long, low type, whitewashed and thatched. The roofs of straw had darkened like old honey.

They followed the track down and along the valley-floor and the people all stopped in turn, leaving their chopping and burning and digging-out of roots, to say a greeting. Old Daire and Finn were very well-liked it seemed; and beneath all the friendliness, there was an undertone of great respect.

Finn had lifted Brigit back on to the ass and she had a good view of all that they passed.

'Are all these your relations and corrections?' she asked, impressed by their numbers.

'Yes,' Finn replied seriously while the other two smiled.

'I hope you don't have to buy them all birthday presents,' she said with sympathy.

'Ah, they're far too old for that,' said Old Daire.

In one of the fields that was well-in from the track and butting right against the base of the rock wall, Pidge noticed a whole herd of donkeys, who left off browsing to watch them go by.

At length they turned in at one of the small fields near the far end and the people there came to meet them. Now as Pidge looked back, the people at the entrance to the valley were the ones who looked small.

There was talk of breakfast for the arrivals. Pidge wasn't at all sure if they had time and mentioned this in a vague way to the company in general.

'You'll be all right for a while, I'm thinking. Throw your length down on the grass and we'll bring the food outside. Isn't it all ready and all you have to do is eat,' Old Daire said reassuringly, and then he went with the people into the nearest house.

Pidge sat on the grass and watched Brigit flash away, chattering to this one and that. He called her but she paid no heed. There she goes not talking to strangers, he thought, laughing quietly. She was following Finn who had gone into the next field to talk with the people there. Everywhere he went, she was behind him; like a pet lamb.

A relaxed feeling stole over Pidge; he lay on his side with an elbow on the ground and his hand propping up his head, as he enjoyed the sun and the air; and the noises the people made while working. His eyes were closing with the languor of it all. From the house there came the homely sounds of crockery being moved and a kettle whistling. He lay flat on his back in the sun and stretched himself out.

Under his head, he heard a sound like a muffled gong. At first he fancied that he was only sensing the vibrations made by the blows of implements, as they struck against stones lying unsuspected in the soil near the roots of the furze bushes; but realizing that it was too quick a rate for a man with a spade to work at, and far more muffled than the sounds around him anyway, he turned his ear to the earth.

As soon as it had taken his attention, the sound stopped and he heard a whispering, distinct and audible though very low.

It said:

'Sow the wheat here.'

It was something like the Voice in the chimney.

Again, Pidge was overcome, but not by shock this time and not by fear; it was pure surprise.

'Do you mean the seed of The Maines?' he whispered back.

'Sow the seed here,' the Voice said in answer.

There are no other seeds, he thought and felt in his pocket. He had wrapped the grains of wheat in his handkerchief. He scraped away a little earth, undid the hankie and dropped the seeds in the hole and covered them. He watched the spot,

196

waiting for something to happen, some marvellous thing to begin.

Nothing at all happened.

'Did I do right?' he asked the earth quietly, as he doubted.

'You did,' the Voice whispered back.

Then from the house came a small procession of people, Old Daire leading. Two men carried a long table and four men carried two benches that matched the table for length. Three women came carrying trays of crockery and food.

'Come on, Your Nibs—your bit to eat is ready!' Old Daire shouted.

'Wait a minute,' Finn shouted back.

'Wait-A-Minute lost the ducks!' Old Daire yelled back. He was surreptitiously heeling in the little patch of seeds with his boot, but Pidge saw him do it out of the corner of his eye.

The table was set and Brigit and Finn came back, and everybody sat down to eat.

There were baskets of boiled eggs, and platters with whole-meal bread, and small dishes of butter for everyone and mugs of hot sweet tea. There were two plates of specially scrambled eggs with herbs of some kind for Brigit and Pidge, and they drank some unusual fruit juice that they had never tasted before. All the crockery had a lovely dandelion pattern; rich yellow and green colours on a cream background in the glazing. Brigit especially admired the egg-cups that the other people were using.

Between mouthfuls, she said:

'It's nice in this place. All the things are nice and the fields are so small and neat, they look like dolls' fields.'

'The same fields have fed the people over and over again from the first; mother and father to us all—the lovely green fields, bless them forever,' said Old Daire gravely.

'More bread and butter, please,' Brigit said.

Daire passed her the plate and took her hand as she reached out.

'This little hand will do something big,' he said, and Brigit reddened with pleasure.

'When?' she asked.

'In time,' he said.

Pidge noted this with a feeling of gratitude; it promised well

197

for the future. As he ate, he looked at the people who had been such good friends. They all had a look of Daire and Finn, and were dressed as they were, in the bluish-grey homespuns. The clothes were all made out of new cloth, it appeared; not even one patch, although they were working clothes. Even as he looked at Daire's sleeveless jacket, a patch was there just under his left arm; but done very neatly. I was wrong, he thought, and finished his eggs.

One of the women was admiring Brigit's brooch and saying how nice it looked. She reached over and touched the little silver bow and arrow with hands that had never known rough work, Pidge saw.

'You'd best be off now,' Old Daire said when they'd finished and eaten all that they needed. 'I'm sure you have a long way to go.'

'Thank you for everything,' Pidge said awkwardly, not yet old enough to say words of indebtedness to older people easily and on an equal-footing, and not young enough like Brigit to just let it trip off his tongue.

'You have lovely plates and eggcups,' she said enviously. 'Thank you for my breakfast.'

Old Daire held out his hand to say goodbye. Brigit settled her satchel on her shoulder and shook hands.

Old Daire then took Pidge's hand.

'You're one of those quiet, steady ones who sees a lot and says nothing.'

'I didn't know that; I suppose I am,' Pidge said, slightly surprised.

'You'll show them the way,' Old Daire ordered Finn, hitting him with his cap.

Finn's gaze was directed back at the spot high up on the rim, where they had first come into the valley. He gave a low whistle and all of the people, even those at the greatest distance away, stopped work and looked at him.

They followed his gaze at once, everyone turning to face the ridge and stare at the hounds on the skyline.

It all went very still.

The columns of smoke that had been rising in straight unruffled lines, suddenly bent at right angles when they were level with the rim and drifted to form a swirling thick blanket, that carried right to the edge where the dogs were now watching. There, it gathered and thickened even more and billowed out at either side; a grey and yellow mass that screened all that was in the valley from the dogs' eyes.

Finn hoisted Brigit onto his back and motioned to Pidge to follow. He then went, not by the road, but through the remaining fields, to the way out of the valley. It was a dark tunnel, hidden by growth, and he silently led the way, out to the countryside beyond.

By a huge thorntree, he stopped and set Brigit onto the ground. He bent and plucked a dandelion clock which he gave to Pidge.

'Run,' he said. 'Keep running until the last seed remains—then stop.'

And then he was gone.

While Pidge took a moment to look about him, wondering which way to go, Brigit began to search the ground in a frantic, angry way.

'I've lost my brooch,' she said furiously.

'Oh no! Not now! We're supposed to be running!'

'I'm not going without it,' she said hotly, as if she thought he might argue with her.

'Of course you can't go without it,' he said glumly, and together they went back through the tunnel, searching all the way.

They had to go all the way back before they saw it lying on a bit of grass, just inside the valley. Brigit snatched it up and Pidge helped her to pin it back on her cardigan, fumbling a bit because he was anxious to be gone.

Naturally, they both had a quick look to see if the smoke was still working, and saw that it was thicker than ever. But all of the people had vanished; perhaps into their houses, and hundreds of hares had come out to play; boxing and jumping about and chasing each other in their usual, crazy way. The donkey-herd was no longer there; instead nibbling the grass, there were well-bred horses; and that was odd too.

They went back though the tunnel and stood again by the thorntree.

'Hold my hand, Brigit,' said Pidge and they ran.

Chapter 12

THEY went swiftly and easily because of the herbs they had eaten; Pidge with the fluffy little dome held out in front, where he could watch it. As they sped along, some dandelion parachutes pulled free and drifted. Pidge snatched a look behind and could not be sure that the Hidden Valley had not changed into a hill-fort, already diminished in the distance behind.

They flashed over moorland, turf-bogs and streams. They pounced at and leaped over ditches, brooks and small boulders. They swept round small lakes and young spinneys and skirted spongy clots of moss, and ran over flat pasturage and lumpy, sedgy ground where water tumbled into suds and made bubbling pools.

And the parachutes blew away, spasmodically.

It was taking a long time.

The sun moved and the shadows changed; the day had a different feeling to that of morning-time. They felt not the smallest bit tired. Brigit chattered about the things that caught her eye as they passed by, but never once asked to stop either to play or explore, in all that time.

It came to it, at last.

Two parachutes remained.

When one went sideways and took off, they immediately stopped running.

'We're supposed to walk now,' Pidge said, although he knew inside himself that they could still run fast if they wanted to.

The last parachute fell and he threw the stalk away.

Close by was a large crag, sheer but for one sloping side. Wishing to know how far they had come, they climbed to its top to try to find out. For a few quiet moments they stood looking back, surveying the astonishing distance they had travelled. There was no sign at all of the Hidden Valley or anything even resembling it.

Even as they watched, the far-off shapes of the hounds appeared, seeming to rise out of the ground because they were so remote; but running marvellously.

Perhaps because he was instinctively looking for them, Pidge saw them first.

'Would you ever believe it; they've found us already,' he said softly.

'Where?'

He pointed.

'Way back over there? do you see them moving?'

'Oh yes. They look so small—like rabbits. I hope they all break a leg!'

'We must walk on as if they're not even there. Right, Brigit?'

'Right!'

They scrambled and slithered down from the crag and set off to walk to wherever they were going.

'How could we run so well, Pidge?' Brigit asked.

'Something in the food or drink that Old Daire gave us, I expect. Funny how Finn knew when *exactly* that we should stop running; yet I don't think those people were Gods of any kind—just a bit strange, maybe.'

At frequent intervals he looked back to check on the hounds' progress and the hairs rose on the back of his neck to see how quickly they were gaining. He saw Brigit shudder.

But the hounds didn't want to catch up, it seemed.

When they reached a certain position in relation to where Brigit and Pidge walked, they stopped running. Keeping this distance, they appeared content to simply track after them. Sometimes they had to trot for a little while to keep the space between them more or less unaltered; but mostly they managed this by just walking. Pidge saw this with the greatest relief.

As time passed, the children became slowly used to the fact that the hounds were following after them. If they turned round some big obstacle or were hidden from view for some time by trees or scrubland, the hounds made no attempt to shorten the gap. Twice in full sight of them, and even though

Pidge said not to, Brigit stopped to pick a flower to find out what they would do. Each time, the hounds immediately dropped to the ground and lay still as carvings, while they waited. A few times, when they knew that they could not be seen, the children ran for a short stretch, always being careful to stop and walk in plenty of time. It turned into a pattern in due course.

Brigit started to lag behind.

Pidge was instantly worried when he noticed that she was limping slightly.

'What's the matter?'

'I've a stone in my sock. I'll have to sit down and get it out,' she said glumly.

'That's all right; they won't try to catch up. I was afraid it was a sprain.'

He smiled encouragingly at her and looked for somewhere nice for her to sit.

There was a massive old fallen tree-trunk to the right of them. Moss grew on it in patches with some green mould and a few baby ferns stuck up like bright, green feathers, and there was a great tough old fungus, sort of blue-grey, that grew at an angle and made the old tree give the impression that it was wearing a cap at a jaunty angle. With all its decorations, the tree looked very attractive. The ground beneath and in front of it was covered with very fine, soft grass, thick and inviting.

They sat there and Brigit took off her sandal and her sock.

A little whispering voice, from somewhere up above them, said:

I think he should be given a good, hard pinch.

A different little whispering voice answered in agreement:

That's what I think. A good old pinch would do him no harm at all.

A whole chorus of similar little voices joined in, all agreeing that what 'he' needed was 'a good, old pinch.'

Some said: *It would bring him to his senses.*

Others said: *There's no cure like a good, old cure.*

Still others said that: *A pinch in time saves nine.*

Then one said somewhat hesitantly:

Far away pinches have long horns.

This terrible remark caused silence.

202

The voice that had spoken broke into nervous giggles and then there was silence again.

Brigit moved in close to Pidge and whispered in his ear:

'Who's "he"? Are they talking about you?'

'I don't know,' he whispered back.

The voices resumed.

One said:

'*My dear old Auntie always used to say: "Pinch first and ask questions afterwards."*'

'*That's just like your dear old Auntie—always looking for a fight.*'

'*Shut up about my dear old Auntie or you'll get such a pinch in a minute.*'

A third voice cut in on this private squabble.

'*We should just tell him he's batty and not pinch him at all—that's my opinion.*'

'*It'll be more than a black eye, if we do. It could be the firing-squad, again!*'

'*Yes,*' a last little voice said sadly. '*He's too batty to be told he's batty, that's the trouble.*'

Pidge stood and looked about. All that could be seen were a dozen or so earwigs enjoying the sun on the tree's bark.

'Nobody there,' he whispered, sitting down again.

The voices continued:

'*He's enough to make your blood run backwards!*'

'*With his little Nappy Hat and his French.*'

'*He says it's French but for all we know—it's Ancient Foolish.*'

'*He prances round something shockin', doesn't he?*'

'*With his battles! Battles? If you ask me, it's all daft!*'

'*I don't know though—he's a good laugh at times. I often get a stitch in my side laughing at him.*'

'*Don't ever let him catch you, that's all!*'

With Brigit's sock and sandal back on, the children stood again. Pidge leaned forward and his shadow fell on the tree.

'*The sun's gone behind a cloud,*' said one.

'*Oh, I hope it doesn't rain.*'

'*I hope it does, then we can all go home.*'

'*Look—we always go on like this and we never do anything about it.*'

'Yes. We always humour him.'

'Poor oul' skin.'

'Anyway, I enjoy it most of the time.'

'So do I—but not all the time.'

'It's the earwigs,' Brigit said suddenly. 'They're the ones who are talking.'

'THUNDER!' yelled one of the earwigs. 'I heard thunder! I knew it was going to rain.'

'Take cover!'

An earwig wearing a Napoleon Hat emerged from a crack in the bark of the tree that went in a narrow split under the elaborate fungus.

'Courage, Mes Braves!' he shouted. 'Stand votre ground. There'll be no Retreat From Moscow here!'

Chapter 13

THE little earwig wearing the hat spoke so commandingly that all the other earwigs stopped their aimless milling about and stood where they were.

Even so, there was a sarcastic mutter of:

'Oh, that's a surprise, isn't it; when there isn't any snow. If there was any snow at all, he'd have us doing The Long Retreat From Moscow up and down this old tree until our pincers was froze off and without a wink of sleep until it thawed!'

Others grumbled:

'I told you he was off his hinges!'

'I said he was under the influence of a High Temperature most of the time!'

And:

'I'd laugh—but it would be pistols for two at dawn with High Stericks, if I was caught with as much as a grin.'

'Seelawnce!' roared the little one in the cocked hat. *'Attention! Gentlemen, you are On Parade!'*

The others fell silent at this and stood to attention.

The children watched, fascinated.

The one with the hat on, walked up and down with his forelegs clasped behind his back.

'Aha!' he cried with an air of having caught them out. They responded to this by shuffling guiltily.

'Ze discipline gets slack when Moi is not around, I notice. Where is Mon Imperial Guard?'

An earwig took a pace forward and said, after saluting smartly:

'They got took in with the washing and they got ironed, Mon General.'

A second one gave an even smarter salute and added:

'It's the third lot this week, Sir. We're gettin' decimated by it!'

The one with the hat seemed to go into a trance of brooding as he paced this way and that.

'What is this fatal fascination with fresh laundry?' he asked himself softly but passionately, and he shook his head from side to side at the mystery of it all. In moments, he solved the riddle to his own satisfaction at least, by muttering: 'Destiny!'; and then he appeared to be much as he was before hearing the terrible news. He faced the others with a dignified formality and said proudly:

'Ze Fortunes Of War, Mes Amis. 'Ats off and a minute's seelawnce for our gallant dead!'

There were weak complaints of: 'We haven't got any hats,' and: 'He's the one with the hat,' and then there was silence.

Pidge took his chance to make sure that the hounds were not in sight. He looked conscientiously in every direction, in case they were playing some kind of soothing trick. He was suspicious that they might creep close and suddenly pounce, knowing that he and Brigit were off-guard. But wherever they were, they were not in view.

'Fall in!' the earwig with the hat shouted, after a few seconds of profound quietness. The others quickly obeyed, tripping over themselves and each other, in their haste. There were cries of: 'Get off me legs, can't ye', and: 'Look where yer going, Dermot', and: 'You're standing on me head, you fool!' and then, they stood in ranks.

'Pidge,' Brigit said, pointing to the one with the hat, 'it's that mad earwig I told you about the other day.'

A great many cries of surprise and panic and some nervous giggles came from the troops at this.

'KEEP CALM!' shouted the one with the hat. 'Do you want it said that we have no discipline; that we are held together with a safety-pin? Back to your positions! Allez!'

The earwigs shuffled back into place.

When they were motionless again, he reared up to his full height and looked closely at Brigit.

'So, we meet again,' he said slowly. 'I know you. Now let me see—didn't we meet at my field-headquarters at ze Battle Of Waterloo?'

'Yes. You were in the old water-butt.'

There was a half-stifled snigger from the others, which he

206

squashed on the instant with a powerful, scanning glare. When order was restored, he turned his attention to Brigit again.

'*It is true that I may have been in an old water-butt—ze redcoats are everywhere,*' he responded haughtily; '*but, it is better than being in a smelly, old boot, what is called Ze Wellington, if I am not mistaken and I never am.*'

'Yes, you're the same one; you had that daft hat on,' Brigit answered back.

'*What?*' he shouted. '*You call my best Sunday Bicorne a daft 'at? No criticism from civilians permitted! Alors! Have you been putting it about zat I am mad? The Emperor Napoleon—for it is I? Moi? Napoleon Forficula Auricularia—Le Wig of Wigs?*' he finished in a passion as he strutted up and down fiercely and proudly, with his chest stuck out like a battlement, before him.

Before Brigit could reply, an earwig jumped to attention and shouted:

'*Permission to reconnoitre, Mon General?*'

Permission was given with a wave of a foreleg and without any interruption whatsoever to the temperamental pacing of the little Napoleon. The other little earwig ran up Pidge's arm and onto his shoulder. He raised himself up on his back legs and pretended to sweep the countryside.

'*Just say that all who are truly great are touched with madness—he'll like that,*' he whispered to Pidge in a very confidential and friendly way.

'Well, Corporal?'

'*All clear, Mon General!*'

'We have heard that all who are truly great are touched with madness,' Pidge said truthfully and not wishing to hurt his feelings.

The little Napoleon halted and considered this.

'*So be it,*' he said dramatically. '*If I have to be loony to be great—adieu, sanity; ze cost is but a trifle.*'

'You should have had that medicine I was going to give you; it would have done you the world of good,' Brigit said reprovingly.

'*Ugh!*' he shuddered with disgust. '*You were going to give Moi ze cough mixture. Don't you know they named a brandy after*

207

Moi? Better than inspiring a smelly old boot, like Wellington! No wonder ze redcoats tremble when my name is mentioned.'

'When he says redcoats, he means the red ants, you know,' the earwig Corporal whispered to Pidge.

'You're an ungrateful brat. I was only trying to make you better,' Brigit said crossly to the little Napoleon.

'From you—always ze insult. How dare you say I have no gratitude!' he shouted back indignantly.

From the earwigs who were standing to attention throughout all this, came many loud murmurs, which were meant for him to hear.

'Tut-tut!'

'They don't know our General!'

'He's a grand lad.'

'Gratitude on legs!'

With a dignified bow, he acknowledged these tributes.

'You can have anything you like,' he said to Brigit. *'Would you like to be King of Naples? Say the word! Chicken Marengo? It can be ready in moments. Anything you wish.'*

'I don't know what you're talking about and anyway I can't stand here all day arguing with you. There are these mad dogs following us and I've been talking to you long enough.'

'Dogs?'

'Yes.'

'Friends of yours?'

'They are not!'

'Mad you say?'

'Yes.'

'Ah, Les Rabides. We will fight them for you.'

'Hear, hear!' the rest of the earwigs cheered.

'Oh good,' Brigit said, delighted. Pidge grinned.

'Sound ze bugles; beat ze drums. Gather Ma Grande Armée!'

The assembled earwigs were extraordinarily perky at this. Drums were beaten and several bugle notes were heard. Obeying these calls, thousands of earwigs appeared from the cracks and crannies in the tree-trunk. Some wore sashes of green which were made simply from blades of grass, and these were the officers for they shouted out orders. The multitude of earwigs scuttled and scrambled in mad, swarming masses. The orders were clear and insistent, and in obeying them, the

208

crowds were soon standing rank upon rank as a disciplined throng.

There was a command of: 'Drummer-boy!' and a small earwig began a low, muffled beat on a little drum made from an acorn cup that had a rose petal stretched tightly across it. Compared with the little drummer-boy who was beating it so well, it looked enormous. The sound seemed to excite and spellbind the army. The earwigs rippled and swayed very slightly, obeying the intoxicating rhythm and seemed ready for anything.

A roll-call was made beginning with: 'First Brigade Old Guard,' and when that was done with, they awaited their leader's words.

'Mes Braves . . . . . ' he began.

'Thrimm-thrimm,' went the drum.

The earwigs cheered with reckless exultation.

'It is time for Battle. Les Rabides are almost upon us and zere is much work before us. Each Wig will do his duty without question, and we have ze advantage of surprise. Our tactics are simple— Ambush And Cling. Zere will be lupin bonbons for zose who acquit zemselves well. Between life and death—zere is but a moment so—go for ze noses. Courage, Mes Braves and Bon Chance!'

Yet another loud cheer burst from the lines; there seemed to be a deep longing to meet the enemy. A thrilling bugle-call was made through a little empty seed husk.

'What an army I have,' the Napoleon earwig said tearfully before crying out:

'Pour l'Empereur et la Gloire!'

This cry was returned as:

'Poor Lumperer Hay Bag War!' because they didn't understand very much of what he was saying and didn't really care, as long as there was going to be a fight.

Orders were shouted by the officers:

'Present . . . . CLAWS!'

Thousands of pincers jutted up into the air.

'Slope . . . . CLAWS!'

'FORWARD . . . . MARCH!'

In trance to the drums, for many more began their tapping, rank after rank followed their leader, who rode astride an extremely large and powerful earwig. They streamed from the tree-trunk onto the ground. It could now be seen, that the drums were strapped to the sides of other suitably large earwigs, and little drummer-boys rode these proudly, as they kept up the hypnotic tapping on the drums that were positioned in front of them.

Many loud cheers, deafening for earwigs, rent the air; and as regiment after regiment passed by, they saluted Brigit and Pidge with an: 'Eyes Right!' and a dipping of pincers.

One brigade sang: *'Pinch The Good Pinch,'* as they marched past and another lot were singing: *'Oh, We Won't Go Home Until Morning,'* in a careless, rollicking way. Some, who appeared to be more serious, sang: *'We Will Pinch With Perfect Pincers,'* very soberly, as if it were some kind of sacred anthem; and individuals cried out from time to time—things like: *'Go for ze noses, lads!'* and: *'Poor Lumperer Hay Bag War!'* and: *'Mind you don't get sniffed up, Johnny,'* answered by: *'You mind yourself, Brian. Cocky!'*

Pidge and Brigit stood watching until the last line of troops had gone.

'I wouldn't have believed it if I hadn't seen it—what an actor!' a voice said close to Pidge's ear.

It was the earwig Corporal, standing at his full height on Pidge's shoulder.

'Oh, I'd forgotten about you,' Pidge said.

'Didn't you want to go with the others?' asked Brigit.

'No. I'm finished with that game. Did you see the way they all came under his power; they're dafter than he is. Talk about mesmerized! Up here, I was on a Higher Plane and it all went wide of the mark with me. Could you give me a lift? I'm going home to me Ma.'

'Yes. Just mind you hold on tight,' Pidge warned him.

They resumed their journey, walking, because Brigit said that her foot was tender as that stupid stone had made a sore place in it.

'Yes,' continued the Corporal happily, *'this time, I stood aloof.'*

'You stood *on* a loof,' Brigit corrected him with a sideways smirk at Pidge who roared with laughter.

'What does a loof mean?' she asked, frowning.

Pidge explained, still laughing.

'Words!' she said with disgust. 'I'll never learn them all.'

The Corporal told them that his name was Myles and said that they could call him Cluas which was the professional name of the clan. He explained that they only used their first names when there was a lot of them together to save confusion and headaches. He said that they were all very proud of their Clan name as it meant: 'Ear': and it couldn't be known how many gifts they had when it came to ears.

Then he said politely:

'I hope you don't mind my asking, but who are these Lay Rabbits you are running from, and why on earth are you running from rabbits of any kind?'

So, as they went along, Pidge told him the whole story and when he had finished Cluas said with regret:

'I'm sorry now that I didn't go with the others. If only I'd known! I wish I had helped you.'

'Oh, don't worry,' Pidge said. 'There are plenty of them without you.'

They stopped for a moment while Brigit grabbed a handful of soft moss and pushed it into her sandal under her foot. Just as she finished, there was a series of distant yelps and howls.

'Can you run now? We've got a good chance to get ahead?' Pidge asked.

Brigit said she could, and warning Cluas to keep a good grip, Pidge took her hand and they ran.

Presently they smelled turf-smoke and saw ahead of them a cottage partly hidden by trees, with a nice sweep of lawn at the front where an apple tree grew. Behind a low hedge, there was a garden strung with washing-lines where a vast amount of washing, blew and billowed like the rigging on a galleon.

'We must walk now. If we were seen running like this, it might look suspicious; and we don't want to have to answer a lot of questions,' Pidge said.

'Where has Cluas gone?'

'Isn't he there on my shoulder?'

'No.'

'He must have fallen off. I told him to hold on.'

'Maybe we were passing his Ma and he jumped; just like anyone would.'

They looked on the ground for him but couldn't find him anywhere.

211

Chapter 14

Nearing the cottage, they were surprised to hear loud howls coming from within.

Suddenly, the half-door flew open and a small man, in his shirt-tails only, ran out; his little thin lark's legs twinkling through the grass almost too fast to be seen.

He was pursued by a big, fat woman—waving her enormous arms threateningly and shouting after him:

'Oh, the baby-bawler! Oh, the little dhribbler!'

The little man reached the apple tree, was up it in a flash and perched on a branch, looking down at her.

'Come down, Cornelius!' she thundered.

'No, Hannah. Not at the moment,' the little man said meekly.

'Come down, ye twelve-sided article!' she roared.

'You'll only bate me agin, Hannah,' the little man explained.

'He spat in me dinner, the little divileen,' the woman said. 'I'll break him in pieces when he comes in for his tea.'

'Ah no, Hannah,' the little man wheedled.

'Yes!' said the fat woman. 'A puck in the pluck is what you're asking for, and a puck in the pluck is what you'll get.'

Having said this, Hannah marched back inside the cottage and slammed the half-door.

'That wan would clane ye beyond soap and water,' the little man said to the children. 'She's forever scrubbin' the skin offa me and whippin' the duds offa me back; and it's washboards, tubs, bluebags and soapsuds from cockshout 'till sunset; and her hands looking like old, grey crêpe and her arms looking like two red bolsters and the look on her face'd stop a clock! That's what she done just now. Whipped the britches offa me, and I just going to sit down to me bacon and cabbage.'

'Did you really spit in her dinner?' asked Pidge.

'I did, bedad!' the little man replied emphatically. 'I was

dhriven to it. In a fair fight, I'm nowhere with her. Ye saw the size of her and the immensity of arms, she has? That's what I done, all right—I spat in her dinner. I was for leggin' it then out the door, only she caught me by the tails of me shirt and it was fisticuffs and buffetings to beat the band.'

'Do you often spit in her dinner?' Brigit asked admiringly.

'Nearly every washday,' the little man replied. He looked thoughtfully at the half-door for a moment and then called out, sweetly:

'Can I come in for me dinner now, Hannah dear?'

'Ye can't! *I'm* ating it!' Hannah bawled from inside.

'There's me bacon and cabbage gone west—lost it again,' the little man said with no trace of anger. 'It's a pity you came on a washday or I'd have asked you inside. She's nice enough when she isn't washing, you know. She's *nearly* nice enough, anyway.'

'Which day is washday?' Brigit asked.

'That is something that is never known until it starts. Some kind of fervour grabs hold of her for soap-flakes and down comes the tub.'

'Well, we'll have to be moving on,' Pidge said awkwardly.

'Where are you off to?' the little man asked.

'On a journey of wonder and fear,' Brigit boasted.

'We're just on a journey, that's all,' Pidge said quickly and frowned at her with meaning.

'If I had me britches, I might go a bit of the road with you. I'd like a little dander along the road on a nice day, so I would. Better than swallowing bubbles and steam with every breath I take, anyway.'

'Can ye get your britches?' asked Brigit. 'She'll break you in pieces if you go in, won't she?'

'She will. She's a woman of her word. But, maybe I can get them without venturing that far into danger.'

He slid down from the tree, picked up a clod of earth and threw it in at the half-door.

'Hannah! I'm coming in there to get me rights!' he yelled.

'If ye come in here, ye'll *get* yer rights! You'll be put in a bottle and corked! If ye come in here—ye'll have as much chance as a stray pig in a prowling of half-starved wolves. The divil nor Doctor Faustus couldn't save ye—if ye come in here!'

the fat woman answered in a savage roar.

'You cross-grained hump of misfortune! I hope me bacon and cabbage chokes ye, so I do!' the little man shouted back and he reached down and picked up half-a-dozen windfalls and let fly with them, straight into the kitchen where they vanished into the darkness inside.

Hannah retaliated and a flat-iron came sailing out to land with a thud a good ten yards to the rear of the place where they were standing.

'She's strong, isn't she?' the little man whispered proudly to the children: 'I'm whispering so that she won't hear me praising her in any way.'

He picked up a great, big gnarl of dried cow-dung.

'Missed me, ye nasty, hummocky lump of Glum! Do you know what you are? You're the greatest Holy Show on earth! You used to have a complexion like milk and roses but now it's more like rhubarb and custard. You used to have *normal* legs under you and now you've got two portions of telegraph poles inhabiting your stockings! You're an oul' monster done up in pink corsets and here's another present for you an' I hope you enjoy it!'

With that, the dried dung followed the apples—straight in over the half-door.

There wasn't a sound from Hannah.

'It's like getting feathers off a frog, isn't it?' the little man said to the children humorously.

After a few moments there came a roaring like that of a bull having his teeth out against his will, from inside the cottage.

'I think she was in shock there for a minute but she's got her wind back now,' the little man said gleefully.

'OH, ME LOVELY DINNER! OH, ME LITTLE FLOURY POPS! RUINED AND BE-DUNGED AND SPOILED BE-YOND ATING BY THAT LITTLE CROOKED-LEGGED EEJIT, OUTSIDE!'

The little man went into a spasm of giggling.

'It's dropped anchor in her potatoes,' he managed to gasp out, being hardly able to breathe. Controlling himself with an effort as tears of merriment started out of his eyes, he called out to the best of his ability and breath:

'*That'll* teach you not to ate my dinner!'

'OH, ME TWO LOVELY DINNERS! ONE BE-SPIT-TLED AND ONE BE-TURDLED! WHAT'S GOT INTO YOU TODAY, CORNY, YE SPARSE LITTLE MORSEL OF NOTHING MUCH?'

'Mutiny—is what go into me today, Hannah—and that's the top and bottom of it, so it is,' he finished as though in some doubt.

'Mutiny, is it? The top and bottom of it, is it? That's what *you* think, my lad!'

From inside the cottage, there was a ferocious commotion of bustling about, punctuated by Hannah bellowing words like: 'DUNG,' and: 'FLOURY POPS,' and: 'DESTROYED'.

A succession of objects were flung out of the cottage in rapid flight and with an amazing frequency, all aimed to flatten Corny to the back of beyond. The aim was as direct as the intention; but Corny took to leaping and dodging and dancing about, so that he was always two jumps sideways or upwards, ahead of Hannah's ill-wishes. Fire-irons, pots of geraniums, jars of jam, a pot of cold porridge, three heavy hob-nailed boots, a biscuit tin, a sack of potatoes, a sack of flour, two duck eggs, a wild-eyed screeching cat that landed on its four feet and ran away, and a linen bag full of washing, came flying out the door.

On seeing the washing, Corny gave a cry of exultation and snatched it up. He tipped the contents out on the ground and rummaged through the pile of clothes.

'Me Sunday britches and dry as a bone! he cried victoriously.

With the slickness of a trout darting for concealment, he vanished behind the tree and pulled them on, bobbing out again almost immediately, now fully dressed.

'Come on,' he said, 'before she roars at me to mangle a blanket, for she has a mouth like a bucket and a voice that could be summonsed for assault and battery.'

'We heard her shouting,' Brigit reminded him.

'You didn't. That was only a hint.'

He led them to the back of the cottage where a broad lane shuttled away from them in a flat twisting ribbon. It went from side to side as though lazily curious about everything of interest in its surroundings.

215

'She's a bit strange, that Hannah,' Brigit remarked.

'She is,' he answered genially. At once he threw a quick look back over his shoulder, to make sure that he was safe: 'She's a quare number, all right.'

'What is she really like?'

Pidge gave her a nudge to behave herself but she shrugged away from him. She felt a curious sort of admiration for this unusual and powerful woman.

'Didn't you see her after me?'

'Only for a few seconds. You can't see much in a few seconds. She looked a bit big.'

'A bit big, you say? She is big enough to stagger a yak. She is so big, that I stole her bedsocks the other day while she was out admiring a daisy; and I trawled a lake with one of them and landed eleven pike, twenty-eight trout and half a water-logged tree. I threw that back. With the other one, I covered a rick of straw against the wind whipping it away and I had enough left over to make a new tarred skin for a boat and blankets for four pairs of stepping mares. She is the type of lady that is Anger and Strength in men's boots; and every washday, she has a burly mind. She is an extremely gorgeous dancer. She dances so fast—that she nearly puts knots in her legs. The steps she uses in her footwork are sure ankle-breakers for anyone at all but herself. It would give you cramps in your stomach to watch her doing her Advanced Slip Jig and everything about her is written on her face, as if it was a headstone.'

'Go on,' Brigit said cheekily, 'you're only bragging!'

Corny roared with laughter and Pidge joined in with him.

'If you ever saw her doing her experimental version of The Blackbird, you wouldn't doubt me. But I might be doing her a great wrong overpraising her like that, with regard to her size.'

Pidge was on the verge of laughing at this, thinking it was a joke; but he saw that Corny was being serious.

'How did she get so big? Is she one of the ones who ate up all their crusts?' Brigit asked.

'To see her eat,' Corny began dramatically, 'would raise a nervous rash on a Dowager. She'll put more than a hundred-weight of boiled spuds on the table for the dinner. Half the time, I can't find me cap for potato skins and I often get colds in the head from it, so I do.'

'She sounds very greedy.'

'Brigit!' Pidge said, making his voice sound cross.

'It's all right—she is only practising her profession. The young want to know everything,' Corny said, with a wave of his hand. 'Hannah is not greedy but hungry. She could ate a side of beef in a sandwich and pull down a tree to ate the top of it, like an elephant. She is nearly as hungry as fire, which is the hungriest thing on land.'

'Is it?' Pidge said, wondering about wolves with sharp teeth and hyenas and jackals, whose very nature seemed to be hunger.

'You may say it is. Haven't you ever seen flames licking their red lips as they consume all before them? Fire is so hungry that the more it is fed, the bigger its appetite grows. Other things can be gratified, but not fire. And the sea is all this and more.'

'Do you really mean that Hannah is nearly that hungry?' Brigit asked, disbelieving.

'I do. And signs on it, because of her appetite, she is nearly as strong as water.'

'Water?' Brigit said, her voice rising in scorn. 'Water isn't strong.'

'I don't believe you're serious but if you are, you're wrong. Water is so strong, it can wear away rocks and shift mountains. Don't you know well, that one man can tame a horse but it takes hundreds or even thousands to spancel water? If a country was a person, the rivers and streams would be its veins with all its life's blood in them. Even when it is harnessed it is never tamed. It can light up cities and turn wheels and if it gets free and throws itself at a town, it can wipe out life like chalk on a slate. It can do all of that; but the sea can do all that, and more.'

'Is she really that powerful?' Pidge asked.

'She is *nearly* that strong, and that's why I'm glad to get out from under her feet while she's washing; you wouldn't know the unlucky moment when she might give a person a belt. Still, she's not the worst, Old Hannah.'

'We know that—we've met the worst,' Brigit said airily.

Except for a very slight flickering smile, Corny appeared to take no notice of this information.

217

'Does she often fight you?' she then asked.

'She does. Every washday without fail. It's a fixture.'

'Does she often be washing?'

'Yes. She is very fond of bubbles—that's why. She forgets everything when she has a cloud of bubbles round her head that she listens to as if they were gossip; and she goes dreamy and that always makes dinner a movable feast and that makes me mad. So, I say things that I know will make her mad. There are three things not to be said to a Hannah on a washday and I nearly always say them; making sure first that I'm near the door for a quick escape, but sometimes she's ready for me and catches me all the same.'

'What are they?' asked Pidge.

'They are: "You're not washing these, I'm wearing them", "Isn't me dinner ready, yet?", and "It looks like rain, I'm thinking".'

'Is she a good runner?' Brigit wondered.

'She is nearly as fast as air when it conceits itself into a wind, and only the sea is faster than that, when it has a finger touching one place and runs in shivers to the far side of the world, to nudge another country with its big toe, at the same time. Only the sea can go that fast and run in three directions at once. Hannah is nearly as fast as the wind—and that's not bad.'

By this time they had travelled a fair way along the twisting road. Every now and then, Pidge stole a look behind and was delighted every time not to see the hounds. He was just thinking how lucky they had been to meet the earwig army, when from somewhere behind them, Hannah let a bawl out of her that shook the leaves on the trees:

'WHERE'S ME BEDSOCKS? WHO'S GOT ME BED-SOCKS? WHEN I CATCH YOU, CORNY—I'LL GIVE YOU WHAT LARRY GAVE THE DRUM!'

A nervous look came into sudden possession of Corny's face. He looked wildly around him for a few frantic seconds, as if thinking that there *might* be a best way to run, and then with a quick, apologetic shrug of his shoulders, he answered with his feet and was gone like a hare.

Hannah came thumping along the road.

Every thumping step she took made the trees shiver and the

218

ground tremble. Now and again a few stones fell off the walls of the fields.

As she came closer, they saw that she was gigantic and that her face was lovely; and before Pidge could restrain her Brigit shouted out:

'Have you got fat blood?'

As she drew near, she seemed so vast that the children panicked and sprang apart to be safe from her boots; and standing on either side of the road, they watched her approaching.

She was a big, beefy, brawny, heavy block of a woman and she came along the road like a ship in full sail. Her dress spread itself out behind her, held up by the slip-stream of her speed, and it snapped and rapped in the wind, for she moved very fast indeed.

When she was almost upon them, she smiled and her whole face was lit up by it; and it was an outward sign of inward grace, as the catechism used to say.

When she was level she bent down and without breaking her stride, she scooped them up in her mighty arms, that were streaked with soap-bubbles, as if they were no more than bags of feathers. And it was gently done.

'He's grown deaf to roaring,' she observed softly, and she leaped over a wall in rigorous pursuit of Corny, who seemed remarkably fast himself.

So she ran for many a mile, skilfully avoiding bushes and trees, until at length, Corny reached the bank of a wide quick river, where he doubled back by skirting round a triangular patch of rowan trees.

When Hannah reached the river bank, she shrugged off her boots without laces, crouched for a second with her knees up under her chin, and, with one powerful spring, she smashed onto the opposite bank. She landed with two loud swatting noises from her great bare feet, on a sloping sheet of naked granite that spread a good length in, from where it lipped the river.

Placing the children carefully on the ground, she almost patted them each on the head with a spade-like hand, but stopped within an inch of touching them. Then she took a mighty leap back, performing a cunning twist while still in the air, so that she landed with the two feet back inside the boots, without disturbing them from their position on the ground. She dipped her hands in the river and worked up a lather of suds. With her hands cupped to her mouth, she blew a sheaf of bubbles across to the children, before turning to run in amazing bounds as she chased Corny again.

They saw him go over a hill and out of view. When Hannah reached the crest of the hill, she stood poised for a moment against the sky, turning to give them a wave before she vanished.

The bubbles had gathered in clusters about their heads.

One after another they began to pop. As each bubble burst in quick succession a ripple of words was released. They sounded like the tremble of crystals on a chandelier hanging in the way of a fingering draught; and they said:

'Olc-Glas-is-safely-held-in-deep-waters-guarded-and-watched-night-and-day-by-one-hundred-of-the-most-savage-pike-in-Ireland-Their-bodies-swaying-in-dark-water-they-are-a-ring-of-yellow-eyes-that-stare-without-pity-or-one-moment's-neglect-And-The-Lord-Of-The-Waters-neither-eats-nor-sleeps-and-is-supreme-over-this-and-most-excellent-guardian-of-all-'

All but one of the bubbles burst and that one drifted away.

At this news Pidge and Brigit threw delighted looks at each other and danced up and down, giving each other many quick hugs of pure happiness.

They sang when they resumed their journey.

They had come closer to the mountains and the hounds were far behind.

Chapter 15

RAIN came.
It washed everything it touched and the hounds were in disorder because of it.

By now they had reached the place in the little winding road where Pidge and Brigit had leaped apart; and with noses that were swollen, they were puzzling at the tracks of Hannah's boots.

'Is it not enough,' Fowler said wearily, 'that we lose the scent of the young pups and find the strange scent of Some Other but that rain must fall to baffle us further?'

'Be silent,' said Greymuzzle.

'Is it not enough,' Fowler insisted, 'that we are beaten on the head by the wands of The Mórrígan whenever the path is not clear; that we are attacked without mercy by a hosting of crazed insects—but that the rain has to fall and increase our troubles?'

'Hush,' Greymuzzle advised again, 'speak no treason.'

'Our lives are miserable,' Fowler said, sighing deeply.

'Be silent. The Great Queen may hear,' Silkenskin said, shivering.

'She listens not—for we are in the midst of sound; all around us, things make their natural noise. Do we not well know that when The Mórrígan listens, her ears suck up all the sounds of the earth, so great is her attention to the thing that she wishes to hear?'

'Even so—in silence there is wisdom,' Greymuzzle said, adding reverently; 'We lie under The Great Queen's hand and through her grandeur, our rank is very high, unlike others of our kind who call all men "Master" no matter how lowly these masters may be.'

Fowler made no reply.

Under Findepath's orders, they resumed their search. They

fanned out across the countryside like the spokes in a segment of a wheel. Leaping a wall where necessary and allowing nothing to hinder them, they cast about the ground meticulously for the merest whiff on grass or stone or leaf, that would be as a signpost to them, showing the way that Pidge and Brigit had gone.

Chapter 16

THERE was a faint air of annoyance in the glasshouse.
It lurked behind The Mórrígan's face.

It was hidden behind a pink and white mask that she had moulded her face into, as if she were made of pale plasticines. She had made her face assume a kind of perfection in which her eyelids were smooth and oval like white sugared almonds and her mouth was a faultless rosebud. Mingled with her annoyance, there was a flickering amusement that she could look so horribly pretty. It was a way of enjoying herself, while she passed the time. She thought that she looked disgusting.

She took an object from her bracelet and set it down a little way ahead of Pidge and Brigit, as they walked.

Melodie Moonlight who was wearing her limp and exhausted shadow scarf-like around her neck, smiled when she saw the object and made some strange passes in the air.

'We will see if The Dagda is strong inside one of our toys,' she said.

Her nose wrinkled to show deep revulsion, Breda Fairfoul was scratching behind her ear with a pencil, as she looked from her textbooks to her flasks and from her flasks to a row of assorted rats. They were sitting on her bench, polishing their faces and whiskers, and they were all quite beautiful. They smelled of lavender.

'You are all quite repulsive,' she told them and with a snap of her fingers, she made them vanish.

She left off her Scientific Work for the moment and she too made some strange passes in the air.

The Mórrígan sneezed.

Out from the dark crimson caves of her dainty nostrils came twin jets of darkish air that turned into long billowing clouds, graphite grey. They spread out and formed a thick canopy over the whole area now reached by Brigit and Pidge.

With a shiver, Brigit looked at the sky. The whole atmosphere of the day had altered and everything had become dark and dreary.

'Is there going to be more lightning?'

'It looks like it,' Pidge said, his heart going nervous as he thought of the blackened walls at the Field Of The Maines.

In the sudden gloom, the trees were gaunt and queer-looking and they rustled loudly as the wind came up. Trees are the worst possible places to shelter under, he reminded himself; I'm not going to do anything silly like that again.

The sky went even darker, turning to black by the second. All about them, the shadows thickened until everywhere was murky without any light at all.

He felt that he sensed something brooding and threatening in the dismal gloom. Even the day smells were gone as well as the sunshine and now there were the damp, earthy smells of the night. It's just the waiting, he told himself; waiting for the lightning to start. Still, his eyes darted everywhere in case he *really* sensed something else.

'It's going to rain soon, isn't it; hard enough to put cracks in our heads,' Brigit grumbled.

'We'll just have to put up with it, unless we find somewhere safe to shelter,' he said firmly.

He looked to try and see if the hounds were visible anywhere, but it was too dark to really see anything.

'We won't run, no matter how bad it gets; right, Brigit?'

'Right!'

By now it was difficult to see where they were going and they stumbled at times over uneven ground and tripped over roots and stones. The wind began to moan, a low and very lonesome sound, that gradually increased in strength to a savage howl.

Brigit was shaking and she held on to Pidge tightly, saying every few seconds:

'What's that!'

And each time Pidge answered as steadily as he could manage:

'Only the wind, don't worry.'

224

Up above the heavy clouds billowed and wreathed and seemed to boil. The sky split apart briefly and a horrid yellowish light shone through, and for a few seconds they could see that ahead of them there was the ruin of a building. The clouds snarled together mightily and the ruin was completely swallowed by darkness. Pidge tried to keep his gaze fixed on the place where it had appeared. No matter how rickety it might be, it could provide some shelter. The blanket overhead was torn aside once more, allowing a shaft of the same ugly light to shine through; and this time, they saw it quite clearly.

Sticking up into the sky, and looking like an old broken and blackened tooth, stood the remains of a castle or a tower.

The darkness returned and was as a cloak between themselves and all that lay beyond a mere couple of feet or so ahead of them. Pidge started to worry that they might fall into a squashy, muddy hole, or a quaking, swallowing bog. In this blackness, it would be terrible and dreadful. Who would help them out if they got stuck? If they were up to their shoulders held fast in the sucking ground, with lightning flashes coming at them like spears of fire, they would be utterly helpless, no better than sitting targets; they could even be killed.

Even without the fearful lightning, there was the danger that they might be swallowed. His thoughts ran wild and he imagined the earth as a monstrous animal with many, many concealed mouths; and he feared it. He thought of mouths, all of them capable of opening under their feet without warning, to swallow them down a muddy gullet into a heaving prison of a stomach. At the back of his mind, he knew that it was all nonsense. All of his life he had been familiar with bogland. Each spring he had gone to help with the turf-cutting and returned in late summer to help cart the dry fuel home. Their own bogland was a place that was heathery and springy, with harmless patches of wetness and straight-edged pools of brown water, that had filled where the turf had been cut. It was a place for picnics, where he had eaten huge amounts of sandwiches because the air always made people very hungry, and he had drunk hot tea poured from bottles that had been heated up cleverly by his father near little fires, without ever having cracked even one of the bottles. The worst that could happen to a person, if unlucky enough to fall into a water-filled cutting, was wet clothes, and that was all.

But now this knowledge was reduced to a weak spark of truth. It was smothered under the weight of his fear, and quenched entirely when he remembered old stories of horror told round the fireside on winter evenings. A shudder ran crookedly up through his body from the soles of his feet; for perhaps bogs in other townlands were more treacherous, and this one could be like the ones in the old stories. Every step became a nightmare of courage. Clinging on to him, and without the slightest idea of what he was thinking, Brigit was mainly worried that she might see a ghost or a Banashee.

'If I do, I'll fling a rock at it!' she said loudly to frighten them off.

Pidge didn't even hear.

The atmosphere was now unutterably evil and terrible. It could hardly be believed that everything had been so splendid such a little while ago.

If only Cathbad the Druid were with us, he thought, bowed down as he was beneath the feeling that he was alone and miserable, and burdened with the care of Brigit as well as himself.

Then underneath the crying of the wind, they began to pick up sounds that were very faint and blown about at first. They stopped moving and listened intently in an effort to find out where they were coming from; and then they were greatly astonished as they realized that they were hearing snatches of music and what might be bursts of revelry with shouts of laughter, rather muffled by distance and battered into bits by the wind.

Oh, how wonderful! There are people here somewhere, Pidge thought.

When they happened on to a paved path and the dread of blundering on to a patch of treacherous ground was gone, he felt even more cheered. Now he kept his head down and watched the path under his feet, for fear of straying away from it in the darkness.

Seconds later, there was a sudden rolling and rumbling of thunder, so loud that it seemed to be right on top of them; and then one flash of lightning. For a moment only, the quality of

the light was stunning, and, looking up in the queer brightness, he saw a castle showing lights.

'Brigit, look! It wasn't a ruin at all. They've put the lights on
now and it's easy to see how fine it is. With any luck at all,
they'll let us stand in until the weather clears.'

But Brigit started pulling at him and shouting that they were
in a whole field of nettles.

'Stingers!' she yelled. 'Stingers everywhere! Oh, I hate them
more than anything in the world!'

Nettles were Brigit's deadliest enemies. Just seeing one,
would always made the hairs rise in coldness on her arms. She
never missed a chance of beheading them and splashing them
down to bits with a stick.

Pidge couldn't understand how they had wandered in
among them without noticing them or getting stung. He
supposed it was because he had been so distracted with
thinking about everything else, and that it was sheer luck that
Brigit hadn't brushed against one in the darkness. He was
mystified to find that they were surrounded, but for the way
forward. It was the only way they could go. The nettles were
even growing behind them, without any sign of having been
walked on. There was just a little bit of path and then, nettles;
so it was certain that they could not go back the way they had
come. He supposed as well that he and Brigit had followed an
imperceptible turn in the pathway, that couldn't be noticed
now as he looked back.

'Do you want a pick-a-back?' he offered, knowing much she
hated being burned and blistered, and how very bare her legs
were with just ankle socks.

'That would only make my legs stick out more at the sides.
If you keep in front of me, I'll be all right. Oh, I wish I had a
good old stick to flatten them, so I do,' she finished furiously.

The nettle-flanked path led them to a pair of imposing iron
gates that were opened wide. Inside there was a driveway with,
on either side, two great stone lions whose manes were carved
ornamentally to look like flames. The driveway made Pidge
wonder if the pathway outside might once have been a proper
road, before the nettles had conquered it.

'This is better,' said Brigit as they walked along. 'All the old
stingers are on the outside, now.'

A short distance in, there stood two boards with painted notices and Pidge struggled to read them in the poor light. Each one was headed by a coat-of-arms, so dim in the gloom that they could barely be seen. The notices, however, were in white on black, so Pidge was able to make them out, although it was difficult.

He read the nearest one, which said:

CASTLE DURANCE
POSH HOSTELRY·TRAVELLER'S JOY
NO ROGUES, RASCALS OR SCALLYWAGS ADMITTED
ALL BREAKAGES MUST BE PAID FOR LATE CABARET
JOLLY SINGING AND DANCING HARPISTS
AND SOPRANOS: (will sing requests)
TOE DANCING TROUPE (from PARIS)
BOOZE in DORMITORIES NOT ALLOWED

They went to the second board and Pidge read it out:

WORLD FAMOUS CASTLE DURANCE
B&B
TERMS VERY MODERATE FOR TOURISTS, HIKERS & RAMBLERS
(No pedestrians unless on business)
School Parties catered for Baths EXTRA
FINE WINES • DRYING FACILITIES • HORSE RIDING
SAUSAGE ROLLS • NO HAWKERS • HAM SANDWICHES
Français Parleyed DEUTSCH SPRACKENED
ITALIANO PARLEYAMOED
Reg: Irish Tourist Board (Bord Failte)
TRADESMEN'S ENTRANCE ROUND the BACK

And there was a note pinned to it that said:

Milkman
50 pints
please
& a dozen
eggs.

Pidge hesitated. He felt very uneasy, but he knew that there
was no real choice for him to make, when it was so terrible
outside.

'What are we waiting for; this sounds a great place. Come
on!' Brigit said and she began walking on ahead of him.

He tried to look back to where the gates and the lions were,
only to find that even they could not be seen, it had grown so
dark. The sky rumbled again and there was the crack of lightning. Brigit ran back and clung to him.

'Hurry up, Pidge; before we get sizzled!' she shouted.

They stumbled along the seemingly endless avenue to the
castle. When they were close to it at last, they stopped to read a
third notice that was very small and just said:

PEOPLE WHO PEDESTER HERE
DO SO ON PAIN OF MEASLES

'What does that mean?' Brigit asked.

'I don't know; unless they don't like it if people come in just to
look around,' Pidge answered, his voice tinged with suspicion.

'It's only a joke. They sound funny to me. I want to get inside,
away from all this horribleness.'

'What else can we do,' he answered, feeling helpless.

They passed by many windows with the glow of lights
behind rich red curtains making the place look inviting and
warm. And then they reached a great door. It was massive and
clasped by iron bands that were fixed to the wood with rivets.
Hard to break into, Pidge thought; and hard to break out of,
too, I would guess.

There was no way to knock except with knuckles, and that
would be like trying to rap at an ordinary door with a feather.

229

A large shield was attached to the wall by the side of the door. An old sword hung beside it, held by means of two strong nails driven into the stone just under the hilt. Brigit looked at it with curiosity.

'Where are we, Pidge? Are we in days of yore?'

'We might be. I don't know.'

As they stood there, the sounds of fun and laughter increased.

Then Brigit saw a gleam of white on the ground. She stooped and picked up a printed card and handed it to Pidge. He felt even more uneasy when he saw her stooped to pick it up; but he didn't know why. He held the card close to his face, peering hard to make it out.

'It says: "Bang For Attention",' he said.

'Bang what?'

'The shield, I think. With the sword.'

'Oh, I suppose they didn't have doorbells in those days,' Brigit said knowingly. 'Can you do it, Pidge?'

'I can try.'

He reached for the heavy sword with both hands, and after a struggle he detached it from its perch. It took all of his strength to aim a blow at the shield. He just about managed it and then jumped with alarm at a very loud crashing noise that leaped out from the shield and rang about their ears.

'What a clout!' Brigit shouted admiringly, as it died away. Now that they were almost in shelter and well away from the nettles, she was feeling more like herself.

When the crashing noise had gone entirely, there was silence from within, but only for a second or two; and when the sounds of merriment started up again, they weren't nearly as loud or as lively as before. I expect we've given them all a bit of a shock, Pidge thought.

The door then swung open easily and without one squeak. It reminded him of something but he couldn't think what exactly, as his attention was drawn to a lady who was advancing to attend to them along the broad passageway inside.

Chapter 17

THE lady was wearing a long, grey dress; tight in the bodice and sleeves, but hanging in folds from the hips. Her hair was trained back from her pale and narrow face, into a top-knot that was skewered into a tight twist from which not one single hair could spring free. Around her waist was a long, corded girdle or belt, with bunches of keys on big, round rings, that dangled as she walked. Some of the keys were big, some were medium. There was one massive key that swung all by itself. Pidge thought that she might be in fancy dress.

Before he had the chance to explain anything, she was talking.

'Ah, here they are at last—the stragglers,' she said. 'What happened to you that you are so late? All of the others on the Charity Walk have beaten you to it and arrived ages ago. We had quite given you up. You'll want some supper, of course, and a warm of the fire. This way. Follow me.'

'If you please,' Pidge said urgently, 'we are not the stragglers. We are not with anyone else. We only want to shelter.'

But she didn't seem to hear.

'You're the last ones expected tonight. You only just made it, you know. Now we can bolt and bar the doors. Otherwise we'll be having burglars, sneak-thieves and prowlers, or even horrid pedestrians, in on top of us without the courtesy of an advance booking, which is a Rule of the House; and that would never do. So vulgar, the way those ghastly pedestrians drop toffee papers and pry through the curtains!'

Pidge said his piece again more loudly. It wasn't any use at all.

The lady had a singular dignity of voice and manner. It was nice to listen to her, even when she said:

'You won't want The Tour tonight, I know; but I'll just mention that this door we are now passing, leads to the dungeons. Down there are the red-hot pincers, the rack and the grid-iron; and other items common to an old-fashioned gymnasium. It's where we take people who don't pay their bills. They are glad enough to cough up, when they see our collection of thumb-screws and toe-squeezers and nose-reformers and such. Any pedestrians we manage to nab, go down there, too. That's a joke!,' she finished, without any humour at all.

She led them up a broad flight of four wide steps and on into the Great Hall. They had never been inside a castle before and they looked about them with interest. From the depth of the window recesses, Pidge judged the walls to be about six feet thick. Suits of armour stood sort of loitering against the stone walls, their well-polished gleam making them seem like superior corner-boys well spruced-up. Secured in some way high up on the walls were shields, battle-axes and spears. Even higher up were poles sticking out horizontally, with flags or banners hanging down dead still.

They've kept it all very well, Pidge thought. Brigit was charmed by the grandeur.

'Come along, don't dawdle,' the lady said.

They followed her.

Some people were in having supper or some other meal and they were sitting in companies of five or six at heavy, wooden tables, each group being distinctly apart and separate from another. Family parties or friends, Pidge thought.

'You can sit here,' the lady said, putting them at a little table meant for two people.

'Excuse me,' Pidge said loudly.

'Miss!' Brigit shouted.

Everyone else in the room turned and looked at them briefly before going back to their own affairs.

'Excuse me. We only want to shelter for a while. We are not the stragglers; and we are not pedestrians either . . . only hikers, who have lost their way,' Pidge said quickly.

But she had her back to them during the first words that they said and she was not listening; and during the rest of Pidge's explanation, she was already on her way to somewhere else.

'It's no use talking to her, she's as deaf as a boiled egg,' Brigit said.

232

They sat for a while.

'What are we waiting for, Pidge?' Brigit wondered in the end.

'I don't know, maybe the cabaret—that's singing and dancing and harps and so on. Someone might come along in a minute who will listen to us and we can explain everything.'

'Is there going to be a dinner-dance? What's a dinner-dance?'

'I don't know. Perhaps. I'm not really sure what a dinner-dance is, exactly.'

'I believe I'll have a glass of champagne.'

'You will not! You're not to ask for it or anything at all, Brigit, please. We can't pay the prices they might charge in a castle. We could end up in prison.'

'Or the dungeon.'

'She said that was a joke.'

'It's all right. I'm not hungry or thirsty. I couldn't swallow a crumb.'

'Neither could I, luckily.'

While they were waiting for whatever it was to happen, they looked about them again.

The room was lit by many thick candles in chandeliers made of spiky iron and there were a good many more in branched candlesticks placed on various surfaces. The best light of all came from the great cave of a fireplace, where enormous logs burned. At a table nearby, some men wearing what looked like anoraks, with oddly, the hoods up, were drinking wine poured from dark, green bottles that were labelled Ruby and Tawny; and they ate meat from platters. The hoods kept their faces in shadow but Pidge knew that they were not the hounds because they were all rather broad and dumpy.

Despite the number of candles and the glare from the fire, it wasn't really easy to see anyone very clearly, since the lights seemed to create unusually deep shadows around what seemed an abnormally short radius. It was all a bit like a vast dark stage lit by hundreds of spotlights that were brilliant but small.

At the far side of the room, some others were rattling boxes and throwing dice, breaking the silence a few times with loud cries of excitement as the dice fell and rolled; and with louder shouts for refreshment. They seemed to be calling for knucklebones to suck and gnaw; but Pidge could not be sure of that: unless, he said to himself, they are rugby players showing off.

He fancied that there were many furtive and sneaky looks in their direction from the groups of people sitting in their colonies, eating and drinking and from time to time huddling together to whisper. And even with the occasional burst of exuberance from the crowd that was at dicing, there was an air of puzzling surliness throughout the whole room. Not what I had expected after that notice about the jolly singing and dancing, he thought. It seemed that what had been festive had gone unfestive; something about giving a Good Example, he decided, feeling that it would have been a lot of fun, if they didn't.

There was a sudden loud banging and they both turned automatically to look towards the place it had come from, wondering what had caused it. It could have been a thunder-ball, the way everything had shaken and shuddered at its force. In a very little time, however, they realized that it was only the door being shut and barred for the night, when they saw a man who had a peculiar shape, coming into the Great Hall. He walked to the lady who was standing close-by now and handed her the enormous key that had been dangling from her girdle, earlier.

For a moment, she held the great key in her hands.

Brigit muttered that everyone looked odd and crazy and Pidge whispered that he thought it might be fancy dress.

They heard the lady say that now all was well, that the last of the Charity Walkers, who were proper little stragglers, were about to have their supper and that they were to be put in the Bloody Turret on their own when they'd finished, so as not to disturb the ones already asleep in the dormitories. The man with the strange shape listened and nodded. Then he went off somewhere and she went somewhere else.

When they turned back to the table they found to their dismay that someone had quietly come and served them some supper while they were not looking. Two warm covered dishes were set before them, and a tray with silver-plated tea things, with a pot of hot tea and a lidded jug with hot water. They looked all around them for someone to take it all away; someone who would listen to what they wanted to explain; but

234

there wasn't anyone serving anywhere, and the groups of guests had stopped sneaking looks at them and appeared entirely indifferent.

'It may be that they will let us wash-up in the morning to pay for the beds if we haven't enough money; but we'd better not even touch the food,' Pidge said.

'It makes me feel sick to think of eating,' Brigit answered. 'But I don't see why we should do their washing-up. I'm for skipping off early, while they are all asleep. It's not our fault that she wouldn't listen, is it? And think of all the washing-up for this crowd and the others who are already in bed. No thanks!'

'Well, I might have enough to pay for the beds; we'll see. If they don't ask too much, that is.'

While they were wondering what to do, Pidge picked up a dead moth that was lying in a crack in the wood of the table and found that his fingers were covered in gold. Nothing unusual about that; but it gave him a peculiar feeling as it seemed to feel icy on his skin, and that was a strange thing to feel from a little dead moth.

From the gloom at the far end of the room, they saw the man with the queer shape coming towards them. He had a large, squat body and short skinny legs.

His head rested directly on his shoulders without any neck at all to raise it up. He was a bit like a two-legged crab. Pidge felt sure that what he *really* was, could not be seen; and that he was probably very skinny but was wearing some kind of framework made of cardboard or wire underneath his clothes, for a fancy dress. It was better to feel sure of that, than to believe he was really as outlandish as he appeared; Pidge pushed aside the unwelcome thoughts about wicked dwarfs that niggled in the back of his mind.

The man stood by the table and gestured at the food.

Pidge stammered and explained everything again. The man just shrugged as much as he was able, as if he didn't understand or even hear what Pidge was saying. He gestured to his mouth.

Does that mean that he can't speak, or that he wants us to eat? Pidge wondered. Once again he explained it all and finished by saying that they were not at all hungry.

235

'WE ARE ON A DIET!' Brigit said distinctly in her loudest voice, adding more normally: 'For Charity.'

The man tried to shrug again and indicated that they should follow him. He took them to a small door, which he opened to show a narrow flight of twisting stone steps; worn down in the middle from centuries of feet. Light shone down from somewhere unseen up above. The man stood aside to allow them to go ahead and they went up, Brigit with curiosity and Pidge with the creeps.

At last they came to an open door that led into a small room and they saw that here was the source of the light. The stairs spiralled on past the door and although not entirely sure that this was where they were supposed to go, Pidge stepped into the room and Brigit followed him.

It was a cosy wood-panelled chamber with a blazing fire, a window with' thick curtains and two small four-poster beds with hangings drawn. By the rosy fire, there were two high-backed, comfortable chairs, each with its own little footstool worked in tapestry. The bare boards of the floor were as rich as satin and reflected in their polish the restless flames of the fire.

When they turned round to thank him and to try once more to explain, the man had gone and the door was closed; again, without a creak or a squeak. A memory was nudging at Pidge but it didn't get the chance to come forward in his mind, for at that moment a blazing log fell from the fire landing dangerously close to one of the footstools. He hurried to lift it back with a pair of tongs that hung with other fire-irons from a bracket on the wall.

'This room is a little dote,' Brigit said admiringly.

'It's very hot though.'

He took off his jacket and parting the hangings on one of the beds, he laid it inside on the quilt, prudently removing the scrying-glass and the bag of nuts, before letting the hangings drop back into place.

'Should we go to bed, Pidge? I'm dying to snuggle in behind those curtains.'

'No. When we are sure that everyone is asleep, we'll creep downstairs and go. We don't really owe anything unless they charge for just sitting down; so that'll be all right. I'll just open the door a crack so we can listen and when it's all quiet, we'll clear off.'

But when he examined the door there was no way of opening it; there wasn't a knob or a latch; there was only a keyhole. He tried to prize it open, grasping with the tips of his fingers for a purchase between the door and the doorframe; but it was hopeless.

Horrified, he remembered the signpost at the crossroads and the silent way it had spun, and the great door downstairs that had opened without even the faintest sound, and now this door that had closed so very quietly.

'We are locked in,' he said miserably.

Chapter 18

'WHAT?' shouted Brigit. 'They've locked us in?'
    'It's true! We've been tricked and it's all my fault,' Pidge answered bitterly.
'Try the window!'

They ran to the curtains and pulled them back. There *was* a window. Pidge had begun to fear that behind the curtains they would find only a stone wall.

It was shut fast. No matter how hard he struggled with it, it wouldn't budge. Outside, it was still dark, without even one friendly star to wink at them from lonely space. From far away came a sound like a woman crying or laughing in the wind. Bad as it was outside, it now looked a far, far better place to be.

He rushed to the fireplace and grabbed the tongs and ran to batter at the glass with his whole strength. The tongs bounced back from every stroke with the glass not even marked.

They went to the fireplace and looked up the chimney, thinking that if the fire died down, there might be a way to climb out. The sides were smooth and unbroken; there was no way out.

He shook the scrying-glass.

When the flurrying snow had cleared, all that could be seen was some kind of old ruin, and though they waited for a while, nothing else happened. He tossed the glass ball on to a chair and feverishly took a hazel nut from the bag and held it on his outstretched palm.

They waited, almost eating it with their eyes.

Nothing happened.

'We're done for,' Pidge said, throwing himself down in one of the chairs with his head in his hands: 'Where is The Dagda?'

In the silence that followed there was only the sound of the fire; a half-burned log falling in on itself, quietly hissing and

238

settling softly; and then, incredibly, from inside one of the canopied beds came a small snore.

Shocked, he cried out:

'Who's there?'

Another snore.

Again silence.

Anger flooded into Pidge, for now to crown everything, it seemed that they were being mocked.

Shouting: 'We'll soon see!' he bounded to the bed, with Brigit as his defiant shadow, and he snatched back the curtains.

The bed was unoccupied but for his jacket lying where he had left it.

'Who was snoring?' Brigit demanded belligerently.

'What's all the fuss?' a sleepy voice asked and to their joy, Cluas crawled out from under the collar of the jacket. He reared himself up and rubbed at his eyes sleepily.

'Hallo, where are we; are we at me Ma's yet?' he inquired. And when he had properly woken up and looked around, asked: *'What's this place? How did we get here? I must have dozed off; why didn't you wake me?'*

'A most terrible thing has happened,' Pidge began, while picking up his jacket, and putting it back on, and holding the hazel nut in his clenched fist all of the time. Rushing his words together, he told of the terrible darkness and the lightning and how they had been led into this trap. As he unfolded his story, he concentrated on giving the exact details of how they had been tricked; and tried hard not to burst out with how he had been feeling while they had stumbled along so helplessly. He thought it best that Brigit should not know; but it was very hard to keep still about it. He grew distracted as well, when he thought of how easily he had been sniggled, for if ever there was a sniggle, surely this was it. And, absorbed as he was in the telling, when he opened his fist and glanced at the nut, he put it back into its bag and into his pocket, with only a small part of his mind taking care of this.

As soon as Cluas had understood everything, he said:

'Take me over to the door: I can get out underneath without any trouble and I'll have a scout around to find out what's what. Just be patient until I get back and don't worry.'

They sat on the floor while they waited. It seemed to take

ages and ages. As the time passed, Pidge continued to blame himself and he went back over everything again and again in his mind. He had even half-known that things weren't right with this castle and he had pushed his suspicions to the back of his mind. He thought himself a fool for doing it.

At last there was a slight scratching from outside and Cluas came back in under the door. He got on to Pidge's sleeve and walked up his arm.

'*You're trapped, all right; and that's not the worst of it,*' he said.

'What do you mean?' Brigit whispered, coming in close to Pidge.

'*I heard things and I didn't hear things; and the things I didn't hear were the worst of all. Firstly, that woman—The Wardress, for that's what she once was—is giggling to herself inside her head, because she's got you for someone she calls her Royal Boss. She is demented with joy and is cock-sure that her Royal Boss will reward her for nabbing you, by letting her off the hook, whatever that may mean. Then, the fella with the nice legs—something like mine but not as good—is sniggering inside his head; and is over the moon with glee, because you've been sweetly had and later on he's going to get the chance to practise his old skills. He plans to sneak in here when you are asleep and rob you of your thorn leaves, Brigit. He says they are a charm against lightning. They dare not touch your other belongings; but they are plotting to accuse you of being pedestrians and then drag you down to the dungeons for a bit of leg-pulling. He used to be a qualified torturer, you see. Oh, many's the foul deed that's been done here in the past! They mean to let you go in the end, although they wish they could keep you for pets. The Royal Boss is relying on you, it seems, to find that "honoured" pebble, because you've got innocent eyes and she hasn't. By the way, the food was drugged, so it's a good thing you didn't eat any of it.*'

Brigit's eyes were like saucers. Pidge looked very pale.

'What else?' he managed to ask after some moments when all was eerily quiet.

'*That was all; and this is what I find so strange—I tried every other head and there was nothing in them. But for the sound of far-away laughter like the noise of the sea in a sea-shell, they were as the dead. I climbed right inside one or two . . . . . excuse me—,*' he broke off in embarrassment.

240

'It's all right, don't stop,' Pidge said encouragingly.

'The brains were just like the kernels of walnuts, brown and shrunken and almost gone. And not even the echo of a soul; empty as husks. They were like dried flowers.'

'What are we going to do? What can we possibly do?' Pidge asked in despair.

'Goodness!' Cluas said, sounding very surprised. *'I should have told you that first of all. I can tumble the lock. It's easy.'*

'What? Can you?'

'Whatever would me Ma think of me if I couldn't do a simple thing like that!'

'Oh good,' Brigit muttered. 'Let them try and stop us after that!'

'No trouble at all; put me to the keyhole.'

Pidge pressed his knuckles against the keyhole and Cluas disappeared inside. Another minute and the door swung open as silently as it had closed and Cluas emerged from the lock on the outside of the door.

'Now say as loudly as ever you can that it's all a fraud and a sham and that you can see through it,' Cluas said casually, as he walked back onto Pidge's sleeve.

They shouted at the tops of their voices.

Immediately, there was the stench of decay.

'Run!' Cluas shouted, and they ran down the stairs.

Up above, the walls began to crumble; and even as they passed, the stones of the walls beside them were being covered in fungus and they became damp and discoloured and smelled rotten.

Pidge felt exultant and Brigit had a smile of pure triumph plastered right across her face.

'We've won! We've won!' she kept shouting.

Running through the Great Hall they saw that everything had gone to rags and tatters, that the furniture was worm-eaten and moisture-stained, and that the whole place was laced with dirty old webs and threads and covered in ancient dust that was as thick and clinging as grated cheese. Stinking pools of rusty, oily water had settled at the feet of the rotting suits of armour in a filthy, stagnant clotting.

They went through what was left of the Great Hall and out into the passage; and the four wide steps were crumbling

241

beneath their feet. Shocked, they saw ahead of them the rigid figures of the lady and the queerly-shaped man, standing before the huge door as if to bar the way. But even as they saw them, there was a fearful groaning sort of sound that might have come from the two people or from wooden beams on the point of collapsing—in his fever to escape, Pidge couldn't know which.

He snatched at Brigit's hand and they ran straight at the terrible pair without altering speed.

'Get out of the way!' he shouted.

Sighing, the huge door fell to sawdust and the solid walls fell apart into a gap and they were able to run round the figures that gleamed hideously into a kind of squalid, golden crust.

And then they were standing on green grass in clear daylight.

There was a muffled falling sound and for an instant they were surrounded by strange whispering.

On the ground a small object flashed briefly before vanishing away.

They stared at the spot where it had been, and daisies and dandelions were growing there. All of the strain left them; it went like a splinter of ice in the sun, as the castle in going took its terror with it.

In a vague way Pidge wondered if the people were trapped forever somewhere, still inside that dreadful ruin.

'I wonder why they were so evil?' he said.

'They must have been bad to begin with, and "Fire burns dry wood" is a true saying,' Cluas answered.

'We won, anyway,' Brigit said.

Before they walked away, Pidge looked for the hounds; but they were nowhere to be seen. We could run if we liked but I'm too tired—and if I'm too tired, Brigit must be as well, he thought.

In a while they found a track in the grass and followed it. Every step helped to make the memory of Castle Durance retreat in his mind to the safe distance between sleep and wakefulness, where a bad dream is first made reasonable and then quietly lost.

'It wasn't so bad, was it, Brigit?' he asked.

'The stingers were the worst of all.'

242

'What about all the rest?'

'A bit like a ghost train in a carnival,' she answered; and he knew that she was feeling all right, too.

The track brought them to a road that seemed to run ahead of them in a straight line to the mountains. Looking back every so often, they followed the road.

Presently they were able to run quite easily.

Chapter 19

BREDA Fairfoul was still sitting at her workbench; still pretending to be a Scientist.

What she was really doing was something very different. She was doing simple enchantments; partly to amuse herself and partly to pass the time. By now, she had decided that when it came to rats, she preferred the good old-fashioned kind, and in a blink, she was confronting several real-looking, greasy rats that stared back up at her, with yellow teeth bared and clever, watchful, distrusting eyes. The glasshouse had suddenly benefited not only from the smell of the rats themselves, but other scents that called up visions of dustbins and old, mouldy cellars and other places not to be mentioned.

The cat that had been so disgracefully used as a duster, started up in surprise. She growled, flickering her tail from side to side, and she glared passionately up at the workbench. Breda slanted a look at her and the cat slumped down and lay on the ground, where she went into a sort of trance that made all of her nature assert itself in the fixed stare of her eyes. Occasionally her jaws would open in a silent growl and she lashed her tail languidly at intervals.

Breda smiled at her rats and she gave them each a bit of tallow to eat. The tallow was nervously snatched out of her hands and swallowed in gulps. When it was all gone, she taught them how to chew tobacco and spit. After they got used to the way the tobacco burned the insides of their mouths, the rats began to enjoy it; but they still watched Breda with suspicion.

She discarded her cap, gown and the horn-rimmed glasses, and she made her scientific equipment disappear.

'I've done with all that jiggery-pokery,' she declared, and the rats looked remarkably relieved—although they still kept an eye on the suppressed cat.

Breda put on herself a green eyeshade and on the rats she put striped shirts with floppy bow ties, under wide-sleeved jackets with many pockets. A small, baize-covered table, with chairs on the same scale, appeared on the top of the workbench and all of the rats sat down. In front of her, Breda laid several decks of new, unopened playing-cards—she split one open, shuffled and dealt. She then gave lessons to the rats on how to play and cheat at poker.

As soon as they received them, the rats' cards shrank in size and they were able to grip them well in their strange hands. Whenever Breda touched a card, it grew back to its normal state; and all through the lessons, the cards never failed to expand or go small as they passed between her new friends and herself. The rats were really enjoying themselves now and they spat tobacco juice at the cat from time to time.

Melodie Moonlight had been pacing aimlessly around the glasshouse.

She drifted over to have a look.

'Little beauties—truly ratty,' she said admiringly. 'Let's hope they don't all get a nasty disease from some fleas jumping off humans, or they could all be wiped out, poor dears!'

She studied the cards held by one of the rats.

'Never draw to an inside straight, my love,' she advised, and moved away again, tirelessly going round and around.

She had reattached her shadow to her heels and it drooped after her as she prowled. It was utterly beaten down with exhaustion, and was no longer able to do its proper job of being a dark copy of her body, that shortened or grew, varying in shape or size as the light came in on her from outside, and with the way she moved about in its shafts. It dragged after her like old rags tied to her feet.

So Breda played and Melodie prowled; but The Mórrígan watched the table.

She watched it with the same enlarged stare and the same single-minded concentration of the cat that crouched on the ground; but the mind behind The Mórrígan's eyes was calm and very cold.

'Where did that hedgehog get to—I wanted to scrub the floor,' Melodie said eventually, and she dropped to her knees to search for him under the table. The lucky little hedgehog was long gone and she found instead a large piece of broken looking-glass. Being a Goddess, she understood everything about it at once; but after snatching a handful of her shadow and cleaning the glass until it shone, and then seeing how well it reflected, she couldn't help giving a loud shout of pleasure.

'What is it?' asked Breda, from under her eyeshade.

'A strange shining,' Melodie answered with genuine admiration. 'A shining flatness that shows a picture of how a thing looks, myself, for example . . . . more so than a still pool, more so than a sheet of polished bronze; the likes of it we have never seen before. It is known as a mirror or a looking-glass.'

She brooded on her reflection for some moments and then broke into a loud, derisory cackle. She stood up and took the mirror over to Breda, and when Breda saw herself in the glass, she got a fit of the giggles.

The Mórrígan withdrew her attention from the table.

Breda passed her the glass and The Mórrígan looked at herself.

With a cool interest she inspected her pretty face and she changed it from being remarkable pretty into being flawlessly beautiful. The other two women sniggered at first and then laughed heartily.

The Mórrígan gazed at her new eyes, so wonderfully amethyst, and she made the pupils into small perfect pansies.

Melodie snorted and went into stitches with the giggles.

A little object appeared on the table. For a second, it shone brilliantly and the glasshouse was filled with ghostly, whispering voices.

Without taking her attention from the looking-glass, The Mórrígan reached for the shining object, put it to her lips and said: 'Hush!'—so gently and dreadfully, that the little whispering voices inside the ruined Castle Durance, instantly fell silent. Completely absorbed in her reflection, The Mórrígan clipped the charm back on to her bracelet, where it swung once again with all the other golden objects against her wrist.

She made the irises of her eyes into real blue iris flowers with lovely black markings, and Melodie was gasping and saying that if she laughed any more, she would fall to bits. Breda made sounds of being revolted.

Absent-mindedly, The Mórrígan scratched her wrist.

Still entranced by the mirror, she turned the pupils of her eyes into little Catherine-wheels that spun and spun and threw out tiny sparks and were fiery and swift and full of splendid colours.

And Melodie giggled and shook and wiped her eyes with her shadow, and then she found that she had to blow her nose on it, before casting it down to the ground with fine disdain.

So they beguiled the time and enjoyed themselves like cats playing in the moonlight; and they gave no thought at all to their landlord, the owner of the glasshouse—Mossie Flynn —who was still patiently waiting for them to come out and do one of their Works Of Art.

They had forgotten all about the Sergeant as well—and as everyone knows, it doesn't do to forget about a Sergeant.

Chapter 20

I T was a day of bright light and trembling heat. Wherever they looked, the children saw a million points of dazzle, as though small bits of the sun's fire had dropped to earth. They were only the quivering raindrops twinkling in the brightness; but the effect was powerful, and the travellers were even more light-hearted than before.

Cluas was singing.

His song was a turmoil of creaks mixed with scrapes and although the song he was singing was: '*Put Them All Together, They Spell Mother*', a song that isn't often laughed at, Brigit and Pidge couldn't help laughing as it sounded so funny.

By and by, the grass verges at the roadside sloped downwards into dry ditches and the land rose again from these little valleys in a gentle slant on either side of the road, wooded and thickly covered with ferns and brambles.

Cluas went silent and he stood up on his hind legs with a wondering air and with growing happiness.

'*Foxglove Flats*,' he cried joyfully, '*summer lettings to careful tenants. No pets allowed.*'

And when, a moment later, they reached a place where tall foxgloves grew, he waved his front legs and shouted gleefully:

'*Ma! Ma! It's Me!*'

'*Who spoked?*' a voice called out, in agitated excitement from inside the largest flower on the very tallest spike. Straight away, numerous other voices from inside other flowers, said:

'*Who spoked?*'

'*Was it you?*'

'*Not me!*'

'*Who, then?*'

'*Must have been Missus-Next-Flower.*'

'*What does she want?*'

'*Search me?*'

'*What for?*'

And for a few seconds, similar remarks flew from flower to flower.

Cluas called again:

'It was me, Ma. Me!'

'Who's "me", I query? Not my little iggsy-wiggsy home from the wars? Not my little diddums come back all debraggled, with pains in his tummock and brain rumbles?' cried the trembling voice from inside the most prominent flower.

'The brain rumbles!' the other voices echoed with horror.

A fat matronly earwig, wearing an apron and an old-fashioned bonnet, appeared at the lip of the flower. As soon as she appeared, hundreds of others that were very like her, peeped out of their flowers, anxious to know who had come.

'Not my snookums with half his pretty pincers gone and shell-shocked into tripe-gripes, from buckyneerin' with his croonies and that daft old Napoleon Barmy Potty?' continued the Ma, still not daring to look up and with her forelegs shielding her eyes.

'Look, Ma. I'm home, all safe and sound,' Cluas said cheerfully.

'You may be,' said his Ma, looking up. 'But while you were away I was so down in the dumps that I wouldn't wish it on a microbe.' Her voice trembled.

'She wouldn't wish it on a microbe, poor old dear,' all of the others repeated one to another, their voices trembling in sympathy.

'The dumps? What's the dumps! I'd go there on my holidays any day of the week,' Cluas said lightly to cheer her up. 'Anyway, I am back home and I'm all in one piece, so everything is all right, isn't it, Ma?'

'All right, he sez. Him that went off without his galoshers! You bold little tiddley-wig! It's a wonder you haven't come back with the tube gallops and the bronichal mufflers. See what bein' a Ma means?' she rebuked him, and tried to look at him severely.

So Cluas said goodbye and Pidge gave him a lift down from his shoulder to the foxglove on the tip of a finger. And the children said goodbye to him, and thanked him for getting them out of Castle Durance. And Brigit declared that he must be the bravest earwig in the whole world and that it was lucky for everyone that he hadn't been afraid of the Wardress or that silly dwarf.

249

And the Ma said that they must excuse her for not talking to them before this, and for not remembering her manners through mother-worry; but that she was deeply beholden to them for sparing her boy the long hike home and for saving him from getting his lights put out in battle. She thanked them as well for saving her from a life of the heart-stutters and the head-warbles, and she said that boys would be boys.

'*I'm grown up, Ma,*' Cluas said when she stopped for breath.

'*If you're grown up, why were you in the infantry?*' she asked tartly, and they linked arms and walked into the pink tunnel that was home.

'*Now,*' they heard her say: '*What's all this about a Wardress and a dilly-swarf? How many times have I told you to be having no truck with the likes of those?*'

'*I did good work for The Dagda, Ma,*' Cluas said.

And that was the last they heard of him.

In a little while they had left the wooded place behind and the open road, white and dusty, ran ahead of them in a straight line. There were no more trees to be seen; just low stone walls, with now and again a sprawl of blackberry bushes and sometimes a few thin hazels.

Chapter 21

BETWEEN running and walking turn and turnabout, they had travelled some miles along the road; not without many a halt to look and listen to find out if the hounds had rediscovered them, or to pick the wild strawberries that grew so abundantly amidst the wayside grasses and wild flowers.

Finally they came to a ploughed hill and the road wound itself like a broad ribbon around its base. The low stone walls gave way to grass and clover as an edging to the road; and as they walked by, the bees were loud in the clover. And then they discovered that the road finished as a single line and had now split into three.

They stood wondering which way to go.

Ahead, there was a wide-stretching sweep of lush meadows and grasslands, succeeded by far-away wheatfields, made small only by distance. And although the mountains still looked like the Twelve Pins, Pidge knew that wherever they were, they were not in Connemara. For there, most of the fields are small and stony and frail, and the earth little more than a thin blanket over sheets of stone. There, too, the little fields are boxed-in with webs of dry stone walling to withstand the gales from the Atlantic in wintertime; for if not, they would surely be whipped away.

He stared at the mountains, certain that somewhere among them the pebble would be found. Then what would happen?

The mountains were not as remote as before. As he stared at them, they seemed to shimmer and change position. He blinked hard and turned his attention to the roads, trying to decide which one to choose. They rolled away and got lost in the distance, making it impossible to follow any of them with his eyes.

Sighing gently, he reached into his pocket for the scrying-

251

glass. At a stroke, he was flustered and shocked to find that the scrying-glass was gone. His heart thumped as he tried all of his pockets and he could not stifle a disappointed groan.

'What's wrong?' Brigit asked breathlessly, catching his agitation and grasping at him with her two hands.

'I've lost the scrying-glass!'

At his feet, the bees fussing in the clover seemed to buzz more loudly.

'What do you mean?'

'Oh, Brigit, I have! I've lost it.'

'You can't have. Where?'

'I don't know. All I know is that it's gone.'

'Is it in the schoolbag?'

He snatched at the bag and had it open in seconds; but the scrying-glass wasn't there.

He stared stupidly into the bag.

'I don't think I can manage without it,' he whispered.

'Don't worry, I'll find it.'

Brigit started to search the ground.

'That'll do no good. We've come too far; it could have fallen out of my pocket miles and miles back,' he said, his voice loaded with fatigue and disappointment.

He suddenly felt very tired. In a daze he turned from the mountains, not knowing at all what to do next. He was so bound up in misery that at times he half staggered. Brigit followed him like a shadow, her face serious and her eyes wide open.

'The Dagda picked the wrong one when he picked me. We might as well try to find our way back home,' he said finally, and he stood still, staring at nothing.

Brigit stuck her thumb in her mouth and waited.

On this side the hill was walled off into a big field with trees growing all round the edges. The furrows ran crossways, so that when rain fell it would be caught and not run down and be wasted. The turned earth smelled rich and fresh and the soil was darker than good plum pudding.

Then, astonishingly, in the centre of the field the earth stirred; it moved like an animal turning over in its sleep.

Unable to believe their eyes, the children watched and saw a second movement close to where the first one had happened.

And then very slowly two mounds of clay and mud rose up out of the field. The mounds took shapes and were man and woman. They were huge figures of earth.

Some birds flew over the field crying: 'Aisling, aisling,' and Pidge knew that they were seeing a vision.

Bits dropped off and the shapes became more defined, and the two figures held hands with a sort of gigantic joyousness that seemed to fill the whole of everything round and about them. It reached Pidge and Brigit and they found that they wanted to shout, as their happiness was so intense.

The figures rose up out of the field and their enormous mud and earth legs danced. They laughed in exaltation. It was as though all that happiness could mean was held in that laughter; and the dance was wild and stately at the same time, as the figures did a lumbering frolic all over the field, still holding hands. There was the feeling that these two were behind everything, behind all life. They danced the lengths of the furrows and seeds began to sprout under their feet. The sprouts grew and, in a moment, all was covered in green. Then the two figures sat down in the centre of the field side by side; and the seeds sprouted all over them.

They beckoned to Pidge and Brigit and fearlessly the children responded; and by the time they reached them, the man and woman were covered with the riches of the earth.

Their eyes were shiny, juicy blackberries that twinkled with lights; their cheeks were russet apples and their hair was made of wheat and oats. Their lips were strawberries; their eyebrows were bushy herbs; and the man had a beard of feathery barley. The woman had clusters of hazel nuts hanging as ear decorations, and necklaces of chestnuts and walnuts hanging in ropes from her neck. Her feet were strewn with gems that glittered and sparkled; and with beach pebbles, for these too are of the earth. Rabbits curled neatly at the man's feet as slippers; and, in the tears of laughter that came from their eyes, were all the fishes of lonely lakes and the sea—in miniature—even tiny, tiny whales.

Birds nestled in their huge laps.

And now Pidge thought: we have been brought to this place by a journey we don't really understand; and I'm glad of it.

He glanced at Brigit and saw that her face was bright with

enchantment and her eyes were alight with joy.

The next moment, Pidge was aware of other movements just behind the two earth figures; and he thought he saw again the thronging people that they had seen earlier walking over the bridge at Galway. They were shadowy and ill-defined and seemed to be formed of clouds.

As he strained to see them more clearly, he was suddenly aware of some slight change in the atmosphere; some difference that caused a brief quivering on his skin. All at once he had the feeling that everything was threatened in some way. He had the impression that the field was filling with shadows that were bringing something treacherous and savage with them. He sensed a great melancholy from the people and he frowned as he struggled hard to understand what he was seeing.

He stole a quick glance at Brigit, but she was still gazing at the man and the woman with gladness.

Looking again at the procession on the bridge, he saw the figures for a few seconds more only, and then they were broken up by a small gust of hot wind that felt unpleasant on his arms. Although he heard no sound, he fancied that the people were shrieking and howling, and that whatever it was that threatened them was hateful beyond belief. He knew as well that he must not think of giving up and going home, and that somehow it was all to do with Olc-Glas and The Mórrígan; and that the man and woman, and everything that befriended them or shared the earth with them, were also in deadly danger.

The people on the bridge became even more vague and uncertain in outline and then quickly faded and finally floated away through the branches of the trees in wisps. In seconds, the shadows had left the field as imperceptibly as they had arrived.

The two figures were now sinking quietly back into the earth, the birds had flown and the rabbits were scampering away. Very soon everything had gone, but the furrows were still covered with grasses and flowers and strong young shoots.

Holding hands, they walked back down the hill.

'What did you think of all that?' he asked her warily.

'It was all lovely,' she said with a deeply satisfied sigh.

It was well that she had not realized all of it, he thought. He

254

looked again at the roads and made a choice.

From somewhere far off, came the baying of the hounds.

'They've found our track again,' Brigit said.

'They were bound to in the end,' he answered, without worrying too much about them.

His mind was calm and clear. He had decided that the road they would follow was the one that looked as if it led to the mountains.

Chapter 22

I T was much later in the day when they reached a finger-post that pointed to a footpath on the other side of a stile, saying:

They paused to read it and then went on, only to find after walking a little bit more that the road came to a dead stop at a thick line of shrubs and young trees. It was odd that it didn't branch either to the right or the left and Pidge wondered if it continued its way on the other side of the living barrier. The shrubs grew as densely as hedging, with here and there a young fir tree or a thin mountain ash struggling for space. At first they couldn't find anywhere that would allow them to look through, to find out what lay beyond. In the end, they were just able to wriggle through a place by the roots of one of the young trees; but they had to lie down and squeeze together to do it.

And then to their horror, they discovered that they were at the edge of an abyss.

It was a deep, sheer, slash in the earth, boulder strewn at the bottom and bare of growth but for a few scrawny bushes. It was a solemn, savage and majestic place and they were subdued by the sight of it.

After they had studied it in silence for a while, Brigit said:

'That's a terrible big hole and I don't like it.'

'Sssshh!' Pidge whispered, imagining the ground giving way under them and what would happen then. Every bit of him that was in contact with the earth was sensitive and trembling. He didn't think it was even safe to speak.

'Pull back,' he whispered. 'Don't do anything suddenly. Be very, very, careful.'

Slowly, carefully, they moved back little by little, and Pidge would not allow Brigit to stand up until they were well out of any possible danger. For a few minutes, Pidge's legs shook with the feeling that things were crawling all over his skin, and then he was suddenly angry with himself for giving in to his imagination. The edge where they had lain had been as solid as granite. Maybe not quite as solid as granite or things couldn't grow there, but solid enough, he told himself sensibly.

'What kind of a place is that?' Brigit asked.

'I think it's an abyss,' he answered after a moment.

It was at this point that the hounds barked to each other as they still followed the trail, and Pidge felt even more furious with himself, thinking that he had chosen the wrong road and that now they were trapped.

'The footpath! There's a bridge somewhere along the footpath,' he said breathlessly; and they ran back and climbed over the stile.

I really must try to stop worrying and frightening myself like this, and take things as they come, he told himself very firmly.

Far away in the glasshouse, a last spark flew from the Catherine-wheels that spun in The Mórrígan's eyes, and it landed on the table not very far from the path where Pidge and Brigit now trudged. In a little while, they got the whiff of woodsmoke. When they came to the end of the hedging they saw the bridge that spanned the terrible abyss.

It was burning.

Chapter 23

'OH no!' Brigit shouted angrily. 'We'll never get across this rotten old abyss now. We're stuck!'

The flames laughed as they devoured the wood.

They crackled as they skipped along the handrails and chuckled as they capered and made merry all over the flooring-boards. Filmy white ashes flew wildly in cross-currents of air, whisked about like leaves in a brisk autumn, while the wood squeaked and moaned.

It was a blazing road of fire where nothing could live for one second.

They stood watching it, feeling helpless and cheated.

The fire roared with an upsurge of flames as it reached a pitch of excited greed and then it very slowly began to be less. Half-hypnotized, they saw it diminish. It dwindled gradually until the ashes no longer flew, but softly floated; and the whole structure was brought to a smoking skeleton where, now and again, embers were fanned by a quiet breeze to glow fluor-escently like deep-sea creatures.

'That's it. We'll just have to try to find some other way,' Pidge said.

'If only we still had the scrying-glass,' Brigit sighed.

Pidge looked at her sharply to see if she was blaming him for losing it; but her face was only wistful and a bit sad-looking.

Mention of the scrying-glass reminded him of the hazel nuts and he rapidly took one out and held it on the palm of his hand. Nothing at all happened.

'Try another!' Brigit shouted encouragingly.

And although he knew in his heart that if help were to come out of one of the nuts, it would be the first one he chose, he tried them all in quick succession. Putting them carefully back in the bag and stuffing the bag well down and folding it over into his pocket, he said:

'There *must* be some other way. If we attempt to go back to try one of the other roads, we'll only walk straight into the hounds.'

They walked on, passing after a while a small flock of sheep that were grazing in the charge of a ram, with a red and white cow keeping them company. The children stopped and looked at them expectantly for a few minutes but the animals didn't appear to take any interest in them.

'This is a bad place to put animals, one of them could easily fall down that abyss,' Pidge remarked.

'I thought they might be put here to help us,' said Brigit, and she looked back at them for some time.

Still there was no way across and no way down except as a stone would drop.

'It might just as well be on the far side of the moon,' Pidge said quietly, looking over to the other side.

At length they saw the biggest tree they had ever seen, growing at a distance of twenty feet or more in from the rim of the chasm. Its trunk was a bulk and a mass and a swelling; its branches were a billowing and a spreading and a stretching; its height was pride and power. It didn't seem possible that such a magnificence was all drawn from the minute things in the earth that feed and nurture.

'Oh,' sighed Brigit, 'if only that tree was a bit nearer to the old abyss, we could easily get across if we walked along one of the branches.'

I wouldn't like to test that idea, Pidge thought; but all he answered was:

'It must be the oldest thing in the whole world to be so big.'

He thought it marvellous.

As they crossed over to it, the tree appeared to grow even bigger; and it waved its branches and rustled its leaves, so that one would think that a ghostly army walked there.

It was an oak tree.

They put their hands on it and looked up to try to see the sky through it, and then they leaned against its trunk and turned to look back at the burning bridge.

Day was now turning to evening in easy stages and dusk was gathering in soft cohesions to the east of them. In the west, the sun was still strong and more brilliant in its going than it was at its dawn. Where Pidge and Brigit stood, the light was still bright and pleasant. They noticed that the animals had stopped grazing and were now watching them intently; and not a stir out of them.

From afar came the cry of a hound, just as Pidge was beginning to think that it was time they looked for a safe place where they could pass the night; and then a voice spoke to them out of the tree:

'Hanging by the neck leaves a deep impression on a person,' it said.

Chapter 24

STARTLED, they looked up but saw no one.

'But,' the voice continued conversationally, 'hanging by the rear leaves no impression at all.'

And a spider—a portly gentleman about as big as a crabapple hanging by a thread—dropped and swung gently before their faces.

'Do you remember me?' he asked genially.

'No,' they said.

'And who was it played yoyos with me?'

'Not me!' Brigit said quickly. 'I never saw a spider your size before!'

'Wasn't it yourself—outside the blacksmith's?'

'No,' she said, her face blank but going pink, 'it must have been someone else.'

'Well, 'tisn't to you I should be talking, so,' the spider said and he pretended to go away up his little rope.

'It was me,' she said then. 'I didn't mean any harm.'

'And no harm done,' the spider said, sliding down again and dangling in front of them. 'I wish I had a fly for every time someone made a yoyo of me!'

He was wearing a shirt that was ruffled at the neck and cuffs, black knee britches, knitted stockings on his lower legs and a pair of buckled hornpipe shoes. On his head was a little hard hat and he smoked a small clay pipe.

'Anastasia knew you would be coming, she read it in the tea-leaves. I was set to watch for you here,' he said.

'Are you going to help us?' Pidge asked.

'To be sure I am. You'll have to come inside the tree.'

'How do we do that?'

'Is there a door?' Brigit asked hopefully.

'No. But if you're as good on your whistle as you are at

261

playing yoyos, there'll be no bother on us at all,' the spider replied, and he laughed mildly.

Brigit took out her whistle, covered the holes as before and put it to her lips. She thought to herself that she would surely play the same tune again; but it was entirely different though equally lovely.

The tree was opening slowly.

It was simply parting with a tremendous creaking and grinding, and for a moment it was as if they could half-glimpse the draped form of a Being with her two arms spread out holding the tree apart, as though she held her cloak open. Then they saw at their feet the beginning of a set of steps that curled downwards.

Brigit was radiant with pride, and then she went very solemn and carefully put her penny whistle back into the schoolbag and buckled the straps tightly. Just to be sure of it, she gave the bag a shake.

'Step inside now and take me with you,' the spider said.

Pidge hooked him onto his finger.

'Down we go,' the spider said cheerfully.

Before starting the journey into the ground, Pidge looked back at the way they had come. The blackened bits of wood still smoked and there was not a sign of the hounds; the flock sheep and the cow had gone back to their grazing.

Fat roots were on either side of the steps and light came in from the split in the tree above. When they had gone about eight steps down, the spider told them to stand still. Almost at once there was a great crunching and rasping as the tree up above them closed itself, and then it went very dark. The stairs had been laid in a natural winding space under the living tree, it seemed.

So dark it was that Brigit, coming down as she was behind Pidge, took a fistful of his jacket and a wad of his shirt as well, pulling it tight against his neck.

'Don't be moving now for a while,' the spider advised. 'When your eyes get used to it, you'll be surprised at how much light there is.'

'Brigit, could you just ease your grip? You'll choke me in a minute,' Pidge said and, reassured by how normal he sounded, she loosened her hold on him.

'Oh, the women are divils for gripping!' the spider remarked laughing fondly, and then added rather more seriously: 'Anastasia and myself have called a truce for the present. She'd ate me another time.'

'I'm sorry I played yoyos with you,' Brigit apologized.

'That's nothing to what some people do,' the spider answered. 'Anyway it didn't take me long to give you the slip, so it doesn't matter.'

Gradually, their eyes got used to the darkness and it was as the spider had said—there was a surprising amount of light. It came in from cracks in the roof overhead and beamed down dustily here and there. One tree root ran continuously at the side of the steps for all the world like a bannister.

'What's this place?' Pidge asked.

'A way in; oh, very old. Used long ago by those who were very wise and skilled.'

In spite of the suspended motes of dust in the light, everything was clean and the root bannister was highly polished. Just by moving his head slightly to change the angle at which he looked, Pidge found that the motes suddenly silvered and glittered and theirs was a constant movement. Exactly like a sort of Universe or Milky Way with its millions of tiny planets and suns, he thought.

'Do they still use it?'

'No. They've gone this long time. This was one of their places, under a holy tree. The world has grown a lot older, but damn the bit wiser, since their day.'

'It all looks clean.'

'Why wouldn't it? Don't we keep it spick and span, and aren't the steps swept and the bannisters dusted and polished with finest silk, every second day?'

'Is this the only way in?'

'No, indeed. There is another way—but like this, it hasn't been used for as far back as history goes.'

'Could hounds find their way in?' Brigit asked.

'Not at all. That tree above us now, hasn't as much of a crack in it as a spider could get a leg in; and as for the other way, it's so tight, I've never even been able to find it—though I know it is there. The distance between an onion and its skin would have to be a gape compared with it,' the spider said, chuckling.

The bannister was with them all the way down to the bottom, where there was a passageway with dry flooring and walls. It was darker there. The spider counselled them to wait again; and soon they saw faint shadows dancing on the walls, created by a light that was somewhere at the end of the passage.

'Step bravely now. No need to think about tripping, for there's nothing to trip over; and there'll be no banging of heads, for the ones who made this were full-grown men,' the spider said encouragingly.

They followed the passageway with him dangling on Pidge's finger and Brigit walking behind. As they came nearer to the source of the light, the dancing shadows grew stronger and soon the space where they walked was wider and they were at the mouth of a huge cave. The dancing shadows were from firelight.

'Is that you I can smell, Mawleogs?' a voice called.

'It is indeed, Anastasia, my dear,' the spider answered, taking his pipe from his mouth and clearing his throat first.

Side by side, Pidge and Brigit stood at the threshold for a few moments, looking in. Across from them, at the far side of the cave, was a fireplace with a bright fire burning under a black pot; and there were stone benches and seats arranged in a wide half-circle before it. Close by, they saw a very fat lady spider covered from top to bottom in Aran knitting. On her head there was a tammy with a fluffy pompom, and her jumper was a mass of bobbles and twists and cables, and so was her longish skirt. Her lower legs were clad in thick stocking done in rib-stitch; but they couldn't tell all this until they were close to her, from the threshold she simply appeared to be covered in spun wool. She was knitting industriously— they could hear the clicking of her needles and see her arms flashing, and she sat on a stool by a large silver web. She looked up from her work and saw them.

'Here you are at last; the tea-leaves never lie!' she cried; 'It's nice to see you. I'm murthered knitting cardigans for the kids!'

'Mind the step and wipe your feet,' Mawleogs said. 'You can put me down now, if you please.'

They crossed the floor of the cave. With every step they took Mawleogs seemed to grow bigger. When they were roughly half-way across, their attention was attracted by many little twittering and swishing sounds, and looking up, they saw dozens and dozens of young spiders who were practising their aerobatics. They were swinging from trapezes and high-flying and looping and twisting all over the place with cries of 'Alley-oop'; and each one had a safety-line floating out behind. A few were walking the high wire. Underneath them all was a great cobweb spread out as a safety-net, and the last rays of bronze sunlight shone through some cracks and looked exactly like spotlights.

'We're part-time circus folk, you know,' explained Mawleogs who was by now about half as big as Brigit.

'Come here till I see you and sit down while there's a seat to be got,' Anastasia said kindly; and Pidge and Brigit sat down. Anastasia was equal with Mawleogs in size.

'We're also weavers,' Mawleogs continued; 'we make blankets for hedges in winter and so on; but mostly we do the high wire and the flying. Anastasia is a Clairvoyant.'

'Yes, Madam Anastasia, Clairvoyant, is my billing, dears. My real name is Minnie Curran, but I'm fond of my professional name and mostly use that.'

'That's a lovely name,' Brigit said.

'I got it out of a novel, dear. I'm glad you like it.'

'The kids are coming along well?' Mawleogs remarked with satisfaction as he looked up.

'They're very clever, aren't they?' Pidge said.

'It's in the blood, lovey,' Anastasia answered and she put down her knitting. They saw that she was knitting two cardigans at once and this was the time when they noticed properly how she was dressed. She was certainly splendid.

She got up from her stool and rattled the silver web with a knitting needle.

'Come on, you little rascals!' she shouted, and all of the kids shot down on silken ropes and sat on the seats. They were all roughly the size of plums, except one, and he was only as big as a small cherry.

Mawleogs, whose pipe had gone dead, began to clean it out with a little blue penknife; an air of domestic peace stole into the cave and a cricket began to sing at the back of the hearth.

'You're in good time tonight, Batty,' Mawleogs remarked, blowing the dust from his pipe.

'I am,' a voice replied and continued its singing.

The little spiders had been staring at Brigit and Pidge, tittering with shyness and pushing each other so that one fell off the end of one seat or another from time to time. It didn't take them long, however, to get bolder.

'We're sittin' beside her,' the ones near Brigit said, and made frightful faces at her. Their voices were squeaky and full of giggles.

'What are you making faces at me for?' she asked indignantly after putting up with it for a few minutes.

'We're sittin' beside you,' they answered and sniggered.

'Stop it this minute! She's not that Miss Muffet that you couldn't look crooked at but she'd have a fit,' Anastasia said. 'We had enough of her with her curds and wheys; not that any of *us* ever met her, but it was in all the newspapers I'm told.'

Mawleogs was lighting his pipe with a great smacking and puffing.

'They're always hoping to meet her some day so that they can frighten her,' he said between exertions.

'We'd put her in a hospiddle!' one of the little spiders said, and immediately was overcome with bashfulness and hid his face.

'You can frighten me if you like,' Brigit said generously, and the little spiders stuck out their tongues and made their eyes cross and pulled their mouths wide with their hands and shouted *'Boo! Got ya!'* And Brigit yelped and said: 'You're horrible frightening,' and put her hands over her eyes so that she couldn't see, and all the little spiders laughed and were delighted with themselves.

'We done it,' they said to each other.

'Did it,' Brigit corrected them and they laughed all the more.

Although everything was happy and friendly, Pidge was wondering about the abyss and how they could cross it; and while Brigit fooled with the young ones, he looked at the huge silver web and at the web that was the safety-net and he pondered on them.

'Spider's web is very strong, isn't it?' he asked Mawleogs after a while.

'Strong! It's an engineer's dream or so I heard one of your

people saying once. For its weight, it's remarkable, I believe.'

'Would it be possible to make a bridge out of it?'

Mawleogs took the pipe from his mouth and laid it down. He brought a paper and pencil out of his waistcoat pockets and did some sums.

'It would; but it wouldn't be done before morning.'

'Even so,' Pidge said, 'it could be done even if it took longer.'

'Say we could spin enough of it,' Mawleogs said kindly and gently, 'we could never be sure of the air-currents for a lift off. I stood three weeks at that place one time waiting to get across.'

'Oh,' Pidge said, very disappointed. 'Somehow, when I saw the web, I was full sure that was the way you could help us.'

'I'm sorry,' Mawleogs said. 'We'll keep you for the night at any rate. It isn't safe at all for you to be outside in the dark.'

On the fire the great black pot bubbled merrily, lifting its hat politely at intervals due to the influence of steam. Anastasia got a big fork and took the lid off entirely and the steam rose in clouds taking the smell of potatoes on a broad journey around the cave.

'The spuds are done,' she said; and with four arms she lugged the pot off the fire and strained the potatoes though a potato basket, and then put them back in the pot and set it near the fire for them to dry off nicely. All of the kids ran and got saucers with big lumps of butter on them and handed them round, giving the ones with the biggest lumps to Brigit and Pidge. They ran again and fetched plates and knives and forks. Anastasia tumbled the floury, yellow potatoes out onto large platters and then gave everyone a mug of fresh milk. They dived in, spearing potatoes on their forks, peeling them and smearing them with butter. They shook a little salt on and started eating; they were delicious.

'Peel me a 'pud,' a little voice said to Brigit and she looked down at the littlest spider of the lot; his little face was so small that it was hardly there at all; and he blushed up at her. She peeled the potato proudly and broke it on the young spider's plate. She ate some of her own.

'Why aren't we eating flies for supper?' she asked conversationally.

'Oh, Brigit,' Pidge said.

There was a surprised silence for a little while.

'Would you have liked flies for your supper, dear?' Anastasia asked anxiously.

'No. Indeed I wouldn't.'

'Well, that's what we thought so that's why we didn't get any,' Mawleogs said simply.

'Why do you eat them?'

'Sure somebody has to, or you'd be up to your ears in them.'

'What do they taste like?'

'Sometimes they do taste of one thing and sometimes another. Roast quail and chicken or sausages, anything the like of that,' Mawleogs explained.

'I see,' Brigit said, and carried on with her potatoes.

Pidge was relieved that nobody was the slightest bit offended.

'These are very good Golden Wonders; we always grow them at home,' he said; and then looked quickly at Brigit, fearing that she might suddenly be upset at his thoughtless use of the word 'home'; but she was drinking her milk and wiping her mouth with the back of her hand, quite untroubled.

'The ram and sheep up above stamped them out of a field and pushed them along with their noses until they dropped through the holes in the roof onto the safety-net. Nora gave us the milk,' Mawleogs said.

'Who's Nora?' Brigit asked.

'A very sweet person, dear,' Anastasia replied; 'she lets the kids do a high wire act between her horns anytime they care to. But we're friends mostly because we catch the flies that drive her demented. We made the butter from her cream. Is it nice?'

'It's great,' Brigit said.

'And all my wool is a gift from the sheep. The flies do terrible things to them, poor creatures,' she dropped her voice to a whisper; 'maggots, you know.'

'Hush, Anastasia—the children!' Mawleogs said.

'We doesn't be often having 'puds,' the littlest spider ventured, and then his bravery astounded him so much that he choked on a particle and had to be held upside-down by Anastasia and slapped gently on the back until it fell out. As soon as he had his breath back he bent his head and searched the ground until

he spied it and then he jumped up and down on the potato particle to get his revenge. He climbed back up onto his seat and drank some milk.

'Isn't the cricket going to have any?' Brigit asked.

'Oh, Batty don't eat this early; he on'y just got up,' the littlest spider said, now fully recovered.

At this, Batty emerged from the back of the fire, brushing the turf-ashes from his clothes and blowing them off his fiddle. He took off his flat cap and beat it against a seat-edge and the dust flew in clouds. Everyone started coughing and when the dust had settled again, Batty stood revealed.

He wore an old tweed suit and the cap, of course; and his small face was almost overshadowed out of existence by a great pair of bulging spectacles.

'Hallo, the house,' he said, taking off his cap briefly.

'Hallo, yourself,' all the spiders answered.

'I'll ate me spuds by and by when you're all snoring,' he said and tuned the fiddle.

'Begob! We'll make a night of it!' Mawleogs said: 'We'll have a bit of a hooley.' He smiled broadly and took a flute, a bodhrán and a set of pipes from a cubby-hole behind where he was sitting. He nodded his head at the young ones.

'But you'll wash the delph, first,' he said, and all the small spiders with the exception of the littlest one, rushed and scuttled and splashed and argued and the dishes were done in a trice. The littlest one climbed up and sat on the crown of Mawleogs' hard hat.

'Who'll give us a few steps of a dance?' Mawleogs inquired as he gave a preliminary blow into his flute.

'I'll do the Fly Land Hing,' a young spider offered shyly.

With a nod to Batty, and a one, two, three of a foot on the ground, Mawleogs and the cricket began to play. With his first pair of legs, Mawleogs played the flute; the second pair of legs beat the bodhrán, held sideways to be out of the way of the third pair of legs that performed vigorously on the pipes. Batty fiddled; puffs of dust rising from him again and again from the energy of his elbow.

The little spider, with more than the usual number of legs at his disposal, danced the most amazing Hing that the world has ever seen. All of the others clapped in time with the music, and

269

on Mawleogs' hat the littlest one drummed the crown with his fists. Anastasia's knitting-needles went as fast as the music and by the time the shy dancer reached the end of his dance, she had done at least five inches on each garment. Everyone clapped and cheered; the dancer bowed low and went to his seat, giggling.

'Next item!' Mawleogs cried; and two more spiders took the floor. One of them played 'The Flight of The Bumblebee' on paper and comb and the other mimed it. Gusts of laughter greeted this performance as all the spiders found it immensely funny.

Anastasia now put down her knitting and went to her silver web.

'Get to your harps, Class Five,' she cried; and a couple of dozen young ones ran to the shadows and sat at small webs part-hidden in corners and waited for their cues. Anastasia played a beautiful haunting air. As she completed each passage, she rested; and gentle echoes of her music rippled in from the little musicians, who really sounded as if they were all masters of their work.

'When Anastasia plays like that, it pulls the heart out of me,' Mawleogs whispered to Pidge, his voice filled with emotion.

The music came to an end in a shower of grace notes and after a hush, there was the wildest applause possible and cries for more.

The harpers all bowed and began a selection of lively dance tunes, sliding from one into another time after time without as much as a single wrong note, ending on a rush of counter-pointing notes that rang around the cave. In the silence that followed, a peal of echoes came back from passages to other caves, unnoticed until this, by Brigit and Pidge.

After all the mad applause had died away, Anastasia and her harpers stood up and bowed and then went back to their places; the young ones all beaming at each other.

'Always keep your limbs supple and your shoulder muscles relaxed, my dears,' Anastasia said, going back to her knitting at once.

'How's the time, Batty?' Mawleogs asked.

'Moving on, as usual,' came the answer.

'Time the kids danced a couple of hammocks,' Anastasia said, clicking away.

'Right. You'll all dance a couple of hammocks for Pidge and Brigit, now,' Mawleogs said.

'Will she pay us?' one young spider asked.

'What?' Anastasia cried.

'He's a money spider,' a small one beside Brigit whispered loudly.

'No I'm not,' the first one said, as bright as a tomato.

'Nothing wrong with money spiders—they bring a lot of luck,' Mawleogs said.

'I'm not a money spider, at all. I on'y meant would she pay us after we do the dancin', by playin' yoyos with us same as she did with you.'

'Of course I will,' Brigit said, and every one of the younger spiders cheered.

'That's settled. Line up for the Haymaker's Jig. We want two hammocks so that's four lines.'

So, after a lot of scrambling, the young spiders formed two pairs of long lines in the middle of the cave.

'Threads . . . out!' Mawleogs shouted when they were ready and every little spider reached behind himself and pulled a thread from his rear.

'Stick them in pairs,' Mawleogs instructed them and as Batty tuned his fiddle, the spiders joined the threads two-by-two and stuck them down on the ground behind them.

'One, two, three and off,' Mawleogs shouted, and away went the first bars of the jig and the little spiders began to dance and weave in and out; and on the floor of the cave, the threads met and crossed and looped. At first, they could hardly be seen but they were getting thicker bit by bit. Pidge and Brigit watched with delight. The dancers danced with grace and agility and they made arches and went under them and swung each other in the centre and did chains.

'The Siege Of Ennis,' Mawleogs cried, changing the music; and the spiders faced each other in ranks of fours, and danced and spun and passed over and under, and the spinning on the floor looked whiter and whiter.

'The Walls Of Limerick—last dance, lads and lassies!' Mawleogs announced; and they danced the dance as thoroughly as possible and by the time it was finished, there was an incredible pair of weavings on the ground.

'Cast off,' Mawleogs instructed them and they released their threads and brought them together in pairs.

'They ought to finish those off with a nice hop jig round the edges, dearest,' Anastasia suggested: 'It would give a pretty picôt touch to it.'

So, once more, there was music and dance and then all was finished.

'Well,' Mawleogs said appreciatively, 'don't talk about Hargreaves and his Spinning Jenny after that! A perfect job in each case. Gather them up with great care now.'

The hammocks were lifted carefully by groups of spiders at the corners and carried nearer to the fire, where they were attached to spaces in the walls.

Anastasia sent other groups to get the bedding from her bedding boxes and they came back with their arms piled high with blankets, some knitted in wool and some made from spun silk, and thistledown pillows, and they gave them to Anastasia who arranged them in the hammocks.

'Why was she spinning, that Jenny?' one of the young spiders asked wonderingly.

'Drunk!' said a little voice from the top of Mawleogs' hat.

'Yoyos!' the spiders cried, drumming their heels on the floor.

'You'll have to help me, Pidge,' Brigit said and they took them in groups of about three and four at a time depending on size. Lifting their hands high, with each little spider clinging on to its thread with expressions of intense concentration, they made throwing gestures and spiders shot out in all directions with delighted cries of fear and excitement; and then they all rolled quickly back up until they were just under the palms of the outstretched hands, and then they were thrown again. Each group got twelve goes; all outdoing each other in thrilled shrieks.

The littlest spider was last of all. Brigit hooked him on to her finger. His tiny legs trembled and he was very scared.

'I be's afraid her'll play conkers with me,' he said, looking round.

'No I won't, don't worry. I'll be very careful,' Brigit said, and she dropped him gently and he rolled back very efficiently; said *'Hurrah!'* weakly; and *'That's enough,'* very quickly.

Everyone gave him a well-deserved round of applause.

Then Batty told a story and they all gazed into the fire, their eyes going vacant as they listened. When it was finished, they still gazed hypnotized, until Mawleogs gave it a dig with the poker and a sheaf of sparks flew, graceful as the tail of an imagined firebird. For a while, the only sound to be heard was the clicking of the knitting-needles and it was all very peaceful until suddenly, Anastasia gave a shriek and went rigid.

'Hark! I hear a voice!' she cried; 'I feel them; the invisibles are here!'

The knitting dropped from her lifeless hands.

The little spiders shuffled in close together.

'Oh, Janey!' they whispered, and all of their eyes stood out in their heads and were like dozens of tiny full moons.

'She's gone off,' Mawleogs said, relighting his pipe: 'Now we should hear something worth hearing.'

'She's gone funny,' one of the kids said while they waited, and he shook with nervous giggles.

'Hush!' Mawleogs admonished him and puffed his pipe, to all appearances extremely calm.

Anastasia's eyes went glassy.

'There's a message . . . . I'm getting a message . . . . the voice is faint . . . . I'm getting "Midget", yes, that's it, I think,' she said.

Pidge gave Brigit a half-smile, thinking that Anastasia was putting on a show for them.

'The voice is saying that I'm not getting it right . . . "Bridge! Midget!" . . . I *see* him! I see him! A tall man wearing white who is shaking his head and wagging his finger at me. Not "Midget" and not "Bridge" . . . I've *got* it! He's saying "Brigit and Pidge". Is there anyone here called "Brigit"? Is there anyone here named "Pidge"? If there is— speak! The message is for you.'

Pidge smiled and nudged Brigit because he thought it great fun.

'She *knows* we're here,' Brigit said.

'Not when she's like this. She doesn't know her own name when she's like this. Answer her,' said Mawleogs quietly.

'Yes,' Pidge said, 'we're here.'

'The man in white is making passes with his hands and

showing me a picture as I'm having trouble hearing him. I see a picture—as plain as anything.'

Her voice changed and she made a solemn chant:

'The One whose bone is made of stone,
The One whose height turns day to night;
Granite hard is now his hide,
But he is still alive inside.
On his head, there are two trees,
And for your sake, he'll bend his knees;
With whelk, you'll find his name doth rhyme,
He's been for Ages trapped in time . . . . '

Here, she heaved a deep, lingering sigh and said more normally: 'Sorry about the last two lines—the man dressed in white is laughing at me. Now he is nodding and smiling and saying that, two hours before dawn, you must go to that One. I've got it right! He's pleased. He's fading, smiling, nodding—fading, fading . . . . he's going, going, gone!'

She fluttered briefly and woke up.

'How was it—was it any good at all?' she asked, taking up her knitting.

Mawleogs had taken his pipe from his mouth and he was staring at her. He looked flabbergasted. All of the kids shivered and sighed. Batty laid down his fiddle very softly with hands that trembled.

'Good?' Mawleogs said. 'You described The Very Lonely One and you did it in poetry. Our friends must go to him two hours before dawn'.

'Who is The Very Lonely One?' Pidge asked faintly, by now greatly impressed.

Chapter 25

'THE Very Lonely One is a great being. I tend to him once a year,' Mawleogs said.

'*Oooooooh!*' all the little spiders said, and they quivered with jittery rapture and snuggled in to each other and waited for more.

'I bring him flowers,' Mawleogs said, staring into the fire.

'*Ooooooh!*' they all said again; and the littlest one asked: '*Does he be liking them?*'

'I don't know for he never speaks; and how could he, poor thing, when he's stone dead.'

This was too much for some of them and there were a few half-stifled shrieks.

Anastasia looked at them sharply.

'Bed for you and for all of us; and well time for it,' she said, 'we have to be up before dawn.'

'*Aaaaaaw,*' they all said, '*we're not a bit tired.*'

Brigit grinned.

'Tired or not, off you go; you're excited enough, and if you have any more of it we'll be kept awake all night with you roaring. Batty, you'll have to be wound up to go off two hours before cockshout, my dear.'

'Whatever you say, ma'am,' Batty answered obligingly.

'You'll see to the fire as usual?'

'Faith, I will, ma'am.'

Pidge and Brigit climbed into their hammocks and settled down. They saw Mawleogs wind up the cricket by turning one of his feelers a few times, knocking on his forehead gently and giving him a bit of a shake to make sure that he was working. Puffs of dust rose from Batty in the usual way. Anastasia had already settled herself in a silken nest a little way off and all of the young ones were safely cocooned and hanging in garlands on the walls near to the fire. Mawleogs wished Batty and everyone else goodnight and away he went to his own bed at the far side of the cave, near the place where they had first come in.

I'll never sleep this night, Pidge thought.

He stared down through the meshes of the hammock at the fire. The hammock was cosy and comfortable. Batty started to play his fiddle very, very softly; and from Brigit's hammock nearby, Pidge could hear her breathing; and knew by it that she was already fast asleep. He got no answer when he whispered, 'Are you awake?'

Presently, there came the blowing and the whistling of dozens of little snores as the young ones slept and, before Pidge could think anymore, he was fast asleep himself.

The next thing he knew was that Mawleogs was standing by him, pulling at his sleeve, saying:

'Wake up, Pidge. The cricket went off five minutes ago, didn't you hear him?'; and that Brigit was already sitting up and rubbing the sleep out of her eyes with her fists.

Anastasia had stirred up the fire that Batty had minded all night; and in a few seconds, they joined her there.

'I never slept a wink thinking of you,' she said to them.

'You're all very kind and good to us,' Pidge said.

'I wish we hadn't got to say goodbye to you at all,' Brigit added.

'Drink a sup of milk before you go,' Mawleogs said, handing them two full mugs.

'All the children are still asleep,' Brigit said, sounding disappointed.

'We would have liked to say goodbye,' Pidge said, wishing that they were awake.

'They're better left alone; they'd be bawling and crying and roaring after you and they'd make you late,' Anastasia said.

And then the milk was finished and it was time to go. Mawleogs held a piece of resinous wood in the fire for a few moments to make a flare.

He held it aloft.

'We'd best be off,' he said.

'Goodbye, Anastasia, goodbye, Batty. Thanks for everything,' they said.

276

'Not at all, not at all,' both replied, and then Pidge and Brigit followed Mawleogs across the cave to where it was darkest, turning round to wave silently before they disappeared after him into a dark tunnel.

Then it came forward in Brigit's mind that she was going to see someone who was dead.

'I don't like this a bit, Pidge,' she said.

'Don't worry. There can't be any harm in it or The Dagda wouldn't allow it,' he answered softly.

The passage twisted and went one way for a while, and then it turned and went another way, and then for a long time it didn't do anything but was just a straight passage. Then it seemed to go uphill for a bit and then downhill and Pidge wondered how far into the earth they were going.

Mawleogs had been very quiet all along.

At last they came to a short flight of steps cut into the ground and they followed him down to the bottom, where they reached a natural archway.

'This is the place,' Mawleogs whispered, and led them into a circular cavern.

It was a place of immense size.

The walls were covered with a substance that was white and reflected back the light of the flare in streaks, like shining mother-of-pearl. As they moved in, the streaks altered as the light struck the walls, bright going dark and dark lighting to brightness. There was the loud noise of water and they came to a place where it gushed from the wall and filled a pool that got no bigger. And then they saw it—the statue of an enormous animal; an Irish Elk. It couldn't be said whether it was wood or stone, bronze or iron; but Pidge knew what it was from his schoolwork. He knew that they were looking at an extinct animal and that bones from such an animal could be seen in the Museum in Dublin. It was a thrilling thing to see.

In front of the statue there was a long table made from stone and the dust of old flowers lay there, where reverence had been done.

'Flowers were always left from long ago, I only copied what was there before,' Mawleogs whispered in the smallest whisper possible.

They tilted their heads back and looked upwards to where

the statue's head was and they saw that two gigantic antlers were on the splendid head.

'They're the two trees,' Brigit whispered, remembering Anastasia's poem.

Without answering, Pidge took a hazel-nut from his pocket, knowing for sure inside himself that it would work. As before he held his hand out flat with the nut lying on his palm. A crack as fine as baby-hair appeared in the nut and it broke open. Lying on the white lining of one half was a minute and perfect silver horn. He picked it out with the nails of his thumb and forefinger and it grew to the size of an ordinary horn. It felt smooth and cold and it seemed to vibrate with the music it contained.

Feeling a bit self-conscious about it, Pidge blew the horn.

The note, clear and sweet, bounded all around the cavern, bouncing off the walls in echoes.

They waited, as the music went all the distance back down the passage and grew faint.

It was such a lovely sound; Pidge couldn't help doing it again. The far-away echoes made it seem that a second horn blew somewhere.

One crack appeared in the statue.

Slowly, slowly, it moved from the neck all along the body. Smaller cracks appeared running out from it and bits of stuff like hard plaster were dropping to the ground. The barest tremble ran through the neck and shoulders and the smallest of ripples ran down the legs. Piece by piece, the covering fell. A stronger quiver, a powerful vibration, and they heard the animal draw in his breath and then the living animal appeared before them.

Slowly he turned his heavy head and looked down at them; then he raised it up on his powerful neck and opened his jaws and belled.

It was a full-throated cry of pleasure, so potent, so thrilling, that Mawleogs dropped to the ground, overcome.

'Oh my!' he whispered, full of a rich, disordering joy.

The Elk moved slowly to the pool and bent his head to drink.

'Blessed be the water,' he said, and came back to them. He bent his massive, ornamented head and looked at them with his soft eyes.

278

'You brought me to life; hurry that I may help you,' he said, and then bent his knees and lay down. 'Climb on me and grip very hard.'

Pidge and Brigit scrambled on the Elk's back and he slowly and carefully righted himself and stood up. Brigit was perched in front of Pidge and they both gripped the strong, dark hair.

The Elk turned and looked down at little Mawleogs.

'My thanks for the flowers, good little watchman,' he said and then he pawed the ground.

'We'll fall off!' Brigit said in a small voice.

'The broadness of your back,' Pidge explained weakly.

Mawleogs came to life.

'If you'll allow me?' he said and hastily climbed up after the children. He took a thread from his body and roped the lower parts of their bodies and legs to the Elk's hide, and he made a small pair of reins which he attached to the lowest branch of the antlers, for Pidge to hold with Brigit in between them.

'Keep these ropes,' he whispered breathlessly to Pidge; 'they might come in handy; and keep a good grip on the hair. You don't have to hold the reins, only I thought they would look nice. Oh my! I must get down now. Such a thing! That I should be the one to see it! Goodbye, Brigit dear; goodbye, Pidge.'

He slithered down to the ground and retreated across the cavern, picking up his flare on the way from where he had left it sticking between two rocks.

The Elk tapped the ground with a forehoof, lifted his head and belled once again. They could feel the surge of sound swelling through them from the vibrations in his body and then the wall facing them was no longer there. It had gone without a sign or sound of how it went, whether it had slid or swung, no one could say. Now there was ahead of them a wide ramp leading upwards to a circle where stars shone and the Elk was taking them up.

There was just time to call 'goodbye' to Mawleogs, who shouted 'Safe journey,' and they were at the top. Barely quickening his gait, and going as smoothly as possible so as not to upset them, the Elk gave a wonderful bound, all the more remarkable for being so effortless, and they found themselves sailing over the abyss as if it were no more than a ditch. They had a glimpse of the awful boulder-strewn bottom and they saw the hounds, snuffling and searching the ground, before being shaken to the heels and running in shock on seeing the Elk rise out of the earth and occupy the air so suddenly.

On landing, the Elk picked up his stride right away and they flew faster and faster over the earth, while he sang the song of his life to them. It told of the days spent with his own people as they ranged over the land, of the softness of his mother, of young being born, and the old ones dying. It celebrated the taste of sweet grasses and herbs and praised the mercy of water that washed away the scent of those who were hunted. His song was about freedom and being, and the joy he had in these two things; it praised the sweet night air as they flew along. And then the song was about the coming of the ice and the long slow dyings; of the springing up of thick forests where many died, trapped by their antlers in the meshing branches; of being near to death himself; and of being found by men who pitied him and took him to a secret and holy place, where they covered him with sweet earth and sang him to sleep with magic. He sang of the whiteness of their robes and the beauty of their chanting and he ran thus through the rest of the night, leaving them when light came delicately to the rim of the world.

Again he bowed down and they slid from his back, nerves jumping violently in their legs from the incredible physical power of the galloping they had experienced. They stood on their unbiddable legs beside a small carthouse.

Pidge gathered the silken ropes and held them in loops in his hands.

'Shelter here until it is fully light,' the Elk told them and then he was gone in the lingering darkness, with a pattering of hooves. They heard him gather speed and burst into a gallop and they listened until the sound gradually faded and they heard him no more. Shakily, they went inside the carthouse and sat on a pile of hay, smiling gravely at each other while they waited for daylight; for the experience with the Elk was too strong to be spoken of, and they were spellbound.

They waited, slowly winding the ropes into balls, until well after the sun had touched the world's rim. They waited all through the morning birdsong, until the dawn was truly complete and the darkness was no more.

Chapter 26

WHEN at last they came out of the little carthouse, they looked about them with very great curiosity. Having travelled such a long distance through the concealing darkness of night, Pidge especially wanted to find out if the Elk had taken them closer to the mountains. But everything far away was still shrouded in morning mist and it was impossible to know one way or the other.

For the moment the carthouse itself took hold of their attention.

They saw that it was unusual in that it had a little spire and a weather-vane on its roof. Such an odd thing must have been built by someone for fun, they said, agreeing with each other.

The weather-vane was of an interesting design—a painted metal man. He stood on one leg with the other sticking out at the back, at a right angle from the knee; and his two arms were stretched out at either side, in a way that might have been graceful if it hadn't been so exact and stiff. Standing on one leg as he was, and with the two arms sticking out as though for balance, he looked exactly like a skater; but one who was badly held back by his nerves.

He had an exceptionally long nose.

So cunningly was he made that his hat looked to be on the point of lifting off from his head, whistled away by a wind that wasn't blowing; and his coat-tails and his long, striped scarf appeared to be billowing out behind him, held up by a non-existent gust of air.

For a while they stood admiring him.

By this time the nervous spasms has gone from their legs and like all normal legs they could be taken for granted; and no doubts at all that they could match, in walking, the stretch of the day.

They had only just begun to move off, when they had the

great good luck to find an old abandoned garden. Pidge had privately decided that they would just walk at random until the mists cleared and then take a bearing; but now he thought that they might as well have a look in the garden instead, to see if they could find some things to eat for breakfast.

It was growing right beside the carthouse which had itself once been part of one of the garden's walls. The walls themselves had been much taken down by time and all that they would have to do to get inside was simply to step over a few stones.

At first they could hardly be sure that it *was* a garden because it was so overgrown with weeds and briar. Hundreds of wild flowers, whose names they didn't know but whose faces were familiar, grew everywhere; and among them was the reassuring sight of dandelions and daisies, the ones in shade still fast asleep. Although he didn't understand the full meaning of these two flowers, the moment he saw them Pidge knew that it was all right to go inside.

Through the wild confusion of growth ran a network of narrow paths trodden into being by the countless small journeys made by wild animals. In following these they found blackcurrant bushes with fruits as big as cherries; and sweet red gooseberries growing on almost thorn-free bushes and they were not much smaller than golf-balls. After their first natural greed was satisfied, they moved in easy stages through the inviting disorder, still following the tracks drawn on the ground by the animals. Their mouths were continually filled with the thick sweetness of jellied seeds and the air was full of the strong scent of crushed blackcurrant leaves.

With the great abyss safely between the hounds and themselves, Pidge fancied that they could spend the whole of the morning there if they wanted to; but even so, part of him still listened and his common sense told him to keep the advantage that they had gained. But not just yet, he thought blithely.

Wandering on, they found red currants that went pop inside their mouths and released delicious bursts of liquid that only made them want to eat more. And then they came to two trees bearing yellow and purple plums that were cool and silky to the touch, and so soft and luscious that the juice spurted in squandering fountains at the slightest, most delicate tasting.

But soon they had eaten their fill and they followed the last track of all and discovered that it took them right back to the broken wall where they had first come in, right beside the carthouse.

They had almost forgotten about the metal man and were taken by surprise when he spoke to them.

'Dear sir or madam,' he said. 'Business as usual. Inasmuch as, heretofore and notwithstanding.'

Even though there was no wind, as they looked at him he spun.

For want of oiling he creaked rather badly and after just a few moments of spinning he came to a slow, gradual stop.

'Oh, what a turn I just gave myself! First today,' he said to no one in particular.

A blackbird landed on a nearby branch and said:

'I hope you are in good spirits, Needlenose?'

Before replying, the metal man slowly lifted his hat with a tooth-watering screech of his elbow joint.

'The best, the best! Please excuse brevity of reply. Yours cordially,' he said cheerfully. He replaced his hat with a clang and said: 'Ow!'

'I've been waiting for you to wake up—I had a row with my wife this morning,' the blackbird began.

'Do you say so?' Needlenose asked in an interested way.

'I do. Now to shorten my story—she's left me. And there I am with three naked, half-starved children with mouths like opened oysters, bawling for food. It can't be done, Needlenose —not with only one pair of wings and a single beak doing the catering. Find her for me, Needlenose—before my children die.'

The painted eyes of the metal man filled with tears of liquid metal that gathered into the corners and became solid and looked rather like ball-bearings. They spilled from his eyes and rolled down his cheeks and they rattled on the slates of the carthouse roof.

Again he lifted his hat.

'Regret to hear of your sad loss; but thank you for your esteemed inquiry. The matter will be dealt with as soon as poss,' he said.

He replaced his hat with another clang and said: 'Ow!' And

with ball-bearings spraying out in all directions, he spun round again.

Pidge and Brigit had to leap backwards to escape being struck by the little metal balls.

The metal man still creaked but not as badly as before.

When he stopped, he said:

'Dear sir, In answer to your valued inquiry, I beg to state that your little woman had gone home to her mother to make a complaint; but that you may expect a happy outcome, as even now, your lady wife is returning to you and the babbies. She is on the wing, sir. Her mother told her not to be silly.'

'There's a deal of power in your nose,' the blackbird said, and he flew away to meet his wife.

'Really?' Needlenose shouted after him. He was so pleased that he stopped crying at once.

'Sunwise!' he cried joyfully, and away he went again into a spin.

'Everytime you do that or lift your hat, you knock water out of my teeth,' Brigit said to him when he had stopped.

'Do you tell me so?' he replied, sounding even more pleased.

'Yes. You make the teeth want to run out of my mouth,' she said.

'One good turn deserves another,' the metal man said by way of answer and he went round and round again.

This time he was facing away from them when he stopped.

'Care for a bearing, madam? North, South, East, West—the Cardinal Points as they're called? The half points, the quarter points—any fraction you like! A course, an alignment, a diagonal, sir?' he called out, apparently to the empty air.

In answer, a group of swallows appeared and flew in darts around the metal man's head.

'What's the news about the winds for Africa, Needlenose?' they asked.

Off came the hat with the now familiar creaking of the elbow joint.

'Beg to acknowledge your most welcome request for information. It will be complied with at the earliest. Yours faithfully,' he said, and back on went the hat with the usual clang and then he said the usual: 'Ow!'

When he had stopped spinning once more, he said:

284

'In reply to yours—beg to state that your request is un-seasonable and winds you require are not in stock at present. Please try again later, in triplicate. With compliments. Your obedient servant!'

The swallows thanked him and flew away.

Now he was facing the children again and he said:

'Good prospects up here, sir. But I know what you're going to say!'

'What?' asked Pidge.

'Everyone's got good prospects when they stand on top of a roof—or a hill. That's right, isn't it, sir?'

'I suppose it is,' Pidge answered doubtfully, not too sure of the metal man's meaning.

'I knew you were clever like me the moment I saw you, sir. I did, indeed. Can I be of assistance? May I help you, madam?'

'Yes. Could you find a direction for us, please?' Pidge asked.

The hat was raised.

'I welcome the favour of your custom. The matter will receive earliest attention,' he said.

The hat was replaced and he said: 'Ow! That's another headache I've got. First today!'

'Do you get many headaches?' Brigit wondered.

'About a dozen every day.'

'You shouldn't take your hat off so often.'

'Politeness can sometimes cost a lot,' the metal man said, and he spun.

'It must cost him a fortune in aspirins,' Brigit muttered sympathetically to Pidge.

The metal man stopped.

He stood silently for a moment and then he spun again.

He stopped.

Once more he spun, going wildly round and around.

When he stopped this last time, he took off his hat and scratched his head in puzzlement. The noise was so awful, Pidge and Brigit had to put their fingers in their ears. They saw him return his hat to his head and say: 'Ow!' Then they removed their fingers again and waited to hear what he would tell them.

'Confess that I am at a loss. Regret, am unable to comply

with your request. Please state precise destination, or nearest town or village.'

'Could you speak more plainly? I don't understand what you are saying,' Pidge said.

'Yes. Stop talking all lumpy. Talk in a straight line, Mr Needlenose, please,' Brigit said.

'Oh!' the metal man said, sounding surprised. 'I'll try. Could you tell me where exactly you want to go?'

'I don't know exactly,' Pidge said guardedly.

'Ah, that explains it. Destination Unknown. Category—Lost Property.'

'You're at it again!' Brigit said accusingly.

'Beg pardon. What I mean is—you must be Lost Property. I could direct you to the nearest Lost Property Office, if you like. You could sit on a shelf until you're claimed, on production of a receipt. See under—"Conditions Of Acceptance".'

'We're not Lost Property,' Pidge said laughing.

'Indeed we're not. We're on a journey for the Dagda,' Brigit said severely.

If I'd realized that she was going to say that, I could have tried to stop her, Pidge thought ruefully.

But he was reassured at once to see that at the mention of The Dagda's name, the metal man's hat went high up in the air.

'Great Guardian Of The Seasons; all honour to the Good God,' he said, with the deepest respect possible. 'You must be Pidge and Brigit.'

'I'm Brigit all right,' she agreed, nodding.

'How do you know who we are?' Pidge wondered.

'I know because the winds bring me all the news. See, it is written at my feet: "NEWS".'

He pointed downwards and sure enough, on top of the little spire on which the metal man was balanced, there were four arrows arranged in a cross and at the tip of each one, there was a letter.

286

'Don't they mean North, South, East and West?' Pidge asked politely.

'They point to the world's ends beyond doubt, as a help for travellers who want to go a little or a long way: and it is from the world's ends that the winds come screaming or whispering to me, gathering up every little scrap of news on the way.'

'We are travellers. Could you give us a direction, please?' Pidge asked.

'I couldn't.'

'Why couldn't you?' Brigit demanded to know.

'I am not a master of the secret way you go. I can find a direction for the whole world but not for you.'

'Why can't you find it for us? Other people have helped us and you should be better at it than anyone else at all,' Pidge persisted, feeling baffled by the metal man's refusal.

'Take my best advice and hold your own course unchanged.'

'I was thinking of going—' Pidge began to say.

The metal man butted in quickly.

'Hush! A wrong ear could be listening. Now I have given you a timely warning and my best advice, and I can do no more.'

This seemed to be so final that Pidge felt obliged to accept it.

'Well, thank you anyway,' he said.

'You're very welcome. Before you leave, may I invite you to come up and admire the view?' the metal man asked, as though it meant a lot to him.

'Well that would be very nice another time, but not now. We should be moving on. I'm sorry,' Pidge said.

'Come up, do. I believe it would do you good, lovely fresh air up here. Please come,' the metal man insisted; and falling back into his old way of speaking, he added: 'Please accept my kind invitation as a refusal often offends. Dress Optional. R.S.V.P.'

'I suppose I could spare a few more minutes. What do you think, Brigit?'

'You go up. I want to do something else myself,' she said, and grasping the hem of her dress in bunches in her left hand, she held it out before her, making a sort of bag or hammock, which she then started to fill with some stuff that was growing near to the garden.

287

From the broken wall it was easy to get onto the roof and then get across to the friendly figure that stood on the little spire. When Pidge was close to him, the metal man bent over with a terrible groaning creak, whispering into his ear through the deafening noise:

'Take a good look and spy out your way, silently. The best of good luck to you and to Brigit.'

'Oh, thank you, sir!' Pidge said in gratitude as he understood now why the metal man had insisted that he should come up, and as he realized how the creaking noise was a hindrance to a wrong ear.

'Call me Needlenose as all my friends do,' the metal man said.

Through a rift in the mist the mountains could partly be seen. In spite of the distance that the Elk had taken them, he saw that they seemed no nearer, but he was pleased to see that at least they were no further away. He examined the country between the carthouse and the mountains for landmarks that they could use as pointers, if the mountains should ever be hidden again. He saw that if they travelled directly cross-country, they would eventually come to what looked like a very large wheatfield; but he couldn't be sure of what lay after that, as the ground seemed to fall away into some kind of valley from an edge. Beyond that, the mist still lingered.

'You've been very helpful after all, Needlenose,' he said.

'Most honoured to be of service,' Needlenose replied.

'Here!' Brigit shouted, her head appearing just above the roof-eaves. 'Stuff this in his hat to stop him getting headaches.'

She had gathered a thick sheaf of long grass and numerous lumps of moss.

Pidge crossed over gingerly, wishing that he had rubber soles on his sandals, and took them from her. He did as she had suggested while Needlenose watched with hopeful interest.

'When the hat is full, put the rest of it on top of his head,' she said.

When next the metal man put on his hat, there was a gentle, muffled thump and Brigit told him that he could always get the birds to gather some for him, from then on.

'This is wonderful,' Needlenose said with his eyes filling. 'What a good, kind girl you are.'

'The winds must have told you,' she said.

'Quickly! Get down! I can't hold back the tears and they could hurt you!' Needlenose said, and he sobbed.

Pidge scrambled down off the roof and they moved away only just in time.

'Goodbye, Needlenose!' they shouted as they struck off across the fields.

'Goodbye! Goodbye!' the metal man cried, as the ball-bearings poured out of his eyes and clattered down the roof to bounce off the ground. 'In conclusion, I affectionately bid you farewell. Your loving friend, Kiss Kiss, Needlenose.'

For a long time they could still see him whenever they looked back. Each time they gave him a farewell wave and he responded by lifting his hat and waving back to them gaily.

289

Chapter 27

I T was somewhat later than midday, when they arrived at the wheatfield.

In the time that had passed since they had left the metal man, Pidge had been trying hard to understand about Needlenose. But no matter how many times he went over it in his mind, he just couldn't puzzle out why the metal man had not been able to help with a direction; and it was all the more baffling when he was so openly friendly towards The Dagda and themselves. In the end, all that he could do was to blame himself, for not properly explaining about how much they had been helped already by The Dagda's friends.

If only I'd told him about the kite and the white birds; and the way that Finn and Daire had taken us to the Hidden Valley and how they helped us, it might have made a difference, he thought remorsefully. I'm sure I made a bad mistake in not trying harder to explain. But it's done now. And it was something after all, to see so plainly where the mountains were, from that good spying-out place on the carthouse roof— and it's no good crying over spilt milk, and maybe we are not doing too badly, I hope.

He followed Brigit in over a dry stone wall.

From ground level, they faced a solid wall of yellow, ripe wheat that had grown very tall, much taller than Pidge. A narrow strip of headland ran between the boundary wall and the wheat; and Pidge said that they would walk along it, to see if they could find a path that would allow them to cut through to the other side. He knew that when the seed was being sown in the spring it was often the custom, if the field were very big, to leave a path unsown for use as a short-cut after the shoots had appeared; otherwise a person would have to walk the whole way around the perimeter.

Poppies grew everywhere and the wheat was the best that he

had ever seen. The day had turned hot and the whole field shimmered and rustled in a slight breeze.

There was a path.

As soon as they came to it, Pidge went back up on the wall to spy out which way it might lead.

The wheatfield was very big indeed; as big as a small lake, he thought. It spread and spread and he could see the line of the path quite clearly. It went straight as a die and could easily be distinguished as a dark stripe all the way across. With this kind of path, all that could ever really be seen was the break between the two walls of wheat; the growth being always too tall, even when the wheat was only of normal height, to allow the path itself to be seen.

He jumped down from the wall and they went in. Brigit, who was going mad for the poppies, hopped in first.

It was like being in a golden jungle. The gentlest breeze hushed the radiant sea of wheat, that seemed to give out a brightness that coloured the air above it, and was reflected on the children's faces. Now and again there was a startled scuttle as they surprised a rabbit or a fieldmouse that happened to be too close to the edge of the path. Mild crowds of butterflies of all colours and sizes, twitched and hesitated about the ripe ears of wheat, and throughout the field millions of insects created a vast drone of life. High above, hundreds of skylarks sang through the stillness of the day. One after another they dropped like stones and, still singing, they hung only bare inches above the wheat. Then they went up again to do it all once more, just for the thrill of it, one would think.

Apart from the birdsong and the soft sounds the wheat made, and the occasional flittings of nervous small animals, there was the creaking of a host of grasshoppers all playing the same tune but on differing notes. The ones nearest were the loudest but the far-away ones could be heard in company with them; and they were all like a great festival of massed soloists, each insisting on competing at once, with everybody obstinately refusing to listen to anybody else at all.

Over all of this, there was a huge langorous stillness that made Pidge go drowsy and dreamy with pleasure. A lovely peace came into him and despite the goldenness of the wheat, he felt relaxed and safe and he knew that it was all natural and real.

291

Brigit was picking poppies as she went along ahead. They all soon fell to rags but she couldn't resist the colour. She was thinking that they were lovely except for the smell they left on her fingers.

'Wouldn't it be nice for these poppies if they smelled like cowslips or roses? Wouldn't they like to? I wish I was a flower with my own perfume and everything, and I'd never have to get washed with soap,' she said.

'You wouldn't like to be a flower and have no legs, to be stuck in the ground and not able to move—and a slug coming along to take a bite out of you,' someone answered from somewhere amid the wheatstalks.

'No, I wouldn't like that,' she agreed, thinking that it was Pidge who had spoken.

'If flowers had legs, you wouldn't like to be a slow little slug, because everytime it saw you coming, your dinner would run away and you'd always be hungry.'

Brigit sighed heavily.

'I wish slugs didn't eat flowers,' she said wistfully.

'We all have to eat something and that's a rule of life.'

'Yes. But I wish that slugs didn't eat flowers all the same.'

'Who are you talking to, Brigit?' Pidge asked, coming out of his trance.

She looked back at him in surprise.

'You, of course,' she said, very puzzled that he should ask.

'No. You were talking to *me* and a nice interesting conversation it was too.'

And suddenly, and without causing the slightest disturbance to the wheat, a magnificent dog-fox was standing in between them on the path.

'I hope you are fond of foxes?' he said with an unmistakable wink. His face seemed to hold aspects of intelligence and humour.

'Oh, very fond of foxes!' cried Brigit with delight. 'That's because I'm not a chicken.'

The fox coughed delicately and was, to all appearances—instantly very deeply absorbed in studying a splendid green beetle with polished wing-cases and quite remarkable antennae, who was taking a casual ramble up a wheat stalk.

Pidge frowned, thinking of Auntie Bina's beloved poultry, and said:

'Who are you?'

'I am a friend and I'll come with you for company's sake if you'll let me. My name is Cú Rua, but my good friends just call me Cooroo.'

'You'll be followed by hounds if you come with us,' Pidge warned.

'It wouldn't be the first time,' Cooroo answered, sighing. 'They're what they call foxhounds, I suppose?'

'No. I don't think so; they're a different kind. Much thinner and all brown coloured.'

'Oh do come!' Brigit pleaded, putting an arm around his neck.

Cooroo laid his muzzle against her arm in a gentle kind of way and said:

'What does Pidge say?'

'Who told you my name?' Pidge asked, interested to know, but hardly surprised.

'Was it the winds?' Brigit asked.

'You told the bees your troubles and they told others until it came to me,' Cooroo replied, as though surprised that they didn't know.

'I never told the bees anything, did I, Brigit?'

'Not a word.'

'Well, they heard at any rate. It seems that they were working the clover near a hill that was ploughed; and the story is—that you had lost some valuable thing—something that was helpful— and you cried out about it because you were very upset.'

'Oh, the scrying-glass—that's true,' Pidge agreed, as he remembered that he had half-noticed the bees.

'Could we be moving on?' Cooroo suggested. 'I never like to stay in the one place too long. I don't even like to be out in the daytime; but if I have to be out, this isn't a bad day for it.'

'Will you let me stroke you sometimes?' Brigit coaxed.

'I'd be pleased,' the fox said, and suddenly he looked shy. Pidge smiled at him.

'We'll go on,' he said.

293

Chapter 28

'WHAT kind of a day is a bad day?' Brigit inquired as they sauntered on along the path.

'A heavy day, with the sky overcast, when the scent sticks to everything. It's better to stay in a hole freezing and starving on days like that.'

'Why?'

'Why is what *I'd* like to know,' Cooroo said bitterly. 'All I do know is—if I'm out on such a day, it's: "Bloody end to you, my fine thief!" and: "View Halloo!" and other strange cries. And horses and hounds and a long run until my heart feels as if it would burst through my ribs. It's my belief that they are all stone mad. And sometimes, there's death in it, on such a day.'

'If you didn't take chickens, they wouldn't hunt you,' Pidge ventured.

Cooroo turned and looked steadily into his eyes for a long moment.

'Oh, but they would. You know it and I know it,' he whispered sadly, and then he moved on.

For a while there was silence, broken in the end by Brigit who had been thinking her own thoughts.

'I like chickens because they're mostly daft, they make me laugh; and I like ducks because they always seem to be smiling,' she said.

'I like ducks too, they taste very well,' was Cooroo's opinion.

'So they do,' she agreed.

'I like to eat as I'm under the impression that it's good for my health,' Cooroo remarked, looking innocently skywards. 'Of course if I were a dog, I could sit up and beg; but as I'm a fox, well sometimes I steal. Now, would I rather be a beggar or a thief, or what is there to choose between the two? What do you think, Pidge?'

Here he gave Pidge a sideways look and Pidge was almost

sure that the fox was laughing at him. With Brigit agreeing with all that Cooroo was saying, he thought that he had better put a word in on Auntie Bina's side.

'About the chickens . . . ,' he began.

'Oh yes?' interrupted Cooroo. 'Why don't we talk about rats?'

'Rats?'

'You know the damage *they* do. And supposing I take the odd chicken or two—what's that to the number of rats and rabbits I eat?'

'I'd eat a rabbit but I'd never eat a rat, yerk!' Brigit said, making a face.

'But the cost!' Pidge persisted.

'Cost? What do you mean?'

'The cost of the chickens and what it takes to feed them.'

'Oh, the *cost*!' Cooroo said in a sarcastic kind of enlightened way. 'Horses grow on trees for the picking, do they? And oats fall from the sky in showers! Hounds can be gathered free like mushrooms on a September morning, can they; and they relish famine and live on moonlight strained through silk washed down with tap-water? And I suppose you've seen cocks of hay floating in on the spring tide to be forked up like seaweed?'

'I never have,' Brigit said emphatically.

'Add it all up and what have we?' Cooroo asked.

'What?' Pidge said warily, feeling that he was losing.

'Saying it plainly, we have the price of the horses, their stabling, feed and tack. We have what is paid for their shoeing at the blacksmith's—am I right?'

'You are,' said Brigit, nodding vigorously.

'Then we have the price of the hounds and the food *they* eat; we have the wastefulness of the rabbits and the gobbling and spoiling done by rats. It all adds up to a big bag of money and it's all to save the price of a few chickens by killing me. What a lot they spend to save a little money!'

'You forgot to say about vet's fees,' Brigit said. 'We know all about these things because we keep horses at home, don't we, Pidge?'

'But—' Pidge tried to say something, but Cooroo cut in again.

295

'They should be *paying* me for all the good work I do. Why—they wouldn't even have to muck out after me, or pamper me with bed and board. It would be more fitting if they would think of what I do to the rats and not what I do to a few hens—if they can think.'

'What I was going to—' Pidge began again, but Cooroo broke in as before.

'They begrudge me my own life—they want my death and they seem to get pleasure out of it and that's a fact.'

'Why do you take chickens at all?' Pidge managed to ask.

'I like the taste.'

'So do I,' Brigit said, defending him, adding reprovingly: 'And so do you, Pidge.'

'Once in a while there's carelessness with door fastenings, and a lucky way left open that's too great a temptation for me, a thief. But there are times when it's hunger-forced work, and if I don't find something to feed the hunger, the hunger will feed on me—and that's another way to die that I'm not fond of.'

Pidge considered in his mind the things that the fox had just said. Hunger-forced work sounds really awful, he reflected in the end, and said nothing.

'In bad times,' Cooroo continued, 'I could believe that all I am is hunger with a nose; but that's only when I'm starving.'

'What do you think other times?' Brigit asked.

'After I've eaten I feel like a cub,' he told her, and he leaped up into the air and then chased his own tail in a small circle on the pathway to show her what he meant.

'But truly, hunger is the sharpest knife. Ah, my poor vixen,' he said, almost to himself, as they walked on.

For a long time there was only the rustle of the wheat in response to the stirrings of the air; and the conversations of insects and birds.

'She was so clever and such a way she had with woodcock,' Cooroo said in a kind of loud whisper that seemed to come from his heart.

Pidge gave him a quick look, wondering if the fox were laughing at him again, but he saw that Cooroo wasn't thinking of him at all.

'Will I never forget that time of hunger and cold—a time

when starvation can beat intelligence—and she ventured out against all reasoning. They were on to her in a flash. I did everything to draw them away from her, barring jumping into their teeth. I flaunted, I barked, I ran across her scent—oh, so many times. But they were like machines. The hunters followed her without mercy all of that day and where she got her strength, I'll never know. She was so beaten in the end that she lost her footing on a small overhanging ledge and fell into a lake. Whatever chance her tired legs had running on land against the softness of air, there was no chance at all in the struggle against the deep water. She swam, very feebly, as far as she could—but she was done-in, and drowned from pure exhaustion. Ah, it is a sad and puzzling fate to share the world with man, but what can we do? My poor vixen—she could charm anything but the hounds, will I *never* forget it.'

The children were deeply saddened by Cooroo's words and Brigit was on the verge of tears. Her eyes shone and her lip quivered. Pidge thought it all very terrible; and to distract Brigit he thought that he would bring the conversation back to chickens.

'Just tell me,' he said. 'Why don't you take just one old hen. Why do you lay about you and kill so many?' he asked, rather unwillingly; realizing that it sounded as if he were picking on poor Cooroo.

'Aw Pidge, leave him alone,' Brigit said, her face looking woebegone and her voice sounding fretful.

Cooroo looked at her with concern.

'I *would* take one old hen if they'd let me,' he said to Pidge though still watching Brigit's face. 'But you know yourself how cracked they are. No sooner do I put my nose in and say: "Good evening, Ladies! Anybody in here got foul-pest?" or any other joke like that—when they're squawking and screeching in a way that'd waken the dead, let alone the man with the gun. You know yourself what they're like. They have only to lay an egg and the whole world must know about it. You know how batty they are, don't you, Brigit?'

'Yes,' she said, beginning to smile.

'Of course you do. Well, then I panic and try to shut them up; but it's always too late, do you see?'

'I see,' Pidge agreed, partly for Brigit's sake—for you could hardly expect the chickens to do anything else but make a fuss, he thought.

'Now that we have all that behind us, perhaps we can be friends?' Cooroo asked hopefully.

'I'm your friend already,' Brigit said very earnestly and throwing her arms around his neck, she hugged him.

'I know you are, Brigit.'

'And so am I,' Pidge said, and he was. And in his heart he wondered how it so happened that a few hens had become so valuable that they could cost the life of a beautiful fox.

Cooroo laughed in short happy barks and went on ahead through the golden radiance of the wheat.

Suddenly, from behind them, came the baying of hounds.

The hairs sprang up on Brigit's arms and her eyes widened. Pidge felt the back of his neck stir in a horrifying way. It was so unexpected. Until this, they were quite certain that the hounds were far, far behind, because of the difficult barrier that the Elk had so easily crossed.

Cooroo was not startled at all as a part of him always listened for this sound; but his neck-hair had a roughened look and his nostrils twitched.

The breeze made a rustling sound in the growth around them and, because everyone was so tensed to listen, it seemed to be much louder than before.

After a silence during which they stood rigidly listening, the howling came again.

Now Cooroo was extraordinarily alive. His eyes were full of sharp intelligence and his body was ready to spring or run or do anything at all that he wanted. Instead of doing any of these things, however, he lifted his head and tested the wind with his nose.

'It's in our favour. We're all right for the moment,' he said.

'What I'd like to know is—how did they get across that rotten old abyss?' Brigit scowled, her voice full of rage.

When the hounds had recovered from the shock of seeing a huge animal appear out of the ground to fly over the abyss like a bird, they had talked among themselves uneasily.

'The strange one with branches fixed to his head like a

298

deer— runs!' Silkenskin had observed worriedly. 'Do the two-legged cubs run also since they are on his back?'

'There are no bonds on us not to hunt *him*!' said Lithelegs to general agreement. 'May we also hunt *them*?'

'The cubs themselves do not run—they sit. I, Greymuzzle, have seen it.'

'Then we must continue to follow only and not hunt in earnest? It is Wolfson that asks.'

'Surely, legs run under them, they speed and the cubs are carried forward. Therefore, do they not run?' Swift inquired.

'Fierce speaks. If we may say that they now run, the condition is broken and the bond is dissolved, since this has happened within our sight.'

'The question is—do they run?' said Findepath.

'The flea on my back runs if *they* run! The flea on my back has a wondrous speed with my legs under him!' Fowler said scornfully.

This was such a ridiculous idea that it caused a burst of unchallenged laughter, and they all agreed that they would continue to trail and not hunt, once they had crossed over the abyss.

They waited for The Mórrígan's help.

In the glasshouse it had been discovered that one of the rats had been cheating unfairly by eating some of his spare cards. He was just thinking privately that there wasn't much nourishment in Kings and Queens but that Diamonds seemed to be slightly better, when one of the rats that sat beside him raised an objection by giving him a smart box in the ear. Bullying broke out then, and soon there was a fist-foot-and-mouth fight in which tails were bitten and noses scraubed, and all the harmony of the poker-game was shattered.

The Mórrígan had long since laid the looking-glass aside, placing it face upwards on Breda's workbench. She had returned her attention to the table landscape, had smiled in amusement to see the children's dismay at the burning bridge and had frowned delicately when they had gone into the tree. Now she turned to watch the rat-fight and she laughed.

Melodie said that she thought them all quite charming.

'How pleasant and refreshing it is to see them being so natural, the vicious little rascals,' she said indulgently.

They enjoyed the fight until it got half-hearted and then Breda separated the few who were still at it and plonked all of the rats firmly back in their places. She declared that the cheating rat had been out of order, on the grounds that the cheat hadn't worked— but that it would have been all right if he hadn't been rumbled.

Melodie had conjured some tiny cigars and she was on the point of giving the first rat a light, when the fun was interrupted by a barely audible cry from the hounds on the table landscape.

They had waited for help that had not come. When there was no response, they had called on the three women to notice thier plight, by throwing back their heads and howling loudly.

The women went to the table, saw the Elk speeding like an arrow away into the distance and the hounds waiting patiently at the edge of the abyss.

'They should have jumped that or died trying,' Melodie said, her voice snappish.

With an impatient movement, The Mórrígan closed the abyss by reaching forward and pinching together the edges of a large crack that ran along the table's surface.

The bracelet, as ever, swung against her wrist.

The hounds got going at once, pushed and prodded into a good start by the women's wands. The Elk, of course, had vanished in the dark distance, but the hounds followed on with fidelity, although they were very far behind indeed. Findepath, Lithelegs, Rushbrook and Swift did well in the matter of scenting, for the Elk's spoor was wide.

During all of the time that Pidge and Brigit had spent in the cart house and the wild garden, the hounds ran. They ran while the children lingered with Needlenose. And still they ran when Pidge and Brigit resumed their journey, half-dawdling or walking at their own natural speed.

This was the way they had crossed the abyss and why they were, by now, not very far behind.

Chapter 29

With Pidge now leading the way and Cooroo acting as rearguard they hastened through the wheatfield, Cooroo having first cautioned them to try not to disturb the high-growing stalks by brushing against them with their bodies as they passed.

'Don't make it too easy for them,' he had counselled.

When they reached the end of the path he stopped and asked the children to wait. He lifted his head and with his ears cocked, he listened. At the same time his nose searched in every possible direction.

'We're safe enough for now,' he said at last; and only then did they emerge from the cover of the wheat.

'Now,' he said, as they went along the headland towards an open gate, 'try to keep in cover as much as you can, even if it's only the shady side of a stone wall. And again, whatever you do, don't disturb anything as you walk, but step throughtfully. If the hounds should happen to be looking your way and you are causing bushes and saplings to move, you might as well be waving a flag at them, do you see? Don't touch anything at all with your bodies to keep the scent slight—then it will only be on the ground. If these hounds are clever, they will allow one nose to do the work; and all of the rest will be content to keep pace with that one until he tires. Then one other will take his place. If they're stupid, they will all be trying to catch a sniff and they'll get in each others' way. If you spread your scent out by allowing things to touch you, you'll be helping them to move faster. To make it as hard as possible, it would be well if we all travelled in a single line.' The fox's knowledge inspired great confidence in Pidge.

They left the wheatfield through the open gate.

'We do things step by step,' Cooroo now said. 'Look out for a ditch, or somewhere that is damp, as a way of going. Never fail to go through thorn bushes and clumps with prickles, and be pleased if you find any. That's the way to give the hounds a few sore noses and make their work uninviting.'

'We haven't got the same kind of skin as you. If we go in thorn bushes we'll get scratched ourselves,' Pidge pointed out.

'Oh, that won't do at all,' said the fox. 'Forget about that bit, so.'

Now they were standing in the broad far-ranging country without walls or fields. A long way off, and growing at a lower level, was a forest stretching as far as the eye could see; and beyond the forest the mountains stood.

Not far from the wheatfield gate there was an evil-smelling dungheap. Cooroo's eyes danced with mischief when he saw it.

'Roll in that! You first, Brigit,' he said.

'No fear!' she answered with a powerful disgust.

Pidge burst our laughing.

'But you should,' Cooroo insisted, 'and be very glad we found it.'

'No, I won't!' she said shaking her head.

'But it would be good fun. It would set the hounds a problem; they wouldn't be sure if they were following us, or wayfaring cows, and the smell would fill their noses. Go on, Brigit!'

'I'm not rolling in it and that's flat.'

'How can you be so foolish? At least get plenty on your shoes—do that much!'

Pidge was laughing so much, he had tears in his eyes.

'Stop laughing, Pidge,' Cooroo pleaded. 'Set her an example and you roll in first.'

'There's no need,' Pidge blurted out, shaking with giggles.

'How can you say there's no need? How can you stand there laughing when we could be running for our very lives at any minute?'

'That's just the whole thing,' Pidge explained, while spasms of laughter still bubbled up from somewhere in him. 'We *dare* not run and we have no need for tricks. We can't run if they're actually in view, and they can't run to catch us unless we do. They're not hunting us at all, they're only trailing us. There are bonds on them or something. And during this journey

302

we've found out that they obey the bonds.'

'What are you telling me!' Cooroo exclaimed. He was utterly astounded.

'We can run now, this minute—if we like, because we can't see them, yet. But I don't think we should, as this country is so open and unsheltered. They could be looking at us before we realized it and got the chance to stop.'

'This is a new thought for me,' Cooroo said slowly.

'You don't have to worry at all,' Pidge said, his fit of laughing over.

'But surely, when they see me they will hunt me, as I am not protected by the bonds?'

'Oh, but you are! Don't you see? While you're with us they can't come at you without running at us. You're safe, Cooroo.'

'This is a moment I'll never forget. This is the best news I have ever heard!' Cooroo said, and he threw his head back and barked with laughter.

'It's wonderful to think that they could hear me and it wouldn't matter,' he said, and he did it again.

'Are they near us yet?' Brigit said fiercely.

Cooroo tested the wind again.

'No,' he said. 'They're still a long way off—but coming.'

'It'll be hard luck on them when they meet me!' she said recklessly, and she made two small fists and waved them about wildly.

Then she stroked Cooroo.

Chapter 30

'SEE our small enemies? The Dagda keeps step with them all of the way, it seems,' said the Mórrígan, her voice rough with exasperation.

Melodie and Breda moved to her side.

'What has he sent now?' Breda asked, scowling.

'A fox. A sly one.'

Melodie shrugged her shoulders and said:

'His skills are worthless in this matter; he will be of little use to the brats. And if they should happen to run, the hounds will be happy to tear him apart.'

No sooner had she finished speaking than The Mórrígan gave a horrified scream. Her eyes sparkled darkly, her knee-caps slipped rapidly up and down her legs, and her toes stood at right angles. She sizzled with temper and was spitting like a sausage in a pan.

'What ails you?' the others asked, as they saw nothing on the table to warrant this kind of anger.

'Something of The Dagda's on my bracelet! Something *good* on my wrist!' she replied in a horrible husky voice that was heavy with offended loathing.

She pointed to a red rash that had surfaced in patches on her skin and then, in the blink of an eye, she snatched at her bracelet and ripped off the little golden Castle Durance. She grasped it between thumb and forefinger and gave it a good shake.

A thing, too small to be seen by the human eye fell out. It landed invisibly on the table and, in time, grew to visibility. It got bigger and was a pale, tiny thing like the smallest seed that could ever be. It grew further still and was unmistakably the scrying-glass.

Quivering with hatred, The Mórrígan used her fingernails delicately and picked it up.

At once, the air was colder.

A small hiss escaped through The Mórrígan's clenched teeth.

The scrying-glass grew even bigger and when she gave it an experimental shake the artificial snow flew.

When the travellers were about half-way across the wide expanse of country between the wheatfield and the forest, the weather changed. One moment the world was at its ease under the sun and the next moment the air chilled and the wind began in a sly way. Brigit was soon complaining that she was perished.

It was a cold wind, a frost-blowing wind, and under its influence the grass swayed and silvered.

The sky had changed. There was a watery-looking sun that looked like a thin shaving of raw of turnip and was pale orange with blue blotches. The sky looked pallid and empty.

It was colder by the second. The sharp wind buffeted them about the head until their ears were singing. It ruffled their hair and chilled the skin on the backs of their necks and bit cruelly at their faces as if it were a frost-wolf with teeth of ice. At their feet the ground frosted and Brigit found a frozen toadstool softly coloured pink and buff; and although it was solid and heavy and rock-hard, she thought it perfect in its strangeness.

They stood shivering in their summer clothes, completely overtaken by the speed of it all.

Pidge looked back and saw the shapes of the hounds in the distance, looking grey in the poor light.

'They've caught up,' he said, and Cooroo bristled.

'I'm freezing to death, Pidge,' Brigit said. Her teeth seemed to rattle as her jaw shook.

He fumbled in his pocket and with stiff fingers he probed inside the leather bag for a hazel nut.

When he managed at last to bring out a nut, it lay jumping slightly on his trembling hand. He thought it would never open, although really it opened almost at once. He had to hold out his arms to take the treasures the nut had contained as they grew in size. And in his arms he held two hooded coats of some

305

kind of white skin, with boots and gloves to match. The bigger coat was lined with some kind of red fur and the smaller one was lined with blue. They struggled into them, relieved to find themselves warming up at once, but their hands were still cold. With numbed fingers they picked laboriously at the straps of their sandals, Pidge helping Brigit in the end, and they put on their boots. Brigit slid her hands into her gloves and the inside fur felt as soft and warm as swans'down, and from the tips of her fingers, her hands warmed up.

'It's like being dressed in a feather bed and we look like eskynose,' she said and she snuggled her shoulders under her hood.

Pidge flattened the sandals neatly in pairs and put them in the school-bag. Gratefully he slipped his gloves onto his hands and they were ready to go on.

Then Brigit started to worry about Cooroo as there was nothing in the nut for him and he had waited so patiently in the cold until they were well-clad.

'You'll be cold with your poor bare paws.'

Cooroo laughed.

'No, I won't,' he said cheerfully.

'But you haven't any boots or socks, and your paws have to walk on the cold ground,' she said, frowning.

'I'm already well-dressed in my own thick skin and I don't need boots,' he said and, lifting a paw, showed her his dark hard pad. 'See? Just as good as those you have,' he assured her.

So they carried on walking on the brittle grass. The pliant earth had gone rigid with the cold and whenever they found a flower it looked to be carved out of coloured ice, and every bush they passed was decorated with transformed cobwebs, the loosely spun ones like ropes of crystals and the tunnel webs were cones of organdie.

Occasionally they looked back and saw that the hounds were keeping their distance.

Again the sky changed and now the sun was like a white peppermint stuck on grey paper. The wind blew against them and they braced themselves inside their coats and trudged on. They passed a small stream that gushed coldly and then a large puddle that already had a skin of ice.

They reached an edge where the ground fell away in a sweeping shallow that spread for miles and miles to the right and left. And there before them was a massive forest of oak and ash and beech. From where they stood, they could see that it really was a wild old forest and not a mere plantation or small wood. Even as they looked, the top leaves on the trees were carried away in great sweeps by the wind, and in a few minutes the bare branches and twigs were like black scratches against the grey sky. Pidge thought sadly of the wonderful wheat and how it would all be destroyed.

'Just what we need, plenty of cover,' Cooroo murmured.

'Won't it be hard to get through with all the undergrowth?' Pidge asked.

'Nothing to the trouble the hounds will have when they're tied to a scent. The undergrowth will make them even slower when they can't see us again.'

Dusk was falling as they entered the forest and the first snows flew.

Inside the scrying-glass the snow had continued to swirl and would not settle.

The Mórrígan lost patience and, using her full force, she threw it away—only to find that it would not *be* thrown away. It travelled no more than a few inches at the remarkable speed her strenuous throw had given it—and then it came to a stop and hovered steadily over the table. It cracked slightly and some of the snow fell.

'A fox and snow, great difficulty for our hounds. The Dagda baulks us at every turn!' The Mórrígan said, her beautiful face crooked with anger.

'If there is a fox, if there is masking snow—let there be hunters,' said Breda.

She went back to her rats, selected four and made the rest go like breath on a cold window-pane. She changed to hunters the pair she had chosen to be hunters, and the other pair she changed into superb horses already equipped with saddles and bridles. The hunters wore belted white tunics and heavy cloaks of scarlet wool. Their hair hung down below their shoulders and it was as fair as silver. In their hands they carried long spears to be used as goads against the hounds; and each one had a hunting horn hanging from the belt under his cloak. In spite of their good looks and the handsomeness of their trappings, there was still something rather pointed about the shape of their faces and this was true even of the horses' muzzles.

They were warned most solemnly to do no more than track.

'You cannot kill as yet,' they were told.

Breda reduced them from rat size to the scale that was suitable to the table landscape and she placed them among the hounds. Their nostrils were already working eagerly and their eyes gleamed.

One of the hunters blew his horn and the other threatened the hounds with his spear. The hounds knew that they were enchantments and that they belonged to The Mórrígan and were therefore untouchable.

Findepath was humiliated and unhappy, but Fowler only smiled secretly deep inside himself where no one could know.

An air of superhuman calm descended on the glasshouse and the little cat grew bored and fell asleep.

Chapter 31

A T first the snow floated like feathers, but quickly changed to come down as a thick blanket that covered the tops of the trees. Some of it escaped the catching branches and after a time Cooroo was covered, and he too had a white coat.

The floor of the forest was uneven and rough in places. To begin with the going was easy, as the undergrowth was shrivelled from the wind's blast, but further in it became more difficult. Where the wind had not penetrated, the spaces between the tree trunks were choked with foliage, and almost covered with bracken and saplings, ferns, brambles and wild fuschia bushes. Brigit kept a constant watch for nettles.

Cooroo was clever and it wasn't easy at all to keep up with him. His head moved constantly as he spied out the best way to go. Sometimes it would be a long finger of short-grown grass, and other times just bare ground where young trees had failed because the growth above had created a lack of light. There were many places where the earth had fallen away, leaving small escarpments and making little hollows where knotted roots were exposed. These were natural dug-outs and much used as homes, as the many burrows and scrapings showed. Sometimes they walked on moss but a lot of the time Brigit walked through dead leaves. Pidge never once noticed the way that Cooroo always looked to him for approval before going forward. At intervals, and for reasons unknown to him, Pidge chose the less easy way; Brigit always grumbled when this happened but Cooroo never complained. The frost glittered on his muzzle before vanishing on his breath, but it stayed on his brow and his eyes were brightly ringed. Brigit said that he had tinsel eyelashes and that he was a Christmas fox. She and Pidge were wonderfully warm now and the boots were soft as well as dry.

They reached a clearing that was like a natural theatre and

gasped when they saw how thickly the snow lay. The children ran out to the middle of the open space, excited by the marvellous snowstorm and overjoyed to be in it. They were exuberant and happy.

Pidge stood with his head tilted back, looking upwards and letting the snow land on his face. He had to keep blinking his eyes. The falling snow made him feel very tall, as if he were a tree standing in its own space.

The snow came powerfully down, flake upon flake. It fell commandingly in its thousands of parts and no power in the world able to stop it. Pidge imagined a policeman standing with one arm raised, saying: 'Halt!', and he laughed and laughed. And then he pictured a grand Judge with his best wig on and his worst face, crying: 'In The Name Of The Law!', and he laughed even more. Brigit was laughing too, as she kept trying to catch an extra fat flake before it landed, and she fell flat on her face into the luxurious whiteness at every second step.

Suddenly they heard the note of the hunting horn for the very first time.

Pidge started in surprise.

'What was that?' Brigit called, only mildly curious.

'I think it's a hunting horn,' he replied.

'What are they hunting?' she asked, looking with anxiety at Cooroo.

'Us,' said Cooroo.

'What? The cheek of those brazen brats!' she said indignantly.

'Not to catch us, though,' Pidge reminded her, hoping that it really was true.

'We'd best go on,' Cooroo advised. 'No!' he added as they began to continue across the clearing. 'Come back here to me and then we'll go around the edge. Let them work for their living!'

So they came back to him, stepping in their own deep footprints, and followed him as he skirted round the edge. Straightaway he found an animal track that went deeply in and, with a glance at Pidge to see what he thought, he took that way. When the track petered out, he found the best way to creep under things to little clearances, and always he found a

310

passage, and each time he waited for Pidge to decide. And still Pidge was not conscious of the many little nods or head-shakes he had given, but just thought that he was following Cooroo.

With their thick coats and boots, they no longer feared the undergrowth. They were well-protected, as long as they shielded their faces from snatching thorns by bending low their heads from time to time.

It was darkening rapidly.

Whenever they reached a glade or small open space, or even a place where timber had been knocked, they looked up and saw the snow whirling. All of the high branches were thickly coverd. There began to be whooshing sounds now and again, near and distant, as the weight of the snow became too much for the branches to hold, and it fell with soft explosions to the ground. Underfoot, the earth was frozen solid and, when they stepped on a stiffened puddle, the ice sometimes cracked like sugar candy; and at other times it splintered with a louder noise that was like the crack of a whip it was so sharp and loud. Cooroo told them to avoid the puddles and he advised them to keep to the quieter parts, and he said that Brigit shouldn't walk through the brittle leaves. Brigit was sorry about this because she thought it was like crunching through cornflakes, with the way the leaves rustled.

Every time they reached a new clearing they found that the snow lay deeper and deeper. In an odd way it made the near trees look tremendously powerful. Pidge discovered that if he kept looking down as he walked, he had the sensation that the whiteness at his feet was coming up to meet him. It made him feel slightly dazed so he stopped doing it.

A hound barked and the sound cut through the air loudly. A horn was blown and they shuddered. Soon after this, they heard far-off crashing noises and they knew that the hunters had entered the forest at last.

They turned anxiously to Cooroo.

'We are still well ahead,' he reassured them calmly. 'The snow is covering up for us, so now they really will have to work hard.'

'But I'm getting so tired,' Brigit said.

'No rest yet,' he answered, kindly but firmly; and they went on, but they were not going as easily and lightly as before.

311

'I hope they all get snow stuffed up their noses when they smell for us. I hope they all get miserable colds in their heads—and I really mean it,' Brigit said.

Pidge, too, was tired. He knew it was worse for Brigit as she was younger and smaller. His legs felt heavy and weak at the same time and he started to wonder if they would have enough strength to drag on to wherever the end was.

Suddenly, the horns of the hunters rang through the forest; and it was terrifying and bloodcurdling because there seemed to be more than one, and they sounded as though the hunters were making good progress. Without another word they hurried on, seeming to gain new energy from fear.

Pidge thought of the plantation of pines that he had imagined was a forest, and he remembered the woodman and his axe; and he was glad that now there was no deception, and that at least they knew where their enemies were, even if they had no idea of what the hunters were like or how many were in the sport.

If we meet up with any person, I'll be very careful, he said to himself; especially after the people in Castle Durance, as well as that woodcutter. Animals and insects seem to be the ones we can most trust and I won't forget it.

The ground had become even more broken and rough. At times they had to scramble over rocky outcrops and make their way round boulders and across frozen streams. Yet, tired as they were, when they happened on a stilled waterfall that dropped from a high edge as a sheet of ice, they forgot their tiredness and stopped to wonder at it. Brigit muttered that it was like the track of a giant snail but for being too beautiful.

From behind a dog barked and almost immediately a second dog howled and then a hunter blew his horn.

'Two strayed—brought back to the pack by the horn,' Cooroo explained.

With the coming of darkness, the wind had dropped and the trees were silent. Now it returned and shook the branches and took some of the snow off the tops in furious billowing clouds. This time the wind was blowing from behind. Cooroo said that this was good because it blew their scent away from the hunters and also it would keep him informed of where their enemies were. He stopped and tested the wind. All at once an expression of disbelief and amusement crossed his face.

'I think I smell my dinner,' he said, and he was gone.

In one second—he was gone! All that they saw of him was the tip of his brush as he disappeared in the falling snow.

The children were utterly shocked and surprised. Pidge felt bitterly disappointed. He felt that Cooroo had deserted them in the middle of their troubles, just to go and hunt for himself. He could scarcely believe it.

'We'd better be going on,' he said gruffly.

Brigit was too surprised to even know what question to ask.

They walked on through the forest.

At last Brigit said:

'Will he be coming back?'

And Pidge answered:

'I don't know.'

With the wind in his face and the snow almost blinding him, Cooroo made his way silently. His nostrils worked continually and the trail he followed was the trail that he and the children had made themselves. He didn't stop until he found a place from where he could get a reasonably good view of anything that might emerge from the surrounding trees into a small clearing. He didn't cross the space but lay down at the edge in a little hollow between two rocks. He waited. Soon he was covered with snow.

It was a terrible wait and he wondered if he were simply waiting for his own death. The hunters and the hounds were coming nearer and the fearful rustling in the undergrowth grew louder and louder. His hackles rose.

Suddenly he half-glimpsed the leading hound as it emerged from the trees and into the clearing. Through the swirling snow, the hound's form was blurred and it was difficult to see it properly. Still Cooroo waited.

Following Findepath, four more hounds came into sight. They plunged into drifts near the trees, half-sinking. Cooroo didn't as much as twitch. The forest seemed alive with the sounds of the horses' hooves although in truth, they were very muffled. And then the two riders were out of cover. Cooroo crouched lower. The figures of the riders, shrouded in their cloaks now turned white, were as obscured by the blizzard as the hounds were. They sat hunched in their saddles and were mere shapes. Fighting his instincts, he waited until they had gained the centre of the clearing, and then he sprang out with his teeth bared and his amber eyes ablaze.

'I know you well! You are RAT!' he said, making a leap at the hunters and their horses.

At once, Breda's magic was broken and instead of the mounted hunters, four rats stood blinking on the hard-frozen snow.

The hounds were struck rigid.

They gazed spellbound at the rats, and then there was a snapping and a snarling and the blind impulse towards action. The rats were no longer untouchable.

With sharp cries of fear they scattered; and the hounds went after them.

Cooroo laughed and he glided away. Then he ran to catch up with his friends, and knowing the way made it easier.

The hounds chased the rats until they vanished as puffs of grey dust, and then disgruntled and tired, they took up their laborious work once more.

314

Chapter 32

THE children were overjoyed when Cooroo appeared beside them again. He was panting but he seemed to be full of something like fun.

'I thought you'd left us for good,' Pidge said.

'Did you get your dinner?' asked Brigit.

'No,' he said, still panting, but his eyes danced with mischief.

When he had got his breath back, he told them what had happened, stopping in his tracks to suppress his laughter.

Pidge felt awful.

'You could have been wrong. You might have been killed. And we would never have known what you did for us,' he said, his voice agitated.

Cooroo pushed against him with his shoulder. It was a nudge of playful good humour.

'I wasn't though—was I?' he said.

'You were lucky the hounds didn't go for you instead of the rats,' Pidge insisted.

'I must have much more than a one-chance life,' Cooroo answered jauntily, and they went on again.

In a while the wind dropped completely and the snow stopped falling. And after a long time, when they left the forest at last, it was really dark.

The night was calm and still and full of silence. It was wonderfully beautiful. Everywhere the snow lay thickly, frosted and glittering. The stars were low in the heavens and they were fantastically large and they glittered as well. The moon was a great shining gong in the sky and it hung in a bowl of brightness and was glorious in its vivid shining.

They stood and revelled in it.

'It's like an ORMOUS marshmallow,' Brigit breathed with the deepest admiration.

As they walked through the snow that had settled close to the forest, they sank at every step; but when they walked in the open where the snow was frozen it bore them well, except for Cooroo. For a while all stayed perfect, and they looked around them and at the sky with the greatest pleasure and feelings of possession.

But in the end the wind came again and found them out. If anything, it was more cruel than before. In moments the snow fell twisting and swirling again.

'Oh well, we creep on,' said Cooroo.

Pidge could well see that even the fox was tired. He sank to his haunches step by step. His head drooped and he was panting slightly. By this time he was completely covered in snow, and it occurred to Pidge that it would be quite difficult for anybody to actually see them when they were all dressed in white.

Now the wind whipped their coats open and played round their bare knees, soon making them numb with cold. Ice needles spiked into Cooroo's nose.

They trudged on, bending into the wind. From a long way away came the faint baying of the hounds.

'They are well-astray and no better off than we are; let that hearten you,' said Cooroo.

The wind stole tears out of their eyes and pinched their faces.

'I feel so tired,' Brigit said weakly. 'Wouldn't it be nice to make a snow bed and lie down for a while?'

'We daren't, Brigit. We must get as far from the hounds as we possibly can,' Pidge answered sympathetically.

By now, he could no longer tell whether or not he had legs. Everything felt numb and mechanical. He listened to the snow creaking under his boots. It let him know that at least he was still walking.

'It's no good,' Brigit said with a moan. 'I have to lie down or I'll die.'

'If you lie down, you *will* die. You're too young to know it but it's true. Snow isn't as soft as it seems and it can kill,' Cooroo said firmly.

'I don't care,' she cried, her knees buckling.

'Come on! You must keep going whatever it costs. Keep

316

moving! Force one foot in front of the other. Keep going!' Cooroo shouted.

Pidge stumbled in closer to Brigit to catch her arm and help her on. More than anything in the world, he wanted to lie down himself, but he knew that Cooroo was right.

A tall shape loomed in front of them suddenly. Because of the falling snow it had been impossible to see where they were going and, as there was a great, natural, muffling silence, they hadn't heard anything approach.

They stopped dead and peered ahead to try to make it out.

It was the Great Elk.

Chapter 33

H E stood motionless in the swirling whiteness, a living assertion of dignity and power.

They looked up at him with gladness as he turned his massive head towards them; already the snow was turning him white.

'I will help you,' he said.

At once Pidge felt greatly comforted. The Elk turned to Cooroo.

'It is an ill thing to be hunted, is it not so, Little Red Dog?'

'Oh thank you, Great Elk,' said Brigit. 'Thank you very much.'

Slowly, carefully, the Elk bent his forelegs and knelt.

'You are still too high,' said Pidge.

The huge animal folded in his back legs and lay on his side.

'Climb up and hold on tight. You also, Little Red Dog.'

Pidge helped Brigit to scramble up and when she was settled he sat in front of her, so that he could shelter her from the savage wind.

'It's no good,' Cooroo called. 'I am not able to climb without footholds. It's because I have paws and not hands and feet.'

'If you don't, you'll never be able to keep up. You'll get left behind,' Pidge cried desperately.

'Then I must follow on after you,' Cooroo said, with resignation.

'No!' Pidge said in a shout. 'We're not leaving you behind now. You'll never find us again if we do.'

'You've *got* to come with us or it's just not fair!' Brigit called to him tearfully.

'I'll give you a lift up—wait a second,' said Pidge and he slid back down onto the snow.

He grabbed Cooroo by the thick hair that grew at the scruff of his neck and with his face set for the effort, he pushed and half-hoisted him up onto the Elk, hoping that he was not hurting either animal. With this help, Cooroo, who was making bucking movements, got near to the Elk's shoulder where he lay in a sprawl.

Before Pidge clambered back up himself, he leaned into the wind and struggled through the snow until he could peer up at the Elk's head.

He screwed up his eyes against the blinding snowflakes and whispered:

'Could you take us towards the mountains, please?'

The Elk was silent and made no sign of having heard.

For a moment Pidge stood in the blizzard wondering if he should risk saying it again in a much louder voice. But he thought he heard Brigit moaning and he turned away.

He gripped and he climbed until he was placed between Brigit and the fox. And then, inch by inch, the Elk righted himself while they responded by shifting and wriggling with matching caution, to centre themselves on his spine when he at last stood upright.

Now Pidge took off his gloves and gave them to Brigit to hold. While the Elk waited he felt in his pocket and found the squashed balls of spider-rope. Taking a kneeling position he passed the ropes several times around Brigit's body, doing his best to make her secure. First he fastened an end of a rope to the Elk's hide by sticking it on, as Mawleogs had done, and he didn't fail to do this kind of bonding as many times as he really thought he should, although his hands were getting very cold.

When he was sure of Brigit he settled back in his place and did the same for himself and Cooroo. He didn't bother with reins. At last he felt that they were as ready as they'd ever be, and he took his gloves from Brigit and with the greatest difficulty, he put them on his now frozen hands.

And now the Elk began his journey.

Soon they were going at a good speed with the Elk galloping as smoothly as he could so as not to shake them off. The wind whipped their faces. Ice crystals fringed their eyes. But it was so much easier now. All the slogging labour of walking had gone and it was simply a question of not falling off and of enduring the cold.

At times Pidge fancied that he was riding and controlling a

horse, and at those times he would press a knee against the Elk's hide and imagine that the Elk obeyed him.

Although he trusted the ropes, he kept his arms stretched out in front of him clutching at the Elk with his gloved hands. In this cradle, Cooroo lay shivering and very soon Pidge's muscles ached from the strain. He worried about Brigit sitting behind him. Even though her arms were clasped about his waist, he feared that she might fall off without his knowing. But when she laid her head sideways against his back and he felt her weight, he was reassured.

Sometime during the journey, it came into Pidge's mind that this was forever. They just went on and on through the storm, with unchanging sheets of whiteness on either side and they seemed to be going nowhere.

Abruptly it stopped snowing and it was possible to really see. Pidge couldn't help but gasp in wonder, not only at the beauty the snow had created, but because at some distance ahead of them, a light was glittering in the moonbright night.

What could it be?

It seemed natural that the Elk should head in the light's direction. The patient animal slowed down and walked. In time they reached the place where the light sparkled in the crisp night air.

It was a lantern tied in a tree and it swung to and fro in the wind.

What does it mean— is it a trap—why would someone tie a lantern in a tree except as a guiding light—or is it a lure? Pidge's thoughts wandered uncertainly, muddled at this new confrontation.

He tried to stare against its light to see if the lantern had any trace of gold about it, but his eyes felt too tired for the effort.

'This place is good,' said the Great Elk. Immediately the responsibility of decision was removed from Pidge's dulled mind.

The Elk lowered himself once again; but nothing could make getting down an easy matter; for, in spite of their coats, they were frozen into a terrible stiffness and every joint, muscle and bone ached unbearably. The Elk held himself very still, until at last they were standing painfully beside him.

'Look!' cried Brigit. 'Smoke!'

It was true.

Just a little way in front of them the snow had formed a long low ridge. From a bump in the middle of the ridge, a thin plume of smoke was rising. At once they realized that there was a house. It was obviously built in a hollow or the roof wouldn't be so low. The whole house was completely covered in snow.

In a second the Elk had started to dig, his forehooves working at a terrific rate. Clouds of snow came flying backwards and upwards, and landed with muffled thuds at the base of the tree.

While the Elk was digging, Pidge glanced around at the near surroundings and was startled to find that they were at last among the mountains and that they were now in a valley. The valley was broad and they had come all the way along it; and it is no wonder, he thought, that we seemed to be travelling through sheets of whiteness for such a long time, when the mountains are completely covered in snow.

He watched the Elk again. It was clear that he had incredible strength. He had already carried them for miles and miles on his back, as if they were no more than straws, and now, even with all this digging, still his breath came evenly and without effort.

As the snow was being cleared away from the hollow in front of the house, great lumps of it dropped from the walls to the ground. A small lighted window appeared but they couldn't see in through it, as it wasn't made of glass. It seemed to be made of thin honey-coloured horn.

A big blob of snow fell from just under the thatch, uncovering a sign. It read:

And then there was a door.

'I will leave you now,' the Elk said, and before they could realize it, he had leaped out of the hollow and was out of sight. The snow was falling again but they could hear him galloping away. They hadn't even had the chance to thank him for all that he had done.

Pidge read the sign, again thinking that he didn't really like signs. Up until this, all of the signs they had come to had always led to something not right. As he was thinking this, the lantern flickered and went out, making his heart jump. Could it be possible that the Elk had brought them to a wrong place after all? But he wouldn't do that, would he—unless, Pidge thought with a thrill of fear—unless he was not the same Elk; and how could we have known for sure with all that snow?

He looked at the door. Good or bad, he decided, we must get inside and get the cold out of our bones.

He knocked, courage in his closed fist.

'Come in! Come in!' called a voice from inside.

Pidge opened the door.

The first thing he saw was an enormous hearth blazing with a luxurious fire of turf and huge logs. On a little stool by the fire sat a tiny old man.

'That's right. Come in. Close the door against the cold,' he said in welcome, and he picked up a quantity of dried furze and threw it into the flames, where it crackled and sent merry sparks flying up the chimney.

He looks like a dwarf, thought Pidge.

Chapter 34

'YOU'RE welcome! Welcome to the Half-Way House and I'm Sonny Earley! Always a smile and a how-de-do here!' He leapt as nimble as a goat off the stool and came towards them with his arms held out in friendship.

And Pidge thought: This time I'll be careful and I'll not be too quick to trust him.

'Let me help the small one over to the fire—you must be near dead with the cold,' the little man said kindly.

He cradled an arm round Brigit and led her to the hearth, where he helped her off with her coat and boots. He drew a small plush armchair close to the fire and he helped her to sit down.

He pulled up another chair ready for Pidge and from a cubby-hole he took a fat sheepskin and threw it down on the hearthstone for Cooroo. With no hesitation at all Cooroo crossed the floor and stretched himself before the generous fire.

'My kneecaps feel as if they're made of concrete,' whispered Brigit, and she shivered.

'Of course they do, my poor child,' agreed Sonny Earley, and his little adam's apple bobbed up and down with emotion like a very fast yo-yo.

He rushed away somewhere and was back in a twinkling with a couple of fluffy blankets in his arms. He glanced at Pidge who was still standing just inside the door, his wistful eyes staring at the fire as if he couldn't see enough of it.

'You're dripping there like a bit of wet seaweed. Get the coat off and come to the fire and unfreeze yourself,' said Sonny encouragingly.

Pidge came to the heat of the fire, shrugged off his boots and coat, and accepted the blanket that was handed to him. He wrapped himself gratefully in it and sat down, while Sonny got Brigit to stand up so that he could drape her well and then he put her sitting again.

'Now take your ease and I will get some food,' the kind little man said, and he reached into the back of the hearth and pulled forward a big iron pot that was hanging from an iron crook. In seconds Brigit and Pidge were staring into steaming hot bowls of chicken broth in which the fat floated like a thousand golden suns. Two lumps of hot bread, on which the creamy home-made butter was already melting, appeared on little blue plates on their laps. Cooroo was already lapping up his bowlful of broth with bread broken into it. Slap-plap, slap-plap, he went—just the same sound as our dog Sally, but she's not ours any more, she's gone, Pidge thought sadly.

Sonny sat on his stool between the two chairs and he helped Brigit to eat her soup, spooning it for her; and she didn't mind a bit. She was able to manage the last of it herself because she was now warm and her cheeks were the colour of ripe haws. From the feeling of the skin on his own face, Pidge knew that his cheeks were glowing too.

On a shelf there was a cisheen of field mushrooms and Sonny put some to cook on a hot stone, sprinkling salt on the tender velvet of the gills.

'Only a scratch meal,' he kept saying.

Pidge stole a look around the room, thinking how cosy and comfortable it looked in the firelight. There was a dresser stacked with sparkling plates and mugs, and on one of the shelves there was a blue jug filled with roses and daffodils, and on a shelf lower down there was a round green pot crammed with primroses. All of the seasons are well-mixed here, thought Pidge, looking at the flowers and the cooking mushrooms, and knowing that, outside, winter ruled.

'These are out of a nearby lake,' said Sonny, and he attached some trout with bright spots on them to an iron spit. He stuck them well in above the heat at the back of the fire, where it was just a living glow without smoke.

'This now is a very muddled kind of dinner,' he said. 'I just grabbed what was near to hand.'

'Don't worry—I could eat leather!' Brigit said, and she sounded very contented.

'Well, don't eat this,' Sonny joked cheerfully and he handed her a kind of leather drinking-cup.

He filled it with a glowing red liquid which he poured from a leather bottle.

'Everything here is nice,' Brigit said.

'I'm glad you think so,' Sonny replied, looking pleased.

He poured out a goblet full of the drink for Pidge, and for himself he filled a drinking horn that was decorated with filigreed silver. When Brigit admired it he told her that he had won it at a fair.

They tasted the drink and it was like swallowing cherries and blackberries and strawberries all at the same time.

'You wouldn't like this, Cooroo,' said Sonny.

'You know his name,' Pidge remarked quietly.

'I wondered when you'd speak,' laughed Sonny. 'But you are right to be suspicious. Friends told me you were coming. From a long time back, like others, I've known of you and your journey. And today I had messages that you were coming for sure.'

'Which friends told you?'

'Last night, a young merlin came and called me from my sleep. "They are still travelling and they've crossed a terrible chasm," he said. At about mid-day, a thrush flew to my door. "I bring you word," he said "they are still travelling. Compliments of a party named Needlenose." And late today, through the white snow came a white owl who tapped on my window-pane to call me out. "They are still travelling in company with one named Cú Rua whose friends say Cooroo; and they are coming into your country," he said. So I got everything ready for you, as you see.'

There was a pause while Sonny took the trout from the fire and gave one each to Brigit and Pidge on little yellow plates, and he put one in a dish on the floor for Cooroo.

'Mind the bones now,' he said.

'That's a bit strange about Needlenose,' Pidge said after a while.

'What is?' asked Sonny, as he shared the cooked mushrooms between the two yellow plates.

'He wouldn't tell us which way to go, would he, Brigit?'

'No, he said he couldn't.'

325

'Well then, he said no more than the truth—mind you don't scald your mouth, the mushrooms are hot.'

'But, others have shown us the way over and over again,' Pidge explained. 'If I'd told that to Needlenose, he might have tried to find a way for us.'

'You were never shown the way.'

'Oh but we were! You don't understand because you don't know all that has happened,' Pidge insisted politely.

'I know every little bit of what has happened. I know that you were taken through the stones at Shancreg by Serena . . .,' Sonny began.

'That's just it. That's just what I mean,' put in Pidge, nodding furiously.

'Serena is keeper of that gateway and she took you the path in. She was only guiding you into this world. The candles are always there to welcome good friends in; for beauty as well. And it was supposed that Brigit would especially like them.'

'Oh I did. They were gorgeous,' she said. She held up a mushroom and popped it into her mouth and she snuggled into her blanket as if she were listening to a bedtime story.

'Then you crossed three waters with Cathbad the Druid; first over one bridge, then back over another and then you went over the lake itself. That was for two reasons.'

'What were they?' Pidge asked.

'Crossing three waters is one of Cathbad's spells to draw good luck, for luck is a thing separate from the Gods and lies in no one's hands; but it might be attracted. Besides that, you only really began your journey when your feet touched the land on the other side of the lake; for you cannot set out on a journey of such importance without first crossing water. Water is one of the two great elements of purity and the other is fire—it is easier to cross water than to cross over fire, so Cathbad took you that way.'

'What about the wild geese that flew over the Field Of The Seven Maines—they gave us a direction?' said Pidge.

'No. What they gave you was the courage to start, *believing* that you had been shown the way. It may be that as they flew, you were looking ahead of them by one or two wingbeats. If so, it was you that gave them the direction, do you see? But it wouldn't have done at all for you to know such a thing so near

326

to the beginning. Everything was new to you then; everything was shocking in its way. If you had known how much was on your shoulders, you might have been too unnerved to go on. So, even though they appeared to be giving you a direction, what they really gave you was courage.'

'Oh,' Pidge said, amazed. 'What happened with the white birds and the kite, could you tell us?'

'I loved that kite but it went away,' Brigit murmured in a little grumble.

'The hounds had reached you then and you were filled with horror,' said Sonny.

'Small blame to them,' said Cooroo, lifting his dozing head from his paws.

'The kite picked you up and the birds hid you from the hounds and then you were set down. It confused the hounds and gave you a new start—for it was always known that no matter where you were placed, you would find your own way again. And it showed you as well that you had powerful help, as knowing this thing would strengthen you inwardly.'

'And there was Finn and Daire and the Hidden Valley', Pidge prompted him.

'Surely it is all very simple? Like everyone else, they had been warned that you were travelling; so like the rest of us, they were prepared. They went out and wandered on the chance that you would enter their country and come under their protection. Like myself, they were honoured when you did,' Sonny replied, and he smiled with immense pleasure.

'There were two wild geese flying just before we went with them,' Pidge said.

'Yes, but they were really saying—"do not be afraid to go with Finn and Daire as they are friends and you are in their country." In the valley they hid you from the hounds for a while and they fed you.'

'It was lovely in that valley,' Brigit said.

'What about Hannah who did all that washing? What about the way she ran with us for miles and miles?' Pidge asked, although he felt he knew the answer.

Sonny's eyes twinkled.

'She broke your scent and took you the miles to give you

327

another start. No one ever said: "Go this way," or, "Go that way," after you had crossed the lake. You always walked on following your own mind,' he said.

'Suppose the journey should have been on the other side of the lake and not this side at all. What then?'

'Why, then you would have crossed back, you would have felt it. Now do you understand?'

'Yes, except for the nuts. How is it that all the things we needed were already inside, if no one knew the way we were going?'

'The easiest thing of all to tell,' Sonny answered. 'Each nut is empty until your need is known. You can crack one now if you like and see for yourselves.'

'Oh, I couldn't do that,' Pidge exclaimed, horrified. 'We might need them all. Do you know what will happen next, after we leave here?'

'I don't know that at all,' Sonny said.

'One more thing. Cooroo showed us the way through the forest, didn't you?' Pidge said, turning to the fox.

'Of course not,' Cooroo answered, sounding very surprised. 'It's *your* journey—yours and Brigit's. I found myself in a strange place and I came with you for company's sake, remember? And then it was fun to know that I could tantalize some hounds, safely! I'm the scout, but you're the captains. I showed you easy ways to go and how to fox the hounds, but it was always your choice.'

'I see. Is this Half-Way House half-way to where we're going, do you think; or could it be half-way to home?' Pidge wondered.

'It's half-way to many places, but no one knows at all where you are going, except that tomorrow you will have to go through One Man's Pass at this end of the valley, or go back the way you came. There are only those two ways from here, unless you go over the mountains.'

'I'm not going over any old mountains! Why is it called One Man's Pass?' said Brigit.

'Because it's a narrow way. Not as narrow as the way into the Hidden Valley, but narrow enough, all the same.'

'Are we still in Ireland?' she asked.

'You are.'

'But I thought you said we were in this world. What's this world?'

'You are still in Ireland, but you are in Faery too. Here it is like, and it is unlike, the same and not the same. Some people call it Otherworld and some people say Tír-na-nÓg. You wouldn't know what Cooroo was saying to you if you were *only* in Ireland. Do you see?'

'Sort of,' she said, and she frowned hard to make her head work better.

'But we were only in Ireland when a frog spoke to us, weren't we?' Pidge asked dubiously, still trying to understand.

'Puddeneen!' Brigit said. 'His name was Puddeneen Whelan.'

'True, you were. But already, even then, elements of this world had touched and come into yours. You'd noticed a lot of strange things before then, hadn't you?'

'Yes,' Pidge agreed.

'Our frontiers are made of mists and dreams and tender waters: thresholds are crossed from time to time. And so, you understood the frog because there was already a mingling, do you see?'

'Are we really in Tír-na-nÓg? Are these mountains the Twelve Pins?' Pidge asked.

'They are the Twelve Pins in Faery, yes.'

'It's all a bit queer,' said Brigit.

'You know the way you can sometimes see someone who looks lost in a crowd?' said Sonny.

'Yes,' Pidge said.

'No,' Brigit frowned.

'Well, he might be in Faery. Have you ever known one person to stop and listen to the cuckoo calling, and the person standing beside him doesn't hear anything, and thinks his friend is only imagining it?'

'Yes,' Pidge said.

Brigit half-nodded.

'Or a girl might look into a river and shout: "Look! There's a fish!" and her friend shouts: "Where! Where! I can't see it!"'

'Oh, yes!' Brigit agreed.

'The two worlds go hand in hand. As you know from going through the stones, you could be walking through a field and a few steps to the right of you, you could be walking in this world.'

They had eaten everything, the delicious juice-filled mushroom caps and the flaky moist trout, the hot bread and butter and the comforting broth. Cooroo had satisfied the last of his cold hunger with a couple of roasted rabbits that Sonny had produced from a pot-oven.

Sleep was overtaking them as they sat wrapped in the soft blankets before the marvellous fire.

'Bedtime,' said Sonny, and he took Brigit up in his arms, and led Pidge and Cooroo to a little bedroom through a hidden door in the wood-panelled wall under the low stairs that led to the loft. The door had opened when he had touched a concealed spring.

'A secret room!' Brigit said sleepily.

Gratefully they fell onto the small-sized wooden beds, already cosy and warm from stone jars filled with hot water. There was even a bed for Cooroo. All three of them fell instantly fast asleep.

Sonny covered them with quilts filled with goose-feathers and then he tiptoed silently out of the room and closed the door. Quickly he set to work.

First he crushed a great quantity of garlic bulbs to a paste and this he smeared all over the wall where the door was hidden, making a terrible smell. Next he went to his storeroom and from there, he rolled three great barrels, one by one, across the kitchen floor and in under the low stairs, where he stood them in a row. On top of these, he piled sacks of oats and flour, and he hung strings of garlic and ropes of onions and bunches of herbs on to nails and hooks in the panelling. A team of spiders came from their little nooks and began to spin webs between one thing and another. No one could even guess at what was hidden. It just looked like a place to keep extra stores.

Sonny now gathered the children's discarded clothes up from where they lay, he removed the flagstone from its place before the fire, and hid the clothes in a deep hole. He replaced the flagstone and he dragged a sack of dead rabbits all over the kitchen floor and he didn't forget to lay the scent of them on the two little chairs and the sheepskin. He took a small shovelfull of dead ashes across to the spider-webs, and after thanking the spiders and making sure they were all clear, he blew the ashes all over the place so that one would think the webs had been there for ages and that the dusty barrels and sacks hadn't been removed for years. The last thing that he did was to wash all the used dishes and he sat himself down by the fire to wait.

All traces of the children and the fox had gone.

In the middle of the night something intruded into Pidge's sleep.

Sounds.

Sounds of feet in the snow; sounds of people coming into the house. He heard voices speaking and Sonny's voice answering. The only thing he could do was get out of bed and listen at a crack in the wood panelling. He stood there, stock still, but even so, he could only hear a snatch here and there of what was being said.

'We are a party of tourists . . .'

'. . . winter holiday . . . hiking . . .'

'. . . need food and beds . . .'

'See what I can do . . .' Pidge recognized Sonny's voice.

'. . . others staying here?'

Then Sonny's voice, quite clearly this time:

'No. The place is empty. The bad weather, I suppose.'

Then:

'Meat! Must have plenty of red meat!'

'There's only porridge and milk.'

'Pap!'

'. . . pap again!'

Pidge could almost see the nostrils flaring and the lips curl; even though they would now have the appearance of people, he knew they were the hounds.

Unreasonably, he felt safe although they were so close. He got back into bed and lay there listening. It's a good job that Brigit doesn't snore, he thought.

For a time, there was the noise of crockery and eating from the kitchen that was only just next door. Later, he heard the sound of many feet climbing the stairs to the loft.

Without caring, he went right back to sleep.

For a long time, the scrying-glass held its place over the layers of darkness that were above the table, and the snow continued to fall.

At first the women had tried to strike it away with the palms of their hands, but The Dagda's skills would not allow them to touch it. The furious women had then tried to melt the fallen snow with gustings of hot air from their lungs; but these hot blasts had always turned cold, as soon as they reached the belt of chilled air that was over the table landscape. Over and over again they huffed and blew at the snow, but they only succeeded in creating bitter winds that tore across the table's surface, that sent the snow swirling all the more and shrouded everything far beyond the talents of second sight.

They knew that their hounds were hopelessly lost in the now completely trackless forest; and they knew that the children and the fox had given them the slip.

As there was little use in matching magic with The Dagda in this, their efforts seemed to be entirely useless and therefore at an end. But once, when the snow had stopped briefly, they had just time to notice where the hounds were, helped by their faint cries of distress, but not time enough to discover the whitely-clad children and the snow-covered fox in the obliterating snow; for they were white upon white and silent. Later, when the snow had stopped again, they had seen the pinprick of light that was the lantern tied in the tree, and this time, they saw the forms of the children, the fox and the Elk as they approached the light. With their wands, they directed the hounds to turn towards the remote light and then the snow fell again.

Gradually the darkness over the table faded and crept away, but it wasn't until the light of the sun came through the glasshouse roof and struck a glare from the looking-glass in reflection, that they at last found a way of dealing with the snow.

Melodie seized the looking-glass and aimed its dazzle onto the table. As if deciding that its work was done, the scrying-glass went small again and vanished. Since the little glass snowball was no longer working against them, the women were able to breathe on the table with better results. Hot winds blew over the snow and the sun glared down.

It was not very long until the snow had all gone, the land had dried out and the streams glittered in the sunlight.

Then the women were satisfied and they threw the looking-glass away.

Chapter 35

I N the morning, Pidge awoke to smell freshly-baked bread
and to see that the darkness of the little secret room was
lanced by many fine spears of light, the strongest ones
being only pencil-thin. They came into the room through
small cracks in the wood panelling and they softened the
darkness.

Even in these modest sunbeams, the teaming motes danced.

Cooroo was already awake and alert; and Brigit was thrashing
about under her quilt, complaining that it was hot.

From the kitchen came the thump and rustling of sacks
being dragged along the floor and the rumble of barrels being
rolled away from in front of their hiding-place. Sonny was
shouting cheerful good mornings and after they had answered
him back, Pidge told the others of the hounds' arrival in the
night and how Sonny had fed them on porridge. Cooroo said
that he had overheard all that had happened and indeed had
stayed half-awake during the dark hours, listening for
suspicious sounds from the loft above them, where the hounds
had slept. This was all news to Brigit—and she was smugly
gratified to think that they had spent almost a whole night
under the same roof as the hounds, without being discovered.

It really was very hot inside the little room. It can't only be
the heat from the fire, thought Pidge; nor was it, for when
Sonny finally opened the secret door and popped his head in,
the sun's light flooded into the room.

'The hounds came in the night,' Sonny informed them.

'We know,' Brigit said. 'Pidge and Cooroo heard them, but
I was fast asleep.'

'They've gone now. They took themselves off at first light,'
Sonny said. He sounded greatly amused by it all. 'I let you
sleep on though—until I was sure that they wouldn't make an
excuse to come back—out of suspicion.'

334

They came out of the darkness, brushing away cobwebs, and into the brightness that filled the kitchen from the open front door. Through the horn window a soft yellow light fell onto the table where their breakfast was already set out. They crossed the warm floor on bare feet, Brigit with her precious schoolbag already over her shoulder. They sat in the same chairs by the fireside, the chairs where they had snuggled under warm blankets the night before; and Brigit unbuckled the strap and took out the socks and sandals. The sun blazed down the chimney, showing all the turf-dust in the hearth and making a strong fire look weak.

'What happened to the winter?' Brigit asked. She handed Pidge his sandals and socks.

'It's gone. The hot weather has come back,' Sonny replied.

'I won't be able to wear my lovely coat and my little boots and gloves; they'd flatten me on a day like this,' she warned. Her hair was damp from the heat in the secret room.

'They've gone too,' Sonny said.

When they had finished putting on the socks and sandals, he told them to pull back a bit and he then removed the hearth-stone to show them the empty space.

'There's where I hid them from the hounds last night but they are not there now.'

'Why have they gone?' asked Brigit.

'Because you don't need them anymore.'

Sonny put the stone back in place. After thinking for a moment, Brigit said:

'They must have been only a loan.'

Pidge eyed a second pot that stood in a corner of the hearth, off the fire. There was a lid covering it, but he saw that a crusted drip on its side was hardening and turning brown from the fire's heat.

'Did the hounds get porridge for their breakfast as well as their supper?' he asked.

'They did!' Sonny said, looking mischievous.

'Good enough for them,' said Cooroo, and a laugh barked out of his throat.

'Were you up that early?' asked Pidge.

'I was by the fire all night,' Sonny explained. 'I was facing them when they came downstairs, never fear.'

'I'm glad they got porridge,' Brigit said. She looked at the breakfast on the table. Sonny had set it out with honey and gooseberry jam, a big bowl of strawberries, a plate of bread and butter and two mugs of milk.

'I'd see no creature suffer hunger—the porridge took that away at least,' Sonny declared, adding: 'There was meat, but that is for Cooroo. Come and sit over now, everything is ready for you,' he finished.

While they sat at the table having breakfast, Sonny took a bowl from the dresser and put it on the ground for Cooroo. The bowl contained cool meat and gravy with bread mixed into it.

'Eat it all up,' Sonny said to the fox.

He went to the dresser again and brought a handful of green herbs that he had taken from a jar, and he placed them before Cooroo, on a saucer.

'Eat these as well,' he said.

Cooroo looked at the green stuff with a disbelieving, comical expression on his face.

'Do you think I'm a rabbit!' he said, with a humorous crack in his voice.

'No, I don't; but eat them anyway,' Sonny answered.

'Ah no,' Cooroo said, regretfully. 'I can't eat stuff like this—I wish I could.'

Sonny touched him on the head.

'We give you this gift,' he said in a serious way. 'No natural hound will ever match your speed once you have eaten them.'

'Can such a thing be?' the fox asked, amazed and looking at Sonny's face, wanting his hope to be confirmed.

Sonny bent right down and looked straight into the fox's eyes.

'Yes,' he said, and Cooroo licked his hand.

'Eat them up,' Brigit's cheerful voice advised him, as he took a first cautious taste. 'We got some of those from Old Daire and Finn in the Hidden Valley, didn't we, Pidge? They made us as fast as the wind.'

There was a very funny look on the fox's face as he ate the herbs.

Brigit was laughing at him.

'He looks just like the hounds when they got the porridge,

336

doesn't he, Sonny?' she said. It made no difference that she hadn't seen it happen, she just knew it.

'He does,' Sonny agreed.

'How long does the effect last?' Pidge wondered thoughtfully.

'As long as it is needed. Cooroo needs it all of his life; but you are luckier than he is.'

When everyone had finished eating and after Cooroo had given a last loving lick to his bowl, Sonny said that it was time for them to go—the day ahead of them might be busy.

'I must tell you now that the hounds have gone ahead of you into the next valley—if that is where you are thinking of going,' he said gravely.

'They'll get a big surprise when they find out we're not there,' Brigit said and she grinned.

'Do you know your minds yet—about going that way?' Sonny asked lightly—without giving urgency or importance to the question.

Pidge looked surprised, because it had not occurred to him to do anything else.

'If we don't, we'll have to go back the way we came, won't we?' he checked to make sure.

'Yes.'

'Somehow, it feels right to go on. What do you think, Brigit?'

She frowned in thought.

'Have we got to go over a *whole* mountain?' she asked, before she made her mind up.

Sonny smiled.

'No,' he said. 'Less than half way. And it's more like a rising walk than a climb. After you've reached the Pass—the track goes down on the other side into the next valley, in an almost exact copy of the way it goes up on this side.'

'I don't mind going half-way up. I wouldn't mind seeing what it's like,' she said then, with an air of giving a verdict.

'What do you think about the hounds being ahead of us?' Pidge asked her to be sure that she really understood.

'I don't give a rap for *them*!' she answered and ate a last strawberry, with an unimpressed air.

Sonny's eyes shone like jewels.

'How do you feel about it, Cooroo?' he inquired.

337

Without any hesitation at all, Cooroo said that he would face the day with his friends and that he was ready to start.

They walked out of the little cottage and followed Sonny up from the grassy basin where his house nestled so very snugly. They went with him to the one lonely tree where the dead lantern was still hanging; and standing in the darkest part of the tree's shadow, they looked about.

They saw no living creature.

The valley was broad at this end, partly grassy and flower-speckled, but otherwise rough with heather. The mountains were huge and they rose in the form of a horseshoe or broken circle, with Sonny's house placed deep within it near to the broad end. Pidge looked back and saw the break where they had come in through the snow the night before. They had certainly come a long way in. It seems ages ago, he thought.

Sonny put a hand on his shoulder.

'This is the first of three valleys. All of them are open in some way so that it's possible to get from one to another. And there's the path leading over into the second one,' he said, turning Pidge round with one hand and pointing with the other to the rise of the mountain on their right.

The path was easily seen. It went up and across the body of the mountain like a sash. The upward curve didn't look steep at all.

'Is the path wide or narrow—is it safe?' asked Pidge.

'Wide enough for an ass and cart all the way. It's a good, safe walking-path, well-used. You can't see the Pass from here; but once you are through it, you'll be nearer to the next valley than to this one. It's not that far, you see.'

Now Pidge, colouring as he remembered how suspicious he had been when he first came into the cottage, took Sonny's hand awkwardly.

'You have been so good to us, when we really needed help,' he stammered. 'We are so thankful to you.'

'Yes, we are,' Brigit agreed. 'Last night I was so cold I was as stiff as a dead fish. And you made us warm and gave us our dinner and the lovely beds and the secret room and everything. Thanks a lot, Sonny.'

'Aren't you going to knit me any socks?' asked Sonny, his eyes twinkling.

338

'How did you know about that?' she asked, going pink.

'Never mind!'

'Goodbye,' Cooroo said, and he licked Sonny's fingers.

Sonny took the fox's head between his hands.

'You're a brave one,' he whispered, and then he released him.

'I won't make a speech,' he said aloud, clearing his throat, 'but it was all a great pleasure to me. Whatever I did is as nothing to the good work that all of you are doing. I'll say farewell now, and may health and courage go with you.'

The three friends walked away, turning once to wave.

Certainly the path was easy. It followed the natural line of the mountain and the way underfoot was even and well-trodden. Cooroo went padding on ahead of the children, pausing every so often while they caught up. His nostrils searched constantly for the hounds and his eyes missed nothing.

It was not until they had been climbing for some time, that they realized the true size of the mountain. They had all stopped to look backwards and downwards at Sonny's house. From where they stood, everything was clear; the cup-shaped hollow, the roof of the house where the turf-smoke curled lazily upward, the tree—but it all looked very, very small. A tiny figure waving to them was Sonny. He looked smaller than Pidge's thumb. They waved back. Now that they saw how far up they had already walked, they were amazed.

The path curved round the flank of the mountain then and they recognized the Pass a little way ahead of them. It was something like a railway cutting through rock and nothing like as narrow as the way into the Hidden Valley. Evidently, in the past, there had been rockfalls there, leaving an accumulation of crags and boulders. Cooroo made them wait while he scented carefully, before saying that they could go on. As they went through the Pass, their feet made echoes as they walked; and they admired the small plants and ferns that grew wherever there was a foothold in the stone.

Coming out on the other side, the mountains to the left of them sloped away; and as they followed the path, lesser heights and ridges were revealed.

Up here they were in a different world, and the differences lay in being amongst the beauty and majesty of the mountains

339

and in walking higher than they had ever walked before. They were in a world of many splendours where the air was beautifully still. Far-away peaks were violet and rose-coloured, and some went up and vanished into white cloud. They could see plunging waterfalls in places that were so far away the waters couldn't be heard; and everywhere there were splinters of light from the flash of the sun on quartzite and water.

As they travelled round the flank of the mountain, new scenes appeared behind the height to the left of them. Once there was a high-level grassy plateau, where calm sheep grazed above a great circular hollow that held a lake of the most intense blue. The random bleating of the sheep seemed to come from somewhere as far away as a star. The sides of the hills were sun-dappled and when the fleecy clouds in the sky moved along, the shadows ran over the hills.

They stopped for a while and stood among harebells and pink-belled heather, for the pleasure of watching the birds gliding and sailing in the sky *below* them. They remembered how it had been when the kite took them away, and they wished that they themselves could really fly with real wings, because it looked such marvellous fun when the birds circled with their wings curved, lazily floating on currents of air.

While they stood, Cooroo waited. His eyes searched and examined constantly and his nose persisted in testing the air. He never stopped studying the world about them, but always in the way that mattered to him. Without even knowing it, Pidge had quite given up his habit of watching out for the hounds, leaving this job entirely to Cooroo who was best skilled at it. It was part of his life's work, after all.

When in due time they moved on, the path took them right to the other side of the mountain, before beginning to slope down gently and, before very long, they were looking down into the second valley.

Part Three

Chapter 1

FROM the place where they stood, a wide and pleasant valley opened out before them far below. It was green and fertile, it was wooded in parts and they could see a shining stream of water falling from a height that seemed remote. The floor of the valley spread for quite a long way and then it went narrow, and curled round the sweep that was the rising bulk of one of the mountains on the left-hand side. It reappeared in the distance as a small glen and then it was gone again, hidden behind the jutting base of a towering spur on the right, where the water fell. The ending of the valley could not be seen. The more distant parts that they could see shimmered in the heat of the sun.

Up here they couldn't help feeling set apart from the rest of the world. There was a most profound silence, so strong that Pidge felt he could almost reach out and grasp at it, as if it were a tangible thing. It made them both feel dreamy. If one spoke, the other felt that the voice came from far away, as the bleating of the sheep had seemed to come softly from the stars.

The earth is quiet, thought Pidge.

'I think I'll be a mountainist when I grow up', Brigit said, her voice drowsy.

Pidge laughed quietly to himself. He didn't bother to tell her the right word to say; it seemed not to matter.

'The world is beautiful', he said. It was as if he knew it for the very first time.

A few moments later, they began their descent. Little by little and step by step, the dreamy state left them and when they were about half-way down, it was entirely gone, and Pidge thought: Now I know why people say 'down-to-earth' and what they must really mean by it.

Again it was easy going.

They stopped just once more and looked up in delight at a

great flock of white birds flying overhead, and among them they saw a pair of swans linked with a silver chain. They knew that they were the same birds that had sheltered them when they flew with the kite, but there weren't as many as before. The birds flew all the way down the valley and then disappeared behind one of the mountains.

'I wonder where they are going?' Brigit said.

But, of course, no one could answer that.

At last they reached the level land of the valley.

After they had walked for a long time, and just before they reached the part where the valley narrowed, they sat down to rest at the side of the path, with their backs against a large boulder that was warm from the sun. Soon after this, a little wind sprang up, and they saw that coloured leaflets or handbills of some kind were being sent all ways by the breeze.

One fluttered against Brigit's sandal and she handed it to Pidge to read. The print said:

BAILE-NA-gCEARD ✿
celebrates
ANNUAL SWAPPING DAY
All the fun of the
FAIR
Merry-go-Rounds
SWINGS
chair o' planes
COME ONE
~ COME ALL ♪

'Oh,' said a thrilled Brigit. 'Swapping Day. At last!'

'Have you still got your box of sweets?' Pidge asked.

'Oh yes!' she answered, shaking her school-bag. 'Come on!'

She jumped up and tugged at Pidge until he was on his feet as well. Cooroo didn't move.

'What does all this mean?' he asked quietly.

They explained all about the swapping sweets to him.

'Come on,' Brigit urged him. 'It'll be great fun.'

'What does this Baile-na-gCeard, mean?' he persisted.

'It means a town of some kind. Baile means town, you know. It sounds like Bally, in English. I don't know what the other bit means. I've never heard that word,' Pidge explained as best he could.

'A town!' Cooroo said, sounding depressed. 'I wouldn't last five minutes in a town. If they don't kill me they'll want me for a pet.'

Brigit dropped down on her knees and put her arms around his neck.

'But you must come—we won't let anyone harm you,' she assured him.

'And this is Tír-na-nÓg—it's different here,' Pidge added.

'No matter. I'd be filled with dread. No. It looks as if I can't come with you,' the fox said sadly.

'But I'm almost sure that no one will hurt you,' Pidge said to him very earnestly.

'Almost is too small a word to put between life and death, Pidge. You don't know how terrible I would feel. I would be defenceless among many people. You can't be sure that everyone here is good. You'll have to go on without me.'

'But last night you walked into the cottage of a man and you felt safer than I did at first,' Pidge persisted.

'Last night I would have put my head in a hunter's lap, I was so weary. And when I smelled the message in that house, I knew that I would not be hurt,' Cooroo explained patiently.

'You don't want to leave us, do you?' Brigit asked, her eyes filling with tears, as she hugged him.

'Indeed I don't,' Cooroo answered, and he licked her lovingly.

'There must be something we can do,' Pidge said. He sat down again and Brigit sat by Cooroo.

'I know,' she said after a moment. 'We could get a bit of string and put it round your neck and everyone would think you were a dog! What about that?'

Cooroo had to laugh.

'See my brush?' he said.

'We could plaster it down with water and it would just look like any old tail.'

344

'Look at my face!'

'It's a bit like a dog, isn't it, Pidge?'

'Not much,' Pidge said.

'I'll get a lot of grass and stuff your cheeks with it and then you'll look fatter,' she said.

'You couldn't make a fox look like anything but a fox. Dear Brigit, it isn't any use thinking about it,' Cooroo said, and he sighed in a resigned way.

A hazel nut fell out of Pidge's pocket on to the grass and it split open. Now they were all relieved and quite sure that in a second or two they would find the answer they needed. But the tiny object in the nut grew to be a wicker basket, and when Pidge lifted the lid, they saw—food. There was a shiny brown earthenware pot, with steam rising out of two small holes in its cover, and other covered dishes; there were chunks of buttered bread and packets of biscuits and a cake; and there was even a large sauce-boat filled with mayonnaise. As well as the food there was a small table-cloth and a mug with daisies on it, a plate, two spoons, a knife and a fork.

Brigit was disgusted.

'What's all this stuff for? It's not long since we had breakfast! We don't want an old picnic, do we? It's a mistake, isn't it. It must be the wrong nut,' she said crossly.

She was full of anger. She looked at the food and at her box of swapping sweets and at Cooroo, and she got up and stamped around, kicking at stones and making fists of her hands and shouting:

'It's not fair! It's not fair!' over and over again.

Cooroo watched her with amazement, but Pidge waited for a few minutes and then said:

'Come on, Brigit. Sit down. We'll think of something.'

'Will you try another nut?'

'Yes. But sit down first.'

While Brigit stamped around in a fine old temper for a bit longer, Pidge took the lid off the steaming earthenware pot to see what was there. It was full of hot soup.

'Would you like some, Cooroo?' he asked.

Cooroo shook his head.

Pidge put the cover back on. He didn't bother to investigate the other covered dishes for he certainly didn't want to eat.

'You see,' Cooroo began, following his own thoughts, 'it's broad daylight and I would be mortally afraid in a town. I am only an ordinary fox. It may well be that I took a step away from the ordinary world and found myself in Tír-na-nÓg—how do I know that I won't do the opposite and find myself back in our own world at any minute? I would be among my enemies and helpless; the dogs in the streets would kill me and tear me to pieces.'

'I understand,' Pidge said kindly.

Brigit, her face flushed, stood in front of them.

'Are you going to calm down now, Brigit?'

'Yes,' she said gruffly, and she sat down beside Cooroo again.

The second nut didn't open. They waited for a fair time and in the end Pidge put it back in the bag and he stuffed the bag well down in his pocket.

'I don't think it's ever the wrong nut. The first one is the right one,' he said.

Suddenly Cooroo stiffened.

'Someone comes,' he whispered, and he was gone like the whisper itself, to hide behind the boulder.

The children watched that part of the road where it swept out of view behind the projecting base of the nearest mountain, curious to see who would appear.

A moment later a figure was there; and coming along the road towards them was a very strange woman. She was big-boned and of a good height, and she would have looked even taller but that she allowed her head to fall forward and rest on the bony framework of her chest. Her yellow hair was wild and matted, her green dress was travel-stained and tattered, and it fluttered at the calves of her legs, in rags. A great thorn held an old shawl in place where it met and overlapped at her breast. She walked in her bare feet.

As she came along, she seemed to be a creature in the grip of two powerful moods that struggled to rule over her. At one moment it would be anger—rather like Brigit's—and she would knock sparks off rocks with her stick and slash furiously at bushes; and the next moment, she would stagger under a terrible burden of sorrow and lurch from one side of the road to the other.

Brigit stared at her aghast. Then she decided that the woman might be drunk and she moved closer to Pidge for safety.

They saw that rain fell on the woman.

This was the strangest thing of all, for it seemed to the children that the rain fell *only* on her; and then splashed down onto the small company of ducks and geese that followed after her, bathering away to themselves in their own language, while they enjoyed the raindrops as they fell from her and onto them. Even when she was at her angriest, the rain never stopped and that was because her sorrow was stronger than her rage.

The children stood up, pressing themselves again the boulder, and they watched her approach with anxious eyes.

Chapter 2

THE woman appeared not to notice the ducks and geese, her surroundings or anything at all in the world as she walked along her road; but she talked all the time to herself. The sad part of her was in charge as she drew near; and this is what Pidge and Brigit heard her say:

'. . . and there's no fol-de-rols in my life at all; no dainties like a pair of boots. And there isn't a pick on me, so there isn't. Hardly the fill of your eye to look at me, and I so light with lacking that you could blow me off your hand. The wind searching in my clothes with hard fingers and the rain sweeping down on me; but if I could get a sup of something warm, I'd care nothing for having only the bare earth under my feet, or the rain, and I wouldn't count this day hard. But I'll not get it and that's as true as the sun blots out the stars . . .

'And I couldn't turn my head this minute, not even to look at a rainbow, for my head is heavy with the weight of my dreams. They assemble in crowds and they ramble where they please in my mind. Some of them are as solid as stone, but they are without meaning—unless hunger has a meaning. And others are like smoke and won't show themselves clearly, but tease me with half-seen things that seem important and torment me . . .

'I'm always like a cow with four stomachs that hasn't eaten for three days; and in one of the clear dreams that I have, there is the soft sinking of my teeth through thick cream with bilberries mixed into it. And it's many a time, in the annoying magic of that dream, I see the salmon, black-spotted and white-bellied and skin-tight with the fullness of himself, go in over the fire and come back with the sheen of worked metal on his skin that's all crisp with little blue places; and the smell rising in the steam off the plate and going into my nose and down into my stomach, so that I was half-fed before I took a

348

bite. And then I see him, the King of the Fish in his bursted coat, and his thick pink wedges and the fat little cushions of pale curd that do always be there. It's as if I can remember the way I'd be cross when the shreds lodged in my teeth, and the way I had to mind the bones. A strange dream for the likes of me; when as far as I know, I never tasted such a thing in my life.

'It's a good thing that my darlings are gone from me; 'twould stand the hair on their heads to see me now, and I every day waiting to fall into a weakness. I wonder where they are? I wonder if they were ever there at all? For that is the shifting dream that gives me most fury—it gives me the fancy that I once had seven strong sons with sweet ways, and that I threw them away after some queer notion I had . . .'

All of a sudden she changed and the ducks and geese scattered to be out of her way, as she leaped up brandishing her stick. Her agility was monstrous.

'Leave me be! Leave me be!' she shouted; and with her stick, she beat at her dreams.

She had passed the children by without noticing them. And then Pidge was not afraid of her any longer. He realized that her anger was directed only against herself and her own thoughts.

'Stop!' he cried.

The woman obeyed.

She stopped in her tracks and turned round. Raising her head slightly, she saw the two of them standing by the boulder. Her surprise was very great and she slowly retraced her steps to look at them.

'There's hot food here and I think it is meant for you,' Pidge said. He knew now that she was supposed to help them in some way but he couldn't imagine how.

'If I had dry boots in your size, I'd give them to you,' said Brigit in a small, subdued voice.

The woman looked at them with astonishment.

'Children!' she said. 'A small, sturdy girl and a fine young boy. Why! I could stand looking at a child all day.'

Her voice was mild and her whole manner had changed.

'My name is Pidge and this is my sister, Brigit; and we are sorry that your life is so hard,' Pidge said. He went rather red as he spoke.

The woman looked bewildered. For a moment a hazy look came into her eyes, as though she tried to grasp at something that she couldn't properly remember.

'Oh, but it seems to me that it wasn't always that way. Once in a while I have notions that there were times that were very good indeed, and even glorious,' she said, with a faint look of wonder on her face. 'You mustn't take any notice of what I'm saying when I'm talking to myself. It's only a bad habit we fall into when we're solitary and we always say the worst to ourselves.'

'What's your name?' Brigit asked.

There was a pause again and the same useless search in her mind.

'I've forgotten,' she said after a while. 'It doesn't matter.'

'Where are you going to?'

'Nowhere and everywhere, child.'

'Why don't you sit down and have some food?' Pidge suggested, showing her the good place by the boulder and pointing to the basket.

The woman left the path and came to sit down. The children stood aside a little way to be out of her rain, and the ducks and geese started to nibble at the grass and whatever else they could find.

'What have you in the pot?' the woman asked, with only the beginning of a splinter of hope in her voice.

'Soup,' Pidge answered, and he dipped the mug into the pot and filled it up. He wiped the drip with a dock leaf and handed the mug to the woman. Brigit passed her some lumps of bread on a plate and the woman laid it on her lap. Then Brigit spread the tablecloth on the ground, and on it she placed all that was in the basket. She was careful to keep everything away from the rain.

'Soup,' the woman repeated quietly. Her voice stroked the word and her eyes looked tenderly at the contents of the mug.

Brigit broke some of the bread that was left and threw it to the ducks and geese. Seeing that she had such good intentions, they all rushed to her with much flapping of wings.

'There's barley in it,' the woman said after a while.

And then she said:

'There's meat in it.'

350

Now her cheeks were slightly pink as the food warmed her.

'There's goodness in it,' she said, and she tilted the mug for the last drop.

Pidge took the mug from her and he filled it again. As he was handing it back to her, he noticed that her clothes didn't look damp, although the rain still fell, and he was a little surprised at this, even though it was Tír-na-nÓg.

'There's other food as well,' he told the woman.

'And you must eat it all up,' Brigit said—partly from kindness and partly because she didn't want any herself.

'That'll be easy work,' the woman said. There was a small sound from the back of her throat like the weakest attempt at a chuckle.

The rain lessened a bit.

'What's in here?' she asked; and she took the cover from a second dish. It was salmon, flaked and moist.

'Try some of this on it,' Brigit suggested. 'It's mayonnaise.'

'Is it nice?' asked the woman.

'It's lovely,' Brigit assured her.

The ducks and geese were listening and looking wistfully at the food. Brigit gave them some cake and biscuits.

'And what's in this?' the woman asked later—and she looked into the last dish. It was filled with thick cream that had bilberries mixed through it. Pidge handed her a clean spoon.

'Why does it rain on you all the time?' Brigit couldn't help but ask, now that the woman looked so much better.

'I don't know that at all, girl,' the woman replied.

Brigit now felt free enough to ask the question that was most on her mind since first seeing the woman.

'What was wrong with you a little while back?'

The woman looked puzzled again.

'I was feeling a bit mad,' she said, after thinking for a short time. 'It got the better of me.'

'I know,' Brigit said, with a guilty look at Pidge. 'I get like that myself sometimes.'

There was a smile from the woman at this, followed by a real chuckle.

The rain that fell on her was even weaker.

'You have nice ducks and geese, anyway,' said Brigit, consolingly.

351

'Oh, they're not mine at all,' the woman said. 'I used to be plagued with them, the creatures, when they first appeared behind me on the road. I wondered if some person would be searching for them. But that's long ago now; and they're still tracking me, though I hardly ever notice them. I forget all about them, so I do.'

'Yes,' said a small, fat brown duck. 'We folly her about. "Don't folly me now", she said once, but we took no notice 'cos we love the rain, don't we?'

'Oh, we do,' the other ducks said enthusiastically, 'we do, we do!'

'And so do they,' the little brown duck continued, and he nodded his head towards the geese who had gone back to nibbling the grass verges by the path.

'Some likes Indian Clubs and some likes Tap Dancing—but it's the rain for us everytime,' the little duck explained further.

'Well! I never knew it!' the woman said, her face now quite rosy from the nourishment of the food. 'I thought they were lost and lonely at first, and after that, I never thought of them at all.'

'We know that all right. We had to learn to do the Tap Dancing ourselves to skip out of the way of your rackety feet. She gets buckin' mad, doesn't she?' the little duck said, inviting agreement from the others.

'Oh, she does, she does!' the others responded, nodding vigorously.

'Ah, you oul' dote,' said the small duck affectionately. 'You left us as free as a cat and shared the rain with us; and what's the odd bit of discomposure from wild feet, when friends travel the road together?'

'It's a long road to be sure,' the woman said with a sigh.

The rain increased again and hopped off her head.

'Long and dangerous, isn't it?' said the little brown duck.

'Oh, I don't think it was dangerous,' the woman disagreed gently.

'Not dangerous? What about all them dogs?' asked the little duck in an outraged way.

'Dogs?' Pidge said, very alert.

'The Water Lady never noticed them but we saw them all right, didn't we?'

'We did, we did! Oh, we did,' the rest of the ducks shuddered.

'Only for the geese, we were halted and completed altogether. It's a hard life being a duck without beak of claw. We've got bills—same as the geese—but we haven't got the hiss and the stabbing power. That's what's missing all right—the hiss. Nor the weight either, we haven't got that. It's as if we were meant to be eaten—born without defence—and about as fit for combat as a tulip.'

'What kind of dogs were they?' Pidge asked.

'Hounds. Hounds is what they were! Skinny hounds. But for the Gander there, we were done, 'cos after they looked, they sort of crept at us. But he sorted them out—sticking out his long neck and hissing like a steam engine. Hey! Come over here a minute, will ye!' he shouted at the Gander.

'To whom do you imagine you are speaking?' the Gander inquired with a haughty and imposing rudeness.

'Oh, come off it, Charlie,' the little brown duck said. 'Stop putting on airs for once.'

'Putting on airs?' the Gander repeated, as if he were hearing the language of a fool that could not be understood by people with a superior intelligence.

'Janey!' the little duck said sarcastically. 'Anyone'd think you came out of a silver cockleshell to hear you talk! You came out of an egg, same as the rest of us—so it's no use being stuck-up.'

'Stuck-up? I beg your pardon?' said the Gander.

'Stuck-up and putting on airs such as would make Ghengis Khan look like a rag-picker. He's always doing that, isn't he?'

'Oh, he is, he is!' all declared.

'I'm sorry,' the Gander said in a supercilious way, 'but the egression of language from your silly beak is an egregious folly from which you should desist.'

'Oh, listen to the rocks coming out of his gob!' the little duck jeered. 'You'll get your neck wrung for Christmas same as others, in spite of it. D'ye know what, Charlie? You give me the pip.'

'Pray ignore him,' the Gander said to thin air. 'He is an object of no consequence and quite below the salt.'

The woman was laughing heartily now; as were Pidge and Brigit.

There was no more rain.

'I thought you were all friends,' the woman said.

'Oh, we're friends all right but we don't hobnob,' said the Gander.

'I'll hobnob you in a minute if you don't watch yourself,' the little duck said, bristling. 'I'll pull your pin-feathers out. It'll be ju-jitsu and no holds barred. He gives me the croup! Somebody hold me back before I have to be dug out of him.'

'I hear you are very brave,' said Pidge to the Gander, partly to break up the argument.

'It runs in the blood,' was the haughty reply.

'Breeding?' laughed the little duck. 'Who ever heard of a thoroughbred goose?'

'It's our History, you see,' the Gander condescended to explain. 'Watchdogs for the Romans, you know—that sort of thing. Military. And we are aristocrats, of course. Odd isn't it, that we never hear of the *duck* that laid the Golden Egg?'

The little duck was fuming.

'Oh? So ducks aren't aristocratic—is that it? I suppose, Charlie, that you have never heard of the Duck of Edinburgh?' he asked with some heat.

'Can't say that I have.'

'Then you don't know everything, do you—not if you've never heard of His Highness!' the small duck finished in some triumph.

'How brave are you?' asked Pidge.

'I'm gifted at it,' replied the Gander.

'I'll say this for him,' interposed the duck. 'Only for him we were bunched. He even sang at them—"Our Dog's Got Fleas"' wasn't it, Charlie?'

'So you really are brave?' Pidge said, wondering if this could be useful in getting them into the town with Cooroo.

'Oh notoriously so,' said the Gander, and he walked around delicately as if the ground might be dirty in some way.

'Are you as brave as a—fox?' Brigit blurted out.

The Gander took a backward step.

'Did you say—FOX?' he asked in a shocked voice.

'It was only a joke, Charlie. She was only passin' a remark,' the duck said soothingly. 'Fox is a word that takes *me* in the gizzard, right enough—but not you, Charlie.'

'Of course not,' the Gander said, but there was a quiver in his voice.

'Of course not,' the duck repeated. 'Not you—that could mind mice at a crossroads. Not *you*, Charlie; not an old Gallowglass like yourself.'

'I have never seen one myself—but it must be a horrid sight,' the Gander said, by now quite recovered.

'Oh it is, it is,' all the other little ducks agreed.

'It's a sight that would have your heart up in your mouth, jumpin' up and down on your tongue. I'm glad you've calmed down and that you're not frightened any more, Charlie; for it greatly misbecomes you,' the little duck said.

'Frightened? Whatever do you mean?' asked the Gander as haughtily as ever.

'Oh, good. Now you are your old stuck-up self again,' the duck said happily.

The Gander raised his proud head.

'Show me a fox and I'll show you a coward, sir!' he said.

'See that?' said the little duck. 'He's not afraid, even though he could get his head snapped off same as if his neck was a bluebell stem. It's all like seaspray on a lighthouse to Charlie —no effect. It's all like hailstones hoppin' off a rock to Charlie—no bother to him.'

'Show me a fox,' Charlie demanded. 'Show me a fox and I'll knock him down with a spit.'

This was the moment that Cooroo picked to wave his brush over the top of the boulder.

The little brown duck was the first to see it.

'Oh, oh, oh,' he cried, almost speechless at first. 'A fox's brush! A fox! Run for your lives!'

There was pandemonium then as the ducks and geese panicked and waddled for their lives, with high-pitched cackles and quacks. It looked as if someone had put spurs to Charlie for he was well out in front going at a good high trot. One of the other little ducks had fainted clean away and he lay beside Brigit, breathing gently. She didn't know what to do about him so she left him alone, hoping that he would recover by himself.

Cooroo stood on top of the boulder.

'Come back,' he shouted, 'I won't touch you. Fainites!'

'Fainites, me granny,' the little duck shrilled; and he gasped as he ran on. 'Oh, me heart! me heart! I'll never be the better of it!'

'Come back, come back! It's all right—he's not hungry!' Brigit shouted.

Pidge thought: I suppose they don't know that people eat them too after their necks are wrung, or they'd never stay near us.

The flight of the ducks and geese was stopped at Brigit's call; but they wouldn't come back and they stood in the roadway in a nervous bunch; one nervous entity on top of several legs.

'It's safe—he won't harm you!' Pidge shouted. 'You won't will you?'

'No, I won't. These are special times. I'll show them I'm harmless. I'll smile the way people do,' said Cooroo, and he smiled broadly, his eyes dancing.

'We know them teeth, don't we?' screeched the little duck.

'Oh, we do, we do,' all of the other little ducks screamed back. 'We know them teeth, all right!'

'Come back,' said the woman. 'You are under my protection.'

This made all the difference to the ducks and the geese and they came back, although warily.

'I'm jumping down now,' Cooroo said. 'There is a flag of truce for the present, and we'll say no more about bluebell stems or knocking people down with spits.'

'You and your big gob,' the little brown duck said threateningly to Charlie. 'Another word out of you and into the mayonnaise your face will go!'

Charlie said nothing but began to nibble the grass.

There was a small moan from the little duck that had fainted and all the other ducks came at once to his side.

'It's Dempsey,' said the little brown duck. 'He must have had another brainstorm.'

Some of the others lay down beside him and fanned him conscious with the skin fans of their webbed feet, until he came back to life.

Brigit dipped some bread into the remains of the soup and offered it to him.

'Can you swallow this?' she asked.

'That could slip down his neck like a mat on a helter-skelter. Thank you,' the small duck said. 'Get it down you, Dempsey, lad.'

'Now, can we go, Pidge?' Brigit said.

'We are in the middle of thinking out a puzzle and I wonder if you could help us in some way,' Pidge said, looking at the woman.

But, it was the little duck that had fainted away, who answered.

'What's the puzzle?' he asked shyly.

'This is Thick Dempsey,' the first little duck said.

'Pour oul' Thick Dempsey,' the other ducks all said, sadly.

'You ever hear of the Speed of Light?' the first duck asked.

'Yes,' said Pidge.

'Well, Dempsey's brain moves at the Speed of Mud, doesn't it?'

'Oh, it does!' came the chorus back.

'He has been this way ever since he was a little yella fella. He was only two days out of the egg when he was chased by a mad turkey cock that wanted to eat him. And while he was trying to dodge him, he banged his little head against a bucket. He was never the same after that. There he was, full of the joys of life, platherin' about on his little webbed feet and sticking his bill up in the air and having a lovely time of it. The next thing is—he's a tipsy-head,' explained the first little duck.

He shook his own head sadly and added:

'He's stone mad but we all love him—these things happen in the best of families. Brains scrambled!'

A horrified shudder ran through all the others at the word: 'scrambled'. The Gander, without lifting his head, murmured: 'Language!'

'Oh, pardon my French,' the first little duck said, embarrassed. 'I don't know what came over me.'

'Poor little Dempsey,' Brigit said, stroking his head with her fingertip.

'But you'd be stretched laughing at the same Dempsey,' continued the first duck. 'Say something funny for them, Dempsey. Go on!'

Dempsey was bashful at first, but he obliged.

'The square of the hypotenuse is equal to the sum of the squares on the other two sides,' he said modestly.

There was a burst of laughter from all the other ducks.

'Oh, himself and his squares,' the first duck gasped. 'Say another one!'

'The circumference of a circle is equal to two Pi R,' Dempsey said, and the rest of the ducks went into fits.

Between sobs of giggles, the first duck said:

'Give us one of your oul' tongue twisters, oh, do! I don't know where he gets them from, I really don't!'

'Antidisestablishmentarianism,' Dempsey obliged and he waited for the loud mirth.

All of the ducks were wheezing with laughter and one of them got hiccups so that he kept going 'Qua-hick.' A kindly friend gave him a peck at the back of his neck to give him a shock and make him feel better.

When they had all recovered, the first little duck said:

'He has the brain of a jelly-fish, but we all love him, don't we?'

'Oh, we do, we do,' the others sobbed and gasped.

'The intensity of light falls off according to the square of the distance,' Dempsey threw in without being asked; and away the others went again. Finally the little brown duck said:

'What a comedian the stage lost in you, Dempsey. Now do you see what I mean about him? He's really daft, poor lad.'

'I think he might be very clever,' Pidge said. 'I believe he might even be able to tell us how to get Cooroo safely into the town among the people.'

Dempsey didn't hesitate.

'Let the fox pretend to be dead and let our dear Water Lady wear him round her shoulders in the fashion of a fur. People are used to that kind of thing,' he said.

All of his friends had a powerful laugh at this, but when the cackles had finished, Pidge said:

'I think that's very clever. Could you do it, Cooroo?'

'Easily,' the fox answered.

'Would you agree?' Pidge asked the woman.

'I'd be delighted,' she said, laughing.

'Dempsey! Me sound man! I always said you were brainy,' said the little brown duck.

358

The woman bent towards Cooroo and he climbed on to her shoulders. He draped himself around her neck, letting his paws dangle.

'How do I feel?' he asked.

'Lovely and warm and cosy,' the woman said.

'You look smashing! He suits her, doesn't he?' said the little brown duck.

'Oh, he does, he does,' all the other ducks agreed.

To Pidge's eye, Cooroo didn't look much like a fur but he kept this thought to himself. With Brigit's help, he assisted the woman to her feet.

'Don't forget—he's only on loan—you can't keep him,' Brigit said anxiously, looking up into the woman's face.

'Sure, I know that, child; and I wouldn't want him any other way but the way he is—alive and beautiful and free,' the woman replied.

Coroo raised his head and looked wisely into the woman's eyes for a long searching moment. Then he touched her face with his muzzle in a foxy kiss and licked her cheek. He then lay against her again and made his eyes go glassy.

They all set off towards Baile-na-gCeard. And Pidge thought: I wonder what it will be like? We haven't seen anything like a town since we left Galway behind.

After they had taken a few steps, the Poor Woman looked at Pidge and asked:

'Have I just eaten salmon? Did I get cream with bilberries?'

'Yes,' he replied.

'I knew what they were!' she said triumphantly, and then they moved on.

Afterwards Pidge remembered the hamper and looked back; but everything had vanished. They followed the path around the base of the first mountain and walked on through the glen.

Chapter 3

I N the real world, the Sergeant was tired of worrying and sick of cocoa. He was very disturbed by feelings in his mind that he was not being a proper Sergeant and that he was not really himself at all.

Several times he half-started out of his chair on an impulse to get out into the streets to ask the first person he met: 'Where were you at ten past three on the morning of December the thirteenth, nineteen fifty-four'; just to prove to himself that he was still the Sergeant and that he knew how to do his duty.

Luckily, he did nothing at all; for in the end when he did go out, the very first person that he saw was the Bishop, who was going round the town looking in shop windows, pricing socks. He had spent a long, long time standing before the sock window at Alexander Moon's Drapery in Eglinton Street, lost in dreams of his native place.

As the Sergeant sat brooding and glumly staring at the dark ring the cocoa had left in the bottom of his mug, his thoughts were broken into by quiet sounds from the front office. There was the sound of a drawer opening and after some rummaging about, the discreet noise of it shutting. This was followed by a loud uncontrolled guffaw of laughter, quickly smothered to badly-stifled sniggers.

What's going on out there? he wondered gently.

'Listen to this, Sergeant; it'll give you a good laugh,' the young Garda said, coming in and leaning carelessly against the wall. He had an old tattered book held open in his two hands.

Oh good, thought the Sergeant; I could do with a good laugh today.

'"The iron-willed Sergeant must be determined, clear-thinking, self-confident and energetic. He must have well-defined values and goals which he pursues with unswerving persistence. He must fully utilize his capacity for hard work."

360

What do you think of that, Sergeant? It's from an old manual,' the young Garda finished with a partly-choked giggle.

There was utter silence.

The Sergeant stood up, flushing very red from his tunic collar upwards.

'You read that very sudden!' he said accusingly, and he strode roughly from the room.

As he went, brushing past the giggling young Garda, he thought that he heard him mutter something about: 'wouldn't say boo to a goose' under the giggles. Whether or not he said it, the Sergeant was inflamed. He stamped out into the yard and bending down he put on his bicycle clips, like a warrior putting on his panoply. He straightened up and grasped the hem of his tunic to pull it down, so that it fitted correctly and snugly about his body. One glance at his brass buttons and his confidence was restored; but other parts of his personality were skittering around untidily inside his brain. He wheeled his bike out of the yard into Eglinton Street and threw his leg over the saddle, as if he were mounting a blood stallion from Arabia. The bike wobbled, but he mastered it and set his face towards Shancreg.

That poor Sergeant looks very troubled, thought the Bishop. He stopped thinking about his lovely native place and the price of socks flew out of his universe completely. Instead, he said a little prayer for the Sergeant. This led him to wonder about who was the patron saint of Sergeants; and throughout the day his mind would return fleetingly to this puzzle. Each time he would say another little prayer.

All goodness is good and the Bishop's goodness was as good as anybody else's; who knows how his kindness may have helped the Sergeant?

Old Mossie Flynn, the owner of the glasshouse in Shancreg, had no idea that a third woman had arrived under cover of darkness; and he had been waiting patiently for the two women to come outside and do something funny or one of their Works of Art. At first he was not surprised that they did not appear.

'For,' he said to his pig, as he tickled her gently behind the ear, 'they do be powdering their noses and all that—they do be dolling themselves up. Or they could even be having a lie-in. Eat quietly now, and don't be disturbing them with loud grunts.'

'And,' he said to the hens as he threw them their grain, 'they do be lacing up their what-nots and pranking around with hot curling-tongs. And putting coats of varnish on their finger-nails. That's the woman's way—and our two ladies have very romantic and mysterious souls. Stop the squawking now in case they are still in their beauty sleep.'

So, he waited; quietly excited at the thought of the fun to come.

He had milked the cow, gone quietly to the well for water and fed all of his animals except for the cat, and she wasn't yet back from her night's gallivanting. Sometimes she would be waiting outside on the step before he even got up; other times she would turn up about noon, perhaps with a rabbit gripped in her jaws, and there were even times when she would stay away for a few days while she visited friends and relations at distant places for weddings and wakes.

Mossie tended the fire, lit his pipe and settled himself to read an old newspaper while he waited. Gradually, however, he found himself wriggling on his seat and heaving a great many sighs and reading the same block of print over and over again, without knowing at all the sense of what he was reading. From time to time, he went to look over his half-door to see if there was any sign of life from his tenants. He was drawn to the glasshouse not by any trick of the women but by his own happy expectations.

Then, as he read the same few words for the tenth time, it occurred to him that the ladies might be thinking that he was still asleep himself, and that they were only holding back from their Art so as not to disturb him; for he had been very quiet and careful in everything that he had done. He had even carried buckets in his arms as if they were pet lambs, hugging them to his chest so that the handles wouldn't clank; and he had stepped neatly in his hob-nailed boots—looking down for soft spots to walk on.

He went to his garden and gathered a lovely bunch of flowers. Then he went and knocked at the glasshouse door.

Looks of fury passed fleetingly over the faces of the three women. Melodie, her eyes as cold as sleet, called out sweetly:

'Who's there?'

'It is I,' said Mossie. He had heard that said on the radio and he thought it sounded very grand and that it would be a kind of compliment to the ladies to hear it.

'Who is "I", might one inquire?'

'Your landlord and friend—Mossie Flynn.'

Melodie opened the door, stepped out and drew the door shut behind her.

'A bunch of flowers for the Artists!' said Mossie solemnly, taking off his cap and handing her the flowers.

There was a short pause of disbelief before she spoke.

'Just what we've always wanted—we're uncommonly obliged to you,' Melodie said coldly and with a look that could fillet a shark.

'When are you going to come out and do one of your lovely Works of Art?' Mossie asked hopefully.

Melodie took a deep sniff at the flowers. Immediately, two hundred and forty nine lightweight insects shot up her nose and met their deaths. She sneezed, and dropped a hot tear that landed on a little worm and gave him a headache.

'Not today,' she said. She could not prevent a slight upcurl of her top lip—an unpleasant sort of smile.

'Not today?' Mossie questioned her.

'No. It's our day off,' she said, and went back inside and shut the door.

Mossie stood doubting himself for a few moments and then he went back to his house. Was it my imagination or was she very rude? he asked himself mistrustfully. Did she sneer?

When a person lives in the country where the population is sparse, he doesn't get much chance to study things like sneers. With so few people about, the one sneer of the week could well be happening in the far side of the parish and he'd miss it if he wasn't there. On the other hand, there could even be six sneers per hour at the farm a half a mile away and he wouldn't get the chance to see them. For as sure as anything, the ones who are good at sneering, become best at smiling when a visitor arrives.

363

Mossie worried in case he was being unjust.

The women went back to their study of the table. They had looked at it for only a second or two when a striking change came over them. The Mórrígan was like one awakening from a long slow dream into quick life, and Melodie Moonlight and Breda Fairfoul were serious and silent.

Studying the table with the greatest attention possible, they examined the three valleys that were mere dips in its surface and the mountains that were little higher than a few minutes' candle drippings. They observed that the valleys led into each other and they noted with sharp interest that the third valley finished in a dead-end. That this was not a trap arranged by themselves, they well knew; but whether that last valley was there as part of a landscape, or by Dagda's wish, they could not tell.

Their eyes went unfathomable, as empty of expression as lizards' eyes.

'What have we here?' they whispered.

The whisper had a peculiar intensity and power and it vibrated in all of the glass in the glasshouse. Almost silent echoes of: 'here, here, here,' came shivering back as though from fragile tuning-forks, and they floated round the table.

Breda and Melodie watched The Mórrígan's face, their eyes dilated with a fierce expectancy. In every other way, they were all marvellously calm; three women of stone.

The Mórrígan returned this avid look and they waited.

A tiny speck of crimson appeared in one of her eyes.

'Blood calls to blood,' they said, and they thrilled.

They knew then, that the children had almost found the pebble that had once hurt that particular eye. *They knew also, that if The Mórrígan swallowed the one drop of her old blood that stained the pebble, she would be strong again.*

Even more, they knew that if she could get Olc-Glas as well, her power would be great indeed.

The eye turned red as it filled with blood.

'I am the Mór Ríagan,' said The Mórrígan, 'I am the Great Queen. I incite men to Battle Madness.'

'I am Macha,' said Melodie Moonlight. 'I am Queen of

Phantoms. I revel among the slain. I gather heads.'

'I am Bodbh,' said Breda Fairfoul. 'I am the Sharp-Beaked Scald Crow. My cries foreshadow the numbers of the dead.'

'We three are The Mórrígna; we are the Great Queens,' they said.

'My heart is an ice-well,' said The Mórrígan. 'Soon, I shall have one drop of my old strong blood. With it, I will dissolve Olc-Glas and swallow him into my cold heart. I shall add his poison to mine.'

'I shall kiss you and have his poison as well as my own,' said Macha. 'For we have grown weak as the years passed by.'

'I shall kiss you and have his poison as well as my own,' said Bodbh. 'For death is my darling and battle my greatest ecstacy.'

'In every human head, there is a seed of evil,' said The Mórrígan. 'It thrives in some and makes them stand out among their fellows for their wickedness and cruelty. The little seed suffocates and cannot flourish when it is choked by love.'

'The little seed cannot flourish,' said Macha, 'when it is smothered by compassion.'

'The little seed cannot flourish,' said Bodbh, 'when it is stifled by tolerance.'

'Truth is nourished by belief,' said The Mórrígan. 'There are many truths. I am a truth.'

'I am a truth,' said Macha.

'I am a truth,' said Bodbh.

'They shall believe in us again. They shall see our greatness and fear us. We shall be nourished and grow even stronger,' they said.

'When mankind cries "mercy", my ears are shells of granite,' said The Mórrígan. 'My child is the blow-fly, the mother of maggots.'

'Time is a slow dream; time is quicksilver,' said Macha.

'The sun rises, the day dawns, the wheel turns—our time comes again,' said Bodbh.

There was a deep silence in which only the unobtrusive breathing of the sleeping cat could be heard. A moment later The Mórrígan's eye was clear and beautiful again. The strange simplicity was over and three women shook themselves physically, as dogs shake off water; and now, they laughed.

'He found the pebble; he did the natural thing and went to the mountains,' Breda spluttered.

'Only a human brat could be so excruciatingly obvious,' Melodie tittered, just as her attention was caught by a movement on the table.

'Look!' she said sharply, pointing.

They looked at the iron-willed, determined, clear-thinking Sergeant who was purposefully riding his bike to Shancreg.

This is a nuisance, the women said to each other silently.

Out of the blue, there was another knock and Mossie's voice came politely through the door.

'Ladies?'

As brightness replaces darkness in a room at night when a switch is flicked, so the women changed. Breda immediately affected cordiality—a thing done often enough in the real world, goodness knows.

'Yes, Mr. Flynn?' she answered sweetly.

'You must come over to my little house for your breakfasts,' Mossie said.

'*Must* we?' Melodie fluted.

'Indeed you must! I know that you haven't any food because you haven't had a chance to go shopping. And even if you had food, there's no way you can cook it in my glasshouse. So I invite you to bacon, eggs and fresh musheroons—ready in twenty minutes—and I won't take "no" for an answer!'

And with that firm message delivered, Mossie scuttled away.

This will not do, the women told each other silently.

There and then, they made the decision to leave the glasshouse *now*, instead of waiting until Pidge and Brigit had led them to Olc-Glas as well as to the pebble.

'One fool an hour is quite enough—two is too many,' Breda said, indicating the Sergeant.

'Good!' Melodie agreed with satisfaction, 'I am bored with this place and more than ready to go, anyway.'

The Mórrígan leaned in over the table and, after examining the land between the mountains and the lake, she carefully selected a likely place. There she placed her thumb and pressed hard, leaving a clear print on the table's surface.

Satisfied with that, she made the table itself disappear—it

was a picture that they no longer needed—but the thumbprint stayed.

She took a pinch of dust from the floor and she blew on it and caused it to swirl above the mark of her thumb. The effect pleased her. Now, the three women made everything that they had brought into the glasshouse vanish as well; and The Mórrígan brought the space inside back to its correct size. Except for the thumbprint, nothing of theirs remained.

They were ready to go.

'Pity about the rats,' murmured Melodie. 'I would have liked a vermin-trimmed cloak.'

Mossie, crossing his kitchen, with a small bowl of eggs and a plate of raw bacon in his hands, was just passing by the open door of his house, when the glasshouse door swung back with a crash and the motor-bike, with *three* women riding it, roared past his line of vision and was gone. He was shaken to the heels and he dropped the eggs. He rushed out to look after his fleeing tenants.

'Three of them—they brought in a squatter!' he said. 'It's my belief that they are not nice crackpot ladies from England at all, but three jokers out from Bohermore!'

He crossed to his glasshouse and went in, stepping over broken glass at the threshold. He frowned when he saw his bunch of flowers thrown aside and he was surprised when he saw his little cat who had woken when the door had crashed.

'There you are!' he exclaimed. 'Dreaming all night, I suppose—instead of catching rats.'

'You don't know the night I've had,' the cat miaoued without the slightest hope of being understood. 'First I was used as a duster and then I had rats spitting at me. Even though I slept, my nerves are still shot to pieces.'

As usual, Mossie thought that she wanted food.

'Can't you wait? You're the greatest devil I've ever met!' he said.

'God help your head,' said the cat. She lashed her tail once and began to clean herself.

Mossie picked something up from the ground.

They made daisy-chains, he said to himself, surprised. He held the wilted flowers in his hand.

'If that's Art—I can do it myself,' he said.

367

'It's enough to turn the hens strange,' the cat remarked.

'Shut up and wait,' said Mossie.

The implacable Sergeant was cycling carefully and legally along the road. A powerful motor-bike raced towards him and whizzed past, making him almost overbalance and fall.

'Oh, me blood pressure!' he cried, clutching at his chest where his heart was. He turned his cycle and went after them.

The motor-bike flashed away ahead of him. With a bitter sense of outrage, he saw it leap over a wall.

'Stunt-riding—even before my very eyes—I am a Sergeant after all!' he growled. 'And at their age! They'll not get away from me this time, the roadhogs!'

When he reached the place where the motor-bike had gone over the wall, he found tyre-marks dug into the road.

Exhibit One, he rehearsed in his mind, visualizing a plaster cast.

He dismounted and lifted his own bike over. Now he was in a field with old rocks. Funny thing! No sight or whisper of the women and their machine. He remounted his bike and rode slowly across the field following the marks on the ground towards the rocks. Looking ahead he observed that they appeared to vanish mysteriously under the capstone; but he deduced that the ground might be hard there and he would find the evidence again, later on.

To his utter horror, the handlebars of his bike took on a life of their own and moved sinuously under his hands. They were writhing under his grip. He yelped and snatched his hands away and held them safely and nervously up over his head, while he stared at the handlebars, appalled.

The instant they were free from his grasp, they behaved as if they were bewitched. They whipped up and down, they lashed to and fro until they went sideways, before sweeping together at the front, where they crossed over each other and stayed rigid.

'It's delirium tremens,' the Sergeant moaned hoarsely.

The bike went through under the capstone and he found that he was in a thick mist. Gathering speed, the bike went like an arrow. As he passed candle after candle, the Sergeant weakly asserted himself by saying:

'Shocking bad street-lighting in these parts—I'll complain to the County Council when I get back.' But he was almost in tears.

In a short while he heard again the sound of a motor-bike ahead of him somewhere and he knew that he was on the right track at least. There was an immediate improvement in his spirits.

When the women came out of the mist and went swiftly through Galway City, nobody saw them but everybody felt a bitter coldness.

When the Sergeant came out of the mist and his bike whizzed through the town, nobody saw him either but his head spun with all that he saw.

The women followed the route taken by Pidge and Brigit when they had followed Cathbad the Druid, and when they reached the lake, The Mórrígan threw a word at the water, taking it by surprise. It turned at once to solid ice.

The Sergeant arrived some minutes later. No matter what he did, he could not regain control of the bike and some force kept him from throwing himself off. The bike went onto the ice and it sped away up the lake.

'I can but make the best of it,' the stoical Sergeant decided, and he put his boots up on the now-steady handlebars and clasped his hands at the back of his neck. He began to enjoy what was happening and to admire his own sense of balance.

'I couldn't do this if I were sober,' he said and he laughed secretly to himself.

The Sergeant's bike left the lake at last and it went over the land on the west side of Lough Corrib, in a streak. He was feeling very happy and he grinned in a foolish way, while he thought fondly of one of his favourite roses. It was a common enough rose; a yellow one with red-tipped petals and not much scent. But, it had always been one of his favourites.

After a time, The Mórrígan became aware that a figure followed them constantly.

'What is that small dark thing that follows us like a chronicle,' she asked.

'It's that limb of the law,' said Breda.

'Sent by The Dagda,' Melodie guessed, in a sudden insight.

'How shall we deal with him.' Breda speculated.

'Shall we let him follow, or take charge of him—which is wisest?' Melodie wondered.

'Take charge of him,' The Mórrígan decreed.

Melodie closed her eyes and went into deep concentration. She sent a mental search back to the Sergeant and she plundered his unguarded thoughts.

It is from little choices like this one of The Mórrígan's that mistakes are made.

Still enjoying himself, the Sergeant said:

'I do believe I am on a mystery trip and I got it for nothing. It's a pity I'm moving too fast to see the view, but it's better than being Up The Amazon On A Rubber Duck at any rate.'

His mind wandering pleasantly like this, he was taken by surprise at seeing a little figure plonked on the road ahead of him.

He squeezed his brakes tightly and dropped his feet, so that his toecaps were in touch with the surface of the road, trying to check the crazy speed of the bike to stop in time.

Two small clouds of dust arose from his feet as they scraped the road's crust; and inside his boots, his feet warmed up like boiled puddings. Sparks flew and there was the smell of scorching leather; but just in time, the bike stopped.

The Sergeant released a sigh of relief that emptied him of air for a few thankful seconds and he regarded the figure sternly. Then he saw that it was a rosy little girl, plump and pretty, with dimples and blond curls. She was sitting innocently in the dangerous centre of the road.

It's scandalous! She's only a baby! the Sergeant said to himself indignantly.

As he came near to her, dismounted and bent down, she smiled at him gravely. Her dimples dimpled even deeper and she offered him a rose with her fat little fist.

The Sergeant was charmed. It was the very rose that he had been thinking about only a few moments earlier.

'Is that for me?' he asked archly.

The little girl nodded and put a finger in her mouth.

'Well, thank you. You're a good little girl, aren't you?'

The little girl chuckled and nodded most solemnly.

'And what's that you have in your other hand?'

The little girl showed him an object made of reeds. It was shaped like a long round lantern—a cylinder—and the reeds lay closely together like thatch. The end that she was holding was tapered and ended in a plaited loop.

'Mine,' she said.

'It's very nice,' he said. 'Is it a doll's house?'

She shook her curls wildly.

'Bufferfly cage,' she lisped.

'And have you got a beautiful bufferfly inside it?' he asked roguishly.

She nodded again.

I think I've got her confidence, he said to himself, as he tucked the rose into the top buttonhole of his tunic. If I win her trust first, perhaps she will let me lift her up and put her on the bike, without too much screeching and bawling and lashing out of legs and fists. You can get a fair belt from one of these little lambs, if you cross them. Then I'll take her home to her mother and give that lady something to think about. Imagine letting a little angel like this sit out on the road.

'Will you show me your lovely butterfly—bufferfly?' he coaxed.

Shyly the little girl held up the cage and the Sergeant bent lower. He put his face close to the reeds and tried to part them with the tip of a fingernail.

The little girl started to laugh.

The Sergeant was mildly surprised to realize that the laughter was not the laughter of a child.

Before he could straighten up and have another squint at her, he found that he was inside something like a massive green stockade, with his bike at his side. The whole structure tapered to a point somewhere high above his head.

Outside the stockade, someone was screeching with wild laughter. He tried to reach forward to prise apart the green columns that imprisoned him, only to discover that he was rapidly going rigid. Try as he might, he couldn't twitch a muscle, apart from being able to blink his eyes.

What next? he asked himself mournfully. And there's me

371

bike turning a funny colour, as if I haven't enough to worry about. Apart from drinking poteen, a thoughtless indulgence, what did I ever do to deserve all these calamities?

Melodie Moonlight stood up and dusted the seat of her dress. She enjoyed one more scream of laughter before catching up with The Mórrígan and Breda Fairfoul.

She handed the butterfly cage to The Mórrígan who undid the top. The Sergeant and his bike were taken out and attached to her bracelet. They were now golden charms. The Mórrígan held out her arm and all three laughed at the effect. They remounted the motor-bike and continued their journey.

On the bracelet, the dangling Sergeant had no real idea of what had happened to him. He knew that he had been picked out of his green prison by an enormous hand; but he was rigid and couldn't turn his head to see the rest of the person to whom the hand belonged. He knew also that he was all gold on the outside and that his bike was in the same condition and that it hung beside him. He sometimes got glimpses of other gold things that were hanging with him, as the bracelet jiggled and swung from the movements of The Mórrígan's arm. He felt like a mackerel on a string.

Occasionally as he swung, he got a peep at a leg below him that seemed to owe little to nature and everything to architecture. The foot of the leg seemed to be resting on some kind of black plinth. It was only the footrest of the motor-bike but he didn't know that and it looked terrifying.

They went like a buzz-saw through the countryside; the din of the motor-bike, as it roared on, was stunningly loud.

He suddenly felt as empty as a sucked egg and very tired. Mercifully, he fell asleep and for a long, long time, he knew no more.

The women rode on, their shadows with them—matching them crookedly on the ground as they went.

Later, the motor-bike vanished beneath them, and a stream of light with a shadow below it was running over the ground and that was all.

Chapter 4

THERE was but one road running through the glen and they followed it pace by pace.

The Poor Woman, who seemed to be seeing the world for the first time, was silent all the way along; but she had raised her head somewhat and she looked about her with the deepest interest and curiosity. Brigit was out in front, skipping along with the ducks and geese; and she was eager to get to the Swapping Festival at last. Pidge was taking stock of the huge bulk of the second mountain where its base jutted into the valley. It was a barrier to knowing what lay beyond; but like Brigit, he hoped that they would soon be at Baile-na-gCeard.

The silence was broken in the end by Cooroo.

'I hope that I am not too heavy for you?' he said to the Poor Woman.

'You're like a bird, a warm puff of very little—no weight at all,' she answered vaguely, as though her mind were elsewhere.

Pidge and Cooroo both knew that this could not be right, for the fox was full-grown and healthy. And even though Cooroo could tell from the movements under his body that the woman wasn't as frail as she looked and that her muscles were strong, he doubted if she really found him as light as she said.

It's only a figure of speech, thought Pidge.

The long silence had made him feel a bit shy. He was aware all the time of the tall figure that walked beside him and he wondered if he should be trying to make conversation, because adults always seemed to expect it; and perhaps if he didn't speak soon she would think him stupid and dull company, or she might think that he didn't want to speak to her because she had been so strange earlier on.

373

And that would never do, he thought gravely; especially if it made her go strange again.

So he said:

'What does Baile-na-gCeard mean, do you know?'

'It means the Town of The Artificers,' the Poor Woman answered, with her head still turned away from him, as she gazed as though staggered at a quantity of meadow-sweet that graced the side of the road. It seemed to beguile her and she was amazed at everything she saw.

'Oh,' Pidge said, and he blushed. I'm as wise as I was before, he thought ruefully.

Artificers!

Here was another word that he didn't know. The Poor Woman didn't appear to notice his difficulty, as she was now entranced by the sight of soft white clouds on the horizon, that rested lazily on nothing.

From a spur high up on this second mountain, the waterfall that they had seen from far away cascaded down in a never-ending streak of silver, and it struck the waters of a small pool and disordered it into giggling bubbles and eddies. They passed a small hazel thicket and then, on seeing the pool, the ducks and geese went ecstatic. They flapped and rushed until they were in the water, swimming and dipping and splashing with delighted cackles and quacks. More and more bubbles jumped into being from the smack of the waterfall and the little brown duck shouted deliriously:

'Oh, it's lovely, it's lovely—come in for a dip!'

But Brigit was too impatient to be getting on and Cooroo was agitated and upset. The uproar of the water overmastered all other sounds and worked against his vital sense of hearing and he was very much on edge. So the Poor Woman called the swimmers out; and they came, though reluctantly, and waddled onwards shaking the drops from their feathers as they went.

Soon Brigit shouted joyfully:

'I think we're nearly there!'

And sure enough, when they had at last circled the foot of the mountain, there was a huge white banner stretched across the road between two trees; with, in brilliant red writing, the words:

And then there was suddenly the sound of a cheerful brass band.

Brigit began to dance. She skipped about, full of excitement. 'Do you hear the band?' she cried.

'More Tap-Dancing,' observed the little brown duck genially, and they all skittered out of the way of her lively feet.

Pidge stole a considering look at the Poor Woman, examining her appearance. He looked at the tattered green dress and the bare feet and he looked at the fox draped over her shoulders. A ragged woman with bare feet wearing a fur, he thought; now we'll get some funny looks.

He was surprised and mortified then, when he noticed her eyes peeping at him and dancing with merriment, from behind the matted hair that had fallen across her face.

Oh dear, he said to himself. I believe she read my mind.

There was a dip down in the road before them and they could now see the little town. It was dressed in sunshine and bunting, banners and flowers. He looked quickly at the Poor Woman again; but she had a bright smile on her face and she was looking eagerly ahead and he was relieved.

Near the town there were many small fields, one with wheatsheaves in stooks. As they were going by, the stooks got up and danced out on to the road. They were strawboys!

'Oh, good!' Brigit said.

Each one wore a suit made from straw and cone-shaped hats, also made of straw, that were bedecked with ribbons; and they carried rattles made of rushes to hit people with, for fun. Two of the strawboys were musicians—one beat a flat, one-sided drum while the other played the fiddle. The group danced up to Brigit and to her great pleasure, their leader gave her a tap on the head with his rattle and then away they went ahead of them, into Baile-na-gCeard.

Hundreds of delighted people thronged the main street and

375

the market square and not one of them gave the Poor Woman and Cooroo a second look. Pidge felt a chuckle bubble inside him. He began to enjoy the idea of hoodwinking everyone with Cooroo posing as a fur; it was part of the celebrations.

Brigit took out her box of swapping sweets and carried it in her hands. Her face was beaming and she tried to see everything at once. She tugged at the lid of her box, but it wouldn't open yet. Pidge said he thought it might open at a special time and that they would just have to wait and see.

The brass band was in its full glory of scarlet and white with gold braiding on hats, shoulders and chests; and it sat on a dais while the individual members blew a frisky gale of music. Their cheeks were puffed out as if hiding small turnips and each face was as red as ten sunsets. All around the sides of the square, people had set up stalls, hung with flags and flowers and selling all desirable things to satisfy hunger; as well as toys and knick-knacks, fancies and farings. The sound of celebration billowed out of the little town and the smells of hot coffee, roasted meats, boiling sugar, oranges and hot currant bread fought each other to prove which was the mightiest and most delicious. The best smells of all came from a cafe called The Amber Apple.

Brigit was wildly excited and Pidge was thrilled. The whole town seemed to be rejoicing. Cooroo had the greatest difficulty in keeping still; the smell of the meat was so strong and tantalizing and he thought the smell of the people so terrible and threatening. Against all his instincts he forced himself to lie still and make his clever eyes look empty. The Poor Woman felt his heart pounding and racing away like a mad pocket watch.

'It's all right—be calm,' she whispered; and he gained courage from her words.

Still nobody took any special notice of the 'fur' around the Poor Woman's neck or the state of her clothing. It was as if they were all quite accustomed to seeing ragged people with the habit of wearing live foxes on their shoulders.

'Keep together, lads—and watch out for The Boots,' warned the little brown duck.

'We will, oh we will,' the others answered fervently and nodded their heads up and down to show how serious they were.

Once Pidge thought for a moment or two that he saw the face of a friend in the crowd—a man that looked familiar, who was selling apples and paper windmills from a cart—but he couldn't find out for sure, as his companions were moving through the press of people and he had to follow them or lose them.

All around, people were having a great time swapping things. They saw a postman swapping three letters for kisses from a blushing young beauty; half a dozen clergymen swapped custard pies as they dodged and hid in shop doorways; two big strong men, stripped to the waist, swapped punches—each swaying rigidly and not budging an inch. The strawboys danced everywhere and there was a fortune-teller's tent where everyone was getting their fortunes told—even a cat; and a man selling those whistling yellow birds made from papier-mâché, that you swing round from a string on a stick as fast as you like, so that they whistle; and the hucksters and stallholders were clamouring their goods.

'Sugar Twists! Lovely Sugar Twists—three a penny!' the nearest one cried.

And there were two small boys, freckled and red-haired, swapping insults and challenges; and two old women in shawls swapping whispers—secrets or recipes or gossip or terrible truths. Three elderly gentlemen in tweed knickerbockers swapped foreign stamps, and a group of young men swapped lies and boasts. A gang of middle-aged ladies stood in the middle of the street and gaily swapped hats, and everyone was wearing a posy or a single flower pinned on somewhere. There were ribbons and streamers and a notice saying that there was a flute competition in one field and that you could climb the greasy pole for a pig in another.

A man with a great cloud of coloured balloons floating over his head called out:

'Balloo—ins! Get yer Balloo—ins. All colours—all sizes!'

And a woman with a basket was shouting:

'Brown Sugar! Paper Pokes of Brown Sugar! Buy a tusheen of Brown Sugar—one penny only!'

Another woman in competition with her was bawling:

'Peggy's Leg and Money Balls. Buy a Lucky Money Ball.' But they were all good-natured and enjoying themselves.

Brigit was trying the lid of her box again, her face fixed in a fierce expression as she used all her strength; but it still wouldn't open. She turned a woebegone look to Pidge.

'I've been very patient,' she complained.

'Don't worry. We just haven't reached that part yet,' he guessed, hoping it was true or there'd be murder from Brigit. She cheered up anyway and enjoyed what there was. They kept moving through the crowds.

Then came the sideshows and fire-eaters and tumblers, and an escapologist, and a man who was so double-jointed that he could knot himself like a scarf and still smile because it didn't hurt a bit. All of the people knocked as much fun as they could out of everything, as if life had no other purpose.

Then, as they turned a corner, a tall thin person was leaning casually against the wall of a shop. With a start, Pidge recognized him as the man who had wanted to buy the book that day, just after everything had seemed to start. *So the hounds were here, too!* A shiver ran through Pidge at being so close to one of them. This one had pretended to be a pedlar. The man bared his teeth in a smile and there were the pointy teeth shining again. The tongue flicked over the teeth and lips, the eyes flicked to Cooroo and a tremor ran through the man. Pidge saw it. Cooroo went as rigid as death, but the woman whispered to him and she glared at the man who forced himself to look away. Pidge shuddered as they passed him by. This was the hound named Fierce—although Pidge didn't know it.

They can't touch us here with all these people—even if we run, he thought after a few minutes, and he chuckled aloud.

After this, he glimpsed many people who were unusually tall and thin and he knew who they were. They were the hounds.

Now, someone had started up a barrel-organ and the throng of people were pressing all around, buzzing with talk and singing with laughter, and rattling the paving-stones with their brogues.

A farmer came and asked the woman if she would swap her lovely ducks and geese for a nanny-goat and kid. There was a moment of panic among the ducks and geese, but the Poor Woman explained very politely that they were not hers at all,

378

and so she had no right to swap them for anything, although the nanny had a lot of personality and the kid was a little darling. The farmer tipped his hat and went away.

Pidge noticed that as soon as the farmer had approached them, three of the tall thin ones had appeared from nowhere out of the crowd, and had edged in to hear what was being said.

So that's their game—spying and prying! he said to himself.

The hounds' eyes kept flicking all the time to Cooroo in spite of themselves. Although they kept control, they were forced by their very nature to watch him and this they did with eyes as big as grapes. They moved away when the farmer tipped his hat.

There was a terrible moment as well when two women admired Cooroo, and a tall thin person was there as if he'd come out of a conjuror's hat. One of the women asked if she could just try on the beautiful fur.

'It's alive with fleas,' Brigit said, and they hastily backed away.

After this they listened for a while to the flute competition, and they moved over to stand on a low wall to watch a troupe of dancers doing hornpipes and jigs on a stage made of planks. The wall was entirely occupied by people all watching the nimble figures. Nearby people were buying gooseberries for a penny a pint and cider for tuppence out of a cask, and there was porter out of tubs, and a Try Your Strength Machine that rang a bell if you were strong, and a Three Card Trick and a Find The Lady stall. From the press of the crowd on the wall, a tall thin person was pushed off and he slipped down into some mud where the ground had been churned up by people's shoes. Before he realized what he was doing, Pidge had jumped down to help him up. There was a strange moment when he found himself looking into startled brown eyes that suddenly took on a questioning and confused expression. Pidge gave a half-smile and went back up on the wall. This tall thin person was Fowler; but Pidge didn't know that either.

They left the dancing and carried on exploring until suddenly, Pidge and Brigit realized that they had somehow lost their companions somewhere among the swarming people. They stood still and looked about, hoping that they could pick

379

Cooroo out in the throng, but there wasn't a sight of them anywhere.

They moved on again towards the music of the swings and merry-go-rounds, and they had gone no distance at all, when a single strawboy came dancing along to them. He twirled around a few times, made a low bow and came to stand right in front of Brigit. She closed her eyes and waited to be hit on the head again, as a favour. But the strawboy held out an opened paper bag and said:

'Swap me a sweet!'

Her face showed excited disbelief as she reached inside the bag and took a sweet. It was a conversation lozenge and the message on it was:

The box of sweets that Brigit had carried so carefully in her hands all through the fair, sprang open. And her face said: 'At last!' if ever a face said anything. She handed the strawboy's sweet to Pidge who read it; and then she peeped into her box and saw that her own sweets were conversation lozenges, too. Pidge put his lips to her ear and whispered that she was to say nothing.

He frowned when a group of tall thin people were suddenly close by and he whispered again to Brigit and told her that they were the hounds. She stared at them rudely and stuck out her tongue. The dog people were near enough to overhear anything said in normal speech, but not near enough to hear the very quiet kind of whisper that Pidge could do, or to get a glimpse of what was written on the sweets. One of them couldn't help giving a little whine of anxiety, only to be softly growled at by another.

Brigit now offered the strawboy a sweet that asked:

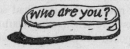

The sweet that she got back was yellow with a blue edge and blue writing, and it replied:

She showed this to Pidge, who whispered to her, and then she offered a sweet to the strawboy again. It was pink and heart-shaped and it asked:

In answer, the strawboy held out the paper bag to her and she took a white diamond-shaped one. It had pink letters that read:

Then he handed her an orange one with words in white that said:

It took only one second for Pidge to search his memory and then realize that these were Boodie's very words. He remembered that day on the island when they were waiting for their father to come back from the Horse Show in Dublin—oh, so long ago. He whispered to Brigit and her face lit up even more. She now knew that the strawboy was a friend to Boodie and Patsy.

They paused to eat the sweets that had been read up to now. As soon as they popped them inside their mouths, the hard sweets melted away instantly like wafers and they seemed to have centres of jelly. And a dot of sweetness was created for a second or two on the tongue before they were gone!

'I could eat tons of these!' Brigit whispered to Pidge.

The hounds had cocked up their ears as she spoke, but looked disappointed when they heard what she said.

Brigit's next sweet was blue with purple writing. It inquired:

A green sweet replied:

Although it wasn't his turn, the strawboy offered another sweet.

it warned, in white on orange.

The blue one Brigit gave him answered:

'I'm going now,' the strawboy said loudly. 'Thank you for swapping your sweets with me.'

He gave one last sweet to Brigit. The instructions on it were:

After bowing sedately, the strawboy danced away.

A sweet that had worked its way up to the edge of Brigit's box fell out and down onto the ground. Quick as a flash one of the tall thin people made a dive for it, picked it up and read it. Pidge watched anxiously, wondering what the writing on the sweet said. The hound looked disgusted and threw it away, and Pidge retrieved it and read it out to Brigit. It said:

They burst into laughter and strolled off through the crowds, pretending as they went that they were only interested in sideshows. But no matter where they went, the thin ones were always close behind them; so in the end they gave up the pretence and went to the place where they had earlier seen the barrel-organ man.

But he had moved from his pitch.

'Now what do we do?' Brigit asked.

'Keep looking,' Pidge answered; and they searched for a little while. Then they heard the music start up in the next street and they weaved in and out of the throng until they got to him.

He was at the opening of a sidestreet, playing and smiling and holding out his cap to passers-by. He had only one leg.

Why! Pidge thought, it could be the man who had the megaphone that time in the railway station at Galway, but he looks much younger.

The man greeted them as old friends.

'Here we are again,' he said. 'I'm very happy to see you and I'm glad you took the job. Have you been well?'

'Yes, very well,' Brigit replied.

The man had let his eyes wander while he was speaking to them. The tall thin ones were lurking close by, letting on that they were only interested in a man who wanted to swap a very sociable pig for a melodeon. The barrel-organ man frowned with meaning in their direction and cut short any further conversation with the children by saying:

'Swap me a sweet.'

The sweet that Brigit gave him said:

Popping it into his mouth, the man pulled a paper bag from his pocket and gave Brigit her choice. The message was:

'Do you understand?' the barrel-organ man asked.

'Yes,' Pidge replied, and they moved away then.

After much searching, they found the yellow bird man having a pint of Guinness at a booth. When he caught sight of them, he searched the surrounding people with quick glances and saw that the tall thin people were skulking within hearing. He laid down his glass, and put his stock of little yellow birds that flew on string and stick, on a clean area of the trestle-counter. A paper bag appeared in his hand, and again Brigit was offered a sweet. Pidge read:

Brigit's sweet in return just said:

'I think these sweets are wonderful,' Brigit said.

The man laughed and went back to his pint.

When they had been walking for some time, Pidge realized that he couldn't really remember the whereabouts of the Fortune-Teller's booth. He frowned and struggled to form a picture of it in his mind, but it did no good. He craned his neck, trying to see past the people who were always in his way. The best thing to do, he decided, was to go to where they had seen the dancers, and try to work their way back from there to where they had first entered the small town, and then they would be sure to pass it on the way.

He explained this to Brigit.

They hadn't gone very far when, to their great delight, they found their old companions. The Poor Woman was sitting on an upturned box in a space between two sideshows and there was dear Cooroo, still draped around her neck. The ducks and geese were at her feet, nestling comfortably on trodden grass, and the Poor Woman didn't see them at first because she was lost in rapture as she gazed at a tethered bull-calf.

'Oh, you little beauty,' she was saying, over and over again.

But Cooroo saw them at once, and he saw the thin people, and he must have either had some kind of muscle tension or a faster heart-beat, because the Poor Woman turned abruptly to look at Pidge and Brigit.

Without stopping for greetings or anything else, Pidge whispered that he and Brigit had to go somewhere, but that they were being followed everywhere by hounds and that they must get rid of them somehow.

'Leave it to me,' Cooroo said; and he jumped to the ground, scattering the ducks and geese.

He went straight up to the tall thin ones, who were now together in a bunch— or pack, as Pidge preferred to think— and confronted them bravely.

'Puppy-dogs!' he taunted them. 'You are base, you are servile—you live for a pat on the head!'

And then he barked a laugh at them and flounced and flaunted right before their astounded and offended eyes.

They stared at Cooroo and their eyes blazed and the lips pulled back from the sharp teeth and they changed in a second from people into real hounds. Cooroo sprang away from them and flashed through the crowds and the hounds streaked after him, baying dreadfully. The crowd opened up for Cooroo to pass. It didn't divide into two lines of spectators making a course so that they could enjoy the sight of an animal being hunted for its life; but the people opened a way for Cooroo and then closed together again, making passage difficult for the hounds. Soon it was impossible to see anything through the block of people.

It hit Pidge and Brigit then that Cooroo was gone!

Tears filled Brigit's eyes; she was sure that she would never see him again, and she felt miserable and sorry.

'I didn't stroke him half enough while I had the chance,' she said, and she sobbed.

Pidge was having trouble holding back the tears himself. This is the second time he's risked his life to help us, he thought. He had a painful, uncomfortable feeling in his chest and a lump rising in his throat.

The Poor Woman stroked Brigit's face gently and she took Pidge's hand and pressed it affectionately.

'You might see him again. Nothing is certain,' she said kindly.

'We think he'll get away, don't we?' said the little brown duck.

'We do, we do; oh *indeed* we do,' the others all said.

'Especially as the hounds are handicapped by such a bunching of people,' Thick Dempsey added; and nobody laughed.

For a while everyone stood silently—one looking at another. There didn't seem to be anything left to say about Cooroo.

With a sigh Pidge decided that he and Brigit had better find the Fortune-Teller and he wondered what to do about the Poor Woman and the ducks and geese.

'Would you like to come with us? We have to find the Fortune-Teller's tent,' he said.

With a shake of the head and a smile, the Poor Woman said:

'No, I won't come. Now that you don't need me any more, I'll be going on my own road again. I thank you for your great kindness and friendship. I'm glad to say that I'm leaving you feeling happier than I was when I found you.'

They all said goodbye then. Brigit tried to kiss all the ducks at once, but they sorted themselves out into a queue and held their bills up in turn. She was surprised when Charlie and his tribe all came and lined up for one as well.

When they had gone, Pidge was left with a very let-down feeling. All the fun had gone out of the day. Brigit felt it as well, because she said:

'I wish we'd never come here. I'm going to miss them all but most of all, I'm going to miss Cooroo. And I don't even care about these swapping sweets or anything. I'm fed up.'

Her voice still quivered.

'I suppose we'd better go and find the Fortune-Teller now that we are here—or everything has been a waste of time,' Pidge said doggedly.

Brigit brushed her eyes with her sleeve.

'I feel the same,' Pidge told her. He looked away in case he might actually cry himself. I'm too old for that, he told himself firmly.

They walked again through the crowds of people who seemed to have thinned out rather, now that the hounds were gone.

But when they found the gaily-coloured tent, the Fortune-Teller too had gone, leaving a pinned sign, saying:

They peeped into the tent through a rip in the canvas and saw that it was empty.

'Now what do we do?' Pidge wondered loudly.

'Look!' Brigit exclaimed, pointing downwards.

At their feet dandelions and daisies grew tightly together in a line. The line began at Brigit's toes and led away from the Fortune-Teller's booth, and it was like a rope of two bright colours on the grass. Pidge understood at once that it was a distinct path of flowers to follow; it was plain as plain.

The flowers ran in a straight course through the remaining groups of people, and no one was treading on them. And when Pidge and Brigit in following them had reached the road, they were delighted to see that the flowers had even pushed up through the compacted surface, to mark the way. The saw as well that the sign was only for them; as they passed them by, the flowers were vanishing, just as the candles had quenched themselves in the mist earlier on.

The stripe of flowers took them all the way to, and past, The Amber Apple. They stood hesitating; the smells coming out were so tempting and they had not eaten a bite since breakfast.

'I tell you what, Brigit. If we miss her again, we'll come

back here and have something to eat. What about that?' Pidge suggested.

'Right!' she said.

Now the path of flowers led them round a corner into an alley. Here they ran down the middle of the road as a bright band of colour. The children followed them down.

At the bottom there were lots of carts and wagons, and there were yards that opened off the sidepaths. When they were near the bottom, there was another smell of cooking. And then Pidge and Brigit were startled to hear a familiar voice say:

'Oh, you Bold Unspiritual! Don't get strigalous with me while I'm forkling me sausages!'

The path of flowers was finished.

Chapter 5

THEY turned a corner and they saw Boodie and Patsy. The moment that he saw them, questions jumped into Pidge's head; but he decided that he would ask for answers later. He kept his questions carefully in the fringes of his mind.

After what had happened with Cooroo, the pleasure they felt at seeing their old friends from the past—so unexpectedly in Brigit's case—filled them with a grateful kind of happiness. They stood for some moments just looking and waiting to be seen, recognized and welcomed.

At first they weren't noticed and they nudged one another and grinned.

Boodie was crouched over a fire, frying a panful of sausages and making half-hearted attempts to fend off a blackbird that was perched on her head. The blackbird was struggling to pull straw from her hat. He was an ordinary enough bird but very cheeky.

On the ground nearby a clean cloth was spread; set with covered dishes and crockery. Patsy was kneeling there, putting a bunch of daisies into a small jar of water. He turned his head and saw them and his face lit up in a smile.

'They've come, Boodie,' he said.

Boodie's hands flew up in excitement and the blackbird flew off, scolding her sharply as he went. Patsy was up on his feet and holding out the tips of his mackintosh hem, he came towards them as he had done once before, that day on the island in the past.

'It was *you*!' Pidge exclaimed, as he and Brigit ran to meet him. 'I thought I saw someone in the crowd that I knew. It was you, selling apples and windmills. I sort of knew you were here, even before the strawboy came!'

And even though he had only just realized it, this was true. He felt a kind of glad surprise.

'That's right,' Patsy beamed, nodding. 'There are things that need to be said; but I couldn't get next, nigh or by you, for them old vaggybones of hounds and their busy, busy ears.'

'They've chased away Cooroo. He's a fox and they want to kill him,' Brigit said. Her eyes glistened and she stuck her thumb in her mouth.

Boodie and Patsy exchanged glances. And Pidge thought that there was a look of sadness in their eyes.

To distract Brigit, he said, while looking at Boodie:

'We're supposed to be looking for a Fortune-Teller. She's supposed to be down here somewhere.' He was sure he knew what she would say in reply. And so he was not surprised when she laughed and said:

'That's me. I'm partial to that diversion once in a way and we wanted to talk without being overheard or lip-read. But I had to give up waiting for you in the end, and come down here to make my fire; or there'd be no dinner at all today.'

She had made a simple hearth of stones and her fire burned brightly within it. With a long fork she turned the sausages in a great black frying pan.

'We knew you'd find us before the day ran its course,' said Patsy.

Pidge and Brigit sat down beside Boodie. The blackbird came back, and now he was trying to tug out a few of Boodie's straggling hairs that stuck out from under the brim of her hat. The hat was still flower-covered and butterflies opened and closed their coloured wings as they rested on the blossoms.

'He thinks I'm a scarecrow,' she laughed, pointing upwards with the fork.

'Small blame to him!', said Patsy, and he passed plates around. 'We hope you like sausages.'

'Oh yes! They smell great,' Brigit said, drawing in a deep sniff. 'Except for the swapping sweets, we've had nothing to eat since breakfast and that was ages ago.'

'Boodie is a qualified artist when it comes to sausages,' Patsy remarked.

Brigit held out her plate and Boodie forked out the sausages.

'About the swapping-sweets . . .' Pidge began with one of

his questions, as he held out his plate in turn.

'We'll have our gossips later,' Boodie suggested, and she poked into the ashes with a long stick and drew out roasted potatoes. 'Don't burn yourselves with these now.'

Tossing them from hand to hand, she wiped away the ashes with her skirt and she broke the potatoes to cool on their plates.

Patsy came with salt and pepper and a dish of butter for the potatoes. Then he brought a covered dish of buttered cabbage. And Pidge marvelled, for the daisies in the little glass jar seemed to turn their faces to Patsy all the time, as though they wanted to see him.

Using their fingers, they started to eat. They had not realized how hungry they were until they tasted the food. Boodie held up a bit of cooled potato for the blackbird. He scolded her again before he pecked at it.

'What have you in the little bag?' Patsy asked Brigit.

'My penny whistle and some hair belonging to the Seven Maines.'

'I lost my scrying-glass,' Pidge said. 'I'm sorry.'

'No need for "sorry"; it was yours,' Boodie said kindly.

'I couldn't really help it—I don't know where it went at all.'

'It did good while it was wanted, anyway,' Patsy said, breaking a second potato on Brigit's plate. 'I'd like to see the hair that's in the little bag.'

Brigit began to undo the strap.

'Oh, after the dinner, will do,' Boodie suggested pleasantly.

As the dinner progressed, Pidge noticed that some dishes on the table stayed under cover, and that Boodie and Patsy began to throw an occasional look at the place where he and Brigit had turned the corner at the end of the Lane.

'Are we waiting for someone?' he asked.

'We hope so,' Patsy replied. 'Eat up now and don't be shy of asking for more if you want it.'

'Last night we stayed in the house of a man called Sonny Earley,' Pidge found himself saying, when they had almost finished eating.

'And what did he tell you?' asked Patsy, with an odd kind of smile.

With Brigit's help, Pidge related all that Sonny had said.

'He's very wise, that Sonny Earley,' Boodie said with a half smile at Patsy, when they had told all.

And then Cooroo came quietly round the corner.

Before they could even get up, he had trotted over to them and they hugged and kissed him with an almost unbearable delight.

'We stood the day's work,' he said with a certain amount of quiet triumph.

'Oh, Cooroo!' Brigit said, her eyes glistening again, but this time for a happier reason.

He flopped down on to the grass. His coat was damp—from sweat, Pidge thought—but he wasn't panting.

Patsy whipped the covers off the spare dishes and brought food for him. A plate of cooled sausages and potatoes and a small joint of meat.

He bit at a sausage and a look of astonishment came over his face.

'What's the name of this creature?' he asked.

'It's a sausage,' Brigit answered, and she gave him yet another hug.

'How ever did you manage to get away from the hounds?' Pidge wanted to know.

'Only for the people helping me and hindering them, I'd never have done it. You were right about it being different in Tír-na-nÓg.'

'We told you so,' Brigit reminded him.

'After I got through the town, I laid a scent all the way back to One Man's Pass. I had a most wonderful turn of speed and there was still no sign of them when I got that far. I looked carefully, you may be sure! I doubled back then on my own scent, and I left the road and my scent behind, by springing up on that boulder where we met the woman and the ducks and geese. After that, I cut across the valley and reached the waterfall before the hounds appeared. My heart was in my mouth at that part—coming back so near to where they would appear, if they were still after me. I ducked behind the waterfall and waited.'

'That's why you're damp!' Pidge interjected.

Cooroo nodded and continued:

'Sure enough, I was hardly there before they came speeding

by with their noses to my scent all the way along the road. At the waterfall the wind was my friend and they didn't get a sniff of me, and I watched them until I saw them go over the Pass. As soon as they were out of sight, I made my way back here and the strawboy told me where to find you. That's it. By the way, you were right—those hounds are not fox hounds and they can certainly cover the ground when they want to—you're lucky they weren't hunting you up till now.'

'You were fast because of the herbs that Sonny Earley gave you,' Brigit said.

'Yes. I know it. When a sausage is alive, does it have hair, fur or feathers?' Cooroo asked, sounding highly interested.

They all laughed at this.

'Tell me!'

'How many legs has it?' he persisted. 'What is its food? Does it graze or does it hunt, and if it hunts—what does it go after? I'd truly like to know.'

Everybody roared with laughter.

'A sausage isn't a creature,' Pidge explained in the end. 'It's made out of meat, spices and herbs—that's all.'

'Oh,' Cooroo said, in a disappointed way. 'I was hoping that I could hunt for a few for my dinner now and again. Herbs, you say! I haven't valued herbs in the past, I realize that. But I'm ignorant of them and I'd better stick to my own ways.'

When Cooroo had finished eating, there was a contented silence as they sat in a half-circle round the fire.

'One way or another, this'll end soon,' Patsy observed after a time.

There was something different about him now. His look and manner were dignified and very gentle, and his face was composed and tranquil.

'Do you mean it's nearly over? But we haven't found that pebble, yet,' said a startled Pidge.

'Oh, but you have,' declared Boodie. 'It's known now that the pebble is in the Third Valley and that's what we must talk about.'

A change had come over Boodie as well. There was a beauty about her face that Pidge had not noticed before; the tones of her voice were different, too—they sounded mellow and her words were said clearly and sweetly. The comic sounds were discarded like worn out garments cast away.

'Oh, that's good!' Brigit exclaimed. 'I'm glad we found it; The Dagda will be very pleased.'

Then there was a lovely moment when Boodie tended her fire with a stick. There was a hallowed feeling, exalted like being in church. There was something about her movements and the expression on her face that was noble and full of grace, as if she were a very great lady. The fire glared and was pale yellow, bright orange and flame red. They all gazed into it with a dreamy abstracted stare.

'You should know,' came Patsy's voice, 'that the Third Valley is strange and secret. No one has been in there for more than a thousand years. The valley itself is an unpleasant place without beauty of any kind. The sun shines there briefly—only for a few moments each day, because the valley is straight sided and narrow.'

Now all of the light seemed to come from the fire. As they listened to what Patsy and Boodie were saying, a dimness fell around them and, except for the fire that they stared into, the world was dark blue.

'It's more a gorge than a valley,' Boodie was saying. 'The knowledge that it is dark and unlovely has been passed from mouth to mouth through the centuries. In that time, some evil thing has crept in there and it keeps out of sight as does a maggot under a rock, and so we cannot name it for you.'

'It sounds a terrible place,' Pidge said softly.

Although he was staring straight at the fire, he was conscious of the blueness that seemed to surround that small bright area. He could see that the blue rim at the edge of the brightness was a darker colour than the rest, and he was allowing himself to examine it with a kind of side vision—still without moving his real gaze from the fire. This was something he had sometimes done in church by fixing his eyes on the altar candles without blinking. He was not dreaming, however, but carefully listening to all that was being said.

'To get there, one would have to pass through the Eye Of The Needle and no one knows what lies beyond,' Patsy said. 'Even the birds do not care to fly over that valley, so we haven't the help of their bright eyes in this.'

'From time to time,' Boodie said, 'creatures have gone

missing, and it is always thought that they may have strayed in there and for some reason, they have not come back. These things we have to tell you before you go further.'

'It is all still under your hand; but if you do not wish to continue, after hearing this, no one will blame you,' Patsy said. It was plain that he really meant what he said.

There was silence again.

Then Pidge asked:

'If The Mórrígan gets the pebble, what will she do?'

'That pebble has one drop of her old strong blood. If she *only* gets the pebble, that one drop will enrich the weak blood she has now and give her back an amount of her old power. If she gets Olc-Glas as well, she will be strong indeed,' Patsy explained.

'Olc-Glas!' Pidge exclaimed. He blinked and lost sight of the dark blue rim for a few seconds. 'I'd almost forgotten about him!'

'You held him in your human hand. He felt the blood pulse under your skin and he awoke from his sleep,' Boodie murmured.

'Who's this Olc-Glas?' asked Cooroo.

'He's an old snake,' Brigit whispered. 'He was in an old book—Pidge found him!' she finished proudly.

'What will happen if she gets *him* too?' Pidge asked.

Boodie and Patsy exchanged a worried glance so quickly that no one else saw it.

'She will use the one drop of her blood on the pebble to dissolve him and then she will swallow him into her heart. Thus she will have his poison as well as her own. It is all very important to her,' explained Boodie.

'What will she do with all the poison—if she gets it?' Pidge asked now.

'She will cast her shadow over the world. As she was once, so shall she be again, whispering her evil to thousands,' Patsy replied.

'You must hear as well that, by this time, she knows where the pebble is to be found. And now she and her two others will be in deadly earnest and will certainly try to get the accursed stone themselves,' Boodie went on. 'Up until now, this has been a game for her—played from far away. She herself has been cool; Macha and Bodbh—her second and third parts—have been merry; partly from mischief and partly to deceive. But the game has grown serious now.'

'Who are *they*? Who are Macha and Bodbh?' Brigit wondered.

'The women who came to dwell in the glasshouse of your neighbour. They disguised themselves and named themselves Melodie Moonlight and Breda Fairfoul,' Boodie still carried on, explaining carefully and patiently.

'Oh, that pair!' Brigit growled. 'I never liked them at all!'

'Now we have told you the dangers that face you as far as we know them,' said Patsy.

Again, there was silence.

In the heart of the fire, the glowing turf popped and exploded into little bursts of flame that looked, at first, like orange coloured sea anemones and there were pale yellow bits that resembled small chrysanthemums, and finally, brilliant yellow dandelions.

Apparently out-of-the-blue, Brigit remarked:

'We've seen a lot of dandelions and daisies on this journey—I wonder why?'

'The dandelion is the flower of the Brigit who is Goddess Of The Hearth,' said Patsy.

'The daisy is the flower of Angus Óg, who is the God of Love,' said Boodie.

'Oh, we heard that about the daisies belonging to Angus Óg from those two in the glasshouse,' Brigit remembered.

'Are the Gods of Love and of the Hearth on our side?' Pidge asked.

'Always,' Boodie and Patsy both answered together.

'I had handcuffs that day—did Angus Óg give them to me?' asked Brigit.

'He did,' Patsy answered with a smile.

And Boodie whispered:

'Both of these Gods are in danger from The Mórrígan.'

There was a pause again and they watched the flowers in the fire.

'If we give up now, she's won for sure, hasn't she? This is my fault again. First I released Olc-Glas and now I've found her pebble for her,' Pidge said eventually.

'If not you, then some other would have done it on some

other day. It might have been a very different story then, if the person were only half as good and courageous as you and Brigit. Then all would have been surely lost,' Boodie said.

'But I am not courageous!' Pidge protested. 'You just don't realize. Brigit is usually far braver than I am. I am not courageous at all.'

'You are braver than you know,' Patsy maintained. 'We knew it from the first—that day on the island.'

Now Pidge remembered the question in the back of his mind and he said: 'I'm baffled by something. You gave the swapping sweets to Brigit that day—how did you know we'd end up here? How did you know it then, when no one knew the way we would go?'

'We gave those sweets in case a time would come when we had need to speak secretly with you, under the eyes and ears of our enemies. It was reasonable to foresee that you might want our help against the hounds—so we made that plan ahead of everything,' Patsy replied.

'Old Daire said that Brigit's little hand would do something big. How could he say that, if he didn't know what would happen?' Pidge asked next.

'Daire is greatly gifted. It may be that he had a half-sight of something that led him to make that prophecy,' Boodie murmured.

'I see,' Pidge said thoughtfully, and he wondered what Old Daire had meant.

'You, Brigit, and you, Pidge, have been our champions in this struggle and now we have Cooroo to thank as well.'

In the fire, the dandelion flames were beautifully alive.

Something seemed to stir in Pidge and a blind obstinacy came into him and he knew that he would not give up.

'I'm definitely going on,' he said, his face set.

'So am I!' Brigit declared. 'I never liked those two and I'll do it for The Dagda.'

'I'll go as well,' Cooroo decided.

'You would do better work, Cooroo, if you stayed on this side of the Eye Of The Needle. You may be able to keep the hounds from following Brigit and Pidge into the next valley,' Patsy suggested.

'Fair enough,' Cooroo agreed.

397

'You have that ornament still, made for you by your friend the blacksmith?' Boodie observed.

'She has. Did you tell him to make it?' Pidge asked.

'Yes, we did,' said Patsy.

'Why?'

'For fear you would need a cunning weapon.'

'Now, show us what you have in this little bag, apart from your penny whistle,' Boodie said.

Brigit undid the straps and took out the ball of hair.

'Take the hair, Pidge. Keep it in your fist and try not to be afraid of anything,' said Patsy.

'It's very hard not to be afraid,' said Pidge, taking the hair from Brigit.

'There are many who will help you,' Boodie and Patsy answered together. Their voices seemed to be moving away.

'That first day on the island—how did you know that we would do all this, when we weren't even asked to by the Old Angler, until after we had met you?' asked Pidge.

'We never doubted you!'

The voices were further away.

'But—how did you know that we would end up at Baile-na-gCeard?' he cried.

'There is no Baile-na-gCeard.' The voices seemed to be a long way off.

'The dandelion is my flower,' Boodie called sweetly.

'The daisy is mine and we are with you,' Patsy's voice came from far above in the sky.

All in one moment, the fire grew brighter; in the next, it had broken into a thousand flowering dandelions and everything was perfectly quiet—except for the shocked blackbird that flew to a bush and hid among its leaves.

Everything was perfectly quiet because they were alone. The town, the people, all of the noise and bustle—everything was gone. The untrodden grass silvered under the touch of a light breeze and there was nothing to show what had been there before, not the print of a heel on the ground, not a matchstick. There was no other life but for the growth about them and the blackbird and a flock of white birds flying away.

'I am not at all courageous,' Pidge was murmuring again.

'There's the Eye Of The Needle,' Brigit said, pointing.

It stood unmistakably at a little distance ahead and upwards. It was like the blade of a stone dagger with a hole through it. A stone path snaked up to it and was a grey thread going through the Eye.

'I'll wait for your return. I'll be somewhere here,' Cooroo said.

'Take very good care of yourself, won't you?' Brigit said, with her arms around his neck.

'It's my nature to,' he answered.

'We'll meet again, Cooroo,' Pidge said very firmly, and after Brigit had hugged Cooroo, the friends parted.

In a very little time they were walking the stone thread. At first it was about eight foot wide but it narrowed considerably as it climbed, with the ground falling away at either side. When they reached the Eye, they stopped and looked back at the Second Valley for a glimpse of Cooroo. He was nowhere to be seen. The landscape was utterly quiet. It looked like a painting.

They continued on the thread and went into the Eye. As they passed under it they were intrigued to see that bright green ferns grew upside-down from its ceiling. They are just like Christmas garlands, thought Pidge.

Emerging from the rock passage, the Third Valley broke before them. The sun shone on the sides and tops of the mountains, but this valley was narrow and unlit. It looked strange and forbidding.

Pidge gripped the ball of hair tightly in his hand, as they took their first reluctant steps downwards to face whatever lay before them.

399

Chapter 6

THE Third Valley was wild and broken and rocky. There were waves and curls and writhings in the grey stone. It was as if the rock had once heaved and surged and had then been petrified in the middle of tumult. There were gapes between the flat grey slabs on the ground where rotten water lay thickly like treacle. This was a blighted, savage and fantastic place, almost bare of life. Strange toad-stools grew there and not much else. It was queer that no tiny green plant made a grasp at life in the smaller crevices in the grey slabs, and there was only the odd patch of whiskery grass, and a few bare thorn bushes warped into strange suffering shapes, and some naked briars that sprawled over the rocks. A stream ran beside the jagged path. It gushed furiously and appeared to be in a fearful hurry to get away from where they were going. The Valley struck badly on their nerves; it was curiously forbidding and evil.

'Boodie and Patsy were right about this place,' said Brigit.

The sides of the mountains rose up steeply as straight as planks, and sharp daggers of rock stood up from the ground. They passed an appalling white fungus that looked like lips or a mouth.

The children sat on a thin flat stone while they thought about how they should try to actually find the pebble.

'The best thing would be to just keep our eyes sharp as we walk along; and if we don't find it by the time we reach the end—we'll just have to come back again and really search,' said Pidge.

'Right,' Brigit was saying, when the rock moved under them. It somehow felt revolting and they leaped up feeling sickened. Frantically Pidge kicked it over. There was nothing underneath but the grey stone floor. Brigit shuddered with relief.

'I thought there might be an evil maggot there,' she said. 'I like being afraid but not too much,' she whispered as they moved on.

The further they went into the valley, the higher the mountains loomed; impossible for any living thing to climb. If Pidge looked up for too long, he had the sensation that they were leaning in over them, and he had to fight very hard against his fears to keep going on. His free hand gripped the ball of hair fiercely.

A small wind sprang up, dismal and moaning, and it made dead leaves patter over the ground like rats. They felt the chill of it on the skin of their arms.

Then the booming noise began.

It was a steady beating sound getting louder and louder as they went forward.

'What is it?' Brigit asked shakily.

'I don't know,' Pidge answered, equally shakily. As best he could he pressed her hand to reassure her.

'I don't like this place—it makes me feel funny,' she said, and she looked around her with frightened eyes.

'I wish Cooroo were here,' Pidge answered; and I wish we had the scrying-glass as well, he finished to himself.

The steady beating noises were getting stronger, louder all the time. They grew more strident, more metallic, bouncing and echoing off the mountainsides, and sending rattles of stones skittering down again and again. It had a ringing note as if a great iron bell were being struck repeatedly in a steady relentless rhythm.

As they went on, the valley narrowed; there were tumbles of rocks and boulders that had fallen in the past and there were signs of mining for metal. The sides of the mountains were splashed with small red lights that flickered and danced. The children were moving reluctantly, as though through a leaden sleep. But in spite of this, they had reached the end of the valley.

A plume of smoke or steam rose from somewhere inside the end mountain that now stood blocking their way. Pidge wondered if it were a volcano and he thought that he couldn't bear to go inside one—not for anything or anyone. The surrounding mountains rose up sheer; there was no way out;

but the children were hardly aware of this as they stared at the glowing reflections that flickered out of a cave. The noise was coming from the cave and the path led in there. It began to be cindery underfoot.

They stopped.

Brigit clutched harder at Pidge's hand and a terrible, shuddering curiosity drew them both to the cave's mouth. They looked about them uneasily and stood there very quietly, wondering what would happen.

The beating noise stopped. The echoes seemed to ring in their heads for a long time and then the valley was filled with an aftermath of silence, in which they now listened to their own hearts vaulting against the substance of their bodies. Slowly, cautiously, they crept inside.

At first there was a wide passage like a road where the stones glinted with scarlet light and dark shadows postured. But very shortly, they arrived at an opening and saw that they had reached an enormous smithy. They stood bemused, trying to be brave as they took in the size of the forge and of the place itself.

Everything was still and quiet except for the breathing of a huge nest of fire. It was going light and dark from the touch of some regular draught that ran somewhere—perhaps along the floor. There was the acrid smell of burning coal and hot metal, and they gazed at a great anvil where rested an enormous hammer and a sword. In a pit by the main fire, a cooking-fire burned under a gigantic pot that was made of rivetted metal plates. Soup bubbled in the pot and sent out a mixed smell—nice, with something nasty—as though an old boot simmered in there, among more usual things.

The smith's great fire lived in a walled semi-circle that was built against a central wall that went up and up. Two arches stood on either side of this wall and beyond these arches, everything was pitch black. Apart from the light of the two fires, there was one other source of light, a solitary but huge beam of sunlight that came down from a crack in the distant roof, and in this bright shaft, the motes whirled and weaved. Everything was set in a natural cave that was a far-ranging stone chamber. There was no sign of the smith.

Pidge and Brigit took a few steadfast steps into the light of the fire, then they stopped. The heat slapped at their faces and pulled the skin tight. And still they looked around.

The bulk of the anvil threw a shadow and they saw that the handle of the hammer was well-worn. Various articles made from iron and bronze hung on the cave wall: a shield with rivets, a spear with barbs, a battle axe. Brigit fingered her silver bow and arrow, thinking of the last time they had been in a forge, when Tom Cusack had made it for her. Pidge was looking at some bones thrown in a heap on the ground at some distance. They were mixed in with other rubbish. They were animal bones, he decided. Perhaps there were some others? Did he see a human grin lying in the rubbish heap? He shuddered and looked away. But now, under the smell of the soup, he fancied that there was another smell, putrid and offensive, like rotting cabbage.

They stood now very quietly, knowing they were waiting, but not knowing what would come.

Behind the fire where everything was dark, some darker thing moved in the blackness. Then surprisingly, a voice began to sing lightly.

'A negg an' some nyamm an' a nonion,' sang the voice.

They were not prepared for anything like this, and they turned to each other with half-smiles.

The voice sang on:

> 'A negg an' some nyamm an' a nonion—
> Oh, what a sight to see,
> Spread on your bread with a nice cup of tea—
> A negg an' some nyamm an' a nonion!

The acridity of the smoke from the burning coal had made the backs of their throats dry and ticklish and they both coughed. At this, there was a great silence and at last a loud whisper came out of the darkness.

'Who is there? What has blown in to me?' the loud whisper asked. It answered itself immediately by saying: 'Two young ones! What an unexpected *treat* to be sure!'

The voice sounded friendly and welcoming and Pidge hoped at once that there was nothing to fear after all. They both took heart and came further into the cave.

'Who are you?' he asked, cautiously all the same.

'I am The Glomach, my dear,' said the voice. 'And this is where I bide.'

'The Glomach,' Brigit echoed, about to giggle. Pidge gave her hand a warning squeeze to be on the safe side.

'You've heard of me, no doubt?' the whisper asked hopefully.

'Yes,' Pidge lied quickly. He didn't want to get on the wrong side of anything called a Glomach.

'What do they say, small lad?' the voice sounded pleased, but suspicious. The owner of the voice stayed in the gloom and they had no idea of what he looked like.

Pidge had gathered his wits by now and he said:

'That you are a greatly skilled blacksmith.'

'What else do they say?' the voice wondered a little nervously.

'Nothing.'

'Nothing of my other skills?'

'No.'

'Nothing of my habits?'

'No.'

'What about my ugliness?'

'We've heard nothing about that.'

'Oh,' the voice said sadly. 'I *am* ugly. I am very, very ugly. That is why I am lonely. I am very, very lonely. Are you sorry for me, little children?'

'I don't know,' Brigit said truthfully.

'Oh, you *should* be—indeed, you should.'

'How ugly *are* you?' Brigit asked. 'What do you look like?'

'Oh, my sweet dote,' said The Glomach, 'I hardly know what to say. I am of the race of the Fomoiri—but I was born wrong, you see. My people all have one hand, one leg, and three rows of teeth. I am a monster with two hands, two legs—and only one row of teeth. Indeed I am a dreadful sight!'

Here The Glomach sighed deeply.

And here, Brigit laughed.

'You must be daft,' she said. 'Everyone looks like that.'

'Do you say—that *you* look like that?'

'Yes—of course I do.'

'Pitiful!' sighed The Glomach. 'So young, so sweet, so pitful.'

'Come out now and let us see you,' Brigit said bravely.

'You might be sorry,' said The Glomach; and the next

moment a monstrous man came out of the inner cave and smiled down at them.

'I am The Glomach,' he said. 'I am so pleased that we look the same.'

They were struck speechless with horror at the sight of him.

He was a bandy-legged, blobber-lipped, barrel-bellied, big-bottomed Giant.

There were ridges on his forehead like thick corduroy lying sideways, and bony ledges densely knotted with black hairs that were entwined and twisted and tangled with each other like ancient briars. They stood out over his eyes. His yellow teeth were as big as shoe-buckles, and there were a couple missing at the front where his tongue showed in a little bulge, like a small pink balloon, when he smiled. He wore a rough tunic of sacking under a leather apron that was marked with scorches and around his fat middle was a broad belt also of leather. Wherever his clothes finished and his skin showed, it was spiked with bristly dark hairs that stood up like black pins.

There was a silence filled with shock as the children stared up at him. Things were happening inside their bodies; all sorts of little signals were preparing their legs for running away. But their brains were several jumps behind normal and the messages were only just getting to their knees when The Glomach said sweetly:

'How very kind you are, to come all this way to visit me here at the back of beyond. Now you see me,' and he shyly turned away and hung his head.

Rolls of fat ran down from the back of his head so that his neck looked like a bloated pink caterpillar.

'Fee, Fi, Fo, Fum . . .' Brigit was gibbering under her breath.

The Glomach thought this a great joke and he roared with laughter and slapped his thighs, creating inferior thunderclaps.

'That's a good one!' he said. 'I do like a good joke. Give us another—it makes things seem more friendly.'

Brigit's mind was running wild. A commonplace saying came into her head.

'You'll be a great help to your mother when you grow up,' she ventured, her voice half-strangled with fear. A deep look

405

of repugnance was fixed on her face.

The Glomach immediately burst into tears.

'Me mother!' he sobbed. 'Me mother! Oh, I miss me mother. Now I have no one to take the top off me egg.'

'You're big enough and ugly enough to do it yourself,' Brigit said weakly—but she had gained a little courage, as had Pidge, at seeing The Glomach cry.

'Ah, but it was so nice when she did it—with a shaking of the salt in it—and the little stirrings with the egg spoon—and the dipping of the finger of bread in the yellow. Mothers do it best, you know.'

'Well, you great big eejit of a baby, your mother spoiled you!' Brigit risked saying.

'She did. She ruined me,' The Glomach agreed, and he wiped his eyes on the back of a massive hairy arm and he sniffed.

'You said I was ugly,' he grumbled in a hurt and accusing sort of way.

'You are the biggest Giant I've ever seen and you're much uglier than you said,' Brigit answered, in spite of Pidge pressing her hand urgently while she spoke.

'Now you will want to run away. But, that would be silly, wouldn't it, when I am the fastest thing in the whole world. Would you like to see how fast I can run?'

Not waiting for an answer, The Glomach bounded out of the cave. For a few seconds there was the loud thump of feet. In the moments that followed, there was a confusion in Pidge and Brigit as to what they should do, where they could hide; and the question—why don't we hear the sound of his feet if he is still running?

In a very few minutes, The Glomach bounded back in to them, shoved a small green fern from the Eye Of The Needle into Pidge's hand, and snatched a huge piece of wood from the ground which he thrust into his fire; then, he raced on lumpishly into the darkness of a second cave behind the fire.

Stupefied, they watched the light going away and very soon a second light was there, followed by a third, and further on a fourth, and further on still, a fifth. They realized that the Giant was running the whole circle of a vast place as big as a small town, and that he was lighting torches set in brackets on the skin of stone that was the hollow inside of a whole mountain. They had only just realized this, when he had completed the turn and was lighting up all the way back to them; and there he was, standing beside them with the wood hardly burnt—and he was not even panting. They gaped at the smiling Glomach and the feat that he had performed, and they were stunned into speechlessness.

They looked at the nearest torches, flaming and smoking—and at the ones further away that were only thumbnails of light in the distance and they knew that they could never run away from him.

'That's my running skill,' he said proudly. 'What do you think of it?'

There was no answer from the children.

'I am the fastest thing in the whole world. I can run the breadth of Ireland during the span of a blackbird's song.'

'But, the sea can do all that and more,' Pidge found himself saying.

The Glomach frowned.

'What?' he said testily.

'The sea can do all that and more,' Pidge repeated in a rush.

'I am the hungriest thing. There is nothing I can't swallow and still swallow,' The Glomach boasted, looking provocatively at Pidge.

'The sea is all you are and more,' Pidge said in answer, and he wondered at himself.

'I am the strongest thing in the whole world. I can crack a rock between my fingers as if it were a nut. I can split a tree with my spit, which goes like sheet lightning.'

'Still the sea is more than that, for it has helped to shape the world and turned rocks to powder—only by licking them. The sea could even swallow you,' said Pidge.

'You're very smart,' The Glomach said crossly. 'Who told you that?'

'I heard it somewhere,' said Pidge.

'But there is one skill I have,' boasted The Glomach. 'No one can overcome me in battle for I can't be killed. In battle against me—all must fail. What do you think of that, Mister?'

'I think it's frightening—if it's true,' Pidge replied.

'It's true, Mister. And as well—the swords that *I* make,

407

thirst for blood. Now—can you say that of the sea?'

There was silence then, until The Glomach spied Brigit's brooch that was still pinned to her cardigan. He recognized it as the work of a smith and he was instantly jealous of the craftsmanship.

'What is that little metal yoke that you wear?' he asked.

'That's mine,' said Brigit smartly, for she had completely recovered herself during Pidge's duel of words with the Giant. 'It's my brooch. It was made for me by a great smith whose name is Tom Cusack.'

'I could make one like that if I wanted to; but you can give me that one instead,' The Glomach suggested.

'Indeed I won't,' she said.

'I must have it. It must be mine. I'll play you for it.'

'I don't know what you mean. Play what?'

'I'll play you at Knucklestones. I always play that with whatever walks in here on two legs.'

'What do you mean—Knucklestones?'

'It's a game where you throw little stones up in the air—pick one or two up from the ground quickly, and catch the others on the back of your hand.'

'Oh, you mean Jackstones,' Brigit shrugged in belittlement.

'You've played before, have you?' The Glomach said, taken aback.

'Oh yes. Lots of times. Auntie Bina showed me how ages ago.'

'Play me for that little thing.'

'What if I don't want to?'

The Glomach smiled.

His eyes went to the huge cauldron that steamed on the cooking fire and then he looked at the children with a horrible sideways look, in which his eyeballs slid to the corners as if moving on grease.

The look was baleful, sly, beastly, poisonous, vicious, spiteful, malign, artful, brutal and treacherous. The look was all of these things in quick succession and then he finally managed to look amiable; but too late. It was all related to the cauldron. Pidge saw it and knew it.

'Brigit will play you—go on, Brigit,' he said in a choked voice.

408

'What's wrong with *you?*' she grumbled, wondering why he seemed to be on The Glomach's side.

'Go on,' he urged.

'How can we play when we haven't got any pebbles?' she said in a derisory way.

A laugh burst out of The Glomach that made all the nasty bits of him shake and tremble, the neck being the worst; and it blew the dust motes that were floating in the shaft of light into small whirlwinds and waltzes.

'I've got my own. I always carry them,' he said, and he unhooked a bag from his belt. His hands were particularly ugly; his finger-joints were like connected small white vegetable marrows, while the backs of his hands looked exceptionally bony with deep hollows between the bones. Despite his stubby fingers, however, he deftly opened the drawstring of his bag and tipped a small pile of stones onto the ground.

'These are my treasures—my little treasures,' he said. 'I have two moonstones, a blue turkey stone, a stone with a hole in it and many others. This is my favourite one,' he said, and he picked one up in his fingers and laid it on the palm of his huge hand.'

Pidge and Brigit looked at it with astonishment.

On the pebble was the bloody print of an eye.

Chapter 7

'IF I win, I want that pebble!' Brigit said presently, her face absolutely wooden.

'*You* win? If *you* win—you can have it,' said The Glomach, and he got down on his knees.

He divided the stones into small piles of five each, keeping the prettiest ones for himself.

'Me first,' he said.

'Why?' asked Brigit.

'They're my stones, aren't they?'

'I suppose so. That's fair!'

He began to play, using his left hand. The pebble with the blood on, he kept carefully in his right hand. Because of the hollows between his bony knuckles, he caught the stones very well, and only once did one drop off when it hopped off a bone and spun away.

'Now you, you sweet dote,' he said and he sat back on his haunches.

'We'll play six games,' Brigit said authoritatively and picked up her stones and weighed them in her hand.

She was quite unconcerned. Pidge watched with his heart up in his mouth, as she began. Almost immediately, there was a rapt look on her face as though she were in a dream. The dream was one of deep concentration and her hands moved in a rhythm as if an intelligence had lodged itself in her wrist. She made no wrong move. It seemed to Pidge that she moved to a sleepy music and there was no hurry and no mistake in what she did. She muttered to herself as she played but Pidge could not hear what she said. In all, they played the six games, The Glomach getting flustered and angry as Brigit's nimble hands won every time. During her last go, Pidge managed to hear what she was saying and realized that each time she tossed the little stones up in the air, she was muttering: 'Ups-a-Daisy!';

410

and he wondered if Angus Óg, who was their good friend Patsy and the God of Love, knew that Brigit called his flower; and he remembered how she had once worn daisy chains on that wrist, calling them her handcuffs and how powerful they became when they had turned to metal.

'There!' she said, at the end. 'I'm the winner. You must give me the pebble now and I keep my brooch.'

Pidge almost burst with pride as he looked at her.

'Never! One more game to decide once and for all!' The Glomach demanded.

'One more game, me granny!' said Brigit. 'I won fair and square.'

'Never!' The Glomach said again. 'You're a cheat. You cheated! You *must* have; nobody ever beat me before.'

Pidge lost his temper. He knew that he had nothing to lose.

'You're a liar—she didn't cheat,' he shouted. 'You're the cheat!'

'See?' Brigit said, scornfully. 'I've beaten you now—so you can just cough up, you bloody liar!'

'No,' The Glomach said. 'I'll cut you up in a minute and pop you in the soup. Two cows, eight rabbits, four chickens, a duck, two goats and a nonion and a carrot. And now I have two noodles! I don't like carrots, by the way—but me mother said they were good for me!'

Brigit treated all this with scorn. She had grown used to The Glomach and now regarded him as a spoilt child.

'Don't be ridiculous,' she said crossly, 'we're people—not ingredients. You're only saying all that rubbish because you lost and you're a rotten cry-baby!'

The Glomach went behind his fire and when he came back, he carried a knife in his hands. Bending for a few moments over his cauldron, he stirred the contents with his knife and then he leaned his back against the part of the wall that formed the arch and he looked at them with glittering eyes.

Brigit got even crosser. She stamped her foot.

'Stop acting the maggot just because you lost,' she said. 'And you shouldn't play with knives—don't you know that? What would your mother say if she saw you messing about with a thing like that?'

The Glomach burst into tears at once.

And Pidge realized that although the Giant had lied and cheated about everything else, he had really loved his mother, perhaps because only a mother could love *him*.

He shouted at him again.

'You are a damned fool,' he said sternly. 'We could have liked you if you'd let us. We were getting used to how ugly you are—but *you're* so stupid—you'd rather be lonely.'

He looked behind them then at the way out of the cave and thought that they should take a chance and make a run for it—make any attempt to get away; because, unlike Brigit, he knew that The Glomach had meant what he said. He could hear his own blood hissing as it travelled through the canals in his head.

The Glomach stopped crying and eyed them both, as if he willed them to just have a try.

What happened next was astonishing, even though Pidge thought that he was well past surprising.

There was a rushing sound and before they could know what was happening, a furious whirlwind burst into the cave and The Mórrígan, Macha and Boðbh, stood between Pidge and Brigit and the way out.

The children drew together in fear.

Chapter 8

FOR some moments the women stood as still as statues. Their hair was unbound and fell in great waves over their crimson-cloaked shoulders, and swept on to well below the golden cords that held their crimson dresses at the waists, to ripple with strange life about their knees. Then a hoarse, exulting cry broke from deep within The Mórrígan, and exactly the same sound was expelled from Macha and Bodbh. The echoes of these cries filled the second cavern and seemed never-ending. The women's faces were twisted with an ugly unspeakable joy and their eyes were terrible. They were so exalted that they could not speak at first.

Behind the children, The Glomach laughed in his turn and, rigid with horror, they realized that they were in a most terrifying trap; caught— with The Glomach behind them and the Three Goddesses before them—and no way out that they knew of.

'Oh, I'm afraid, Pidge,' Brigit moaned quietly, her face white. Pidge tried to give her hand a comforting squeeze, but he was past being able to move once he had heard the cry of the women. He thought that surely everyone could hear the furious pounding of his heart. It felt swollen, as big as a football; and it banged away painfully inside him, thumping against his ribs and filling his head repeatedly with its echoes. It made his body shake violently.

In a dead silence, the fire was the only thing that made any sound; it seemed to be breathing.

The Glomach spoke.

'Three old hens to pluck—a good day for me,' he said.

The Three Women gave him a domineering stare.

'You will deliver up the stone,' The Mórrígan said imperiously.

'A hard one,' The Glomach said to himself, consideringly.

413

'She'll take a bit of boiling before she softens.'

'You will deliver up the stone,' The Mórrígan said even more commandingly.

'It's mine!' he roared, and the force of his voice made the ground tremble.

'Base-born lump! Do as we command,' The Mórrígan said, her eyes as sharp as emeralds.

'Ah, don't be annoying me, little woman,' The Glomach said, with an exaggerated yawn of boredom. 'The pebble is mine and tantrums won't get it for you. And that is my last word!'

'Then be ready to welcome your death, blockhead; for it rushes towards you this day,' The Mórrígan said; her voice cracked and went ugly as it lingered on the word: 'death'.

The Glomach let out a roar, a great bellow of laughter; it rumbled crazily around the far-ranging second cavern and its sound was full of his contempt for her.

'My death? Oh my dear! If I die at all, you'll make me die laughing! No more about it now; not another word!'

The Mórrígan stepped closer, Macha and Boðbh by her side, and every movement was a threat.

Fear flashed through Pidge like a hot wet fire. It seemed that he and Brigit were turned to rock and were totally unable to move.

The Mórrígan reached forward and with a finger of rosy-tipped marble, she stirred the motes that still floated lazily in the shaft of light that came down from the hole in the roof. From the glittering specks, six and twenty she-warriors sprang into being and burst forth to stand before the three Goddesses.

They were hard, brawny and wild-eyed.

Their chins were square and strong and their powerful legs and arms were as hard as mahogany. They were dressed in short tunics and cloaks, the cloaks being fastened at each left shoulder with a great, enamel-worked pin. These mighty shoulders bulged with an immensity of muscle that quivered with a fearful promise, and the muscles that filled the rippling skin of their arms were like huge spoons. Every she-warrior had a mass of coarse dark hair, held back from the face with a clasp of iron, and each was armed with sword, spear and shield.

In the manner of all warriors, they shook their spears and raised a terrible cry and struck a further terror in Pidge and Brigit. They brandished their swords and beat their shields with ringing blows and they pranced and leaped and were wilder than a storm. The Glomach was not impressed and he scratched himself lazily.

Suddenly, Brigit screamed because it was all too much for her.

At her scream, there was a flaring in the Giant's fire and a shower of sparks shot up into the air. Everyone watched as part of the fire collapsed in on itself and a dandelion as big as a plate appeared in this cavity. It grew and it spread until it filled the whole fire. The ball of hair came alive in Pidge's fist and it squirmed. Too terrified to move or speak, he stood stiffly, but his hand moved of its own will and threw the hair into the living fire.

In the heart of the glowing blaze a small curl of green smoke appeared. It went upwards like a plume and spread outwards like a fan and the fire was covered with a steady dome of green haziness. Now a picture formed within it: they saw the Hidden Valley.

From the place where Pidge had sown the seed, the Seven Maines sprang and they were comely and full of life and dressed in princely clothes. Their tunics were of pale yellow and their cloaks were of purple, ornamented with gold and silver borders, and each cloak had a clasp of pure red gold. Their hair was long and flowing and held back from their faces by thin golden bands. Around their necks were the ropes of twisted gold that Brigit had polished; and on their backs were silver shields and these were rimmed with gold. Each of the Seven held two spears with shafts of elm and there was silver veining in the shafts. They came riding on horses. The horses they rode were royally styled in breeding and dress; they had collars of gold and their bridles had a ball of silver on one side and a ball of gold on the other. The Seven Maines rode with fury through the haze until they bounded out of the fire and leaped from their horses and faced The Mórrígan and her forces. The horses herded together and rushed in a body into the second cave.

These things were seen in seconds only; and there was a

sudden wild surge of hope in Pidge and Brigit as the Seven took their positions in front of them and stood between them and all that threatened them, holding swords that they had drawn from under their cloaks.

At this mark of defiance, the six and twenty she-warriors beat a din on their shields that was answered with an equal dinning by the Seven Maines.

Bronze war-trumpets were blown and the Poor Woman with the proud Gander at her side appeared running in the green smoke. As they ran, their appearances changed and the Poor Woman was a tall proud one, with a beautiful face that was pale and long. She looked wonderful in her speed, her yellow hair sailed out behind her and her green cloak flew. She had a great brooch of gold pinned over her breast and she held a straight, shining red spear in her hand.

The Gander had become a big man with flaming eyes. His cloak was blue of the skies and his tunic was blue of the violet; his sword had a golden hilt and his spear was tipped with silver. They were Queen Maeve and her husband, Ailill.

And when the Seven Maines saw her, they sent up a cry of joy to see their lovely proud mother again and to know that she was fighting with them.

And Maeve rejoiced at seeing the sons that she had once lost in a war that she had caused over The Brown Bull of Cooley—an animal that she had coveted beyond human reason—and she let out a cry that made the she-warriors retreat a step; for she was a fair match for them, even without the help of her husband and her sons.

'The Royal Nine from Connacht stand between you and that stone of blood,' Maeve shouted and that was her challenge.

The battle began.

As they fought, the ducks and the rest of the geese appeared in the green smoke. They were flying at first and then they were running and changing as they ran. And they were warriors and Maeve's Men and, with their swords flashing, they were out of the fire and fighting at her side.

Sword struck sword and shield faced on to shield. A spear from a she-warrior, spitefully aimed at Pidge, was deflected by Maine An-Do, The Quick, and passing the children, it went into The Glomach. The Giant collapsed on to the ground. As 'soon as he fell, his shadow broke into pieces and was shattered.

He lay dead and the relief to Brigit and Pidge was beyond telling.

The battle went on. The Mórrígan's wish now was to get to the dead Giant and take the pebble from his hand and then snatch Pidge and Brigit to force them to lead her to Olc-Glas. But the Seven Maines fought and Queen Maeve and her men fought; and they kept the she-warriors from advancing one step, without any great trouble.

The Hidden Valley was in the fire again. And there was Daire, a proud chieftain, frosty-haired in his age, but strong and powerful. And there, too, was Finn. Behind them, their people were gathered in a Tríoca Céad—Thirty Hundred men in a military force. All were mounted on good horses and the bridles were hung with little bells. Three harpers rode with them and a man was beating a rapid march on a flat skin drum. They came with their music and their bells ringing and they had embroidered silken banners that fluttered in their wake. Four deep they came and one would think that they would never end, for it was the Hosting of The Sídhe.

They came with a fine carelessness and in a leisurely way; but still they arrived in seconds only; as if it were only the eyes of the beholders that were slow in their seeing. They stood with the group from Connacht, after streaming from the fire. As each man sprang to the ground his horse went into the second cavern, until a large snorting herd had gathered in there. In every lull, the children could hear the jingling of harness and the tinkling of bells.

Now the people of The Hidden Valley had joined the fighting, but The Mórrígan, Macha and Boďbh only laughed.

The Mórrígan reached up and snatched ten ribs of hair from the crown of her fair head. She cast them to the ground and ten warriors who looked exactly alike, with each man having the same face and build and each one wearing light yellow, stood and fought by her six and twenty she-warriors.

Macha reached up and pulled ten ribs of hair from her blue-dyed head—and ten blue warriors all looking alike joined the ranks that faced the children's protectors. Boďbh then drew ten red hairs from her red head—and ten red-clad warriors stood with the rest. There was something inexpressibly terrible

417

in the way they all looked the same, in the way they were all replicas of each other, without the individual spark of creaturehood that shows uniquely in every human being.

In the centre of the green dome of smoke, the Old Angler appeared. He was running swiftly over vast distances towards them. The nearer he came, the more he changed. Old age fell away from him at every step and he straightened and grew stronger, until he was a youth in a white tunic carrying two spears, a sword and a sling in his hands. He leaped from the fire and put himself before everyone to face The Mórrígan. Seven lights shone in each eye and there were seven lights shining round his head.

'Cúchulain!' she screamed; and she bared her teeth like a wolf.

'I am your enemy. I was your enemy in the past. I am still your enemy. My hand gave you all of your wounds. Here I am to do it all again—and more!' Cúchulain said.

In the midst of the battle, he went against her the first time and he threw his casting-spear. It went through four of her yellow warriors; but The Mórrígan herself evaded it by taking a sideways leap. He went against her the second time and a stone flew from his sling. It made red holes in five of the blue-clad warriors; but she herself evaded it by flying upwards. He thrust his sling into his belt, his sword into its scabbard and the remaining spear he laid on the ground with his shield. Now he went against her the third time with bared teeth and his two bare hands. He had eight of the red-clad warriors pulled asunder before he reached the spot where she had been. She had gone small and rolled herself out of his way. He gathered up his spear and shield.

The Goddesses were pulling hair from their heads by handfuls now, and hundreds and hundreds of their strange warriors sprang from the ground. Some of the fighters had spilled out into the Third Valley where the clashing of their swords could be heard. Others had spread well into the second cave where The Glomach's torches flared and lights flashed from the tips of swords and spears. The horses were screaming now; they reared and plunged fearfully; some made a mad dash and escaped to the outside world and scattered hysterically among those who fought there. Cúchulain, sword in hand, was

all the time hacking and slashing as he tried to get close to The
Mórrígan; but she was able to dodge him again and again, and
her six and twenty she-warriors were always near to her and
they were fierce and merciless in their work.

Now The Mórrígan slowly raised her finger-tips to her lips
and blew the half-moons off her finger-nails. Ten metal
crescents went spinning and whistling round the cave in an
attack on the warriors—*no matter which side they were on*. And
when they at last embedded themselves in the cave walls, they
were red-stained and dripping. They split the rock, so hard
they were and so fast they flew.

Twenty more crescents flew from the fingers lifted to the lips
of Macha and Boḋbh. Cúchulain raised his sword and shattered
half of them to fragments before they could do their fearful
work. And still, The Mórrígan evaded him and she heartened
all of the warriors to fight fiercely and fervently. A kind of
madness touched them all, and at this, her face expressed a
most ferocious delight.

Brigit had turned to Pidge and hidden her face against his
chest and he had opened his jacket and wrapped it about her
and he cuddled her. They shook from the thumping of each
other's hearts.

And The Mórrígan gloated at everything.

'I am War,' she said.

Even though the battle might go against her; she gloated
that she had been its cause. She chanted for blood and flecks of
foam fell from her lips. Her blood leaped fiercely and coloured
her face. A shrill babble came from Macha and Boḋbh; a
litany, a dirge, a song of destruction and death. Pidge was
filled with terror and a bitter anxiety raged over his mind. He
was conscious of Brigit's warm breathing against his chest and
his hands shook as he held his jacket around her.

The Mórrígan's face took on a strange aspect. Her face was
horrible now. The soft contours had fallen and drawn in and
her bones stood out as a death-mask; but the mask was that of
a beast. The face had lengthened and come forward; the bones
were long and white and they gleamed. On top of her body the
skull of a horse shone whitely and her eye sockets were black
holes. The spittle hung in droops from her teeth and weirdly
gutturally sounds came from her throat. She was lurching

through the battle, watching the men as they died sharp deaths.

A fearful tremor ran through Pidge and he forced himself to look away. But then he saw that Macha and Bodbh had changed too, and that Macha was howling like a dog.

There was a low moan from Pidge and he edged backwards, holding Brigit and turning his back on the frightfulness. Brigit came out from under his jacket and he roughly turned her away from the fighting too; he would not let her look behind and they stared instead at the ground.

Then out of the corner of his eye, Pidge noticed a faint movement on the floor by the dead Glomach. A bit of his shadow was moving. He glanced at Brigit and saw that she stared at it too.

All the pieces of The Glomach's shadow were slowly moving towards each other and pulling together. They locked into each other like a jigsaw.

When the shadow was complete, The Glomach stirred himself and rose alive from the floor. He plucked the spear from his body and threw it into the struggling mass.

'Tickle me again!' he roared.

He had been dead, or as the dead. The shadow held the key to his life and that was the skill in battle of which he had boasted; the Giant was deathless.

He bawled out a roar and again the ground shook at its strength. He called his great sword to life and it jerked off the anvil into the air. It fought on its own and, thirsting for blood, it flickered through the fighting men and caused red destruction. Many fell before its evil magic. The Glomach laughed and his laughter was a roar of power and scorn. He made a spiteful snatch at Pidge and had him by the collar. Pidge's tongue was glued inside his mouth and he wasn't even able to squeak.

The Seven Maines rushed from the thick of the fighting and attacked The Glomach, but he held Pidge in front of every attempted sword thrust, still laughing.

Brigit screamed again. She was sobbing as she pulled her brooch off her cardigan. She fumbled at it with shaking hands and she fitted the tiny arrow to the bow and drew back the string made from the hair of a horse's tail. There was the merest whizz of a noise and the arrow went into the Giant's elbow. The little stab annoyed him, he was caught off-balance and he fell against the wall, banging his head very badly. Again his shadow shattered to bits. Pidge made the greatest effort of his life and he leaped to stand beside Brigit.

The Glomach fell to the floor slowly and the shadow pieces scattered around him. But for one fragment, all of the bits lay on the floor. That one piece fell into the bubbling soup pot, where they watched it melt. It went like black gelatine and dissolved into dark bubbles. The smell was awful and it was the end of The Glomach. He was truly dead.

The evil life went from his sword and it too, dropped to the floor. Pidge went over to take the pebble from the still-warm hand, so ugly, so huge. His flesh crept and he was shuddering uncontrollably.

All around the battle raged, while the Goddesses shouted with savage joy. They slobbered and they didn't try not to, and they were crying out that even the trees would tremble and bleed and the stones of the earth would weep. They walked through the fighting mass, saying words of sly sweetness like flowers of poison. Dropping their voices to a deep and artificial huskiness, they fawned over the warriors and said the old words that incite men to murder. It was the whispering of death to life, of old bones to warm flesh, a deadly mist of words sprayed out of their mouths and the more they were listened to, the stronger they became. Cúchulain continued to search for The Mórrígan among the deranged.

And the terrified children stood, not knowing what to do. Pidge's mind was in utter turmoil. We are lost among all this and The Dagda has abandoned us, his mind was saying over and over in a wild gabble.

But Cathbad suddenly appeared in the fire and he wore his druid garments of white linen. In his hand was a slender wand of oak and he leaped from the fire and came to the children, saying:

'The Dagda has not abandoned you.'

He raised his wand and formed a broad sweeping pattern in the air around them while he said queer stiff words.

A shroud came about the children, a shroud of protection; and they knew that they were safe within it from the battle and The Mórrígan. The terrible sights that were before their eyes grew confused and blurred, like something seen through a

421

rained-on window. The fighting continued, however, for they could still hear the clashing of swords and the groans and shrieks of the men.

Cathbad turned to them and wordlessly Pidge held out the pebble with a hand that shook; but the druid smiled and shook his head.

'It is still for you to do,' he said.

He took hold of each of them by the hand and he walked with them to the fire, where all three leaped in and walked through the green haze.

Cathbad went with them through this strange shrouding and they realized that they were going through the fighting that had spilled outside into the Third Valley; but everything around them seemed completely unreal.

He went with them all the way to the Eye Of The Needle. There he stopped. He placed his wand under his arm and then he held his cupped hands out to the children, low enough for Brigit to see.

'Look!' he said.

In the cup of his hands there seemed to be a rippling movement and a drop of water was there. In the drop of water they saw something that was green and pink. In a moment they saw a rosebud and it split and unfolded until a complete rose was there, with all its wonderful enfoldings of soft petals. In a second it was gone and Cathbad's hands held a vision of the blue and purple sea, where snow-white seagulls wheeled and dived and the sleek heads of seals and the smiling faces of dolphins appeared in the shining water. The vision rippled away and now there was a thrush on its nest in Cathbad's hands. She flew away and the sky-blue eggs with black spots were there. The eggs cracked and four naked babies came into the world. Another moment, they were fully feathered; and testing their wings, they flew away. Now there was a field with a mare and her foal, and the foal did marvellous things with its unsteady legs and its wild little head, tossing its mane and biting at the empty sky. They saw snow falling and the green spike of a daffodil rising through the whiteness of the ground and then, underneath it all, they saw the humble worm turning the earth and keeping it sweet.

And while they were watching, Cathbad's voice asked:

'What lies within my hands?'

'Magic,' Brigit whispered.

'An enchantment,' Pidge said softly.

'What is the battle?'

'An enchantment,' Pidge said again, and he squeezed Brigit's hand gently.

Again there was a rippling in the hands and in the drop of water a minnow swam. It was perfect in its littleness and, when it turned sideways to look out at them, they saw the wonder that was a minnow's eye. A peacock came next and he spread his splendid tail and rattled it for them proudly. The tail shivered and the peacock was gone and now they saw the children on the swings in Eyre Square, laughing and carefee. Another moment came and they saw again the people on the bridge in Galway and it seemed that children from the whole world walked there, smiling and hopeful.

Now in the hands were two flowers fast asleep. The white flower opened and Patsy, the God Angus Óg, stood on the thick yellow carpet that was the heart of a daisy; and the yellow flower opened and Boodie, who was the Goddess Brigit, stood on the tongue-shaped petals of the dandelion. They held out their arms to Pidge and Brigit and it was an appeal and a sign of love. Boodie's hat was still covered with flowers and butter-flies and, at the front, there was a little moth with a jet-black body of velvet; his wings were red with black spots and he showed them off to the children. One of the spots grew bigger and bigger until it filled Cathbad's hands making a cup of soft blackness. They gazed into it, and it seemed to be as deep and never-ending as space. In it there were suddenly tiny pinpoints of light and the light was brilliant white. All at once the lights were shivering and twinkling stars and they showered out of Cathbad's hands like fireworks. They filled the air a little way above with white sparks, and there was the smell of carnations. Some drew together to write the word:

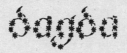

A shudder of happiness ran through Pidge and Brigit.

'You have not lost your courage,' said Cathbad.

The stars winked for a few seconds before fading away.

'Cooroo waits by the waterfall,' Cathbad said. 'Keep your courage. The Mórrígan will follow you, but she will be patient until you lead her to Olc-Glas. The Lord Of The Waters will rise only to your bidding—Olc Glas is in his jaws. I leave you now, to go back among the wounded with my healing powers. After you find Cooroo, go home.'

He was gone and the green haze was gone.

Brigit looked at Pidge and she gave him a sudden smile.

'We got the pebble,' she said.

Chapter 9

THEY began to run.

Down the snaking grey thread of a path they ran, going faster as it broadened. Before very long they were on level ground and running through the Second Valley.

They went over the patch of dandelions where the Goddess Brigit had made her fire, and elation was rising in them at every step. By the time they found Cooroo, they were bright-eyed and flushed. At the waterfall he was waiting patiently; keeping out of sight in the small hazel-thicket that grew beside the joyous pool.

'You're safe!' Brigit shouted; and she threw herself on him and hugged him.

'So are you!' the fox exclaimed, and he licked her enthusiastically.

'Oh Cooroo!' Pidge cried. 'I'm so pleased to see you! You don't know the dreadful things that have happened!'

Cooroo glanced quickly at Brigit.

'Don't try to tell me, Pidge,' he said prudently. 'You're both safe and that's what matters. Are you bitten, cut or wounded? Are you hurt in any way? Are you lame in any leg? Tell me that?'

'No,' they said.

'You haven't been touched! I can tell by your faces that you got that pebble you were after—you did, didn't you?'

'Yes,' they said.

'Good! Then the work hasn't been wasted,' the fox said with a quiet satisfaction. 'Not wounded, not lamed, and fresh as the morning. When these things exist together, it's always a new day.'

It was now that Pidge grasped at an understanding of Cooroo's life; they were free, they were unhurt, their legs worked and there was always hope.

'Listen to me now,' Cooroo said, giving a serious weight to his words. 'The hounds are lying in ambush at One Man's Pass. Can you smell them?'

They shook their heads.

Cooroo looked amused.

'What poor examples of noses you have!' he laughed, and then went on: 'They believe they have you trapped because they think that there is only one way out of this valley.'

'There *is* only one way, isn't there?' Pidge asked, instantly attentive.

'No. I've found another way.'

'Where?' Brigit asked, conspiratorially.

'There's a small passage behind the waterfall. It's dark in there; but while you were gone, I went all the way through it, and it will bring us out on the east side of these mountains. East is the way to Lough Corrib and your home—is that not right?'

'Yes,' Pidge told him.

'We don't have to go over the Pass and out through the First Valley after all,' Cooroo said. His eyes were twinkling again when he added: 'And if I may say so, the hounds are foxed nicely, this time!'

Pidge smiled broadly. Cooroo seemed able to make anything seem normal.

'Now, as we go through,' the fox went on, 'keep one hand stretched out above and ahead of you, Pidge. You're the tallest, and I don't know how high the roof is, so you must explore ahead by touch. Everything else is all right. It's a bit wet underfoot but you'd expect that. The air is good and it's quite a short way through.'

With Cooroo taking charge like this, the relief to Pidge was wonderful. It was just so comforting to have someone he could trust, who would simply take charge and give his mind a rest.

'All right?' the fox asked.

'Yes,' they answered; and then they followed him in under the waterfall.

They were in a niche or small chamber that was narrow but high enough for a full-grown man to stand upright. Facing them now, a short way in, was an apparently blank wall that was the rising mass of the mountain itself, the niche being only a tiny bite out of the living rock. They went directly to this wall.

There Cooroo made a sharp turn to the right and slipped into a division in the rock and the children followed him in. It was dark almost directly, so Pidge did as Cooroo had suggested and, with one hand upraised, he carefully searched the way ahead for any lowering of the ceiling, while his other hand gripped the pebble tightly. Brigit came last. She clutched at the hem of Pidge's jacket and kept as close as she could to him without treading on his heels. They went in silence. Sometimes there was a drip of cold water falling unpleasantly on their necks. Occasionally they splashed in small pools that felt cold. Now and then they kicked a stone or a pebble and it clattered. Always there was the sound of Cooroo's paws padding and splashing ahead of them.

The tunnel didn't go through the wide base of the mountain. It was like a slice cutting across the curve of a great irregular circle, and so, very soon, there was a greyness in the dark and then a lightness in the grey and then an opening that brought them out into sunshine and the three valleys were at their backs, and left behind.

Brigit heaved a huge sigh of relief and she wiped the water from the back of her neck with her hand.

'We've fooled them all,' she said, and she skipped.

Pidge looked around him in bewilderment.

The open countryside was before them now; but another range of mountains stood ahead of them, not very many miles away.

He had quite lost his bearings and he didn't know which way to go; but Cooroo nudged him and said:

'Those are the Maamturks!'

And in Pidge there was conflict. His heart leaped with happiness because he knew these mountains so well by sight. He could see them every day from his home. Once they were past them, there would only be seven or eight miles to cover before they reached Loch Corrib; and at the same time he was thinking—not *more* mountains, haven't we done enough?

'On we go,' said Cooroo.

As before, they ran through countryside that was lake-dotted and stone-walled and wooded. They stopped once to look back; but as yet no one followed them. The fox urged them on; and presently they reached the rising ground of the Maamturks. Cooroo studied the way up, moved along a bit, and he wasn't satisfied until he found a dried-up gully, and then he said that this was a good place to start the climb—as Pidge and Brigit had only two legs each.

'It's no use worrying about our scent—so we won't bother our heads about it,' he declared. 'The main thing now is for us to gain distance.'

Flat stones projected from the floor of the gully where the water had long ago washed the soil away; and they stood out like steps and were climbed without much difficulty. They found a sheep path then and Cooroo led them upwards as they followed it. After a long climb on this path, they found a broad shoulder of heathery ground that led them easily to the high top. Now that they were at the very top, they stopped and looked back again.

'The Twelve Pins look like ghosts of mountains instead of real mountains now,' Brigit remarked, wonderingly.

They examined the countryside that they had already covered and they were pleased when there was no sign of anyone moving there.

Cooroo faced about and he took in a deep breath of air. And although there was no wind to carry scent to them, he said:

'I can smell the fresh water of the lake; its softness comes across to me in the air! On we go, again!'

They began their descent.

It took a fair bit of time as they had to be careful—not so much of falling, as the going was quite easy, but of twisting an ankle. Near the bottom, they found a grassy slope and they half-ran, half-slid down it. Then, over a last bit of tufty, heathery land and across a stream by stepping-stones, and they could really run again.

With no other great natural obstacle between themselves and the lake, they went light-heartedly and easily. They ran so well that they almost danced over the ground. Elation was rising in them again and their eyes sparkled. They felt that they could bite and taste the air. Again, now that they wanted to go fast, they found that they were very fast indeed. Cooroo was overjoyed at his wonderful new speed. Pidge knew that it was entirely because of the herbs they had eaten, of course; and he wondered, fleetingly, if it were all too easy. But he was exhilarated by his swiftness and he felt a sense of power.

Once Brigit said:

'Is there anything in sight?'

And they stopped for some seconds and stared hard at everything behind them.

'No,' Cooroo decided; and they ran on.

Another time, Pidge said:

'What now? Is there anything in sight, this time?'

Again they stopped and searched the distance between themselves and the Maamturks. Nothing moved, so they ran on.

Now they were laughing and full of hope.

Chapter 10

EMBROILED in the battle, The Mórrígan did not see them go. It was a long time and they were a long way off before she missed them and knew that they had gone away with the pebble. For a moment she stood amongst the carnage, before going swiftly to stand with Macha and Bodbh. She communicated with them rapidly; they listened intently—and in the next moment, they had melted into her and become one with her again; their three shadows combining into a single dark shape.

For a few seconds, she stood with the blood lust gone from her and her beauty was even greater than before; for she had been greatly refreshed.

She gave a soft call and her six and twenty she-warriors struggled to her side. Bunched around her, they fought their way into the second cavern where each one grasped a shuddering horse by its dangling reins.

Dragging the screaming horses after them, The Mórrígan and her warriors gave a leap into the sunbeam and escaped into the motes. No one could tell which of the millions of particles they had now become.

Presently before the mouth of the cave, a troop of horsewomen descended from the sky and started along the valley with a clatter of hooves over grey slabs. At breakneck speed the frightened horses raced, swerving as best they could to avoid the sharp daggers of rock that stood up from the ground. Every living thing scattered before them as they rode in a wild burst towards the Eye Of The Needle. The Mórrígan was smelling the way that Pidge and Brigit had gone. Her purpose was to follow their trail exactly. Her reason was simple—it was in case that, in their great fear, the children might have cast the pebble away, to be rid of her. She knew that the blood on the pebble would not allow her to pass by, without revealing itself to her; and as she and her warriors galloped crazily along, she was ready to receive its silent message.

She charged ahead to take the lead as they approached the way out of the valley; and in single file, they dashed up the path and swept through the Eye of the Needle and thundered down the snaking, grey path, regardless of danger to the horses or themselves.

They rode boldly through the deserted Second Valley.

Their pace was the incredible hurry of a race. The horses' ears were laid back, their nostrils flared widely and their tails streamed out behind them. Great veins stood throbbing on their heads and necks, and their manes were like flames of fire. Still, the riders wished for even greater speed and they kicked into the horses' flanks with their heels. Before very long, they were wheeling past the base of the mountain where the water fell; and there, The Mórrígan pulled cruelly on her reins. Her horse reared madly, plunged and reared again and then stood, quivering and snorting, while the other horses milled about in panic.

The Mórrígan called her hounds.

Slim shapes appeared on the crest of the far mountain where the pass led over into the First Valley; and they ran in haste to obey her.

Again there was rapid communication.

Smell! was the command when they arrived. *What means this?*

The hounds scented the children and the fox, and were too confused to answer. They abased themselves before her.

My enemies have slipped through here with the fox—is this how you watch? she questioned, her face impassive.

The hounds rushed to explain that One Man's Pass was the only known way out of the valley.

Who guards One Man's Pass now? she wanted to know.

'It is unguarded—we, all of us, came in answer to your call, to serve you' Greymuzzle explained.

Fools! This could be a trick of The Dagda's. At this very second, the brats and their companion could be out of hiding and sneaking through the unguarded Pass above. You, Findepath! Take one other and follow the scent that is here. If my enemies have found a way through at this place, do likewise. Wait on the other side until

431

we arrive. Mind! Keep your noses sharp in case my bloodstone lies discarded on the way. And woe betide you all for this piece of stupidity.

'Yes, Great Queen,' the hounds answered, lying in abasement on the ground.

Findepath and Fowler then went behind the waterfall. As they left the main party, one of the she-warriors leaned from her horse and gave Fowler a slap on the hindquarters with the flat of her sword, to encourage him in his duty.

Once he was in the dark, he bared his teeth briefly but plodded on after Findepath as he had been ordered.

Again the riders drummed the horses' sweating flanks with their heels; and, followed by the remaining hounds, they charged on through the Second Valley. They sped past the huge boulder and urged their horses up the sash-like path. Sensing extra carefully, The Mórrígan led her forces at unbroken speed through the Pass and they followed the line of the mountain and poured down, into, and through the First Valley.

Where the cottage of Sonny Earley had stood, there now grew a wide and thick ring of daisies. The Mórrígan's eyes flashed fire and there was a deep scowl on her lovely face as they galloped past.

Soon they had reached the far end of the horse-shoe shaped valley and they charged out into the open. They turned sharp left, still driving their horses unmercifully. On they went, obsessed with hurry, until they at last had raced parallel with the mountains to the place where Findepath and Fowler had emerged from the rock passage, and where they now stood waiting.

They reined in for a little time while she questioned as to whether the pebble had been abandoned by Pidge in the tunnel. On hearing that it had not, she scowled; and they all set off again following the trail.

Now that they were in open country, the hounds kept pace with the galloping horses. In time, they reached the point that Cooroo had chosen as an easy way over the Maamturks. Only The Mórrígan and the hounds used the gully as a path upwards. But the she-warriors kept in line with her and forced their horses to throw themselves at a rougher ascent. Without a definite path to follow, the horses laboured up the slope, digging in their powerful back legs to thrust their bodies forwards and upwards, while the she-warriors beat them with the flats of their swords. The horses' hooves knocked down stones that clattered like falling slates in a high wind. Fowler looked at the cruelly-used horses with something like pity.

They reached the top at last and reined in to scan the countryside spread out before and below them. In the distance three small figures could be seen, running.

A slight smile played about The Mórrígan's lips as her thoughts dwelt fleetingly on the thumbprint that she had placed on the table in the glasshouse.

Chapter 11

A faint and distant drumming of hooves made the children and Cooroo pause and look back a third time. They saw a small cloud of dust moving at speed between themselves and the Maamturks.

'Here they come!' Cooroo said.

A spasm of dreadful fear struck Pidge before they ran on.

'Keep your courage; keep your heads!' Cooroo was saying; but they scarcely heard his words.

It was like running from a bad dream.

They ran over pasture land, they skirted round and ran through small clumps of trees. They ran over cut-away bogland, avoiding the deep pools of brown water. They crashed through the green blades of rushes, they scrambled over low stone walls; they ran up small hills and raced down the slopes, leaping over grassy hummocks, just missing rabbit burrows. Once, they followed Cooroo over a deep stream that was narrow enough to jump, holding hands.

They were not conscious of any of these things; but one appalling thought struck Pidge as he ran—he and Brigit were now running in full view of the hounds and the bonds restraining those relentless and slavish animals were now broken.

Brigit was flying over the ground in a blind trance, the whole of her small being intent on putting the greatest distance possible between herself and The Mórrígan. She was totally, utterly, silent. The strap of her precious schoolbag snapped and the bag fell to the ground behind her; but she would not stop and she didn't want Pidge to stop—when he hesitated in his stride, she gave a small scream. He read the fear in her face, so he ran on.

After a long time, Pidge dared to snatch a look back. He was immediately sorry for he was sure that their enemies were gaining on them. Later, he felt compelled to look again; and he was even more certain that the distance between them had shortened. The truth was that it had shortened; but not as much as he feared.

And then Cooroo did a strange thing. He made a snatch at Pidge's hand—the hand that held the pebble in a tight grip—and then he ran away from them at an angle, going northwards and eastwards.

The children were so stupefied and shocked that they stopped running. Pidge was overwhelmed with the miserable feeling that they had been betrayed. A few seconds elapsed before he realized that the pebble was still safe in his hand. It had all happened so suddenly.

There was one backward look of farewell from Cooroo, and then he was moving swiftly with his legs going at full stretch and his head up.

Still half-dazed, Pidge and Brigit watched him go, and then they saw that the Mórrígan was dividing her forces. In moments, the six and twenty she-warriors with half the hounds at their heels were swerving to follow Cooroo. Pidge understood that the fox was risking his life again and he felt a sharp stab of sadness and regret. He said nothing to Brigit, however; and they were both running again now, driving themselves to go faster and faster.

And even though they knew that The Mórrígan wanted merely to keep them in sight until they had led her to Olc-Glas, as Cathbad had said, their fear was terrible. Pidge's greatest wish was that they would find somewhere to hide in this open country; but it seemed quite hopeless. Another look back and he was very slightly cheered to feel that the distance between themselves and The Mórrígan was more or less the same. It seemed that she was not gaining on them.

But now he knew what it felt like to be hunted, *finally, they were quarry*!

And then a small wind came from before them to add to their troubles. It wasn't a cold or a strong wind, but it was rather horrible in the way it carried sharp dust to throw at them and blind them. No matter which way they turned their heads, the wind found their faces. It seemed to swirl all round them and they were forced to run with heads bent, to protect their eyes. And Pidge thought: this wind has nothing to do with Needlenose—it isn't friendly, it isn't full of air.

Under their feet, the grass became withered and thin. The wind prevented them from seeing where they were heading; and all that they could really notice was the ground as they ran over it. There was a sudden change and the grass was grey and blackened; and in the end, they reached a part where the grass failed and the earth had a dark crust like burnt bread and puffs of black dust powdered at their feet at every step.

In spite of the wind, they managed to look around them.

Everything was stricken with a kind of blight. The bushes and rare scraps of grass looked sick and ailing and there was an oily, shiny look to things. On the crippled bushes, the leaves hung like smuts on cobwebs and there was a peculiar smell, half-sweet, half-nasty, that was unlike anything they had ever smelled before.

They stopped moving while Pidge shielded his eyes and looked behind to see if they could possibly turn back and run a different way. But The Mórrígan's hounds had fanned out into a half-oval. Pidge realized that they were boxed in, because every hound was in a position to run at them in a straight line whichever way they went. It was something like the way sheep are penned.

Even though the distance between the hounds and them- selves was still great, he was terribly afraid to make an attempt at changing direction, so they faced on again.

Ahead of them now, they could dimly see a pale grey rock formation of low ridges. A hope jumped in Pidge that it might be a place where they could hide, or where they could dodge their pursuers. At the very least, they would get away from this horrid scorched place.

'It makes me feel sick,' Brigit said.

'There must have been a terrible fire here,' he said, guessing an explanation.

When they reached the grey rocky place, they found some- thing like an avenue created by the rock rising on either side of an empty narrow space like a path. The walls made by the rock were not very high; just a bit taller than Pidge.

Just before going in they noticed a bubble, like half a giant Easter egg, that was resting on the ground. It was revolting because it wobbled with the movement that was inside it. It looked like a blister. They were glad to walk into the avenue to get away from the sight of it.

Inside the avenue it was humid and damp; and in there, the smell was more persistent. The sky pressed down on them like a heavy blanket, the atmosphere was entirely oppressive, and they could hardly breathe. No sooner had they gone inside than Pidge felt that he had made a dreadful mistake; but he comforted Brigit by saying that when they came out on the other side, they would surely have left this awful area behind and they would run on grass again. There was no question of being able to run now; the ground was slippery from an oily moisture. They plodded on and on through this disgusting place, passing the glistening grey walls with a shudder, and from time to time, a blister that wobbled. The avenue seemed endless.

Some time later Pidge began to suspect that they were following a way that looped back on itself, or that they were going in a circle that was getting smaller. Although it was sweetish, the smell was almost choking them now and they were half-stifled by it. The wind still came and treated them roughly; but it had no effect on the smell.

'This is another rotten place and I hate it,' Brigit said in the end.

But Pidge was silent.

For he now realized, that in spite of all they had been through—they had arrived at a place that was a dead stop, where there was no way through the grey stone.

This was the most appalling blow.

Telling Brigit to wait and to try not to be too frightened, he bent his knees and launched himself at the wall. Even though one hand was clenched because of holding the stone, he managed to grip the top of the wall and he then dug his toes in and somehow scrambled up. He swung one leg over and sat; and shielding his eyes against the wind, he looked about to see where they were.

His heart almost failed him then. He saw line after line of grey stone wall extending in stern enclosures all around the point they had reached. His stunned gaze travelled over them; and they were so many that he might be looking at the frozen wave-crests of a filthy grey sea, that went in a huge loop or whorl to a central place, and he saw that he and Brigit were in the lifeless heart of it. His courage went weak and he was filled with despair when he realized that there was no way out that he could see. If only the nasty little wind would drop, then he might see an escape! His head felt hot and he was incapable of thought. He stared a little while longer, before he was completely thunderstruck with a certain realization.

'Oh no!' he cried in deep despair.

'What? What?' Brigit shouted at him quickly.

'We are in a maze!' he answered, his voice entirely wretched.

Chapter 12

'COME down! Come down, Pidge!' Brigit screamed and he jumped down and stood looking at her. He was in a stupor. It might even be that if she hadn't shouted to him, he would still be uselessly astride the wall. He was unable to think of what to do. Crazily, his mind strayed to Cooroo and he wondered if he were lying dead somewhere by now. Quite suddenly he had an impulse to throw the foul stone away; to lob it as far as he possibly could over these grotesque walls. They had been through too much. If he threw it away all this would be over, he thought, feeling utterly depressed and without a spark of hope. The Dagda would lose the fight then, of course; but shouldn't he be helping us? he thought miserably. Why doesn't he help us?

And this was followed at once by:

Of course! The hazel-nuts! I must try a hazel-nut!

He was conscious again now and his hand tore frantically at the bag in his pocket. He found a nut and picked it out between finger and thumb. It cracked before he could lay it on the palm of his hand and one half fell to the ground. In an instant, the part that was left showed a soft greyness that was lovely and in it there was a mixture of iridescent colours. One half-second more and a plump pigeon was perching on his fore-finger, calmly fluffing his feathers and blinking his eyes.

'I am Raðairc,' he said. 'Homing-Pigeon, First Class at your service. Allow me a few moments to spy out the land.'

He looked enormous as he dipped briefly on Pidge's finger before taking off. His creaking wingbeats seemed to fill their ears.

He seemed to be gone forever but in reality he was back in a few seconds, and he came to Pidge's finger with his wings fluttering creakily as before.

'It's not as bad as it looks,' he said, reassuringly. 'Some of

439

the walls are broken and I can guide you out. All of this is a trick of The Mórrígan's, but if you do as I say, it might not work as well as she hoped it would.'

'What does she hope for?' Pidge asked very anxiously.

'She has put this here to delay you, so that she will be in striking distance if the Great Eel is waiting for you at the lake. It's not to snare you; it's just to slow you down so that she can get closer. Do you understand?'

'Yes,' he said grimly.

'But what is it?' Brigit asked in a frightened voice.

'We won't worry about that now, Brigit. Will you just do as I say?'

She nodded and Pidge nodded.

'Right! First of all, you will have to retrace your steps a little way. Ready? Follow me!'

Raḋairc took off again and, flying very low, he led them back along the path for some distance and then he perched on one of the walls. They hurried to keep up with him, feeling that he was their one desperate hope.

'Climb over here,' he counselled. 'The part of the wall that is directly opposite to this in the next path—is broken down.'

Pidge scrambled up the wall by his tried method and, when he was safely astride it, he reached down and grabbed Brigit with one hand, while she grabbed the wrist of his other hand, the one that held the pebble. He pulled, and she clambered, and in this way she got to the top. Pidge jumped down on the other side and held his arms out to her. Grim-faced and with her jaw set tight, she threw herself at him.

'Oh, that was well done!' Raḋairc said encouragingly. 'No time to lose—come on now—straight across to the gap opposite you!'

They ran to the gap, cutting across one avenue. Pidge felt disheartened again when he remembered how many more there were; all those folds of grey stone.

'This way!' Raḋairc said; and again he flew before them along a path, to stop once more where there was a wall to climb that would help as a short cut.

'There is no simple way out of here,' he warned them as they climbed. 'It'll be hard work. But I have spied out the way that is shortest and where you will still face Loch Corrib. So look on the bright side—you are under my wing now and I will take you home.'

Far away in Shancreg, Old Mossie Flynn was still in his glasshouse.

His attention was suddenly drawn to his little cat. Something behind Mossie had fascinated her and she was staring at it with the deepest intensity, Mossie turned to look, following the line of the cat's vision.

He saw what he thought was a cobweb and he went over to have a look at it, and to find out why his cat was so interested by it. It was an odd thing; but he wasn't able to see any guy-line of silken thread that might attach it to anything. His curiosity was aroused more fully and he bent his head to look under it. He turned his head and peered at it from a sideways viewpoint. After this he walked all around it.

It hung in the air without support.

Mossie concluded that he had made a wonderful discovery in Natural Science. The Hovering Shancreg Cobweb, he said to himself.

He checked it all again, noting a little dust storm that was active just above it.

'This is a very queer thing!' he exclaimed, at last. 'I'll see if it floats!'

He filled his lungs and blew at what he still took to be a cobweb.

It didn't tremble or float away in his breath, but to his disappointment, it collapsed in on itself and fell to dust.

Quite suddenly, just as Pidge and Brigit were about to climb over yet another wall, there came a warm gust of air and all of the grey walls broke, whispered, and went to powder. The smell was gone, the rocks and blisters were gone; and the dusty wind was no more.

Raðairc flew above them, shouting:

'Splendid! Splendid! Come on! One good burst of speed! You can do it!'

He's exactly like a trainer of athletes, came the thought into Pidge's weary mind.

In a great hurry now, they ran eastwards.

'Follow me! Follow me!' Raḋairc cried incessantly.

Pidge wondered fleetingly how The Mórrígan had created her maze. It was well that he didn't know that he and Brigit had been inside her thumbprint, that the strange bubbles were beads of her sweat and that the glistening on the rocks was a coating of the same sweet and evil-smelling moisture.

He took one fearful look back and in his horror he was sure that The Mórrígan and her hounds had come closer. Terror stimulated him to even greater speed and he was matched by Brigit as he was holding her hand. They gratefully obeyed Raḋairc in everything he commanded. Although their speed had greatly increased again, the dread that The Mórrígan was shortening the distance between them filled Pidge with terror. In his mind the hoofbeats were louder and he could hear the laboured breathing of her horse and the slap of her legs against its sides.

And now, at last, they reached the lake's edge and they were fighting back terror. Because of the delay in the thumbprint, The Mórrígan had indeed gained on them but she was not as close in reality as she was in Pidge's fevered thoughts.

Raḋairc flew over the lake, calling:

'Hurry! Hurry!'

Pidge scrabbled frantically in his pocket for a hazel-nut. A greater anxiety seized him when his fingers discovered that the bag was empty, and he pulled it out and shook it, before throwing it away and trying his pocket again.

Down in a dusty corner he found what was the very last hazel-nut and his breath trembled out of him in relief. He held out his hand and the nut danced on his palm with the shaking of his nerves.

The nut split open; and then misery and grief flooded through him when he saw two completely empty half-shells, jiggling about on his hand.

442

Chapter 13

PIDGE went rigid.

His eyes stared as he foolishly waited for something to appear in the empty shells. The Mórrígan was getting closer with every second that passed and his whole mind was a riot of confusion and fright.

Surely, surely, something would happen?

Surely, surely, their need was known?

At last he was forced to admit somewhere inside himself that the nut was empty and useless, and with a groan from his soul, he threw the shells away.

He didn't know what to do; he didn't know which way to turn.

In vain his hands searched his pockets in the useless hope of finding just one more nut; and even while he was doing this his eyes were fixed on one of the shell halves that was bobbing gently on the surface of the lake where it had landed.

Brigit, who was looking behind her all the time, hardly realizing what was happening, was saying: 'Why doesn't it hurry? Why doesn't it hurry?'—but her words came nowhere near him in his panic. Through the disorder in his brain came the realization that the half-shell that floated on the lake was growing.

In the time it took him to draw in a wonderful breath of air, the nut-shell had become a small round boat, and Pidge grabbed Brigit's hand and they jumped into it. He looked for oars or paddles but there were none; they had barely settled themselves when the boat started to move. It went as straight as a line in Geometry, right across the dark green, glassy and unrevealing surface and it seemed to slide over the water rather than cut through it.

What will she do when she gets to the lakeside? he wondered. He clenched his fist tightly on the pebble. She's not getting it!

Never! I've seen what she really is and I'd rather die than let her take it.

There was a commotion back on the land as the hounds reached the water's edge where they spilled over the ground, snuffling and whining.

And then She arrived—the Three-in-One; and she threw herself from the back of the badly-winded and reeking horse, and she was very tall and beautiful and full of anger as she stood at the side of the lake. The horse immediately shied away from her and ran off, although he was so done-in.

Pidge's eyes blazed with light. He raised up the hand that held the pebble.

'The lake is bottomless,' he screamed, 'I am dropping this pebble in.'

This threat astounded and infuriated The Mórrígan even further. Pidge's bold words were ringing in her ears. That this moment now contained the unbelievable possibility of her defeat was the thought that dominated her mind. It beat like a pulse in her head and stung her to action.

'Hold!' The Mórrígan screeched; and the blood on the stone yearned towards her—and some of its evil came into the little boat. It faltered in its movement.

Pidge could feel The Mórrígan's eyes on him. They seemed to burn into his head. Everything went to a dreamlike state.

The blood on the stone assumed a power over his head. He felt a vibration under the curl of his fingers and his grip was loosening. Against his will his hand began to slowly rise even higher in the air.

Suddenly, The Mórrígan threw her arm up over her head and cast what looked like a line or a whip, out across the lake. It rose very high and snaked over the water in a long thin streak.

She had raised her hand against the children.

Brigit moaned and cowered down, making herself very small in the bottom of the boat.

Then, fingers and a thumb as fine as wire reached and plucked the pebble from Pidge's now-feeble grasp.

The boat stopped moving.

He was completely overcome by horror and revulsion, as he realized that she had sent her own hand across to them and that *she* had come so close to him.

444

The Mórrígan held the pebble high and shrieked a laugh of triumph at the earth and the sky and at The Dagda.

It was a terrible moment, full of evil insinuation, and Pidge, cowering now, gave a loud moaning cry for help.

The cry for help by chance coincided with a movement The Mórrígan made that brought her foot down heavily on Fowler's paw. In all of his service to her, he had been walked on like all of the hounds, and now, a flashing remembrance that Pidge had once been kind and the fire of the pain inflicted on him by the Mórrígan's foot, came together in a crazed feeling in his head. He was overcome with a courageous madness and he bit The Mórrígan on the leg.

In her anger, The Mórrígan screamed a different scream and she dropped the pebble into the lake. It fell right beside the boat, but Pidge and Brigit were beyond having the ability to even think of catching it as it fell. The pebble vanished into deep, deep water that might truly be bottomless.

Without losing its magical thinness her arm came back at her like a spring, and she smote Fowler and turned him to a small pillar of stone. Her charm bracelet flew from her wrist as she swiped at Fowler and it landed on the earth.

As soon as the bracelet touched the earth, the Sergeant and his bike, which were the only things clipped on to it that were not truly owned by her, returned to their full size. The Sergeant looked in a bewildered way at The Mórrígan; and what he saw was a beautiful woman, more lovely than any rose. He looked at her without reserve at first, and then he blushed to see her perfection. The truth of his feeling lit his eyes and from his buttonhole he took the yellow rose with the red tips and held it out to her.

'Peace,' he said; for that was the name of the rose.

He stood humbly before her, wondering if she would accept his mild offering.

The Mórrígan received the word as if she were pierced by the stab of a sharp needle-tipped knife and, for a time, she spun away from it screaming.

Anger swelled up in her even more. She had lost the stone into the pure water and now this creature dared to stand before her, distracting her during the most vital moments in her struggle for the stone and her old power, and saying the one

445

word whose meaning she hated and feared because it threatened her very existence. Her face turned olive-coloured and then white.

She trembled and went into a spasm and stood in the full horror of her ugliness.

The Sergeant's eyes filled briefly with compassion before he lost two-thirds of his strength and his knees buckled. He dropped as a petal drifts from a flower and a leaf floats to the ground; he fell like a gently unwinding bolt of navy blue silk. A fearful sense of loss filled his whole being; and he fainted away into unconsciousness. Nearby, the back wheel of his fallen bicycle spun slowly and to no purpose.

Without understanding any of it, the children had watched what was happening.

When they first saw the familiar figure of the Sergeant, a man from their own world, someone they had often seen winking and smiling when on point duty and directing traffic in Galway City—or leaning against a wall having a chat with a friend or two, Pidge had felt greatly comforted. Now the Sergeant was lying on the ground and they didn't understand why.

The Mórrígan, however, was not finished, although the pebble was gone. There was still Olc-Glas and his poison and she would have that at least, if nothing else. She would follow Pidge and Brigit forever if need be to get it.

She again threw a word at the lake to freeze it; but The Dagda's great invisible hand scooped it up and flung it to the sky, where the sun burned and it sizzled like a spit. Her hand had been lifted against the children. Now The Dagda might raise his hand against her. A blow for a blow.

At this the waters of the lake murmured against her. They went in angry ripples to the lake shore and formed little eddies there that spoke to the earth in low whispers.

'Listen to us,' they said. 'What were the words of the ancient scribe? What did he say? "Man's flesh is of the earth, his blood of the sea, his face of the sun, his thoughts of the clouds, his breath of the wind, his bones of the stones, his soul of the spirit." Thus he said, did he not?'

'Yes,' the earth agreed.

'Is he not my child, your child, the child of the wind and of the fire? Is he not born of us and nurtured by us, as is everything that lives on this bright ball? Of them all, he is our brightest child. In the hope that one day he will truly remember and love us as he once did—give me your strength. As I have drenched and refreshed you when you were parched, give me what is in you that makes trees grow tall; give me that which makes trees strong.'

And the earth sent a message to the fiery heart of the world that said:

'Thou fire! Give us what is in thee that cracks rocks and bursts mountains that we may rise against her.'

And the fire and the earth gave their strengths. The water rose up in a glittering sheet and stood as a mountain of light before her. It stood between The Mórrigan and the little boat, and she could not go through it, for its clear purity would do her very great hurt.

Pidge and Brigit looked at the shining wall and marvelled. They had seen the woman in her hideousness; but the ugliness couldn't touch Pidge as he was not yet a man. Now all was quiet. The ripples, where the stone had broken into the water, had subsided and everything was calm. The only sounds were those of the little wavelets that wetted the sides of the boat with mild pattings.

'She didn't get it,' Brigit said at last.

'No. But we failed just the same,' Pidge answered, full of weariness.

In spite of all the help and all we've been through, the pebble is gone. And Olc-Glas exists somewhere and we were supposed to destroy him. It's all been for nothing, he thought sadly.

He gazed sorrowfully at the water.

He went back over all their adventures in his mind and he came back again to the knowledge that they had failed.

Brigit was full of angry wishes.

And then, their attention was taken by a tiny point emerging from the lake's surface, causing small ripples of its own. It came up a bit more and was blunt and not a point at all and a small face came out of the water and a familiar voice said:

'Who drop dis on me noddle? I cum up to complain.'

The frog, Puddeneen Whelan, came swimming in close to

447

the boat, clutching the pebble to his front.

So once again there was great hope and happiness.

'Oh Puddeneen! It's you!' Brigit exclaimed.

'It is!' he agreed. 'But doan talk to me about weddings and da bride wore broderie anglaise!'

'I thought this part of the lake was bottomless!' Pidge, light-headed, exclaimed, ignoring Puddeneen's last remark, and looking at the deep glassiness of the water.

'Bottomless how-are-ye,' said Puddeneen scornfully. 'If it wuz bottomless da water would all fall through to da other side of da world.'

Pidge reached out and took the pebble.

'By da way, I doan sing no more love songs,' said Puddeneen. 'Listen!'

And he swam silently away.

He was only a small movement in the water close by, when he happened to turn and he saw the wall of water for the first time.

The children saw his little body rise stiffly out of the lake for one moment of pure horror and then he dived and was gone from sight.

They had the pebble again now and the boat began to move. Raḋairc was flying in circles waiting for them to land, crying:

'This way, Pidge! This way, Brigit!'

The boat took them to land and then drifted away.

Pidge looked at the soft mud at the water's edge and saw the tracks of cattle and other animals that had come to drink; and it was a homely sight that gave him comfort. He knew that The Mórrígan was somehow held back by the water and every step was taking them nearer to home. He still had no idea at all of what to do with the pebble, and he didn't know that The Mórrígan would still try to pursue him with the wish to get Olc-Glas.

Then they walked into mist again.

'I wonder when we'll see the first candle?' Brigit said.

Raḋairc came down through the mist and said: 'Straight on!'; before flying back up again.

'Maybe there won't be any candles this time. We've got Raḋairc to make sure that we don't go astray. He knows where we are because he directs us,' said Pidge.

It felt wonderful to be in the mist again and the way it filled all the space around them made them feel protected.

'What about Serena?'

'I don't know. She might only be in charge of the way in and we're going out now.'

As they walked on, no candle appeared; and of Serena, there was never a sign. But from time to time, Raḍairc would suddenly descend through the mist and tell them to go a little to the left or to the right and then he would disappear up into the mist again.

Pidge was even more sure that everything was now all right and that they were heading for the stones at Shancreg; the gateway that would bring them safely back to their own world and home.

Suddenly, Serena *was* there; and they both hugged her and hugged her before walking beside her, each with an arm around her warm, soft neck. They were moving through the gentleness of the mist and all their happiness came back to them.

Pidge started to daydream about what it would be like seeing Auntie Bina and their father after all this time. He was wondering how he could possibly explain to them about why they had been gone for so long, and most of all—why they had gone away without telling anyone.

He wondered just how cross they would be because of getting a fright. Grown-up people were always cross if children gave them a fright by going into some danger or other, or being missing when they should be home. He was just arriving at the idea that the Sergeant had been notified of their absence and had somehow come to search for them, when Brigit said:

'Listen!'

There was something behind them in the mist.

The mist thickened at once. Serena, moving faster, said: 'Don't stop!' but they had already stopped, letting go of her in their horror, and she had moved on ahead of them before they realized it. They had stopped because they were shocked with fright.

There was something coming. They could hear sounds, but the sounds were puzzling and didn't explain themselves. No one could tell where they were coming from, as the heavy mist distorted all noise.

They could hear Serena calling them, but again the mist had the same confusing effect on their learning and they didn't know where she was. Pidge took Brigit by the hand and they ran to try to find her. Radairc must have dived through the mist to help them only moments later—they could hear him calling to them as well—but they couldn't even guess where he was.

Quite suddenly they realized that the puzzling sounds were coming from behind.

Chapter 14

THEY heard the terrible breathing of an animal that was running a desperate race.

In a fearful instant their legs became nervous, twitching like the legs of foals, and they made half-starts at running themselves, but still not knowing which way to go to find Serena. In the end Pidge gave a sort of tug at Brigit, jerking her along and they were running.

Pidge threw many glances backwards before he saw out of the corner of his eye, the shape of a dog or a wolf labouring and straining to cover the ground. He knew that the animal would be upon them in seconds and that they would be caught. Holding Brigit's hand in a grip of iron, he forced his legs to go faster and faster, until it seemed that the main purpose of existence was to cover the ground and eat up miles.

We've just got to make it as far as the stones, we'll be safe after that, he thought desperately.

Still the animal gained on them, panting and making terrible noises of exertion. Pointlessly Pidge wondered which of the hounds it would be, which of them would be the one to capture them; for the animal was gaining on them through the energy of its will. Quite sure in his mind that if the animal caught them, it would be all over, he felt a jumping in his throat and tears stood in his eyes.

Then a voice behind him panted in frightful gasps, saying:

'Don't slow down. Keep going. The she-warriors are close behind!'

It was Cooroo! Brave Cooroo. He must have run the whole incredible distance that was the perimeter of Lough Corrib and now he was running beside them. The hot salty tears spilled from Pidge's eyes.

Behind them again, further away but getting nearer, was the

muffled sound of galloping hooves as the she-warriors rode their horses pitilessly.

And then, as if that weren't enough, the air above them was filled with The Mórrígan's horrible exulting laughter and they knew that she was overhead.

Pidge felt a stronger vibration under the curl of his fingers and the stone turned and turned in his grasp.

'Keep going!' Cooroo cried in a voice that sounded as if his chest were tearing.

New speed came to them. Pidge ran like the wind holding on to Brigit who matched his swiftness.

The Mórrígan had confronted the water and commanded it to lie at her feet; but the water strengthened by the earth and the fire had had not obeyed. Her anger had been an explosion of power and in her pride she had wasted some moments in conflict with these great things. But they had not given way.

The Mórrígan, quickly now, reduced herself and diminished to nothing. She went small enough to hide in the centre of an inert speck of dust. The dust was a dead thing and couldn't feel that she was there and so it could not betray her presence. The wind's fingers searched for her everywhere and in its searching it touched the dust motes but it couldn't feel her. From the wind's touch, the dust flew. It was blown high up over the water and over the lake. In this way, The Mórrígan had defeated the water and now she flew above The Dagda's mist, searching for Pidge and Brigit.

Brigit was sobbing and Pidge realized that she was trying to be quiet and suppress the noise of her sobs for fear The Mórrígan would hear and so find them in the mist. And this awareness of Brigit's fear and of her bravery, of Cooroo's great efforts, of the way they had seemed to win at the lake and the knowledge that an evil, destructive, fearsomely hideous Goddess and her terrible warriors were hunting them in a blind mist, he felt it was finally and truly beyond him and he must give in. By now the tears were pouring from his eyes.

The Mórrígan, however, and the she-warriors were not able to hear them through The Dagda's magic mist. Unfortunately, the sinister hounds could still scent Cooroo and the children in spite of it.

The ground suddenly went from under the feet of the children and the fox—and they were falling.

All three screamed.

Chapter 15

THEY tumbled and rolled down a smooth slope for what seemed an eternity of fear and confusion.

When they stopped falling at last, they found themselves on the floor of what looked like a quarry. His eyes blinded with tears, Pidge couldn't see that it was more like a man-made stone bowl, with sides that were shaped and smooth and bore the marks of tools. Here there was no mist and through their tears they saw that it was an empty place save for a large brass bell and some kind of grid.

He drew his sleeve across his eyes to wipe away some of the tears and he tried to comfort a terrified and choking Brigit by putting his arm around her.

They saw that at their feet there was a great pool covered by the enormous circular grid made of metal. The centre was a smaller circle and radiating out from it were spokes. To one side of the grid a great brass bell that was green-stained stood on the ground.

It made no sense at all. They were trapped. All three knew it, for there was no place at all where they could hide. Even if they had the strength necessary to lift the bell and get in under it, they would be found in the end, for it was the only place to search.

They looked around at the forbidding stone bowl that they couldn't possibly climb out of and they were convinced that they were in a prison and that it was The Mórrígan's doing. Pidge, listening, thought he could hear the horses still running somewhere in the mist and he knew that it was only a matter of time, now.

We may be killed here, he thought and his mind felt numb.

So at last, they were trapped.

Cooroo dropped to the floor, beaten. His rib cage rose and fell, his tongue lolled and he lay stretched out on the ground, looking up at them with bloodshot eyes full of pain.

Brigit looked around her at the still forbidding stone and she seemed to crumple. As Pidge looked at her he understood that almost all of her courageous spirit had gone. There were no words left to say that could have any meaning; and all he could do was keep an arm around her in a useless gesture of protection. In his other hand he still gripped the squirming pebble. He could hear the horses still galloping somewhere in the mist and he knew that, sooner or later, the fearsome she-warriors would discover them. One last obstinate spark glowed to life within him. Let them take it from me! he thought distractedly. Let them take it from my dead hand, as I had to take it from the Glomach's hand.

Shuddering uncontrollably, he thought of the dogs whose teeth were made to tear and of the terrible she-warriors with their swords and spears.

The tears of regret and fear and just sorrow fell from his eyes, and he thought how pointless everything had been.

'Do not be afraid,' said a voice. 'The Dagda is my father.'

'What?' Pidge said, looking round him blindly, thinking that he had imagined it.

'You have almost defeated her, do not be afraid. Take the serpent.'

It was the eel! The Great Eel from the water spout. His head had appeared through the centre circle of the grid. In a moment the iron case was there in his jaws and Pidge made a snatch at it. He struggled to keep hold of the pebble with one hand, while Brigit helped in a fumbling way to get the iron case open. He snatched out the page with Olc-Glas and allowed the case to drop to the ground. The page began to struggle to get away from him. It fluttered wildly in his hand.

Without thinking at all of what he was doing, Pidge opened the hand that held the pebble and his tears fell onto it. Suddenly there was a most foul stench and on the stone's surface, the red stain softened. In his other hand, the page struggled even harder to escape, and Pidge brought his hands close together one above the other. He seemed to be obeying an unspoken order.

The softened blood on the stone went thick and slimy. It moved slowly and gathered into an expanding, gluey clot.

Pidge tilted the pebble and the glob of blood slid to the edge and hung as a drop. The sticky slop fell—first lengthening like elastic—and it landed right onto the drawing of Olc-Glas on the page, covering his head completely.

Just before the blood landed, the page screamed. The smell then was frightful and it made the children feel faint. For two or three moments nothing more happened and then a tremendous heat filled the quarry as the energy of the evil snake was dissipated. In those few moments The Mórrígan would have swallowed the snake and taken this energy into her being, if things had gone her way.

The whole sheet of paper had gone to nothing but stink; there were no remains. Not a fragment was left.

But all was not finished yet.

For when Olc-Glas screamed, there was the loud drumming of hooves up above them, as the she-warriors reached the rim of the quarry. Huge iron spears rained down on them from all sides, piercing the swirling mist that was a layer overhead. Through all that was happening, Pidge found himself noticing that, oddly, the spears were painted green.

The she-warriors could now be seen through small shiverings and partings in the mist.

The screaming of the snake had also brought The Mofrígan.

She alighted at the edge of the quarry in her hag form and looked down. In a glance she saw that she was beaten, and she knew that the snake Olc-Glas and the pebble's blood-drop, were lost to her forever. A strident sound, raucous and harsh, yet dismal, came from her throat and she changed and towered as a monstrously huge, three-headed bird, that was as black as pitch but with red eyes burning. She was Scald Crow.

The noise of her voice coming from three widely-gaping beaks, filled the quarry with sickening echoes and froze the children to the marrow. They huddled down together, as near to the ground as they could get, fearful and terrified of what she would do.

But part of her terrible screeching cry was because she knew that she could do nothing, take no revenge. For if she lifted her hand against them a second time, The Dagda's reply would surely be swift and she might be overwhelmed.

The three baleful heads, branching from the one neck of the

odious bird-body, glared down at the children for a few moments more, and then the filthy creature, coal-black but with few real feathers, flapped its great wings.

Still crying as though partly in reproach, she circled the quarry once, before rising through the mist and taking to the sky, her she-warriors rising with her on their horses. There, high up, she dissolved into a mass of billowing black atoms that was an uneven sprawl of cloud—the Queen of Phantoms.

Her lament at losing tore through the sky, before she rose, dark and shapeless, even higher into the air and travelled away, her she-warriors riding in a wide arc around her. And the still faithful hounds were there, mutely following their Queen and her warriors. Slowly and silently they all moved away from the world, the unbound hair of the she-warriors floating and waving and streaming out behind them, as they rose and fell massively in their saddles, responding to the movements of the horses beneath them, without the whisper of a sound.

There was a long hush during which the mist rippled softly and then it cleared and was gone; and a suffusion of peace hung over the stone bowl.

Radairc swooped down to them.

'She's gone,' he said. 'You've won for The Dagda and everyone.'

Everything happened rapidly then.

The quarry seemed to be shrinking. It closed in as it shrank and, in the end, the children and Cooroo had only just time to leap out of it, before it became impossible not to topple over in the little space that was left. They looked about them with great amazement.

They were standing in Eyre Square.

The quarry had become the stone bowl of the drinking fountain and the large brass bell was really only a copper drinking-cup and the grid at the bottom was only to let waste water run away. The green-painted spears of the she-warriors had been the iron railings, for the railings were gone. So that's what happened to them, Pidge thought dreamily.

All the evil had gone.

It was even possible to feel the lack of it everywhere.

The first thing Pidge did was to fill the drinking-cup and

457

offer water to Cooroo, and the fox lapped it gratefully. After he had drunk enough with Pidge refilling the cup as needed, Cooroo went on his hind legs and licked Pidge's face and then he went to Brigit and licked her face too. When he padded off silently in the shadows, they realized he had been saying goodbye. As he went, he made himself small and kept in the shadows. Some people would say he was slinking; but all that he was, really, was a small animal being wise in the care of its life.

The square was utterly empty and the shadows lay deep blue like spilled ink.

The children looked all about them and up at the sky.

The sun had gone behind a vast puffed-up smokey cloud. The edges of the sun cloud were lit up by it and seemed like beautiful silver tissue; and that was ordinary and wonderful. Rain began to fall softly and the sun came from behind the cloud; and the light touched the rain so that it fell in glittering drops. Raḋairc circled through it, and he came to them and said:

'It is really all over.'

A rainbow appeared then and Brigit reached for Pidge's hand, for the rainbow had brought music with it; and that was not ordinary, but marvellous indeed. Each colour had its own pure and beautiful sound—music beyond imagination or dream. They seemed to be listening with every pore, every strand of their hair, with their finger-tips and the skin at the backs of their necks. As they stood exalted, the half circle of the rainbow straightened out slowly, slowly, and reached down to them. It enveloped them in its radiance and they could feel the colours tingling and dancing on their arms and faces. Tiny beads of violet and green were clinging to the small fair hairs on Brigit's bare arms and on Pidge's face too; and they sparkled like minute lights on a Christmas tree. The clear unearthly music was a mist and a storm and a tranquillity of sound at their feet. Raḋairc was a blissful ball of feathers. Then the colours began to flow like a river of magic and the children found that they were moving with it. They wanted to talk; but they didn't know what to say. At last Brigit said:

'Pidge, we are riding a rainbow.'

And Pidge found that all he could say was:

'Yes.'

For this was The Dagda loving them and thanking them and it gave the children the greatest-ever joy.

Gently the rainbow flowed through the sky, until in the end it carried them through the grey stone doorway at Shancreg. For a few seconds more the rainbow and the music swirled round them and then they were gone.

Pidge looked up at the sky and noticed without surprise that the plane was still there, still making its vapour-trail; the trails it had made earlier were only now drifting in wisps. He glanced at the ground and saw an apple-core, still fresh but browned a bit, lying at his feet, and he knew that they had only been gone for an hour or so.

They both looked back through the doorway and saw a soap bubble coming towards them. It was the last bubble that had been on Hannah's hands—the one that had floated away when all of the others had burst.

The soap bubble came and hovered above them. It grew bigger and expanded until it was like a transparent dome, and it came down over them and enveloped them. It was as if they stood inside a glass ball like the scrying-glass.

Their friends now came to say goodbye—they saw them all again.

First Cathbad was suddenly there, tall and proud in his white robes. He smiled broadly. As they looked at his face, it changed and it was fleetingly the face of the old scholar that Pidge had met on the first day in the bookshop. And then it was Cathbad's face again.

Hannah and Corny came laughing and dancing. As they came, their outlines trembled slightly and they dissolved to become their old friends, Boodie and Patsy, for a short space only; and then they were transformed into figures of great beauty and light. The children saw them as they truly were. Brigit, Goddess of the Hearth had brought her humble dandelions; and Angus Óg, the God of Love, had not only his daisies but a ring of white birds that flew in a circle round his head.

The Seven Maines came and each one cupped the children's faces in their hands for a moment, before leaving a light kiss on the crowns of their heads. And the Poor Woman with the ducks and geese was there, and they changed as they had changed before, so that Queen Maeve and Ailill and all her

459

men now stood before Pidge and Brigit. They honoured the boy and girl and showed respect by laying their swords, shields and spears on the ground at their feet.

Then the Old Angler came running as a speck in the distance; and standing before them, once again, was Cúchulain, the warrior and hero. He bent down, and with an arm around each of them, he set them onto his shield and he lifted them up in the air high above his head and they could see Daire and Finn and all of their people. And as Cúchulain held them aloft, there were three great bellowings of praise. They were being saluted as heroes. It was all tremendously powerful and it quickened Pidge and Brigit so that they were shouting with excitement too.

Cúchulain at length put them down and Angus Óg came to them and they looked into his eyes. These lovely eyes had the blue of a bluebell wood trapped in them and his gaze held them while everything darkened about them. And with a wonderful, tender love he gently made them forget, until very suddenly the bubble was no longer there and everyone was gone.

The children stood wondering why they were in the field with the tumbled stones and why they felt so happy. Brigit's schoolbag was lying on the ground. She was surprised by this and by the fact that the strap was broken. When she opened it, she was not at all surprised to see that it was empty.

They set off for home, but their eyes were bright and dancing and they were full of joy.

When they got home, there was great excitement in the house.

Sally was back and she was jumping all over them and licking them.

'We think she was in the horse-box and slipped out before we noticed,' Michael, their father, explained.

But Auntie Bina was even more excited about some travelling-people that had called to ask for a little food. She had invited them in for a cup of tea; and the woman had sung songs and played a banjo first and then a concertina; and the old man had danced while holding out the tips of his coat-skirts. The old woman had told Auntie Bina's fortune and had left presents for Pidge and Brigit, for she had seen that they existed when she read Auntie Bina's hand.

'It was the greatest fun; what a pity you missed it,' Auntie Bina said.

For Pidge they had left a glass snowball with an alpine scene inside it; and for Brigit there was a penny whistle and a whole set of china. There were six egg cups in the set; the china was decorated with dandelions and daisies and Brigit loved it at once.

Sometimes Pidge would see a frown of concentration on Brigit's face as she tried hard to remember something that she couldn't name, and he would frown and try to remember with her. Other times, he would feel something in his mind, a picture that wouldn't quite form, and he would try to grasp after it, finding as he gave up, that Brigit would be staring at him at such times, with a great frown of effort on her face too.

And there were times when Pidge shook the glass and, as the snow was falling and beginning to clear, he fancied that he saw strange yet familiar things through the snow, but only briefly, and never long enough to be certain of anything. It was intriguing and mysterious, and he was always excited when it happened and called Brigit to look.

And from time to time they would both meet a dog-fox; the same one every time, they were sure. He would stand and let them come quite close before walking away. They knew that he was not afraid of them at all. Every now and then he would stand still for a long time, and they would all three look at each other with puzzlement and affection and feelings of *knowing* that could not be explained by the children. If ever they went on a picnic, he would appear. They would throw food near him which he accepted and ate with perfect ease. On winter days, they particularly went for his sake and he was always waiting for them. In time, to their delight, they found that he trusted them enough to eat the food from their hands and even let Brigit stroke him. One day they found out by accident that he relished sausages above everything; and Pidge never forgot to buy some especially for him, whenever he was in Galway.

They often heard him bark in the night.

There were times as well, when they were aware of faint, mystifying and joyous echoes that made them stop in the middle of doing something to gaze at each other.

And whenever Old Mossie Flynn spoke of his former lodgers, the children were always deeply interested in what he said, and would sit silently and stare at him with widened eyes.

And on windy days there was a kite. It was splendid and always flew beautifully. There was a picture of an old ship painted on it and it had long ribbons of violet satin flowing out from it and these always danced in the breeze and sometimes glittered as though with silver. Pidge had made the kite himself. He had found the design and instructions in a book that he had happened on in the library in Galway. Auntie Bina gave the ribbons. She had found them at the bottom of an old trunk, and said at the time, that she didn't even know that she had them. Brigit always said that the kite was hers and that Pidge had made it especially for her. Somehow he never minded, when she said this.

Many times later he tried to find the book again but he never could, even with the librarian's interested help. It wasn't in any catalogue and all trace of it had vanished.

Last of all were the rainbows.

From that time out, they always saw lots of rainbows; and occasionally when they were with other people, there would be one. If it were particularly magnificent, they would cry out:

'Look! There's a rainbow!'—and the other people would say:

'Where? Where?'

And the children would be surprised.

Epilogue

WHEN the Sergeant fell he had dropped onto the entangled nests of waterbirds. Over the years the flat nests had come away from their moorings in the reeds at both sides of the lake during storms, and drifted to land at this spot, carried by a current that was changeless. They were massed in a great bed at the Sergeant's feet, like a raft. He had landed on his back, legs in the air, still clutching onto his bike by the handle-bars. The wheels continued to spin gently as he slowly floated across the lake.

Now when the Sergeant came to, he was on his bicycle and riding in circles round the stones in Shancreg. From the deep grooves his wheels had made in the ground, he concluded that he had been foolishly cycling in this way for some time. He pulled himself together, dismounted and wheeled his bike across the field and he lifted it over the wall and went out onto the road.

He was thoughtful as he cycled back to the Garda barracks in Galway.

The young Garda was surprised to see him and remarked that he hadn't been gone long. The Sergeant reached over to pat the young man on the shoulder and he was cut to the heart when the young Garda flinched and drew back. He was stricken with remorse for the harshness he had shown in the past, and from that day out he became the nicest Sergeant that the world has ever known. Hardened criminals used to break down and cry in the streets when he passed; and in later years, people were known to say that when God made that particular Sergeant, he broke the mould.

Only once did he mention something of his experience to another person. He confided in his Lovable Auntie Lizzie. He described with tears in his eyes how the beautiful woman had been stricken with a most terrible disease. Auntie Lizzie made him put on a warm dressing-gown at once, and to comfort him she broke bread into a bowl and sprinkled spices and sugar over it. Then she covered it with hot milk and stirred it with a big spoon.

'Eat your goodie, child,' she said.

'I wonder where she went?' the Sergeant said in puzzlement, after a while.

'I think that she went off round the world to forget you,' Auntie Lizzie said, looking at him fondly.

'Do you know,' The Sergeant said, knitting his brows: 'I never even knew her name.'

He finished his goodie and licked the spoon.

'I think. . . .' he began, and broke off with a bashful look.

'What?' Auntie Lizzie asked encouragingly.

'I think I'll call her My Angel,' the Sergeant said shyly, and he blushed.

Acknowledgements

I would like to thank Roger Langley for his unfailing encouragement and enthusiasm, also Barbara, Ruth and Eric. Danny Rigby, my young reader, deserves thanks too, as does Maggie for her practical and invaluable help.

Books that have helped:

Celtic Heritage by Alwyn Rees & Brinley Rees.
> Thames and Hudson, London 1961.

The Celtic Realms by Myles Dillon & Nora Chadwick.
> Weidenfeld and Nicolson Ltd., 1967.

Irish Folk Ways by E. Estyn Evans.
> Routledge and Kegan Paul Ltd., 1957.

The Mountains of Ireland by D. D. C. Pochin Mould.
> B. T. Batsford Ltd., London 1955.

Cúchulain of Muirthemne by Lady Gregory.
> John Murray, London 1902.

> (Lady Gregory's book is a translation of old Irish manuscripts. A lot of the description of how the Seven Maines and others were dressed, and, various horse-trappings etc., comes from that book).

Glossary of Gaelic Words

(To show pronounciations, the words have been broken into parts. This shows syllables only, so if you decide to try saying the words, say them quickly by running the parts together. For example: Millskuhuch, Bowrawn, Knowneenee, and so on.)

Ailill	Queen Maeve's husband	Al-ill
Aisling	A dream-vision	Ashling
Angus Óg	Young Angus. The God of Love	Angus is just Angus. Óg is pronounced to rhyme with 'brogue'.
Baile-na-gCeard	Town of The Artificers	Difficult to say, but try it as: Bollya-nah-Gayrd(th). The 'd' has a slight 'th' sound.
Banashee	Woman of Faery	Banashee is phonetic for Bean-na-Sidhe.
Bodbh	One of three aspects of evil of the Queen/Goddess, the Mórrígan	Bowv. Bow rhymes with 'now'.
Bodhrán	A round one-sided drum	Bow-rawn. Bow rhymes with 'now' as above.
Breac	Speckled or spotted	Brack.
Cathbad	Chief of the Druids	Koth-bod. The 'd' at the end has the slight 'th' sound.
Cisheen	A basket	Kisheen.
Cluas	Ear	Kloo-ass.
Cúchulain	An ancient hero	His name means Culain's Hound. Pronounce it Koo-(c)hullin (hull rhymes

467

		with gull). The dot on the 'c' is an aspirate. To get it right, you have to make a sound at the back of your throat—try breathing out while sounding the letter 'h'.
Cú Rua	Red Hound	Koo-Roo-a.
An Dagda	The Good God i.e. good for everything—a leading magician, a redoubtable warrior, an artisan, a farmer—all powerful and omniscient. He is *Ruad Ro-Fhess*, 'Lord of Great Knowledge'.	Something like Dogda but give the 'd' the 'th' sound.
Daire	Oak tree	Darra. Again you need the 'th' sound. Try it with the 'th' as used in the words 'there' and 'then'.
Fidchell	An ancient board game	Something like Fid(th)kel.
Finn	Fair or blonde	Fin (like Finland).
Fomoiri	A mythological race of giants, half-human and half-monster	Fo-mo-ree. Fo and mo rhyme with 'go'.
Glomach	This creature was supposed to live down Biddy's Lane in Galway. He was said to be a huge man with black hair and his principal job was to catch children who were out after dark.	Glumuck.
Maamturk mountains	Name means Boar's Pass	Maamturks. Maam rhymes with 'balm'.
Macha	One of the three aspects of the evil Queen/Goddess,	Moh-(c)ha. Rhymes with 'lough' in Lough Ness.

	Morrigan known as Queen of Phantoms	
Maeve	Queen of Connacht. It is said that her name means 'drunk woman'.	Mayv.
Morrigan	Great Queen (Mór Ríagan)	More Ree-an (People usually say Morrigan in English
	Great Queens (Mórrígna)	More Reen-yah
Nóiníni	Daisies	Known-een-ee
Olc-Glas	The Evil Green (One)	Ulk Gloss
Poteen	Name given to illegal whiskey	Putcheen. The Gaelic way of spelling it, is poitín— means little pot.
Radairc	Sight/vision	Ryark
Seven Maines	Queen Maeve's sons. The names are explained in the story.	Three of them are hard to pronounce at first sight: Mathremail—Moh-roo-al Athremail—Ah-roo-al Milscothach—Mill-skuh-huch.
Sidhe	Faery People	Shee.
Tír-na-nÓg	Land of Youth (Otherworld)	Cheer-nah-Nogue. Nogue rhymes with 'brogue'.
Tríoca Céad	Thirty Hundreds (of men in a military force)	Three-aka Kay(d)th